THE OCEAN MINDS

Howard Matthews

MINERVA PRESS
LONDON
MIAMI RIO DE JANEIRO DELHI

THE OCEAN MINDS
Copyright © Howard Matthews 2000

All Rights Reserved

No part of this book may be reproduced in any form
by photocopying or by any electronic or mechanical means,
including information storage or retrieval systems,
without permission in writing from both the copyright
owner and the publisher of this book.

ISBN 0 75411 065 6

First Published 2000 by
MINERVA PRESS
315–317 Regent Street
London W1R 7YB

Printed in Great Britain for Minerva Press

THE OCEAN MINDS

Prologue

The gathering dark clouds loomed low on the eastern horizon, the menacing woolly tendrils slowly unfurling under the morning sun like the tentacles of an octopus slowly reaching for its prey. Initially the sun repelled the invaders of the blue sky with immense yellow shafts of sunlight, but the rapturous clear sky was slowly and steadily relinquishing to the insurgent menace. The sea was very calm though, and so he felt confident that the weather would remain clement, for the time being – he concluded that he had sufficient time to complete the task at hand and return to the marina.

He eased back the throttle control lever and turned the wheel of the small wooden fishing boat, directing the prow towards the thickly clawed mangrove swamp. The momentum of the boat slowed to an equivalent walking pace and he noticed that the fresh sea air was accompanied now by an intermittent warm breeze that was becoming stronger and increasingly constant; the wind managed to ruffle his short black hair with intensifying insistence, disturbingly indicating to him that it would not be long before the weather worsened.

The engine continued burbling quietly as it slowly pushed the ageing wooden hull towards the path in the watery maze of roots that, even from a very short distance was not visible. An intense green gloom enveloped the skilfully piloted craft when it eventually entered the dense sanctuary afforded by the mangrove swamp, now that the already disappearing light from the sun was significantly obscured.

The interior silence of the swamp sanctuary was suddenly pierced by the loud call of early morning birdsong, accompanied by the continual background sound of the muffled buzzing wings of an insurmountable number of unseen insects. The clamour of the swamp did not startle him, but the quiet sound from the engine of the small boat had became unusually loud in the festooned confines, so when he decided that he had entered the swamp far enough he shut the motor off with a sense of relief. He listened in earnest for any extraneous noise in the humid, still air. Presently he felt satisfied that there was nobody else at sea, on shore or flying above that could observe him; only the camouflaged wildlife could see him and regard him with wary eyes. He turned about his person and bent down next to the large sheet of tarpaulin that was weighted down behind the small open wooden wheelhouse of the craft. He began removing the pieces of meat from under the tarpaulin, piece by piece, leaning over the side of the boat and then plunging the individual pieces between the tangle of roots immediately below the surface of the water.

The exertion in the humid confines was making him sweat profusely and the pungent stench of decay was making him feel nauseous. He involuntarily gagged. Stopping what he was doing for a moment, he tied a towel around his head so that it covered his nose and mouth and then continued in his labour.

He mused as he toiled that some of the pieces were quite large and he wished he had cut them smaller. However, he eventually completed his task with considerable effort and stood up to survey his work. Already, he observed unhurriedly, there were fish nibbling at the flesh, quickly devouring small pieces and then nervously darting away, only to be replaced by another equally nervous mouth at the table. He knew from experience that it would not be long at all before the flesh was stripped and only the bones remained, which would soon sink and form the sediment that would lie undiscovered for all eternity.

A misplaced finger pointed accusingly at him from below the surface of the water and the contrasting paleness of the flesh caught his eye. He leaned over the edge of the boat and brutally slotted the severed limb further and lower into the roots, vigorously and quickly ridding himself of the mockery and condemnation. He then took a final look at the tangled roots and the assortment of discoloured, dismembered body parts that were now surrounded by the frenzied movement of shiny watery creatures. Satisfied that all was positioned correctly, he smiled to himself and pushed the starter button, firing the engine which clattered back to life. He slowly eased the throttle control forward, deftly guiding the boat back through the maze and returning along the quiet coastline to the island of Key West.

Chapter One

The bar had not adopted a name since it had been built over a century ago. This historical fact – that also served as a convenient novelty historical fact for the tourists – was inexplicably and deeply entrenched in the minds of the current local community.

The bar formed part of a small parade of two-storey wooden buildings that formed an equally small section of the main thoroughfare of Duval Street, which is approximately one mile in length but is densely populated by residential properties, tourists and the accompanying businesses of Key West, Florida.

The interior decoration of the bar was that of a stereotypical mock Irish bar. The rustic and intentionally simple interior had a welcoming and relaxed atmosphere, mainly due to the abundant use of dark wood decoration: wooden beams, wooden furniture and an uneven wooden floor that creaked when one stood on it – like a creaking wooden sailing ship being pressed by the powerful and ever swelling ocean that supported it.

On most days of the year the bar was warmly lit by the strong natural sunlight that streamed through the large front windows, enhancing the interesting drifting patterns of smoke that swirled in the still air amongst the happy voices of the many patrons. Not today, though, because a thick blanket of dark cloud had covered the sky and obscured the sun to the very end of every horizon. The cool darkness of the bar was accentuated by the silence and, paradoxically, by the feverish drumming sound of the falling rain outside.

Christine stood behind the bar, her rear resting on the edge of a high stool and her elbows resting on the heavy oak surface of the bar in front of her. She gently smoothed the fringe of her long black hair from her dark brown eyes and listened lazily and with detachment at the sound of the rain through the open back window. The minutes passed like a growing tree as her mind imperceptibly drifted and sifted her various thoughts.

Situated at the rear of the building immediately at the bottom of three stone steps was a small swimming pool. She absently decided that the surface looked reminiscent of the Atlantic Ocean under the domination of a raging storm, creating unusually mountainous peaks and troughs in the water – from the point of view of a small insect, had it been swimming in the pool. The rain was so heavy and constant, in fact, that she suddenly stood upright with considerable concern and wondered if the level of water would rise above the edge of the pool and up to the steps of the bar. However, she quickly concluded that there was nothing she could do to prevent it and so she would just have to wait and see what transpired. She relaxed somewhat and resignedly settled back into her former position, finding it difficult to locate the warm space that she had previously occupied.

Her eyes fell on the abundance of leafy trees that stood in the relatively small garden, and how they looked weighty under the strain of the heavy morning downpour. The leaves drooped under the extra weight as each heavy raindrop pounded the branches and leaves with a loud and constant slapping sound. The branches of the trees slowly and dutifully swayed in the direction of the downpour, like a multitude of bowing servants in a leafy courtyard.

She shook her head to clear her mind and once again forced her attention to the book that she was reading. She had read the same line time and time again and on each occasion she had not comprehended what was written. She read the line again, slowly this time, allowing the words to embed themselves into her imagination and elevate her mind into a literally different world. It was unfortunate that the rambling text and complex sentences of the novel demanded her full and undivided attention, otherwise she could have immediately lost herself totally in her creative imagination. The slowly passing day would have then given way to an equally quiet night and then closer to the end of the inclement weather.

As she neared the end of the page and her imagination was finally beginning to lift her from the present watery bombardment, her concentration was broken by the sound of hurrying feet splashing in the street outside the front of the bar. She looked up from the pages with a sigh as the rushing figure ducked unnecessarily into the open door of the bar, with a folded broadsheet newspaper positioned barely protectively above the head. The middle-aged gentleman shook the rainwater from the sodden newspaper and palmed his short black hair into some semblance of tidiness as he approached her with a pleasant smile. The day, despite the heavy rain, was very warm and humid and his hairy legs below his shorts looked as heavy as the rain sodden branches on the trees.

'Hello Jim,' Christine said in her Irish lilt. She automatically took down a glass from the shelf above the bar and moved towards the beer pump. 'The usual?' She smiled.

'Yup.' He returned the smile to show his gratitude and greeting. He dragged a wooden stool away from the bar, causing a loud scraping noise on the wooden floor as he did so. He seated himself at the polished wooden counter and began to speak amiably, saying somewhat rhetorically, 'I can't believe the weather. How many more days will this damn tropical storm linger?'

She tilted the pint glass under the tap as she pulled the pump lever and looked up as she continued her well practised pouring method without looking, 'In my opinion, 'bout a week.' She waited for the liquid to settle. After a minute or so of silence she filled the glass to the top and consequently placed a perfectly poured pint of Irish stout on a beer mat on the bar in front of him. She continued in same unhurried fashion, 'It doesn't matter really, Jim. The humid air'll clear soon and the storm will pass us by. The tourists'll be back and you'll sell hundreds of your wonderful paintings.' Her clear brown eyes smiled honestly at him.

Jim owned a small art shop at the seaward end of Duval Street. The paintings contained within, he painted in his studio above the small shop. Many art shops are prevalent in Duval Street, as well as bars and other tourist shops selling paintings, books, and ornaments that have a strong theme of the moon and stars – for a reason unknown to the majority of visitors to the island.

He swallowed a large quantity of his drink and then smiled, 'I've always admired your attitude.' He paused for thought and contemplated her smile. 'You always have a bright and sunny outlook on the world, don't you, Chrissie?' He laughed a slow and deeply comfortable laugh; almost like a department store Santa but not at all false. 'You always brighten my day, even when the sky is low and dark.' He gestured to the front windows with one hand as he quickly took up her hand with his other hand and kissed it ever so gently.

She warmed to the jovial compliment. Jim, although he was a former policeman in Miami, was a charming and gentle man, when he was not engaged in being very forthright. Jim believed in speaking his mind and made no apology for this personality trait that, locally, he was very well known for.

'The way I understand it,' she replied with a thoughtful look, 'is that a problem is not a problem if it'll be gone in week or two. Before you know it, it'll be warm and sunny again and it is unlikely that you'll look back on these terribly dark days with much recollection. It could be far worse, Jim.' Her eyes shone like a light behind clear glass, accentuating her clear complexion that was as smooth as the head on the pint of stout that she had poured moments earlier.

'You're right, of course.' He paused as he contemplated the taste of the stout and the words that he had listened to. There was a silence as he paused uncertainly. 'How's your pop? Have you heard from him?' he said as though the thought had just bitten his leg.

Christine's time was filled with looking after the bar/hotel while her retired father, who owned the bar in name – or no name, as was the case for this particular bar – spent his retired days fishing and walking his dogs in his native Ireland. While her father was away, Jim, a long-time friend of the family, regularly looked in on the bar to ensure that Christine was not in need of anything. She very rarely required the assistance of others but she appreciated the sentiment and Jim's fatherly attentiveness.

'Oh yes,' she answered cheerfully. 'I heard from Father the other day actually. He's still at home, in Ireland. He's spending his days fishing, walking through the hills and drinking plenty of stout. You know, the usual things he does!' She laughed gently as she pictured in her mind's eye her father doing all the things that he enjoyed: she could almost feel the wind pulling at her hair as she walked beside him on a grass covered cliff overlooking the tempestuous sea; she could almost taste the sea on her lips, taste the stout, smell the familiar smells of the grass and wild flowers and hear the silence as she sat next to her father while he fished in silent thought.

Due to the fact that her father had retired, she did employ part-time help in the bar to assist with the workload when it was busy. She enjoyed meeting the public, apart from the tourists that came and went. The local people that frequented the bar were her friends. It was not that she disliked the many tourists that visited all year round on her island, neither did she become resentful of their encroaching on her tranquillity, but she enjoyed hearing the stories from people who, to her, were from the outside world.

Due to the geographical position of Key West, she felt that the island where she lived was somehow detached from the pressures of the world. When she had lived in London, studying English at Greenwich University, she enjoyed her stay in the metropolis, but had longed to get away from London and live again in the tranquillity of Key West. She was at home in the family owned bar and enjoyed being surrounded by the quiet, peaceful, trouble free community. However, just talking about her father at his home in Ireland took her mind to the distant land and at the same time brought to the fore her memories of his presence. Her eyes shone brighter and her smile lengthened with contentment.

'He undoubtedly is enjoying himself.' Jim broke her reverie and his seemingly similar distant thoughts. 'I guess that it's nothin' to worry about!' He took a pipe from the pocket of his tailored shorts, filled the small bucket at the end of the stem with tobacco from a leather pouch and pressed the leaves down with his thumb. He lit the small basin and puffed contentedly on the sweet smelling smoke. 'Who else 'as been in here today? Anyone I know?'

'Umm…' She slowly woke from her daydream and thought of the present as she watched the smoke drift and hang in the still air of the bar, while the sound of the falling rain splashing on the ground outside reached fever pitch. It seemed to her that, for some unknown reason Jim always asked this question. Most people have a well worn question, though, she considered, like 'What have you been up to?' when they meet someone they have not seen for a number of years.

Jim's question was not quite in the same league, though, and so she answered without further thought, 'A group of tourists came in here earlier, waited a minute then carried on running down the street, and...' She had to raise her voice slightly above the sound of the rain. 'Oh yes, Mo came in at midday too, with her son Philip.' She looked pensive. 'They didn't stay for long, only the one drink. You know those two, don't you? She mostly keeps herself to herself but occasionally she makes many an appearance during a single blue moon. He's a bit of a regular here, though – more's the pity.'

'Mo and Philip,' he said contemplatively. He took the pipe from his mouth and cradled the basin in the palm of his hand. 'Is Mo that mad old psychic woman, whose son is a little keen on yer? She owns the small curio shop near Sloppy Joe's bar.'

'That'll be the same two, but she's not mad,' she added with a tired expression, slightly raising her neat eyebrows. She busied herself by fastidiously wiping the bar surface with a damp cloth.

Jim watched her almost angry actions as he continued puffing on his pipe. He removed it from his mouth as he formulated his thoughts into words, 'You don't have the same feeling for him, do yer Chrissie. Why's that? He's a strong and good lookin' fella. He has a good sea fishing and tourist business, and yer pop likes him too if I remember rightly – yer pop liking someone must be a bonus in anyone's book.'

She stopped what she was doing and wrung the cloth out over the sink. 'Philip's not my type,' she explained. 'He's far too cocksure and a philanderer. I'm too busy to concern myself with someone I can't trust. He seems to be pleasant enough and sure, all the girls think he's *dreamy*,' she said cynically. 'But I'm definitely not interested. The problem now, you see, is that my attitude makes him even more interested in me. Anyway,' she sighed, 'I wouldn't date anyone just because he achieved my father's approval.' She tutted and continued wiping the bar.

'Do you want me to speak to Philip?' he asked protectively.

'No, Jim. I can look after myself all right. If the worst comes to the worst then I'll give him a right hook.' She finished what she was doing and flashed a confident smile.

'That's my girl!' he laughed loudly.

'What's so funny?' came an old, yet loud and clear voice.

Jim turned on his seat towards the door and Christine saw that Mo had returned to the bar, which struck her as unusual, considering that she had left but an hour earlier.

The old woman helped herself along with the aid of a wooden stick. The large yellow rainhat that she was wearing appeared shiny with collected rainwater, which dripped onto the wooden floor as she slowly and carefully approached the bar.

'Care to share the joke?' old Mo said as she looked up at the two of them, causing even more rainwater to cascade noisily the short distance from her hat and onto the wooden floor behind her, thus creating a sizeable puddle. She obliviously continued her careful approach to the bar.

Jim opened his mouth to speak at the same time as Christine threw a quick glance at him. She shook her head ever so slightly and Jim, out of nothing but respect for Christine, put aside his honesty and replaced it with very dusty tact. Had it been for anyone's sake but Christine's he would have been honest and explained Philip's behaviour to Mo and not cared if he had offended her. He reluctantly and moodily uttered, 'I was just tellin' Chrissie a story 'bout my days with the Force in Miami.' He visibly relaxed as he changed the topic of conversation, which he was not comfortable with doing at all, 'What'll you have, Mo?' He sighed regretfully.

Mo finally reached a stool and gingerly hauled her small frame onto the soft cushion on top of the long wooden legs. Jim offered a hand to assist her but she chose to ignore him and his offer and completed her determined actions unaided.

'Glass of stout, please, and one for yourself, my dear,' she said sweetly to Christine as she removed her rainhat, that was now devoid of rainwater, and placed it on a stool next to her. She liked Christine and always spoke to her like an old aunt would to her favourite niece, and understood that her son Philip liked Christine and that Christine did not share the same feelings for him. However, it was rare that anyone in Key West knew what Mo knew, or even what she was thinking at any time, which meant that she was not known to become involved in anyone's business – but she knew it all anyway. She sometimes found it very necessary to become involved, though, despite the fact that she preferred to observe from a distance.

'How come you're making a second visit in one day, Mo? I don't usually see you from one month to the next.'

'Don't you like me in your bar?' she asked firmly, without revealing the humour that she felt.

'Sorry, Mo. I didn't mean to offend you. It's just unusual, that's all,' she replied honestly and with regret.

Mo smiled an almost toothless smile, 'That's okay, dear. The weather has unsettled me, that's all. Philip's working elsewhere today, and, well, there are not a great deal of tourists around and you know I like people to talk to.'

Jim looked at the old woman with a certain degree of amusement, as she offered drinks to other people with his money. He was a very generous man but was flabbergasted and amused at her ambivalent attitude when he offered to buy her a drink.

Although Mo drifted in and out of the local social scene, the whole community knew of her and her idiosyncrasies and found her intensely curious – like a curious piece of antique machinery or something intriguingly similar. Mystic Mo, she was *creatively* and commonly known as throughout the community.

Christine did not take a drink for herself; she rarely drank alcohol. She instead continued to silently pour a slow glass of Irish stout for Mo.

'How are you, Mo? I haven't seen you for months,' Jim said a little too loudly.

Mo was never one to mince her words either and she went to great lengths to set people straight on overlooked facts as well. In many respects she was very similar to Jim, which meant that their respective personalities became abrasive when they were together, which fortunately was not too often. To some people visiting the area it would seem strange that two people in a community so small would have so little contact with each other, whereas in a city, two neighbours could live side by side for years without even meeting each other once, and not deem it unusual. However, Mo and Jim's unspoken distrust for each other was spirited and their lack of contact not at all unusual.

'I'm not deaf, Jim.' She clasped her small, bony hand around the full glass as soon as Christine set it down on the bar. She wore a look of concentration and she slowly and carefully raised the glass to her pouting, waiting lips and took an interestingly large quaff. 'I've been busy in the shop, right up until this infernal weather started,' she said as she rested the glass heavily on the top of the wooden bar. 'This foul weather means that the tourists have taken off. They *had* been busy buying all my stock and having their cards read, but now the numbers of tourists have left me with idle hands – and you know what the devil does with idle hands?' She now had a dark froth covering her top lip.

Jim stared at her, nonplussed, and he slowly gestured to his own top lip, prompting her to slowly wipe her own. She glowered at him.

'It's only a little heavy rain. We're used to that here, aren't we? It'll be gone soon enough,' Christine offered, a little uncomfortable now because of the atmosphere which was developing before her.

Mo leant closer towards Christine and said seriously, choosing her words carefully, 'It's more than that dear – much, much more.'

Jim and Christine looked at Mo intently as they waited for her to continue. It was soon apparent that she had finished.

'Whatever do you mean, Mo?' Jim said incredulously as he continued to study her gnarled face. 'The Weather Channel on cable is saying nothing unusual about the weather, and they use satellites and computers to help them to predict the weather.' He teased her, 'What do you use? A crystal ball? Hardly the cutting edge of technology,' he guffawed loudly.

'Listen, young man,' she turned on him. 'A storm is already blowing. A storm that will cause trouble and scuttle dreams, not one that they will report incessantly on cable television. If I am right and you don't believe me until it's too late, you'll be sorry you mocked me.'

Jim immediately wore a facial expression of surprise and disbelief, as if he had silently sat on a sharp object.

'No, Jim,' she cackled softly, 'I'm not going to turn you into a frog or any other hideous creature. I mean that you'll be sorry inside your being that you didn't heed my warnings.' She continued gravely, 'It won't hurt your business or your life in the long run if you take steps to protect yourself, will it? Or are you too arrogant and pig-headed to listen to me?'

He chewed on Mo's words for a minute. He did not have an inkling what she was rambling on about and his mind was working overtime trying to fathom her meaning. Besides, why is she so concerned about my well-being? he pondered. He was too bemused and open mouthed to even rebuke her unmasked insult. Instead he just looked her up and down and waved his hand with dismissal, believing that she must be slightly insane. 'You're right, I won't listen to you but it's not for the reasons you said,' he scoffed.

Christine looked at Jim and then at Mo, who returned Christine's look with a penetrating gaze with her small grey eyes, accentuated by the colour of her long grey hair. The gaze felt so strong to Christine that time froze but momentarily, in which she struggled to break the connection.

'You believe what I say about this storm don't you, dear?' Mo issued as a statement rather than a question, before continuing without waiting for a response, 'The weather determines the mood for any sentient being in any part of the world. For instance, when it is bright and sunny then people are happy. However, in parts of Scandinavia and Russia, where it is in complete darkness for months at a time, the number of suicides increases dramatically.' She spoke her words slowly and deliberately with each syllable and letter pronounced precisely. 'I have been having these dreams recently, about water and metaphorical floods of deep water invading parts of my every day life; filling my view from windows; filling my bed and cupboards with deep water that threatens to engulf me and sink me to the depths. Recently I have woken in the middle of the night, sweating with fear and trepidation,' she said seriously, 'and I have judged that the dreams have been created by this storm that surrounds us.'

Christine answered carefully from the top of the proverbial fence, not really daring to comment specifically on Mo's obscure words, 'I was looking out of that window earlier,' she gestured to the window at the rear of the bar, grateful for the opportunity to tear her eyes from the grip of old Mo, 'and at the rain that was beating down the leaves on the trees, causing the trees to sway with the strain. I'm no meteorologist, and I hope that it will soon pass, but I wouldn't be surprised if this weather will last longer than normal. Yes, it'd be right to be better safe than sorry. As for the storm being a harbinger for something else, I'm afraid that I am not at all qualified to comment on that and I bow to your more informed mind.' She smiled triumphantly.

'Very diplomatic,' Jim said.

Mo, looking diminutive in stature seated on the stool that was too high for her, said authoritatively, 'When Chrissie passes away, her days on this earth will be remembered and defined with clarity and fulfilment. This storm is an omen for change, for clearing out the dead wood in the lives of some. Embrace change and hardship, for it will make you a stronger and better person.'

Jim had lit his pipe again and was puffing smoke into the air, 'What are you going on about now? They are irrelevant words, Mo, but I suppose they could be prophetic,' he conceded, 'But don't write Chrissie off yet – all knowing old one.' He stifled a smile, 'She's plenty of years in her yet.' His voice wobbled with increasing humour, 'You sound like a woman spouting inauspicious words in a corny meteorological disaster movie, warning of an imminent disaster and nobody will believe you.' He laughed openly with wide smiling eyes.

'How dare you insult my intelligence. I'm everything but superficial,' she scoffed intelligently and unabashed, demonstrating that she was surprisingly well informed about modern day cinematic dross. She paused and took another large sup from her glass. 'None of us really knows when our time is up – not even me.' She retained a serious and authoritative expression, then an even more thoughtful look which caused more wrinkles to appear on her countenance. 'Treat each day as if it were the last, for one day it will be true, but bear in mind that what you do will still have consequences for you, even when you live on in the minds of others. Every day that you are alive is a wonderful day, no matter what the circumstances.'

'Oh, you're nuts, you are, and you're indeed a mystic,' he mocked when she had finished, believing that she was definitely mad. 'Bordering on the mystifying. None of your sentences follow each other. I don't know what you're on about,' he laughed.

Christine bit her lip, with the accompanying thought that he may now be upsetting old Mo too much. Mo was an old woman, after all, and the agitation of a confrontation with Jim could cause her heart to beat too fast and her blood pressure to rise fatally.

'Not really,' she interjected hastily, deciding that the conversation had gone farther than she was comfortable with. 'I understand what she means – I think,' she added under her breath.

Christine, working as a bartender, was ever trying to diffuse potential arguments and offer advice in times of trouble. If Jim had been at the receiving end of sceptical comments then she would have turned her own attention to his defence with disarming subtly. Today, though, it was Mo who needed her assistance, she felt.

'Of course you do, dear,' she said, then continued after a short pause, 'I have been inside your mind.'

It was Christine's turn to stifle a smile.

'Now you're just being really downright silly,' he said irritably aghast, and had evidently reached the pinnacle of scepticism as he listened to the old woman behind the rambling voice. He quickly drained the remaining contents of his glass and picked up his paper, ready to leave. 'I wish I could stay and listen to you all day, Mo, and look at Chrissie's enchanting smile, but I have to get back and finish the painting I'm workin' on.' He rose from the stool and said farewell to Christine before turning his attention to old Mo sitting emotionless on her stool. She looked reminiscent of a garden gnome fishing by an ornamental pond, trying to hook somebody on to her tales of impending emergency, so he mused to himself. 'See ya, Mo,' he said petulantly as he patted her firmly on the shoulder before he disappeared into the prematurely failing light and pounding sheets of rain.

Mo said nothing in reply.

'Bye Jim,' Christine called out, as he disappeared into the streaming rain with the newspaper once again placed uselessly above his head to shield him.

She was not left feeling uncomfortable in the presence of Mo because she had been in the presence of Mo's prophecies many times over the years. She also knew that Mo would not stay long in the bar because she rarely drank more than one pint at any one visit, and the pint that she did drink was smoothly dealt with and at an alarming speed. Mo did not speak at length to tourists who were not paying her money for her mysticism either, so there was no danger that Mo would scare customers away – should any venture from the dry interior of the board and lodgings. It was best to humour the old woman, she thought, although, in the distant areas of her mind she believed that there was some unfathomable truth in the mysterious and enigmatic words that she spoke. Whether or not Mo was psychic, she was prepared to keep an open mind on the subject, in case she experienced definite evidence either way. Christine was an intelligent woman without any kind of prejudice and believed that any human being had the right to believe anything they wished, provided they did not try and ram their beliefs down the proverbial throat of others. She was a realist and would not be swayed by conjecture or prejudice of the majority, even if that left her in the minority.

'What'll you do for the rest of the day?' Christine enquired.

Mo looked at her intently, 'I will return to my shop, my dear,' she said before she took a final draft of stout, leaving only froth on the sides of the now empty glass. She slowly wiped her mouth with the back of her hand and climbed off the stool that she had been seated on. 'Philip is at his boathouse repairing one of his cherished wooden boats. I think I'll stop by and see if he needs anything first,' she said distantly. She bent down and grasped her walking stick, securely positioning it in the claw of her hand as she prepared herself for the journey ahead of her.

'Okay, Mo. You be careful out there. When'll we see you again?' Christine enquired compassionately, wondering if months would pass before the old woman returned. She preferred to know the plans of old Mo at this particular time of inclement weather, so if Mo did not keep to them then she would know that something was possibly wrong. Christine would have liked to have made regular visits to Mo's home when she did not see her from one month to the next, but the inevitable unwanted attention of her son made the proposition too unwelcome. She often asked others to check on Mo, but not Jim as he would intrude too much on Mo's existence and ridicule whatever she said or did.

'I am unusually restless. I'll be back soon, and regularly so until this storm passes.' She looked contemplative as she leaned towards Christine, almost whispering, 'You be very careful too, my dear. If you need anything then just ask me. Although it pains me to say, obnoxious Jim will also be there too if you need him.' Her expression relaxed and a tired and haggard look took hold of the skin around her eyes as her forehead furrowed into a constant frown. She sniffed loudly and turned slowly, walking carefully towards the door.

'I always look after myself,' she smiled after the old woman, 'and make sure that *you* look after yourself in this weather. You must call me if I can do anything for *you* too.'

Mo nodded as she continued to prepare herself for braving the elements.

Christine watched Mo leave and wondered how she could be the mother of Philip. Philip was at the age of thirty, or thereabouts, and Mo looked at least ninety years old, which would have made her a mother at the age of sixty. Highly improbable, she mused.

Old Mo suddenly turned and looked at Christine when she reached the door. Mo stood at five feet tall, was bent slightly over her stick and her long grey hair was tied neatly in a ponytail. She stood stock still in the strong breeze that blew in from the street outside the bar, ruffling the edges of the yellow hat that she had pulled tightly on her head. The rain fell heavily and the only sound was the loud continuous pitter-patter of the large droplets on the road and on her large rainhat. Christine balked at the thought that she had spoken her mind aloud, as the look on old Mo's face was that of nodding comprehension and a sympathetic understanding of Christine's thoughts.

'You'll have to stop by my shop, dear. I must talk to you. You understand more than anyone round here, even my young Philip,' she said above the sound of the downpour.

Christine looked at the old woman and said unsurely, 'I'd like that. Next time I pass by I'll drop in to see you,' she found herself replying.

'Good,' Mo said firmly as she looked intently at her, 'I'll see you soon then.'

Christine was puzzled by the old woman but decided that she would make the effort and visit her within the next few days, even if Philip was there too she would have to confront him. She took her book up and set about turning her mind to the contents of the pages. However, the constant pitter-patter of the rain distracted the silence again and Mo had peculiarly disturbed her thoughts and her ability to concentrate on the pages.

The light had become very dim in the interior of the wooden bar. The almost single dark grey quilt of clouds, low in the failing light of the day had securely obscured the limited natural sunlight that remained in this most grey of days. She set down the book, approached the panel of light switches on the wall and switched them on, gently illuminating the quiet, empty interior of the nameless bar.

The rain fell from the now blackened clouds with renewed vigour, as though it had a purpose for falling so forcefully. He was standing in the leeward shelter of a small wooden building and yet the heavy rain had managed to saturate his body through sheer force. Rainwater dripped constantly from his short black hair, running down his forehead and dripping past the raven eyes that mirrored the blackened sky.

He stared unceasingly through the falling sheets of rain. He had been standing unnoticed in this statuesque position for the past hour, his eyes piercing the occupant of the bar that was located on the opposite side of the narrow street. There were no other people about to notice him standing there, and even if there were, they would have had scant regard for a lone figure sheltering from the torrential rain. Had a pedestrian passed close to him, though, if they were very conscious of the world around them, they would have immediately sensed that brutal intent dwelled in the pools of infinite blackness that filled the eye sockets of his skull, the same powerful intent that one can sense if one stumbles across a powerful and dangerous wild animal; the same powerful intent that strikes intense fear and dread into the bowels of other beings.

He slowly moved forward towards the interior lights of the now illuminated bar. He watched with growing excitement as Christine turned away from the window. He approached the bar with a malevolent smile.

Chapter Two

Denise's mother would have instantly disliked the King of England if her daughter had brought him home to meet her, so it was not that Allan had earned the hostility that he had incurred from his future mother-in-law. The problem was that his future mother-in-law was fiercely interested in ensuring that her daughter would be provided for in the manner that she was thus far accustomed, for the remainder of her life, without her precious daughter ever again having to work for a living. Unbeknown to Allan, this was his prospective mother-in-law's sole purpose for living and was the extent of her aspirations, hence her resolve. Moreover, although the King of England was more than capable of fulfilling this requirement she would probably have found fault with the size of his feet, be they too large or too small. Allan was just about capable of fulfilling this single most important expectation of his future mother-in-law, and his feet were of an averagely acceptable size too. However, anything else that could be considered good about him she actively sought to deny or belittle. Without any rational reason, she vehemently disliked him and never attempted to be pleasant to him or, for that matter, even be civil to him. In her opinion, the only good husband was a dead one who left a sizeable life assurance policy – she would most certainly be damned to Hades, (if she ever even managed to reach the gates of heaven) doomed to perpetual marriage to a slovenly layabout with no money of his own and a penchant for untidiness.

Denise struggled from the living room to the hallway with a bulging pink sports bag, struggling to shrug the long strap from her shoulder she finally let it fall and it hit the carpeted floor with a thud. She set down the oversized heavy suitcase by the front door too.

Her mother watched her and tutted when she looked at her own watch again. She stood imposingly between Denise and the door. 'He's late,' she announced with well rehearsed panic in her voice. She bit her lip. 'Perhaps he has had an accident or his car won't start. You'll miss your flight! All that money – wasted. I told you he is no good.' She folded her arms tightly over her floral dressing gown, which covered a heavy high-necked nightie. Her look was distant as her mind gleefully and secretly tried to imagine the worst possible scenarios; almost surreal scenarios involving deranged and angry mobs carrying axes and cut-throat razors.

Denise heard the sound of a car pulling up outside and she quickly opened the front door. She watched through the gloom of the dim, orange streetlit early morning shadows as Allan quickly stepped out of the car and quietly jogged with a lumbering gait along the path. She watched her fiancé as he fleetingly stole a glance at his watch.

Allan opened the car door and peered through the dim morning light at the open front door. He subconsciously noted how much alike the mother and daughter looked as they stood with folded arms in the open doorway. He did consciously notice, however, as he hastily made his way to the open door, that they were both wearing the same angry scowl. Why, he thought to himself, would Denise be annoyed and angry on the day she was flying to America for a two week holiday? He looked at his watch as he hurried along the tree-lined path towards the open front door. His watch silently informed him that he was late by a few minutes, which he did not equate to being actually late.

'You're late,' Denise hissed quietly when he arrived softly in the open porch, 'I was beginning to think something awful had happened... like the car wouldn't start or something.' Denise's mother looked distant as her daughter spat forth her forced castigation.

Allan listened with well worn disregard as he lifted the waiting suitcase from inside the door into one hand and the pink sports bag into the other.

'Well, you must be the most thoughtless man that I have ever met in my entire life.' His soon to be mother-in-law glared at him, her arms tightly folded in an almost self-inflicted bear hug.

'Sorry,' he whispered excitedly, not really comprehending her words, and then immediately fearing that this one word spoken in a whispering apology would have woken the entire well kept suburban London street at this early hour of the morning. He consequently stooped lower to the ground as he lumbered quietly back along the path, after emitting an almost imperceptibly apologetic farewell to Denise's mother.

She did not answer his farewell. Instead she immediately seethed at the missed opportunity to verbally abuse him, partly because he had not taken offence at the accusation and also because her mind was engaged in conjecture – did Allan have a life assurance policy? She refrained from hurling verbal abuse that would wake the neighbours, besides, that was not how she conducted herself in public.

'*Bon voyage*, precious.' Denise's mother quietly sniffed away a tear as she kissed her daughter on the cheek.

'Bye, Mum.' She cajoled as she reciprocated the affection. 'I'll telephone you when I get there.'

Allan jammed the large suitcase and sports bag into the boot of the car and climbed into the driver's seat before quietly shutting the car door. He looked across, through the passenger window and watched as Denise's mother held her precious daughter tightly. Was she going to let Denise go? he thought to himself.

It was late October and Allan was due to be married to an attractive woman in the middle of the following year; to the woman that he was watching say goodbye to her mother.

Allan and Denise's relationship had snowballed since the six months when it first began. Earlier in the year the happy young couple had bought a house together, which they were planning to move into after they had married. He was very enthusiastic in the preparation of Denise's new home – the happiness of Denise was most important to him – but he also wanted the home to be created for his own benefit. He was looking forward to being with her when he woke in the morning, when he came home from work and when he went to sleep at night. The only part of starting his own life that he was not happy with was leaving his mother, who would now be left alone in a large house that echoed the past and allowed the winds of time, past and future, to blow openly through old doors and windows. However, she still worked part-time and she had a hectic social life and so his only concern was not based on rational fact, only unavoidable sentiment. She would be given a new lease of life, he sometimes mused to himself to give him comfort.

The holiday that they were about to embark upon had been planned before he had proposed to Denise, so the following two weeks were an ideal coincidental opportunity for them to be together before their life took the turn into the straight road that led to the distant horizon. He had been due to take the holiday with a friend but the friend had pulled out of the arrangement a few months previously due to increased financial commitments. Allan had initially felt let down by this but had readily agreed to Denise's suggestion that she utilised the available holiday place.

Denise jogged in an unnecessarily girlish manner towards the car and when she reached it she placed her hand on the car door handle and turned to wave to her mother again. Allan quickly leaned across and lifted the door lock, allowing her to climb in without incident. He started the engine and slowly pulled away from the curb, allowing Denise maximum time to wave energetically to her mother until the last possible visible moment. He watched in the rear-view mirror as her mother stood at the front door, then she quickly moved to the end of the garden path and waved until the car disappeared from view. He looked at Denise. 'Are you okay?' he asked attentively.

She sniffed and touched her nose with a small lace handkerchief that she pulled from the pocket of her immaculate white jeans. 'I'm fine,' she said as she adjusted herself in the passenger seat and sat erect. She tried to conceal the fact that she was upset. She touched his hand that he had rested on the gearstick. 'I'm glad I'm going on holiday with you,' she said affectionately as she looked at him.

Allan, with eyes fixed straight ahead as he concentrated fully on the task of driving on the empty road towards Gatwick Airport, smiled at the windscreen and said, besotted, 'Me too.' He rarely embarked on lengthy conversations when he was driving because he preferred to concentrate. However, he could sense a deliberate and uncomfortable silence descend after only a few minutes, for she usually did the talking for both of them.

Eventually Denise ventured, seemingly ambivalent at first, 'Why were you late?'

He broke his concentration and quickly and quizzically looked at her. 'Eh?' he asked with surprise.

'This morning – picking me up.' She smiled as she replied, prompting him to answer.

'I wasn't late. I was only a few minutes over the time we agreed. Our flight doesn't leave Gatwick until midday and the time now,' Allan tilted his wrist towards him in controlled panic, 'is six thirty.' He was dimly aware that he was being reprimanded.

'Well, it's not fair. I was worried,' she continued with an adult, childish wine.

There was momentary silence. 'Sorry,' he replied defencelessly, not wishing to pursue the matter further. He leant across and carefully touched her hand. 'I'll make it up to you,' he expressed with devotion.

Allan, Denise and the luggage eventually arrived at the long stay car park outside the vast area that the sprawling Gatwick Airport encompasses. It was then necessary to take the courtesy bus that transferred them to the airport terminal.

Dawn was beginning to break as they rode in the courtesy bus through the glow of the orange streetlights. The artificial light that immediately evokes *early morning* in the minds of city dwellers all over the world was slowly being dissolved by the natural sunlight of early autumn. Quiet had again descended on the couple, for when Allan had taken the wrong turning attempting to locate the long stay car park, Denise had been forced to shout at him and take control of the situation by barking instructions while she authoritatively read from the map. Navigation and sense of direction had never been Allan's strongest points, which his future mother-in-law would be more than happy to dwell upon if she knew.

'Where would you be without me?' She forced a smile at him as they sat side by side on the bus. She would not have normally been the one to break the silence because it had not been her who had created the air of tension. However, pointing out his need for her presence was equally as satisfying to her ego as maintaining an awkward silence. Besides, she was on her holidays and she allowed herself to be unselfish.

'I don't know what I would do without you,' he said honestly, relieved that the silence was over. He leant over, kissed her on the cheek. Denise smiled but he failed to notice her spuriousness.

They arrived at Gatwick Airport four hours before the flight to Fort Lauderdale was scheduled to depart. Denise enjoyed arriving at airports early because it gave her the chance of visiting the many duty free shops – at least twice. Allan did not care much for shopping but, seeing as Denise did, he had no choice in the matter. He would have liked to have suggested that they could have passed the time by having a leisurely breakfast, then taking a look at the CDs in the music shop, a while spent looking at the duty free cigarettes and the rest of the time spent drinking a few beers in the pub. Denise would never agree to wasting valuable shopping time, and unless he wished to be verbally humiliated in public he had to keep his mouth shut. The quiet life beckoned and Allan had the backbone of an octopus. He did not try to acquire one either – she would never allow an octopus in the house.

A comparatively high percentage of Denise's few friends had recently married, and shortly after marriage they had each started a family. Denise was now ready to give up work and fall pregnant just as soon as she could and begin the remainder of her life with her friends – such were her aspirations.

She had met Allan six months previously in one of the many nightclubs in the City of London, where Allan could have been seen most weekends dancing frantically and whittling away his youth by drinking beer and having a good time with his male colleagues. Denise soon realised her luck in that Allan was subconsciously looking for a long-lasting relationship; she rapidly and expertly manipulated him with ease into a fast-moving relationship. His social life took a nosedive, which he willingly accepted now that he had a serious partner. They appeared inseparable to all Allan's now distant friends and acquaintances.

After Allan had checked their suitcases in at the airline check-in desk, the young couple made their way through the modern airport terminal and into the shopping area that visibly increased in size and the number of shopping outlets every year. The area was relatively devoid of people at this early hour of the morning, which suited Denise as she could maximise the available shopping potential by not queuing in changing rooms and waiting in queues of shoppers at the tills.

Traipsing around the shops at such an ungodly hour in the morning seemed most bizarre to Allan, if not most heinous.

Once inside the first shop, Denise casually pushed items of clothing along the rail, indifferently contemplating the suitability of the items while Allan stood behind her with his hands linked behind his back. Intrusive dance music throbbed annoyingly in Allan's ear – like the sound of a droning vacuum cleaner – together with the sound of a woman's voice relaying to her colleague the difficulties she was having with her current girl-friend. He eavesdropped on this particular conversation with considerable interest.

'Allan, can you hear me? For goodness sake, Allan.' She looked sternly at him and followed his gaze to the two women behind the counter. She reached out and held his chin between her fingers and physically turned his head to face her saying deliberately and sternly, 'Allan, for the third time, what do you think of this bikini?'

He enthusiastically began offering his opinion on what garments she was contemplating. He suggested that he assist Denise in trying out the finalists in her selection. She offered an almost sarcastic response. 'No, Allan. You can help me get out of them after we return from the beach in Fort Lauderdale – if you're lucky.' The last part of the sentence she said deliberately and precisely, almost with venom.

Allan had an eager sense of humour but did not often have the confidence to express it with Denise because he sensed that she found his humour immature. He had not really meant what he had suggested to be enormously funny and would have expected anyone else to return a single snigger and then walk off with a smile. He was indeed eager not to give an impression of immaturity through fear of losing her, and so he simply said nothing in response.

Denise slunk off in the direction of the counter to pay for her item. He thrust his hand into his pocket and followed her with his hand on his wallet, not keen on the fact that a nearby shopper was smirking at Denise's sarcastic comment. He wordlessly paid for her bikini as he curiously yet surreptitiously studied the assistant behind the till.

Once a rather pointless few hours had been wasted, in Allan's unspoken opinion, Denise decided to pass through passport control and into the duty free area where further shopping opportunities awaited. Fortunately for Allan, the amount of shops did not sufficiently allow Denise to expend all her time doing as she wished, which was just as well because he was genuinely excited about the day being the day he went to America. He found that airports contained an exciting unsurpassed atmosphere, and the damned shopping was making him impatient as he was not sampling enough of this atmosphere; which Denise could sense but was purposely and stubbornly unwilling to do anything about. He was unwilling to suggest to her that they do something else and so, as was common in his life, he suffered in silence.

The morning had eventually run towards midday and so, after she had managed to persuade Allan that cigarettes were cheaper in America than in the duty free shop – even though she only said this to prevent Allan from purchasing two hundred cigarettes and had no idea whether her statement was true – she reluctantly suggested that they pay a visit to the bar before the flight was called.

Allan was dumbfounded with her suggestion and he spluttered, 'Are you sure?'

'There's no need to be sarcastic, Allan. We are on holiday,' she replied, feigning well practised affront.

He had not intentionally addressed her sarcastically but he was so flabbergasted that he replied needlessly, 'Sorry,' and without thinking about the reasons for saying so.

'That's okay, Allan. As I said, we are on holiday.' She was satisfied with her various purchases, which Allan was now carrying together with her bulging pink sports bag, and so her mood was light and without antagonism.

The heavy bag was making the long shoulder strap hang tightly on his jacket and almost cut into his skin but he was spurred on by the thought of a rest and he ignored the discomfort. Having got out of bed very early this morning, not having slept very well, and because excitement was draining his energy, he was now feeling rather tired. However, he veritably skipped ahead into the bar like a happy dog that had been let off its lead in a field of other playful dogs.

'A pint of lager and a sweet white wine, please,' he requested cheerfully from the attending barman. The interior of the bar was decorated in the typical wooden fashion of an archetypal English pub – a Japanese owned stereotypical English pub – with a myriad of framed black and white photographs adorning virtually every available space on the surface of the walls. From the ceiling hung the obligatory assorted horse paraphernalia, including bridles, stirrups, horseshoes and various unfathomable brass ornaments. Quiet chart music played in the dimly lit but at the same time cheerful surroundings. The smell of beer tickled his nostrils while Denise stood behind him in quiet reluctance. It was her turn to feel slightly bored but she made no attempt to hide this fact. She folded her arms tightly.

Allan, leaving the bags at the bar, took the drinks and the two of them found an empty table in a flora and fauna festooned conservatory that adjoined the bar area.

He returned to the bar to retrieve the bags once she had sat down on the chair that he had chivalrously pulled out from under the table. The two of them finally sat at the table together in the near empty conservatory. The sound of the music had become barely audible in the excited open atmosphere of the airport, partly because of the increasing tannoy announcements preceded by loud doorbell sounds, and partly because of the general hubbub of travellers and the working airport contributing to the background noise and the air of excitement. The smell of jasmine perfumed the air, mixed pleasantly with the smell of freshly ground coffee. Allan felt almost uncontrollable excitement and happiness in every atom of his body and thought that he might burst at any minute.

'This is nice,' she admitted, as she relaxed in the wicker seat and looked about her person. Her high-pitched, quite loud voice filled the capacious, airy room. The interior of the conservatory was a leafy oasis in the almost clinical airport and could not fail to impress this fact on any person who entered.

He nodded as he set his glass down and took out a packet of cigarettes from his pocket.

She crossed her arms and looked out of the window at the hive of activity, dominated by the large white taxiing aircraft that curiously contrasted brightly under the now grey midday sky. She did not particularly enjoy the anticipation of flying, but, once the aircraft had taken off and climbed to its cruising height, her concern would dissipate as she became accustomed to the fact that she, like the other passengers, was flying by the seat of her pants. She wondered how it was possible that the aircraft successfully defied the laws of gravity, and she realised that Allan probably would know the physics behind aviation but she decided that she was not sufficiently interested in his undoubtedly thorough explanation. Her thoughts were usually along the lines of: what she did not know could not hurt her.

'I hope there aren't any thunderstorms in those clouds,' he thought out loud, 'I don't really fancy flying through heavy turbulence. It makes my stomach churn. I don't like or enjoy roller coasters or anything like that.' Allan generally preferred to air his fears as it gave him comfort.

She looked uncertainly at him with her arms tightly folded. 'Thanks, Allan. I needed that to calm my nerves.'

'Sorry,' he apologised in a lowered whisper, without thinking much about what he had said, and continued with another story. He remembered something that he had witnessed not so long ago and he hoped that it would cheer her up, and perhaps put her at ease. 'My friend, when he went on holiday last year, had an unusual experience on his flight to Spain.' He chuckled and she looked at him wide-eyed and with an almost disinterested expression, with her arms still tightly folded. 'When the aeroplane finished taxiing and started really fast down the runway to take off, the stewardesses were huddled around the door, straining really hard to force it shut. It was stuck in an open position, you see, and they had real trouble closing it. I mean, you would have thought that the captain would have asked the chief stewardess before the plane started to take off, if the doors were shut.' He took a drag on his cigarette, exhaled the smoke away from the cross-armed Denise and drank a mouthful of lager. 'The take-off was aborted and the plane grounded.' He laughed.

Silence.

'What?' he smiled excitedly at her as she glared at him. He was so excited that he was trembling slightly.

'Allan, do you have any other horror stories? Perhaps you would like to tell me about the time a friend of yours flew on a plane and the wings fell off, making the plane crash into the sea where the survivors swallowed large amounts of poisonous sea water,' she said with an acrid tongue.

He looked thoughtful for a brief moment. 'Toxic waste you mean? Yeah there is a lot of that in British coastal waters, apparently... no,' he coughed nervously, 'I just thought it was funny that a captain would even consider taking off without checking that the doors were shut.' His blue eyes suddenly shone brightly. 'Actually, I have seen three old ladies fall out of a car as it pulled out from a petrol garage!' He began to laugh very loudly as his vivid memory reminded him of what had happened.

She was not surprised at all by the sudden addition of a thinly related story, for he talked a great deal of nonsense when he was excited, she noticed critically.

'What happened, right,' he was laughing so much that he could hardly speak intelligibly, 'is that this car pulled onto the main road and obviously the passenger door was not shut properly.' More laughter. 'As the car turned sharply the three old ladies and their handbags came tumbling out and were strewn across the garage forecourt. They were gently rolling about as they attempted to find their handbags. I was sitting outside a pub opposite and I almost wet myself laughing. A few friends and me rolled on the grass holding our sides, we were laughing so hard. Actually—'

'Didn't you go and see if they were all right?' she interjected, not amused at all.

Allan had tears in his eyes. 'We could hardly stand, we were laughing so much,' he blubbed but he managed to calm himself eventually. 'Somebody came out of the garage and helped them back into the car. I am telling you, it was the funniest thing that I have *ever* seen.'

'It doesn't sound funny at all, especially after the horrible aeroplane story.'

'Oh. I suppose you had to be there really,' he said when he eventually stopped laughing and he wiped the tears from his face. 'Sorry.' He stifled a final snigger.

The disturbing roaring and rumbling sound of the aircraft wheels on the tarmac caused the entire cabin to shake violently. Denise held Allan's hand and squeezed it tight. He was busy peering through the small window when the loud rumbling noise stopped as the wheels left the runway and the nose of the aircraft lifted towards the sky. The jet engines continued their high-pitched, constant scream. It was now the only sound that dominated the other passengers' minds as they worked hard to defy the laws of gravity – both the engines and the people, straining physically and mentally to keep the aircraft airborne.

She relaxed her grip on his hand when the aircraft eventually levelled its rate of ascent to a less noticeable gradient.

The lit overhead 'no smoking' and 'seat belt' signs went dim with an accompanying 'ping'. Allan wondered what possible benefit there would be if the plane did crash and the passengers were wearing seat belts. He imagined the crash investigators' surveying the crash site.

'Now look, Bill, sure, all the passengers are horrifyingly burned, crushed, dismembered and dead but at least some torsos are still in one piece and are sitting in their allotted seats. We know who they are, even the ones without a head!'

He smiled to himself and pressed his face against the toughened plastic safety glass that separated the cabin from the external window of the aircraft. He strained to watch the towns, villages, roads and fields gradually becoming smaller and smaller, then finally being wholly concealed by the blanket of grey clouds that had initially whispered past his view.

He then turned his attention to the cabin and rubbed his hand that she had been squeezing so hard. He looked at Denise as she ordered drinks from the stewardess: Denise Poulden, for that was her maiden name, stood at 5'7" tall – when she stood up, which she was not at the time of ordering the drinks from the stewardess – with a very slim figure, stern expression, thin face and shoulder length, slightly curly, mousy brown hair. She was dressed in white jeans, light blue fitted top and a three-quarter length leather jacket. She wore only a minimal amount of make-up yet applied it with precision and aplomb so that only a little was actually noticeable. She was quite unremarkable at first glance. However, when one engaged in conversation with her it was immediately apparent that the saying, *first impressions last* is very true. Notwithstanding, she made the best of her appearance and managed to look synthetically attractive.

Allan had a quietly intriguing but barely perceptible smouldering look. This look was often disguised by his lack of self-confidence but when he was actively engaged in conversation with friends his intense blue eyes and smile revealed an interesting person lying inside the bashful, pleasant exterior. Denise did not concern herself with what he could make of his personal qualities but instead valued and wished to keep the Allan that could make money and keep them both happy with a minimum amount of hassle to herself.

She took the drinks from the tray and passed Allan his soft drink in the small, transparent cup.

'What's this?' he asked her curiously.

'Cola,' she answered firmly. 'It's a nine hour flight, and I don't want you drunk and embarrassing me.'

He had no intention of behaving thus and added pompously, 'Actually, in an aircraft cabin the atmosphere is very dry because of the air conditioning. You must drink as much fluid as possible to counter the effects of the false atmosphere, steering clear of alcohol because it dehydrates you.' He sipped his drink as she looked at him doubtfully.

He could sound quite pompous at times and his indomitably sensible nature accentuated this. She wondered if he had ever acted out of spontaneity or had committed an exciting act. However, she quickly came to the conclusion that this was unlikely, if not inconceivable, and she could not actually imagine anything herself that was exciting at that particular moment either.

She did imagine – perhaps even rather irrationally hoped – that he had a very dim view of the essence of excitement. Allan was as dependable as German engineering and she did not, at this time, wish to compromise reliability with excitement.

Denise declined to play cards with Allan when he produced the pack from his rucksack, and instead she placed her headset on her head and watched the small television situated in the back of the seat in front of her.

He looked at her face as the screen illuminated her with a flickering blue hue, then he rummaged turbulently through his rucksack again, searching for something to do to occupy his mind. He found his personal stereo, which he listened to for a short while. He soon became bored with this and resumed rifling through his rucksack. He found his crossword puzzle book, which he looked at briefly, then read the first page of his holiday novel without comprehending the words. He then joined Denise by placing his headset on and watching his television screen. He soon became bored with this too, and realised that he had disappointedly exhausted his carefully collated myriad of pastimes within the first hour of the flight. He selected the television channel that displayed the position of the aircraft on the globe, the graphics displayed on which, showed that they had travelled barely beyond the United Kingdom and eight hours of the flight remained. He shook Denise's arm to get her attention.

'What?' she glared at him, somewhat annoyed.

'Denise, I'm bored already. Talk to me or something would you?' He whispered mischievously in her ear, 'Perhaps we could adjourn to the toilet and join the mile high club?'

She took the headphones from her head, 'All right then.'

He stood up with the look of someone who had won the lottery.

'Let's talk.' She smiled and placed her hands in her lap. She turned in her cramped seat to face him and removed the headphones from her head. 'What do you want to talk about?'

He sat down with a resigned look of dismay, but inwardly acknowledged that Denise would never have been likely to agree to his suggestion. 'Well,' he said, not really wanting to talk about anything in particular, 'let's go through the itinerary for what we're going to do again.'

'Allan, we've gone through this a million times already. Surely not again?' she said incredulously, preparing to return the headphones to her ears.

'Now, tell me if I've got this right,' he continued anyway, 'We pick up the hire car…'

After five minutes of listening to him prattle on, she closed her eyes and her mind wandered off from his attempt at conversation. She had never spent whole days on end with Allan and already he was beginning to annoy her. Her life was enhanced by being with him, and his idiosyncrasies could be overlooked by her and even ignored if she so wished. After all, she thought, nobody is perfect and she had the rest of her life to alter him in some ways to suit her better.

'You're not listening, are you?' he asked her after a few minutes. He had noticed that her eyes were closed and her head was leaning back.

'Yes, Allan,' she answered casually, her eyes still closed.

A seed of doubt briefly threatened his mind but was quickly engulfed by the powerful seas of contentment, mixed with a healthy surf of lust. The pattern that he had drawn in the sand of the beach in his mind's eye, was quickly cleared by the tide of love and lust – although various other seeds existed on the expansive watery horizon. However, love and lust are too blind to notice such small, distant seeds that may never actually reach the shore of consciousness. He happily returned the headset to his ears and flicked through the channels using the buttons on the side of the armrest.

Denise was now distracted so she looked about the cabin in her immediate field of vision. Her mind contemplated the good looks of a nearby male passenger. She studied his well formed biceps that bulged from his short sleeved T-shirt and wondered what he did for a living. To her, he had the look of a builder, because of his physique, but she had no way of finding out. She watched as he stood up and made his way to the toilet. In a rush of impulsiveness she clicked open the seat belt in her lap and quickly explained to Allan she was going to stretch her legs. She joined the good-looking passenger as he stood outside the toilet door.

'Hello,' she said as she stood close to him, 'On your holidays too?'

The good-looking man looked at her.

'No ma'am, I'm going back home to Miami.' He smiled, flashing his white teeth and causing his strong stubbled chin to jut out – a chin that any man would be proud of.

Denise shivered involuntarily as her conscience voiced immediate approval to her mind. 'I see.' She bit her lip, shifted her stance and leaned casually towards him. 'What do you do there?' She opened her eyes and her pupils automatically dilated.

'Oh, I own a bar in South Beach.' He continued to smile as he looked with nothing but interest at her unusual green eyes.

To Denise he did not seem very talkative but she was now quite interested and so persisted, 'You'll have to tell me where it is. Perhaps I could visit?'

'I really don't think it's your scene.'

'Why not?' She was disappointed by the challenge.

The man chuckled and touched her arm, 'Well, it's not a straight bar, ma'am.'

She paused and looked distant as her mind processed what he said. 'Oh, I see.' She laughed nervously, initially thinking of shapes and buildings. 'Are you, ermm, are you gay?' she whispered, 'if you're not then I am really, really sorry if I have offended you.'

He nodded with an even broader smile, 'Don't insult me with an apology.'

She was grateful when the door opened and the good-looking man disappeared into the small room.

'What was all that about?' Allan said to her when she returned to her seat, for he had seen her lean close to the broad man and whisper something to him before he had watched her disappear into the small room when it was vacant again.

She put the headset on and looked at Allan, 'Oh, nothing really. He just started talking to me. Don't worry, I told him that I was engaged.' She smiled.

'I see.' He was slightly jealous. Denise was obviously attractive to other men, he mused and looked pensive as he thought. 'That's all right then, I suppose,' he could only reply, secretly rather pleased that other men found his future wife attractive.

'And what if it wasn't?' she pricked him.

'I don't know,' he replied uncomfortably, 'I suppose I would have had to confront him.'

'Yeah, all right, Allan, whatever you say,' she replied superciliously, not believing that he was capable of behaving in such a way.

Chapter Three

The boat drifted slowly around the outcrop of rocks at the end of the relatively small cliff face. The twenty or so silent occupants of the vessel gravely observed the flotsam and jetsam that was beginning to sink slowly beneath the surface of the murky blue water. The assorted remnants of what could only have once been a wooden boat, bobbed gently upon the surface, surrounded by a multitude of oxygen bubbles rising from the depths. The heaviest pieces of wreckage slipped through the silken surface of the now quiescent water. It was this vivid scene of hopelessness and destruction that was obviously the result of such wanton ferocity which deposited an aura of fear that hung thickly in the air.

The unintelligible babble that could be heard constantly from the two-way radio speaker suddenly burst into panicking clarity, shattering the quiet, uneasy and expectant atmosphere.

'Get the hell out of there!' came the unseen excited voice. The passengers sat up straight with a renewed air of surprise. How much more could go wrong? they wondered in silence.

The man at the helm stood up from the panel beneath the wheel and hit the starter with force. The engine of the boat reluctantly burst into life and the vessel surged forward, accompanied by a relieved cheer from the passengers. Within seconds, though, a loud thump reverberated solidly on the hull of the boat and the passengers were momentarily lifted off their seats. A multitude of screams erupted that threatened to penetrate the hull of the vessel as well as whatever else had physically struck it. Tom looked at his partner, who blankly stared ahead with a look of wide-eyed surprise, whereas she was wearing a look of utter astonishment. He wanted to say something to her but he could not stop himself shouting wildly at the top of his voice.

The skipper of the boat, standing at the helm in the bow of the vessel, pushed the throttle lever forward and the sound of the engines reached a more urgent pitch, then he stood with one foot on the prow of the boat and with the rocket-propelled grenade launcher primed and cocked, he scanned the water left and right. The skipper suddenly launched one grenade after the other. They left the barrel of the gun with a loud, resounding, popping sound, followed by a loud explosion as each grenade exploded beneath the water and sent a fountain of spray that twinkled like diamonds high in the bright morning air. The boat continued on its course to the shore as the bottom of the vessel was being continually and violently jolted, as were the nerves of all the passengers.

The man at the prow continued firing the rocket-propelled grenades into the water, which greatly rattled the nerves of the men, women and children with each and every explosion. A bowel breaching moment threatened when an exploding grenade ruptured an underwater pipeline leading to a nearby onshore petroleum refinery, sending an unseen fiery charge to its centre and causing an almighty explosion that erupted in a mountain of fire. The heat from the fire, despite being about one hundred feet away from the boat, was so intense that Tom was compelled to shield his face with his hands from the searing heat that so threatened him. However, the boat continued on its journey remarkably unaffected.

Suddenly, and much to the delight and terror of the other passengers seated under the canopy of the pleasure craft, the flashing bloodstained teeth of the great white shark loomed out of the depths, horribly burnt, scarred and disfigured from the effects of the explosions under the water. The leviathan was dead, at last. Everyone aboard cheered as the boat reached the quayside, much to Tom's relief.

'I thought that the ride had gone wrong or somethin',' Tom explained excitedly to Tanya – his partner – as they disembarked.

'That was absolutely fantastic!' she enthused. 'The explosions were terrific! Totally terrifying.'

'Yeah, man. I nearly crapped my pants when that gas station went up.' He laughed as he adjusted his ponytail. He smoothed the water back over his hair that had collected on his head from the effects of splashing water, 'If I was a kid, man, I would have!' he confessed rather unnecessarily.

'There were kids on it, you know.' She looked behind her to watch the disembarking hoards to ensure that she was not mistaken, 'I reckon, though, that kids these days are used to that kind of excitement,' she pondered aloud as she lit a cigarette and exhaled smoke. 'They probably just reckon that theme park rides like that are adequate, though, because they're used to violent films and video games at a much earlier age these days. I mean, when I was a kid, which was only about fifteen years ago I suppose, my vacation entertainment was watching cartoons and riding my bike and that was about it, you know. The most exciting film I saw was *ET* and that film now is probably shown on daytime television on a crap cable station. Kids now watch death, violence, sex and swearing – and that's just what happens to their folks and neighbours!'

He laughed, 'Not quite.' He paused, 'I was a skateboard man myself. Hey, I was a diva on the skateboard.' He jumped forward and adopted a stance on an invisible skateboard. 'You know, tricks, stunts and stuff. As a matter of fact, I may have a mooch around the garage when I get back home and see if I can find it.' His arms were outstretched as he kept his balance.

She playfully slapped his bare arm. 'Okay baby,' and walked slowly past the stationary Tom.

He looked at her through an overly emphasised frown. 'Are you patronising me, woman?'

She turned and smiled coyly, 'Me? No way, baby.'

He took her comment in the good humour that it was offered and lunged forward to grab her. She neatly sidestepped him, turned and pushed him in the small of the back.

'Too slow, fat boy,' she teased.

'Hey, not fair. First you call me a baby and then you call me fat boy.' He feigned affront and made his bottom lip curl over his top lip in a kindergarten fashion. He stood still with his hands in the pockets of his shorts and buried his head into his chest.

She laughed and hugged him around his waist, for he was considerably taller than her.

'Hey, I'm sorry.' She tilted her head and stood on tiptoe so that she could kiss him. She laughed, 'I'll make it up to you when we get back to the apartment,' she hissed.

He scratched his goatee thoughtfully. 'Mmmmm...' he paused, 'Yep, I can just about manage that.' He smiled and suddenly panicked, 'Jeez, is that the time?' He pointed at his watch dramatically, 'We should be heading back! Come on!' He grabbed her arm and started running.

'Tom!' She struggled free and laughed gleefully. 'It's early in the morning already!' she called after him. 'We only just got here!' She watched his long legs stride effortlessly ahead.

'Shit. I thought I could try,' he admitted. With open palms facing towards the radiant sun heed turn to look at her from a distance. He jogged back to her side.

They continued hand-in-hand as they made their way around the now busy Florida theme park under the blazing sun that hung higher in the clear blue sky, happily discussing their childhood.

Theme park workers dressed in the costumes of various past and present famous movie stars such as Elvis and Laurel and Hardy – whose films were a particular favourite of Tom's – wandered the period building sets and streets that surrounded the large man-made blue lagoon at the centre, upon which powered two speed boats zooming from one end to the other, splashing tourists with a refreshing spray of cold clear water.

'About going to Key West after the weekend,' Tom began. 'Have you rung your uncle yet?'

'Yes and no,' she explained cryptically. 'I rang this morning but he wasn't in. I'll call him later. Whatever happens, though, we're going,' she said assuredly. 'I haven't been there for years and I'm really looking forward to it. You know, a few beers, watching the beautiful sunsets, the restaurants, the bars, the night life.'

'Oh, I'm there, man.' He looked distant as his imagination whisked him away. 'I went there when I was a kid, with my folks – when they were still together. I can't remember what it's like, just that it's real busy and everything is really close together – you know, all the houses and yards and stuff.'

She paused momentarily, not sure whether Tom would want to talk about his past.

'Your mom, she left home when you were what age?'

'No Tan, she didn't leave, my old man *told* her to leave.' He shook his head and sighed, 'He was up to no good with his secretary. One night he came home late from work and said to my mom that he wanted to divorce her.' He looked distant. 'I remember that the shouting lasted for days and days. She left in the end, after about a week of shouting, screaming and throwing stuff. Best thing she ever did, you know.' He managed to laugh. 'And I don't mean throwing the ornaments. You see, she took him for half of everything he owned and started a promotions company with the money. Since then she hasn't looked back. I mean, look at what she has done with her life – her happiness and success – and to think that none of that would have come about if she had stayed married to my old man.'

'I didn't realise that it was that way round,' she said. 'Still, you don't seem to have been adversely affected, and neither does your mom – or dad, come to think of it.'

Tom's father was a director of a transport company and lived happily with his second wife in New York. Tom spoke to him every other month – usually, but not religiously – and the distance suited the relationship of father and son. Tom had found it very difficult to forgive his father at first, but ever since the failed marriage of his parents, he had witnessed his mother blossom on her own, then he found that he could eventually begin to forgive him. However, if his mother had suffered as a consequence of the marriage breakdown then he would have found it difficult, if not impossible, to forgive his father. His parents very rarely spoke these days, though, for the ending of the marriage was anything but civil and they were both scarred for life in that respect.

'At the time, when I had just started my teens, I rebelled and was a real handful. The thing is, though, I had received discipline as a younger kid and, although I was bad, I would not skip school.' He laughed. 'That seems weird to some, but at school I could behave badly and go against the other kids and the teachers – you know, fights, detentions and that. I suppose I was lucky in a way because the only reason they didn't kick me out of school was because I was good at football.'

'I didn't know that.' She looked surprised.

'Yeah, I was good at it but I didn't really like it.' He shrugged his shoulders. 'Although I was a rebel, I was only a rebelling rebel and not a full-time rebel. After a few years, once my home life became settled and I lived with my mom but saw my old man at weekends, I worked hard, graduated and took all my exams – and now I am the successful man you see before you today.' He stood still and erect, proudly, with his fists on his hips and wearing a large cheesy, comical grin.

She laughed and they continued walking slowly.

'So, do you think that kids today have it easier or harder, you know, with all the strong influences that they have? That is, if you were growing up today, do you think that you would have turned out the same?' Tanya was a deeply thoughtful person, in that she thought about matters very deeply and enjoyed serious discussion.

He wore a serious expression as he thought.

'Everyone is different,' he said eventually. 'If a kid receives strong discipline at home and at school; if they are reasonably intelligent; if their peers have had the same upbringing then they have a good chance of living their lives as they wish without making a mess of things. The thing is though; if they aren't disciplined at a very early age; if they do not receive a good education or if they are not averagely intelligent or without common sense; if they are not shown forcefully the difference between right and wrong at an early age then they'll play video games and watch violent films without judgement. The line between right and wrong is then blurred and they'll probably begin murdering the people around them, commit crimes and other acts of violence just because they do not know any different – and violence is basic and raw human nature that hasn't been tamed by society – only hidden in the closet. They'll be nothing but savages and will have to be treated as such,' he said resignedly.

She looked thoughtful. 'No, you can't say that because each person is different and each child will react differently – some will rebel and some won't. Perhaps I agree, in part, but there are many people who wouldn't agree with you and would say that you're just a pessimist – perhaps that you even have fascist tendencies.' She raised her eyebrows doubtfully at his strong choice of words and at the same time injected realism into his thoughts.

'And they are the one's who are causing the problems – the people who are too afraid in case they upset a lone single parent in Wyoming,' he moaned sarcastically. 'I'm a realist and what kids need is firm discipline, not weak-handed liberalism. I don't mean that their parents should hit them – that should only ever be used as a last resort – and they should not spoil their kids for no reason either. These, I reckon, are the basic laws of parenthood.' He laughed without humour, 'I'm going to be the dad from hell, aren't I?'

'No, I think that you'll be a good father – even though you reckon that it's going to be that black and white. You know, you're gonna be in for a shock,' she squeezed his hand. 'Just make sure that you don't turn out like your pop or a fascist dictator,' she said seriously. 'I believe that being unfaithful is the sign of an untrustworthy and flawed character, and being a dictator is just warped. As long as you are true and just, then you have the chance of being a good parent.'

He sighed, 'There are too many psychologically flawed people on this planet who are parents and dictators, and you are fortunate enough to be with one who isn't one of them – and I know this because I studied psychology for a few years before I decided to change to computer engineering. Damn weirdos freaked me out in the end.' He smiled. 'I'll be a good dad then. Thanks for that.'

'Yeah, but people change,' she goaded.

He held his hands up in submission. 'Hey, I accept that, but a person's fundamental character remains the same. However,' he continued to look thoughtful, 'it's very unusual that a person who never lies, who is always trustworthy one day commits murder or robs a bank – but it does happen. They usually have a part of their character that is a bit odd – a part of their character that you can single out and say, "There. That's what gave the game away. I knew there was something odd about him."'

'So, you reckon that an untrustworthy streak is detectable, even in the most disguised character?'

'Absolutely,' he said with finality. 'With the benefit of hindsight,' he conceded.

'Well, that's the human character explained away in a few sentences.' She smiled doubtfully. 'You know, you should be a politician.'

He thought for a moment. 'Nah, politics is different to just standing on a soapbox. A politician has to talk to dickheads and suck up to the people in power – hey, often they are one and the same.' He chuckled at his aside before continuing. 'If I got involved in politics I would change it all. For instance, at a summit of world leaders I would insist that everyone brought a bottle and that rock'n'roll was played loudly and constantly. Each leader would have to down a glass of beer or a spirit before he said anything. Old Boris would have loved that – he would have ruled the world!'

She smiled her reservations and looked at him. 'I have never met a man who I can discuss serious stuff one minute and then watch as he behaves like a total kid the next minute.'

'And I have never met a woman who is as erudite as she is attractive.'

'I'm averagely intelligent but I wouldn't say that I'm massively academic,' she replied quickly and modestly. 'Thanks for the compliment, though.' She frowned. She poked him hard in his firm chest and suppressed a smile. 'Hey, you'd better not be implying something else,' she said angrily.

He shrugged off the hard poke that he had received and laughed. 'How could you even think that! If you were a book you would be a literary masterpiece.' He bent down in front of her on one knee. 'If you were a painting you would be a Rembrandt,' he said, with his hand placed on his heart.

She kissed him firmly on the lips. 'Nice cliché, baby, but I guess that's okay. Your heart's in the right place.'

Further along they stopped at an ice-cream vendor and purchased two ice creams. He waved one in front of her nose and she pulled away quickly.

'Don't you dare ask me to smell that!' she threatened.

'Now would I do a thing like that?'

'You have done! Remember, in that mall near where your mom lives?'

Tom frowned.

'You remember. You bought two big soft ice creams and you sniffed it then passed it to me to have a sniff. I leant forward with my nose in the tub and you pushed it in my face!'

He laughed. 'Darn it. That's one of my favourite gags.' His face lit up. 'I remember once, when my mom had a garden party when I was young, a distant aunt came over and I was carrying a huge cake to put in the shade outside. I asked my aunt to sniff it and then whacked it in her face.' He laughed loudly. 'Man, the shit hit the fan that day but it was as sure as hell worth it.'

She laughed and gingerly took the ice cream from him.

They soon wandered into a nearby film exhibit situated in a large building, reminiscent of a newly built brick warehouse. The interior was split into two levels, the second level being a balcony that overlooked the first level. The spartan decoration, the silence and the coolness of the air gave the impression of a movie theatre. However, one exhibit stood out in the very dim lighting and took the form of a model condominium, the exterior of which was best visible on the first floor balcony.

Tanya and Tom ascended the gently sloping flight of stairs and stood at the part of the balcony that overlooked the scene from the well known thriller movie by a famous English writer and director. From where they were standing, an onlooker could observe the model apartment block opposite and peer through darkness and into the lit windows, which were in fact cleverly, but simply disguised television sets that formed part of the facade of the building.

Binoculars placed in small holders fixed to the balcony, were available for the visitors, so that it was more comfortable to the eyes than straining to survey the small windows that were as far from onlookers as the screen at a movie theatre. Tom noticed a young man next to him, perhaps in his mid-twenties, put a pair of binoculars to his eyes and so he decided to do the same.

'What can you see?' she asked Tom curiously.

'Well,' he paused as he scanned the windows, 'not much. Hey, wait a minute, a woman's taking her clothes off in that window.'

'Which one's that?' the man next to Tom asked, trying not to sound too interested.

'Eh? Oh, ermm, right hand side, fourth window down,' he replied. He turned to Tanya and revealed a guilty grin. He returned the binoculars to his eyes and periodically instructed the man next to him as to which window was the most interesting.

'Tom, stop being such a perve. Let me have a look.'

Tom laughed. 'Oh, I see. I'm a perve but you can have a look.'

'That's right. Anyway, I'm looking for *men* who are undressing.' She smiled and took the binoculars from him. 'I can't see anything interesting going on. There are no men or women undressing,' she said after a short while.

'Let's go, then,' he said nonchalantly.

She replaced the binoculars in the holder and turned to leave. It was then that she noticed that a large crowd of tourists had assembled behind them. They looked at her and then Tom disapprovingly, for they had witnessed all their actions since Tom had been using the binoculars.

The bright sunlight contrasted powerfully with the dark interior and they were forced, respectively, to hastily adorn their sunglasses.

'Tom,' she began, 'could you see anything or were you geeing that man up?'

'Well,' he confessed, 'there was one window with a woman undoing a blouse. You couldn't see anything but I thought I'd have some fun.' He grinned.

'I guessed as much, and I didn't know those people were behind us.' She groaned. 'At the age of twenty-eight I felt so immature, like I had been caught singing in a hairbrush by my mom.'

'That happen to you too? I knew they were there.' Tom smirked. 'Anyway, you'll never see them again and I know that exquisite experience, intelligence and inner beauty is belied by your youthful exterior.'

Tanya stood at just five and a half feet tall, with long, dark, undulating hair that cascaded to the small of her back. It was tied back loosely today and had ever so subtle hints of auburn. Her eyes were large pools of fresh cream infused with silky milk chocolate pupils. The remainder of her appearance was as appealing, accentuated by her intelligence and almost constant smile. She was an enchanting woman and no man could pass her without fixation.

She started after him. 'I can't believe you didn't tell me they were there!' she called after him as they chased through the park. They ran past the same group of tourists that they had seen in the exhibition and had to stop running because they were laughing so much. The group of tourists ignored them.

Tom stood on the chair, the chainsaw leaping to life as he pulled the cord that started the engine and laughed maniacally as he raised the throbbing machine above his head – the smoke from the tiny engine enshrouding him in an eerie lustre. A constantly smiling waitress obliviously walked past the chair that he was standing upon and he suddenly swung the revolving blade towards her neck, decapitating her in an instant. The expression on the severed head that landed on the plate, was halfway between a frozen smile and surprise. The body slumped to the floor and the last remaining beats of the heart pumped thick red blood onto the floor, as the body quivered in the throws of death.

'Tom,' Tanya enquired. 'What are you thinking about?'

He broke from his murderous day dream. 'What?'

'The lady asked if you would like another drink.'

'Errr… no thanks. Shall we go?' he said hastily, somewhat disturbed by the way his mind was working. He embraced the idea of leaving the unremarkable purple restaurant, the external shape of which was like an unfeasibly large purple boil.

'Okay.' Tanya was puzzled.

The smiling waitress soon returned to the table with the bill, which Tom paid. He looked at the waitress's neck and smiled.

'Tom?' Tanya looked at him and then at the waitress.

'You wouldn't believe me if I told you,' he confessed as she left the table. She returned his gaze and smiled encouragingly. 'But I'll tell you in a minute,' he said as they stood up and left the restaurant, descending the flight of steps from the purple boil. He took a deep breath. 'I was just thinking,' he began, 'how annoying that place was, and what would happen if I took a chainsaw to that waitress's head. I was having a daydream in that damn atmosphere of contrived enjoyment and I just wanted to spoil it by doing something that would get everyone's attention.'

'Murder?' she asked, a little perturbed.

'I was thinking symbolically,' he said absently. 'It annoys me, that's all, that the people in power think they can arrest my attention with a large purple boil-shaped restaurant and crappy burgers on a weird plate. Are we that dumb? Has the human race reached an end to which it must subject itself to inane leisure time?'

'Well, you suggested to go in there, and you are the one that suggested visiting Orlando,' she explained.

'Yes I know. I thought that I would still find all the kids' stuff entertaining, but it's taken on a universal appeal that is meant to cater for the young and old alike. Okay, I admit that the rides are, generally speaking, outstanding, but it's just the way it's all packaged. It's like a really superbly drawn cartoon with a crap story. Does that make sense?'

'Not really,' she replied pragmatically. 'If the parks were badly packaged then it would detract from the enjoyment. If you don't expect too much then you won't be disappointed. You should just view the package for what it is and accept that you understand what lies behind the shallow and glossy facade. Like you said earlier, about those people that were behind us when we were messing about in that exhibition, it didn't matter what those people thought of us because *we* knew what had happened, and the fact that *they* didn't know is of no consequence to us. Similarly, we can be safe in the knowledge that we can enjoy the intense hype and gloss around us every minute of the day and extract what we find enjoyable – and that only.'

He remained thoughtful. 'You know, if I didn't have you to bounce my thoughts off then I would probably drive myself nuts thinking about these things.' He leant forward and kissed her.

'You're having one of your thoughtful moments,' she said. 'You know, you shouldn't have a spliff before you go out; you know it sends your mind into overdrive, thinking about the universe and life,' she chided gently.

'Yeah, I know, but I like thinking about all that stuff,' he confessed quietly. 'It makes me feel even happier about myself, reminds me of how lucky I am being with you and how society takes us all for stupid animals that believe anything that we are told.'

'You're starting again.' She raised her eyebrows. 'C'mon, let's get a drink and I'll phone my uncle from the hotel bar. We're going away next week to where life is how it should be lived.'

'Hey, you're right.' He lightened his mood instantly.

They sat at a table near to the circular bar that occupied the centre of the establishment. The soft lighting and dark furnishings created a peaceful and secluded ambience. They had arrived back at the apartment and showered and changed before venturing out for the evening. The day had been long, hot and exhausting but nevertheless enjoyable.

'Great,' Tom exclaimed. 'I'd like to stop off along the way on the east coast of Florida, stop for one night at home and pick up some clothes and stuff. Heck, it's quite a drive y'know, It'll make it a more leisurely journey. I hate rushing around and being rushed, as you know.' He raised the glass to his lips.

'Too right I know,' Tanya said under her breath as she raised her eyebrows. She had just returned from making the phone call to her uncle in Key West, hence Tom's enthusiasm. 'Anyway, he's expecting us in two days time, so we'll leave here tomorrow; leave in the morning and stop for the night at home and then drive to Key West the following day.'

'When was the last time you were there?' he asked.

'Must be—' her eyes rolled upwards to the sky as she thought. She looked up at the fan that revolved slowly and silently on the ceiling and let the gentle breeze cool the small beads of sweat from her brow, 'Jeez, must be about five years ago. My folks, brother and me went to stay with my uncle for a week in the apartments that he lets out to people on vacation. Hey, it's a real nice place – wait till you see it.' She patted his knee to emphasise the point. 'Anyway, I remember that I didn't really want to go but I was between jobs at the time and I wanted a vacation and so I went.' She leant back in her chair as she reminisced. 'That was *the* most relaxing week of my life. We didn't do much: we just sat drinking in the shade, and eating and talking for the entire week. On one day we ventured out on a boat for a bit of sea fishing, but we spent most of the day eating, drinking and talking then, too.'

'There's a lot to be said for doing nothing, just taking a step back from life to contemplate everything and take stock of the things in life that matter. I have a feeling that I'm going to live in Key West some day,' he said confidently. He currently lived with

Tanya in Fort Lauderdale, in a plush house that adjoined the many waterways that snaked through the opulent suburbs. He was employed as a computer engineer and was in demand all across America and Europe – such was the rare extent of his expertise. He was so in demand that he could work when and where he wished and take vacations when it suited him, and was well paid to boot. At this moment in time he had decided to take a three week vacation.

Tanya, on the other hand, was the creative half of the partnership and was self-employed as a freelance writer. She wrote articles for magazines and newspapers but could not bring herself to be tied down to a specific area of the country and work for one employer. She was happy with her portable computer and cellular phone, thereby allowing her to travel with Tom, when it mutually suited them both, and basically she had the opportunity of working from any country on the planet if she wished. It was this sense of freedom that suited her personality and enhanced her ability to write. She was now, after five years in this line of work, creating a good reputation with the major national newspapers and popular magazines, ranging from entertainment magazines to travel publications. It was her intention to write an article on Key West, not because she was a workaholic but because she enjoyed writing. She enjoyed the fact that other people would be reading her thoughts and her observations. In effect, readers of her work would be reading a written fragment of her mind. She shared her intentions with Tom.

'That's not a bad idea. Hey, you could do a piece on me,' he suggested. 'You know, rich computer engineer and his favourite ways to relax.'

'I don't really think that sex, drugs and rock'n'roll are really a suitable exposé for a man in your line of work.' She smiled.

'Hey, that's a bit strong.' He frowned. 'Anyway, I doubt if anything could dent my reputation as being the best in the country,' he said very modestly.

'Watch your head on that fan way up there.'

He laughed. 'I didn't mean to sound quite so arrogant,' he confessed. 'That's probably partly why I dress like I do and adopt this appearance.'

Tanya looked puzzled.

'Well, it's partly the rebelling rebel that's still in me. I want the good things in life but I refuse to conform. I want people to judge me incorrectly by my appearance and choose not to like me, because then I know that I don't have to waste my time talking to those particular people.'

'So, if someone does talk to you and seems to get along with you, then you know that, essentially, they are the type of person that you want to know?'

'Exactly.'

'And if they turn their nose up at you then you know not to bother?'

'Exactly.'

'I suppose it almost makes sense.' She frowned doubtfully. Sometimes he went a bit far.

'I think so, provided it's not taken too far by having everything pierced and tattooed.' He laughed, 'I think that subtlety is the best method, so that it's not quite so obviously rebellious. I also think that you have to have the right personality to carry it off. For instance, if I was really obnoxious to people I didn't know, then people would have grounds to judge me unfairly.'

The bar in which they were seated was quite busy with people on their vacation. Most patrons were dressed in shorts and loose clothing, for the day was very hot and sunny. The exposed flesh of many people had been burned a bright red by the intense sun, despite the fact that the smell of sunblock was thick in the air and it had been applied liberally by them all.

Tanya winced as the exposed red back of a passer-by went past them.

'Why do people do it?' She shook her head.

It was Tom's turn to look quizzical.

'Sunbathe,' she explained.

'Give it a few years and nobody will sunbathe, once they realise what exposure to strong radiation does to you. Actually,' he said, 'each to their own I suppose. As long as it doesn't affect me, I don't care what people do.'

'But what if I liked sunbathing and in a few years time I was diagnosed with skin cancer? Wouldn't you regret not ever having stopped me?' she probed.

'That's nothing but conjecture and I can't comment on that. You could be hit by a bus next week and killed, but I don't think about that either,' he said matter-of-factly.

'Thanks a lot,' she said with disappointment.

'All right then, I could be killed in a plane crash next month, therefore I wouldn't be around when you were diagnosed with skin cancer.'

'Are you saying that you don't care?'

'Of course I care,' he said vehemently. 'I'm just making the point that hypothetical questions of this nature do not warrant a realistic answer. Of course I'd be upset, you know that, but I wouldn't waste time wishing that the past had been different. Look,' he picked up her packet of cigarettes, 'you smoke these and it's highly probable that, at some time in your life you'll get some kind of cancer.'

'Right, so I might get hit by a bus next week or I may live my life until I'm about fifty years old, only to be struck down by cancer and die a slow, painful and lingering death,' she countered.

'Exactly,' he said. 'Enjoy!' He took one for himself and then passed her the packet. She took one without guilt and raised her glass with an accompanying smile.

'Here's to being killed when you least expect it,' she said ambivalently.

He mirrored her wry smile and slowly shook his head as he contemplatively returned the glass to the table.

Chapter Four

The aircraft landed at Fort Lauderdale Airport at five o'clock in the evening, local time. The flight attendants had completed the job of looking after their passengers and dampening their fears of flying in an aircraft. Now that the aeroplane had landed on terra firma, the passengers immediately ignored the unspoken fears that they had had nine hours earlier. Now, they eagerly and confidently gathered their belongings from the overhead lockers and ignored the flight attendants' adamant requests that they remain seated until the aeroplane came to a complete halt.

The flight crew, unlike the passengers, were not excited and were not impatient to get up and walk around after spending nine hours in a cramped seated position; for the flight crew it was just another tiring working day *and* they had more work to do, whereas the passengers had a holiday to embark upon.

The passengers disembarked from the aircraft and stampeded excitedly through the connecting tunnel to the airport terminal. Allan briskly followed the tide of passengers and looked at the scene beyond the window of the articulated tunnel. He reluctantly observed that the American sky was also grey, like the sky was above the south of England when Denise had looked out of the window at Gatwick Airport.

'We brought the weather with us,' he remarked inconsequentially as he turned to her.

Denise merely looked out of the window at the clouds.

'Mmm,' she could only muster in response.

He was quite tired after expending nine hours in the cramped conditions of the aircraft, without sleeping or stretching sufficiently. Why was doing nothing so tiring? he mused to himself.

Conversely, Denise had slept for a number of hours, despite Allan making a nuisance of himself – in her opinion – and she was not feeling too tired but was sleepy after having been woken not long ago. She had a feeling that the tiredness was brought on by the champagne that Allan had ordered. Although she initially forbade him to drink alcohol on the aircraft, she favoured the idea of drinking champagne at ludicrously inflated prices as she believed that it impressed the passengers immediately about her – what she did not realise was that the majority of the passengers on the charter flight did not take any notice at all.

The Gatwick flight was the only flight in the arrivals area but the queue for the seemingly over-bureaucratic passport control extended to a considerable waiting time. Sniffer dogs, under the guidance of armed policemen, were being led along the queues of people.

'Denise, do you reckon they're looking for a bomb or a terrorist?' he said to her in a lowered voice as he comprehended the scene before him. He was not really expecting her to give him an informed answer because he assumed that she would not really be interested. However, he sensed that she was unhappy about something and so decided to make conversation.

'No,' she replied tiredly. 'When I came here a few years ago the police were doing the same thing then. They have tough immigration rules in this country.'

He watched as the large Alsatian dogs, happily – because he could not fail to notice the vigorous action of the dogs' tails wagging rhythmically – walked up and down the queues of waiting passengers from the single aircraft.

'What, do some passengers have a stowaway stashed in their hand luggage?' he said facetiously and laughed to himself.

She ignored his quip.

Neither Denise nor Allan noticed the policeman with the dog walk back nonchalantly along the line of passengers. Allan looked up and saw that the policeman was looking at him as he slowly passed. Allan looked at the dog, whose tail was wagging and tongue was lolling out of his open, panting mouth. He held out his hand for the dog to sniff with his large, black and very wet nose. He ruffled the dog's head, causing the two thick velvet ears to waggle from side to side.

'Hello boy,' he said in an artificial high-pitched voice.

The policeman looked at him quizzically, then smiled uncertainly as he shook his head and continued his last walk along the queue of passengers. The policeman considered that the young Englishman was too wrapped up in his partner to be at the apex of committing a crime, and his well trained dog was no more interested in the couple than he was in a tomato.

Allan and Denise eventually came to the head of the queue and at the counter filled in a form, which are necessary – for some unfathomable reason – to be completed before entry into the United States. Presumably they can recognise the handwriting of known criminals, Allan mused: This is the handwriting of that international terrorist. Look at the letter 'A' and the way he strikes the stem of the seven through! He smiled to himself as he handed over the completed form and passport to the member of staff.

Denise had witnessed the same procedure when she had visited Florida with her mother while on a two week holiday four years previously, and they had both enjoyed their stay immensely. Her mother had enjoyed her stay because she busied herself by complaining about everything. She consequently received a constant stream of sincere, yet meaningless, apologies and assistance from managers of restaurants, shops, tourist offices and hotels all over the state of Florida. She was rather disappointed that they had been so helpful; she did not really comprehend the fact that America was the quintessential home of complaining about consumer dissatisfaction of all magnitudes. Had her complaints been met with hostility then she would have been happier because she did relish an argument. If she had thought about the situation at length, though, she may have realised that the American population have the right to bear arms, as detailed in the American Constitution of 1776. This right would probably have been exercised to the full extent if Denise's mother had been allowed to reach full fettle.

It was Denise's turn to hand over her documents and Allan looked about him. The décor of Fort Lauderdale Airport appeared more subdued than the interior of Gatwick Airport in that the lighting, carpets and furniture were of a darker ambience and not at all like the clinical white tiles and bright lights of Gatwick Airport. Fort Lauderdale Airport was fully air conditioned but it did still feel uncomfortably humid to him, for he was not used to hot, humid climates; dressed as he was in heavy black jeans, white

T-shirt and a three-quarter length leather jacket. His short dark hair, brushed and waxed tidily forwards as was the norm amongst most young men in their mid-twenties in the 1990s, finished off the smart, well groomed yet casual appearance.

Eventually, once they had convinced the immigration staff that they were not terrorists or intending to disappear into the wilderness when they left the airport, they made their way to the baggage reclamation area. He removed his jacket and placed it on the baggage trolley that he was pushing. Due to the comparatively small size of Fort Lauderdale Airport, he soon parked them both in a suitably quiet area and then walked off to take a position by the carousel, where the suitcases were due to be loaded from behind the walls and out of view of the expectant, patiently waiting passengers.

It seemed to him to take an eternity for the suitcases to begin their journey into the airport terminal, and his tiredness and waiting in the warm temperature was forcing him to begin to feel more and more irritable. He heard his name through the background cacophony of spoken words over tannoys, passengers talking and the first sounds of suitcases bumping around the conveyor belt.

'Allan!'

He turned to face Denise.

'What's happening?' she mouthed, together with a gesture of open arms. He shrugged his shoulders and turned his attention again to the conveyor belt.

'Allan!'

'What?' he shouted loudly as he turned around again.

She was taken aback by the abrupt tone of his reply. She was going to ask him, quite unnecessarily, to hurry up and get the suitcases. However, she could see the look of irritability on his face and decided to say nothing instead.

Allan, unusually, for he would have ordinarily abandoned his position to ask if she was all right, returned his attention to the revolving suitcases. Other passengers standing about the wide, circular conveyor belt briefly turned to see where the shouting was coming from. Observing that there was nothing to see but a slightly embarrassed young man, they returned to leaning dangerously forward to retrieve their luggage, while Allan waited patiently for a sight of their suitcases too.

It was not until the majority of the passengers had walked away with their luggage on their trolleys, and Allan was one of the few people still waiting, and after he had stretched the elastic tags attached to many of the suitcase handles and let them go with a resounding slapping noise – even those suitcases that he knew were not theirs but had by chance metamorphosed into a different size and colour – that he became quietly annoyed. He very rarely became annoyed and if he did, then it was because he was tired. Patience was one of his strengths but again, in this instance, his resistance had been dramatically whittled away by his tiredness. He did have a mild and not unreasonable temper but it was on the end of a very reasonable fuse.

Why, he pondered, did it always seem to him that his suitcase was the last to arrive? Had the American baggage handlers lost it? Was their luggage currently revolving alone around the conveyor belt of a Mediterranean airport-cum-hut? He decided not to think so negatively, but Denise had long ago embarked on such a train of thought.

The suitcases were very thin on the belt and so he immediately noticed theirs when they finally appeared through the thick plastic curtain on the other side of the carousel. He grabbed the handles of both cases when they eventually came into reach. Allan, at six feet tall, was an averagely strong person. At this moment, being somewhat flustered, he was able to exert his pent up frustration by using his strength to lift both sets of luggage clear of the belt at the same time. What little anger there was in him soon dissipated when he saw Denise smiling. He was altogether cheerful now and he knew that they could get under way and their holiday would begin properly. He placed the suitcases heavily on the trolley that already had the hand luggage settled on it, and smiled at her.

'Aren't you annoyed?' she fumed.

'About what?'

'About what! How about how long it took for us to get our cases? I'm going to complain.' She stomped in the direction of a nearby lost luggage counter.

He watched as she approached the innocent smiling airport staff. She launched her complaint, visibly causing the staff to blink and physically stand back from the ferocity of her verbal attack. He pushed the trolley to where she was standing as slowly as he could and stood silently behind her. He looked around the airport, choosing not to make eye contact with the airport staff who were attending to Denise.

'Well, it's not good enough,' she spat.

'Is she with you, sir?' the supervisor asked – for he had noticed the name tag of the tour company on Allan's suitcase. Allan nodded almost apologetically, raised his eyebrows and smiled inanely.

The man behind the counter nodded and gave a knowing smile.

'Okay, madam. All I can do is apologise. It was caused by a breakdown of one of our vehicles on the tarmac. I'm very sorry that it has inconvenienced you. What would you like us to do?'

She stood with her arms tightly folded. 'Right, I've got your name and I'll be writing to complain about your attitude. You should know what to do and you didn't have to be so rude about it. You may as well have said, 'So what are you going to so about it?' You'll be in trouble for this.' She stormed off in the direction of the automatic doors.

The man followed her with his eyes and looked at his colleague. She shrugged her shoulders and smiled and they both looked at Allan.

'You should be thankful that her mother's not here!' He managed to laugh nervously.

'Well, she's probably tired,' the supervisor said kindly.

'So am I,' replied Allan, 'but I'm still reasonable. Sorry about my fiancée,' he said apologetically and made to follow her.

'Wait a minute, sir,' the supervisor said. 'Here, take these vouchers. You can use them at the restaurant when you return to the airport. That should placate her some.'

'Thanks very much.' He took them and put them in his pocket. 'Have a nice day!' he said with a grin, pleased that he was able to have the chance to use what he perceived as a colloquialism.

Allan watched as the young boy who, perhaps at the age of five or six years, enthusiastically dealt a barrage of karate kicks and chops to his unsuspecting mother, who was engaged in conversation with the woman behind the main reception desk of the car-hire office. The mother's body gently bucked and swayed as each playful blow landed upon her but, quite remarkably, she continued indifferently with her conversation.

For goodness sake, he thought. When will this woman discipline her child? Was she immune to the annoying blows that the child was inflicting upon her?

He quickly concluded that the behaviour of the child was probably the norm and that the mother frequently ignored her child in the vain hope that he would soon become bored and consequently stop annoying her. He also presumed that the child was misbehaving in order to attract his mother's attention, and her ignoring the child was no doubt making matters a whole lot worse for her and everybody else in the office. However, an obvious member of the family, each of whom had the same mass as an elephant – juvenile and adult alike (human and animal alike) – grasped the child's waist with hands the size of manhole covers and lifted the boy effortlessly out of harms way, thus putting an end to the commotion that had attracted the attention of the entire office for the past ten minutes. The little boy immediately ceased the blows and the accompanying 'Ya!' sound and looked unashamedly scared, as he struggled and kicked his legs ineffectually in the outstretched arms of his seemingly immovable captor.

He then turned his attention again to the large open-plan, airy office that he and Denise stood in – which they had reached via a courtesy bus that had transferred them the short distance from Fort Lauderdale Airport. After the half an hour that they had waited in the office, they were now at the head of the queue that snaked through two rows of specifically roped-off sections, immediately inside the automatic doors of the single storey building surrounded by carefully designed and equally carefully placed shrubbery.

The interior of the office consisted of numerous symmetrically positioned desks situated under the many bright fluorescent lights. The desks were occupied on one side by the office workers wearing their smart red uniforms, consisting of ill fitting suits for the male workers and a matching jacket and skirt for the women. On the other side of the desks stood assorted groups of tourists engaged in the transaction of car hire.

'Allan,' Denise said suddenly. 'That woman at that desk over there is free.'

He hurriedly picked up the suitcases and struggled with them towards the vacant desk.

The woman smiled a helpful smile as they approached and invited Denise and Allan, with a gesture of her hand, to have a seat. They sat down gratefully and he gave the woman the documentation that they were given in England, which they had received, when they had paid for their fly drive tickets. The woman tapped the keys on the computer keyboard in front of her and then dipped her hand into the desk drawer and produced a file. She proceeded to show them a well worn leaflet detailing photographs of the cars on offer and the actual car they had paid for with the flight tickets.

'What, that one there?' Denise pointed abruptly with a nail varnished finger at a small, bright green coloured photograph of the compact 'city car' that the woman indicated to them on the leaflet.

'Yes,' began the woman. 'The vehicle that's included in the ticket price is the basic car. Most people decide to upgrade when they pick their vehicle up from this office. However, you can take this car if you'd prefer.' She continued smiling when she had finished her patter.

Allan wondered what she was sitting on to make her smile so.

'I wouldn't be seen dead in that car,' Denise said in a disgusted tone. 'Allan, we're not having that one. What are you going to do about that?' she challenged the woman without waiting for him to reply.

The woman on the opposite side of the desk did her best to stifle a smile at the response she had expected from Denise. As soon as the couple had sat down she had sensed that she was an angry person, partly because of her body language and partly because of her stern features.

Denise pointed out a red convertible car pictured on the leaflet. 'We'll have that one,' she said firmly.

Allan looked with surprise at the car she had chosen so certainly, without question.

'Well, how much is it first?' he suggested sensibly.

'That doesn't matter,' Denise replied quickly. 'We've enough money to hire a car each if we want to. I'm not driving about in a car that I'm going to look silly in for two weeks. I suppose *you* would choose a boring car and prefer to use the extra money to buy cigarettes.'

He smiled uncertainly, bemused, not knowing where to look. What Denise said was not true because he would gladly have spent his last penny on someone close to him rather than spend it on himself. Denise wore a very determined and challenging look as she faced Allan, who avoided her confrontation and instead, bowed his head and looked again at the leaflet showing the various cars on offer. The convertible was not the most expensive car, and even if it was he quickly decided that resistance was futile. He was not against the idea of hiring a sporty-looking convertible, but his inherently sensible nature meant that impulsiveness always took a second place to adopting the careful approach. They most certainly had the money to afford this particular superfluity and so the decision that she had made was not really a foolhardy one. It was no use arguing anyway, though, because Denise had decided.

The woman behind the counter now looked at Denise with bemusement and even her smile dropped – she would have to practise in front of the mirror when she returned home. She decided to progress the conversation as she had been trained, and her thoughts of the role playing situations that had been created in the training seminars made her smile, for she had never had the opportunity to use them before.

'The convertible isn't the most expensive car.' She eagerly offered a line for Allan to grasp hold of. She detailed the price of the car for two weeks hire.

He quickly looked at the tariff and noticed out of the corner of his eye, that Denise had folded her arms. He grabbed the line with both hands.

'It is quite reasonable,' he said with relief as he sensed Denise unfold her arms, yet she said nothing and he knew that she was glaring at him. 'We'll take it,' he said, as if his decision held the deciding vote.

Denise sat up straight and her lips formed a satisfied smile but her eyes remained impassive.

Allan handed over the travellers' cheques and signed the necessary papers. The woman withdrew a set of keys from the drawer of the desk and offered them to Denise with her outstretched arm, for it seemed to her that the female half of the couple wore the proverbial trousers.

'Oh no,' she said, waving both hands at her wrist, 'he'll be driving.'

The woman moved her outstretched arm so that the keys dangled in front of Allan. He took them slowly and said thank you to her before he stood up, and heaved a suitcase into each hand. As he stood up he smiled at the woman, who was very attractive and he sensed her to be a warm and kind person. She smiled sympathetically in return and watched him struggle to keep up with his partner, as they made their was through the automatic doors and into the night.

Outside, the rain had abated but had maintained vast puddles of water that littered the tarmac of the car park. The car park contained four or five rows of cars, with about twenty cars in each row, Allan estimated absently. The area was lit sparingly by the presence of scattered tall streetlights and any other light that would have ordinarily been afforded by the moon was obscured by clouds that raced across the night sky. A billowing breeze sent ripples across the lakes of water, which the two of them were forced to skirt widely because of the unknown depth.

Denise walked ahead as Allan struggled along behind, beginning to feel the strain of carrying the large heavy suitcases for a lengthy period of time. His eyes fell on the back of Denise, and then on her tight fitting white jeans that stretched taut over her *petite derriere* that she moved deliberately as she walked – it had taken her many years of practise to perfect the walk and make it look natural. He wondered if he would get a chance to reach into her back pocket and caressingly retrieve any contents therein, because she had her hands full. He longed to do so and he probably would, when she was not in them.

'Here we are,' she turned and said when they reached a large red car that was the same as the picture they had been shown in the office.

Allan smiled as he appraised the appearance of the car, with the accompanying knowledge that he would soon be seated, even though he had been cramped in an aeroplane seat for nine hours already in one day. He released his grip on the suitcases and removed the keys from the pocket of his jeans inserting them into the lock on the boot of the car. The boot – or 'trunk' as it is known natively – would not open and so he tried the second key on the key fob. That key was also ineffective.

'You're useless,' she said as she moved him away from the keys and the boot with her *petite* yet powerful bottom.

'If you open it,' he managed a fatigued smile, 'then I must have loosened it.'

'Idiot,' she said under her breath as she fumbled with the keys unsuccessfully. 'They must be the wrong keys.' She tried the keys in the driver's door of the car. Nothing. 'Go back inside, Allan, and ask the stupid woman to give us the right bloody keys.'

'I'll have another go.' He held out his hand.

She pushed the keys abruptly into his hand. 'If I can't do it,' she said, 'you certainly won't be able to.'

He held the keys in his open palm and looked at her seriously. He considered asking her not to take that tone with him. However, after a pause and a sigh he wordlessly made his way back into the car-hire office.

'Allan,' she called out as he reached the automatic doors. He turned and looked at her, standing, as she was, below a streetlight. She shouted wearily, 'Hurry up, I think it's going to rain.'

He turned towards the building and headed inside in the direction of the woman who had initially dealt with their transaction. She was serving another customer but looked up when she felt the breeze blow in as the automatic doors opened and she heard Allan as he approached her desk.

'I can't find the car.' He mustered a grin for the woman, who smiled weakly in return. He stood beside the people who he had interrupted and blushed slightly as they looked accusingly at him. He apologised, for they were no doubt tired and eager to get to their hotel too.

They tutted and looked at him even more accusingly when the woman said, 'It must be out back somewhere,' and pointed to the car park outside the window.

He rolled his eyes and blushed deeply with approaching anger.

'Well, there's me looking in the gents' toilets.'

The woman looked puzzled, not having yet grasped the concept of irony.

'I know it's out there,' he said loudly. 'Where out there? There are about a hundred cars!'

The woman looked somewhat perplexed by his determined yet tired face, for her training had not dealt with this situation. She was pleased that the woman Allan was with had not confronted her with the problem, for she seemed a proper handful. The female employee was reaching the end of her shift that had started many hours ago at the beginning of the morning. She too was tired and tutted very softly as she rummaged in the drawer of her desk.

Allan quietly fumed at the woman and was even more angry when she disappeared for five minutes into a back room. After an indeterminate amount of time – as the saying goes, a watched pot never boils – she returned with a fixed smiling face and an apology.

'I'm sorry about the delay. Here you are, sir.' She passed him another set of keys and took the one's he held. 'You have the wrong set. The car will be in bay sixty-seven. Sorry for the inconvenience sir. Enjoy your stay.' She smiled, revealing two rows of immaculate teeth.

His anger was diffused by the smiling face of the attractive young woman in the red skirt and jacket. Five minutes ago, he had wanted to pick her up by the lapels and manhandle her outside into the car park and say to her, you bloody find it then, smart arse.

He quickly broke off eye contact with her and said, 'That's okay.'

He was always close to being assertive but was always a sucker for a pretty woman and an agreeable solution. Being angry after an experience did not give him any satisfaction either. Instead he took the alternative set of keys and hurried into the welcoming coolness of the night.

The rain was now falling quite heavily and as he quickly approached Denise standing in the dim glow afforded by the streetlight, he could see that her hair was now plastered onto her face and forehead.

'I'm wet,' she said accusingly as he neared, as if it was his fault that the rain had started again.

He was tired, annoyed with not being able to obtain the correct car keys in the first place and he wanted to sit down and have a nice cup of tea. He most certainly was not in the mood to be on the receiving end of one of Denise's tantrums.

'*I've got the keys.*' He pronounced the words slowly and precisely.

'About time to. What took you so long? I'm soaked!' she said with growing anger, fuelled by his apparent composed exterior and lack of concern.

'They gave us the wrong set of keys. What can I do about that? It's sorted now, and I'm tired, hungry, thirsty and becoming wetter by the minute arguing about nothing.'

'You bastard. Anyway, you *are* wet,' she shouted across the roof of the car as he opened the driver's door and climbed in.

'Pardon?' he asked tiredly when they were both seated. The rain pattered rhythmically on the soft roof.

'I said that you *are* wet,' she unkindly offered again in a disinterested tone, daring him to answer her back with an angry look that would have challenged the face of a spoilt child.

'That's what I thought you said,' he decided to say obliviously.

'You should have complained to the manager and we could have demanded a reduction in the price. We might have got some money off or some vouchers like we got at the airport,' she persisted.

'You correctly said that we had enough money to hire whatever car we wanted. Why should we waste time trying to save money that we don't even need?'

'Don't you raise your voice to me. It's not my fault they gave us the wrong keys.' She turned on him.

He was puzzled as to how their conversation had taken this turn against him.

'If I had stayed in there arguing the toss with the manager then you would have been out here for longer, and out in the rain for even longer and then you would have been even more wet than you are now.' His voice steadily rose, 'I have the keys now.'

She bowed her head and rested her forehead in her hands. Tears welled in her eyes and then rolled down her cheeks.

He looked at her and almost panicked.

'Sorry,' he said, 'I didn't mean to upset you.' He placed his hand on her knee, which she quickly brushed off.

'If you raise your voice to me again,' she said aggressively, 'I'm going home and I'll never speak to you again.'

'I'm sorry,' he professed. 'I'll make it up to you. Perhaps we can go shopping tomorrow and I'll treat you.'

'That'll be a start.' She sat up in her seat, trying to hold back her feeling of pleasure so that she could milk his sensation of guilt.

He began to press switches on the dashboard with increasing intensity.

'I can't find the lights,' he said from under the steering column.

'Well the switch must be there,' she flustered. 'I can't believe that anyone would be stupid enough to make a car without headlights.'

'We are in America, Denise,' he offered uselessly, as he appeared from under the dashboard.

'What does that mean?' she asked with disinterest as she helped press all the buttons on the dashboard of the hire car.

'I mean that the switch is probably in some ingenious and convenient place.' He started the engine just for something positive to do and the parked car in front of theirs became illuminated by a flood of light from the front of their hire car.

'*Et voila!*' he exclaimed with surprise. 'There must be a light dependent resistor that automatically switches on the headlights when the daylight is poor.'

'Great,' she offered. 'Now, shall we go? Or would you like to fascinate me with other features that this car has to offer, or shall we try to discover if there's anything you've missed?'

'Sorry,' he replied as he selected reverse gear from the steering wheel mounted gearshift. He turned in the large seat to look out of the back window as he put his foot on the accelerator. 'Whoa!' he exclaimed excitedly as the car shot backwards at an alarming speed. He applied the brake adroitly. 'I'm very sorry, Denise. I'm not used to the power, or an automatic gearbox.'

'That figures. Just be careful,' she said with folded arms.

He carefully selected the drive gear and they slowly pulled out of the car-hire car park entrance – instead of the exit – and onto the main road.

He had never experienced driving in a foreign country until now and driving on the wrong side of the road created a certain amount of nervousness within him. The length of the car bonnet was also alien to his limited driving experiences, in that a considerable amount of shiny red metal was prominently visible in front of him, reflecting the bright lights of shop signs, advertisements and bars that they passed in the night.

However, 'This is great,' he enthused with quickly growing confidence. 'It's easy driving these big cars on wide, straight roads. It's not like driving in London, where you have to have your wits and tip-top driving skills to hand all the time.' He turned the radio volume a little higher and began singing.

She turned the volume down. 'It doesn't mean that you can't concentrate,' she countered. 'I don't want to end up in a crash and ruining our holiday by spending it in hospital.'

He quickly glanced at her and tutted softly.

'Allan, I was only saying. Fine, if you want to drive like a lunatic, go ahead. Let me out of the car first, though,' she retorted angrily.

Allan was on holiday, driving a sports car with his attractive fiancée beside him and expectantly looking forward to an enjoyable two weeks. He was in a happy mood and thought to himself what would happen if he pulled the car over and asked her to get out – after which he wheel spun the car and watched the reflection of Denise and her suitcase by the roadside rapidly becoming smaller in the rear-view mirror. He laughed at the preposterous thought and the hypothetically disastrous consequences.

'I wouldn't do that, Denise.'

She scowled angrily at him and looked somewhat shocked.

'I know you won't,' she said, almost as if she had been watching his imaginary sequence of events.

He daringly turned the volume of the radio to the level that was more audible.

'And I won't drive like a lunatic,' he explained.

An uncomfortable silence immediately fell, creating an atmosphere where, undoubtedly, the last person to speak was the winner. She folded her arms tightly and stared intensely through the windscreen into the bright lights that they passed.

Allan was not good at this particular game, primarily because he was an intellectually mature person and also because he was inherently a decent person who preferred to argue openly, if at all.

'Sorry, Denise,' he offered after a minute of trying.

Conversely, Denise was a past master at the waiting game and persisted by not replying to his almost immediate apology.

'I said I was sorry.'

'That's not good enough. So far today; you began by picking me up late; you shouted at me in the car on the way to airport; you told me scary stories at the airport that really frightened me; you annoyed me on the aeroplane; you abused me in the car-hire place and now you're being really horrible to me.' She sniffed dramatically. 'I just wonder what you're going to do to me next.'

It was his turn to be aghast for he had not realised that he had committed all those heinous crimes against her. His mind rapidly processed the incidents that she had mentioned.

'I didn't,' he offered indignantly before formulating a more reasoned response.

'If you can't see what you've done,' she spluttered, 'then you've got big problems.'

He bit his lip as his mind finished processing the incidents and conversations of the day. He most certainly had not intended to upset her but it was apparent to him that she had taken offence, however innocent his intentions. Perhaps he was not attentive enough.

'Denise, I'm truly sorry if I've upset you.'

'Well, you have!' she said emotionally.

'Then I'm sorry that I have been horrible to you, but I didn't mean to be.'

'Well, if you didn't mean to then that's even worse.' She turned angrily on him.

'What can I do to make it up to you?' he entreated.

She wiped the tears from her eyes with her lace handkerchief. She always impressed herself with her well honed ability to turn on the tears instantly. She maintained a lengthy dramatic pause, further indicating her potential as a thespian.

'For a start,' she began, then with increasing volume in her voice, 'you can find us a nice place to stay for tonight and stop bloody driving around this damn city all night!'

The timeshare apartment that they had booked was for the two weeks, starting from the following day. Tonight it was down to them to find their own accommodation for the single night, in a luxurious, plush and expensive hotel, Denise angled.

'Right,' he said in a kind voice. 'We'll try that place there.' He decisively manoeuvred the car off the main coast road and onto a quiet side turning, which was bordered by low-rise motels, hotels and small shopping arcades.

Fort Lauderdale seemed to him to be a clean – occasionally a rather exclusive – and sprawling holiday town. He did not equate Fort Lauderdale with being a city because high-rise buildings were not in abundance and because of the large areas each building occupied, rather than plots of land barely large enough for the building – which were his pre-requisites for cities like London, Leeds or any other city in Britain. He also did not consider Fort Lauderdale as being a city because he had so far not encountered clusters of buildings in a compacted area. To him, Fort Lauderdale seemed to have no outskirts or central area because it all had the appearance of the outskirts of a conurbation. Perhaps he had lived and worked in London for too many years of his life and his expectation of a city was very narrow, he mused. He decided that he should be more open-minded.

He parked the car in silence in a vacant parking space in an empty parking lot. At his chivalrous insistence she remained in the car, as he had suggested that it was not necessary for them both to make a potentially unnecessary short journey through the rain and then back to the car again.

He swiftly stepped out into the rainy night, running quickly towards the glowing light of what he assumed to be the reception of a select hotel, set in opulent green gardens and surrounded by palm trees. It almost had the quiet and exclusive appearance of a well-to-do golf club.

He halted his run with a few heavy steps as he arrived in the dry, brightly lit interior of the building. The décor was spartan, with a few potted plants strategically placed on the floor adjacent to a wooden desk. All was quiet. He looked for a bell to ring to gain a hotel workers' attention. He looked over at an open, glass and wooden double door, when movement attracted attention through the corner of his eye. A middle-aged woman, dressed in white, walked past his view. Curiously, she was in the process of removing a pair of plastic gloves.

She detected Allan's presence and looked at him.

'Can I help you?' the woman asked, with surprise, as she changed direction and approached him.

He sensed her surprise and, although he knew not why, alarm bells rang in his head.

She stood in front of him and looked at him quizzically.

He began to realise that something appeared unusual about the premises he was standing in. However, he ventured tentatively, 'Have you a room for the night?'

The woman frowned. 'Not really.' She paused. 'Did you know that this is a retirement home?'

'Oh!' he exclaimed, too bemused to be embarrassed. 'It looked like a nice hotel from the road. I do apologise,' he politely explained.

The woman said tiredly, 'That's okay.' She turned away from him and went about her business, leaving him standing in the reception area feeling rather foolish. He ran back to the car. He had left the engine running to facilitate the continual running of the air conditioning for Denise and, after he had dived in from the rain, he quickly shut the car door to prevent the cool air escaping – he was not used to air conditioning.

'Well?' she asked.

He looked up and noticed a retirement home worker standing on the steps of one of the nearby accommodation blocks, set as they were in lush green and dense gardens, who was looking at the couple seated in the red sports car.

Allan turned to look at Denise. 'No luck I'm afraid. This place is a retirement home. We're not ready for this type of accommodation yet are we?' He laughed as he pulled the gear lever into reverse.

'Typical,' she replied. 'You can't do anything right can you? I suppose *I'll* have to find us somewhere.'

He felt offended and ineffective. He said nothing in response to her taking charge of the situation, yet smiled to himself as the worker on the steps watched the car pull away into the rainy night. He noticed that Denise had turned the volume of the radio lower while he had been in the retirement home, but he did not say anything to her or bother altering the volume.

The coast road began to wind its way away from the sea. The number of buildings and lights decreased hastily into a virtual non-existence of the dark night. The view from the interior of the car altered from civilisation to that of pitch blackness, highlighted by falling rain in the beam of the headlights and the existence of dark shadowy trees lining the now single carriageway.

'We had better go back the other way.'

She suggested what he was already thinking and he wordlessly performed a U-turn and accelerated the car back towards where the lights and buildings beckoned. He was reluctant to start a conversation with her through fear that he would somehow upset her in a way that he had not imagined.

'Are you cross?' she asked.

'No,' he said with an effort. 'Why?' He briefly turned to look at her face, which was intermittently illuminated now, by the car headlights of vehicles travelling on the opposite side of the road. To him, she had the all too familiar look of someone who was ready to start an argument, as was apparent by her frown, intent staring eyes and folded arms, yet assuredly collected expression.

'Well, you've gone awfully quiet and so you must have the hump about something,' she said finally.

It was useless to try to deny that he was in some way cross, because the more vehement the denial, the more he would appear to be grumpy and the more perplexed he would become.

'Well,' he began.

'I'll forgive you, Allan,' she interrupted, 'but please don't be annoyed with me for something that wasn't my fault,' she challenged.

'I didn't want to upset you, Denise. I thought I would say nothing for a while and concentrate on looking for somewhere to stay. I am truly sorry,' he murmured apologetically.

She shifted her position in her seat and sat up straight, looking ahead.

'Okay, Allan.' She smiled. 'Let's try this road coming up on the left, on the other side of the road. You'll have to come back on the other side of the road, though, otherwise you'll block the traffic coming behind us.'

'Right,' he replied cheerfully, pleased that normality seemed to have finally descended between them.

He found a safe place to turn the car, and travelled back on the other side of the road with the beach and the sea now on the side of the driver's window. He turned off the coast road and drove past a bar, that she had pointed at on the corner of the side road. He wistfully looked through the window as they drove past. He was hopeful of locating accommodation nearby because he liked the look of this particular bar, which caused him to enthuse about how pleasant and quiet the surrounding area appeared to be, whilst being careful not to suggest anywhere in case it turned out to be unsuitable in some way – for instance, the owner's feet being too small!

'Let's try in that small hotel there. It looks nice and exclusive, surrounded by those lovely gardens,' she said cheerfully, as they neared a small hotel and pool, surrounded by palm trees and green bushes and illuminated pleasantly by lights concealed in the shrubbery.

He parked the car in a space behind a pick-up truck.

'Shall we both go in?' he suggested after he had considered the definite presence of a sign displaying the word, *hotel*. 'It's not raining and if you don't like the look of the place we can try somewhere else.' He was intelligently thinking ahead now, and had already pondered the possibility of paying for a room for the night which was unsuitable, and Denise then blaming him for not realising that the place was not what she wanted.

She considered following this course too but she was now tired of driving around and was willing to sleep anywhere and could not be bothered to find fault.

'I'll come with you, if I must,' she said tiredly, as she opened the car door and stepped out into the night.

Once they had followed the path through the well kept gardens, they arrived at the main building, outside of which was a sign clearly marked 'Reception.'

Allan knocked on the patio door, which seemed a rather odd entrance to a hotel reception. Immediately after he did this, he wondered if he had committed another *faux pas*, for the curtains were pulled back and an unshaven man in a string vest and shorts, stood in the light that radiated from the room behind him. Allan thought that he may have inadvertently knocked on the door of a paying guest and he urgently turned his head, scanning the area around him for another sign.

The man slid open the door and spoke gruffly.

'Yeah?'

Denise prompted Allan with her elbow and he reluctantly looked at the man, wondering briefly if he had again stumbled on the wrong type of accommodation. However, he could not imagine what type of accommodation the man would be the owner of, except an open prison for reformed murderers.

'Ermm,' he began uncertainly, 'have you a room for the night?'

'Sure,' replied the man, as he held the curtain back and beckoned them in.

Allan and Denise entered the premises dubiously. Once inside, Allan observed that the room was sparsely decorated with tacky wallpaper and furniture that had a distinct 1970s appearance. A woman was seated on a two-seater, well worn couch opposite an old television with a large manual tuning dial. She turned to appraise Allan and Denise at considerable length, before wordlessly turning her attention back to the flickering television screen.

Allan sensed that Denise was not greatly impressed but the interior of the room was at least clean, if a bit distasteful in decoration. The thought leaked into his mind that he had inadvertently walked into a scene from a Quentin Tarantino movie. For some reason, only known to the inner most thoughts of his mind, he felt unusually threatened in the presence of the couple, essentially because it was the first American home he had been inside and he imagined that the coarse-looking couple could be capable of pulling a gun on both him and Denise and robbing them at gunpoint – he had seen far too many American movies.

'Double room?' the man asked obtusely.

The woman remained too impassive towards the English couple because she was obviously listening.

Allan – unsure whether the meaning of the man's words had a different meaning to those in England because it was obvious that they required a double room – replied hopefully, almost in the form of a question.

'Double, please.' He presumed the unkempt man to be the proprietor.

The man busied himself by bending down and searching inside a cupboard before eventually producing a set of keys, which he gave to Allan.

'That'll be thirty dollars for the night, payable now,' he said indifferently, without asking whether they wished to see the room first.

Allan looked at Denise for confirmation of her wishes. She finished a yawn and nodded her head in agreement. She was obviously tired and just wished to have a place to sleep for the night, and, provided it was clean, it did not matter too much how the room was furnished.

The man looked at Allan and held out his hand. Allan produced his wallet and secretively gave the man thirty dollars, for Allan still perceived a threat. The proprietor smiled as he took the money.

'The room's past the swimming pool, up the stairs on the second floor. The number is on the key.'

'Thanks,' said Allan who immediately turned and slid open the patio door. The rain had stopped again, thankfully, and they both stepped outside.

The proprietor shut the door after them and watched them walk up the path.

'Weird, those Limeys,' the proprietor said to his wife. 'Anyone would think I was goin' to mug him or som'at'.' He laughed as he let the curtain fall back into its natural hanging position.

Allan walked ahead of Denise and turned to her when he thought they were out of earshot of the 'reception'.

'That couple seemed rather odd,' he said. 'I thought they looked rather menacing, didn't you? I couldn't wait for the transaction to finish so that we could get out of there.'

'Allan,' she replied incredulously, 'don't be silly.'

'Yeah, but nobody knew that we were here and they could have pulled a gun on us and robbed us,' he said, as he stopped by a set of stairs adjacent to the swimming pool. She sometimes surprised him with her lack of concern when it mattered most, yet he could be a few minutes late and she would be terribly concerned.

The strong smell of chlorine unpleasantly cleansed the air, despite the fact that the sea was literally yards away and the wind was billowing nicely. Denise pushed past him and quickly climbed the stairs. He followed, slipped on the wet wooden steps and fell onto his knee. She turned at the top of the stairs when she heard the thump.

'Are you all right, Allan?' she said, with a small degree of delayed concern and her hand over her mouth to stifle her giggle.

'I think so,' he said. He grabbed hold of the railing and hauled himself into a standing position. He bent down and rubbed his leg before looking for assistance and sympathy from Denise, who called out from along the open corridor.

'Hurry up, Allan, I want to see what the room is like.'

'It's all right, nothing's broken,' he said under his breath. He carefully ascended the remaining stairs with a slight limp and finally reached the door of the apartment, where Denise was waiting impatiently. He inserted the key in the door and turned the handle before entering the room. The interior of the room was dimly lit by the lights in the grounds outside the hotel, so he easily located the light switch on the wall and flicked it on.

'My God!' she exclaimed when the thin door swung open and revealed the interior.

'It's not that bad,' he said as they both looked about the hotel room. The walls were decorated plainly with grubby cream paint. A double bed, pushed up against a side wall was draped with a purple counterpane, and brown lamp shades covered the two lights positioned roughly and unevenly above the head of the bed. A small air conditioning unit, which he switched on, hung obtrusively on the wall opposite the bed. It sprang to life with a gurgle, and was followed by the continuous rumble of a small electric motor as the whole unit shook the wall, threatening to work itself loose and escape through the flimsy door of the apartment. It did not, however, fall off the wall but produced a generous amount of cold air, thereby forcing the humid interior of the room to a much more comfortable level and making them put up with the din.

Denise briefly disappeared into the bathroom and then she returned to the main room and faced Allan.

'At least it's clean,' she remarked, as she wiped her finger along the top of the television that mirrored the one situated in the room of the couple who had so threatened Allan's rationale. Her finger was covered in grey powdery dust as she held it up to inspect it.

She hurumphed and said, "ish.'

'So, we're staying here?' he asked hopefully as he tested the bed. He was tired and did not desire to be aggravated further by confronting the Tarantinoesque couple and asking for a better room, or alternatively by spending the entire night driving the streets of Fort Lauderdale looking for suitable accommodation that satisfied Denise. He would have settled for a cockroach infested hovel, almost, or even a retirement home, for that matter, because he was so tired.

She paused, seemingly for dramatic effect, enticing him to think that the probability that he had to confront the threatening people in 'reception' was becoming more likely. She laughed teasingly as she watched the look on his face, which had an expression like a teenager waiting hopefully for an affirmative answer from a parent to the question, 'Can my girlfriend stay for the night?'

'Well,' she said doubtfully, remembering how eager he was to please her at the moment because he thought that he had been horrible to her. She toyed with the idea that they should find somewhere else – just to make life difficult for him – but she was tired now and abhorred the thought of driving again through the streets of Fort Lauderdale looking for a suitable place to stay. She was also mindful of the fact that this had been her choice of hotel.

'We may as well stay,' she said finally. 'I couldn't put up with you driving around Fort Lauderdale and taking me to more retirement homes, hostels, monasteries or any other stupid places.'

'That was an easy mistake to make,' he said, with considerable relief, opening the door of the apartment. 'I'll just go and get the suitcases. I'll lock the door behind me.'

'Why?' she called out abruptly when he stepped back into the night. He came back into the room. 'Who do you think'll come in here?' she said. 'Not the string vest bogey man and the wicked woman from the reception of horror?' she offered, with raised hands, clawed fingers and an accompanying unearthly croaky voice.

'They do have guns in this country,' he replied, in what he saw as a justifiable defence. 'I'll lock it just the same.' Regardless of her obvious disdain, he protectively closed the door and left her standing by the 1970s style television set, wordlessly twiddling the dial, the flickering screen illuminating her face in the poorly lit room.

She soon became bored with unsuccessfully tuning the set and instead, sat on the bed and thought to herself, How sweet it was of Allan to think of protecting her. His constant pandering to her every whim meant that she could ask him to do anything and he would usually embrace her wishes with acquiescence. If Allan was the caged animal then she was the keeper with the food in her hand, she mused. She lay back and smiled contentedly and almost immediately, as her head touched the pillow, she began drifting into sleep – the clatter of the noisy air conditioning unit becoming a distant distraction as she shrank from consciousness.

Allan *carefully* descended the stairs this time, through the chlorine filled warm air, following the dimly lit path through the well kept grounds of the small hotel. A warm wind blew strongly through the dark, humid night and the sound of the nearby Atlantic Ocean impacting on the beach was the only other dominant sound he noticed; the other sound being the leaves on the surrounding trees rustling furiously in the wind. He licked his lips and tasted the salt that was being carried by the wind as it skimmed off the surface of the sea.

He opened the car boot, taking out the suitcases and hand luggage, which he struggled to put into position on his arms and shoulders before shutting the boot and heading back to the room. The suitcases and bags were knocking heavily on his legs but he was determined to return to the room as quickly as possible, without stopping for a rest, even though his stretched arms complained bitterly.

He reached the bottom of the stairs and looked up at the short flight of damp, slippery, dark steps. He started his ascent carefully, trying to tread firmly and fully on each step so as to avoid an accident. He reached the top of the steps and eventually stood in front of their room.

'It's only me,' he said as he fumbled with the key in the lock. He turned it but the door was already unlocked. Strange, he thought to himself, for he was sure he had locked it. He grabbed hold of the suitcase handles and pushed open the door with his foot as he bumped his way through the door frame.

A presence was missing in the room. Denise was not there. He put the suitcases down, sliding out of the rucksack and shoulder strap of the pink sports bag.

'Denise!' he called. No answer. He knocked on the door to the bathroom – no answer! He nudged the bathroom door open. 'Denise!' he said, as he looked inside and saw nothing but an empty bathroom suite.

His thoughts began to take onboard feelings of dread and fear that she was apparently missing, which was especially distressing as he had even had the forethought to lock the door before leaving, which she had scoffed at.

'Why didn't I double check the door?' he said aloud to himself. 'No, think rationally.' He tried to compose himself. He decided to check outside first to see if she had opened the door from the inside and gone for a walk. If he failed to find her he would then confront the couple in the reception area and then, if all avenues had been briskly walked down, he decided that he would call the police.

He checked the door handle and quickly discovered that the locked door could have been opened from the inside. His thoughts rapidly processed another idea that jumped upon him, Perhaps someone duped her into opening the door and then abducted her when she had opened it to see who it was?

'I was only gone for five minutes,' he said and slipped as he hurried outside again, tripping over one of the suitcases inside the door as he did so.

'Shiiiit,' he cried, as he stumbled forward, holding on to the railings that had fortunately interrupted his potentially fatal fall from the first floor landing.

His heart was beating fast and threatened to leap out of his ribcage as he approached the stairs. He slipped on the first unsafe step and began to fall forwards through the darkness, down the stairs. His stomach lurched and his mind screamed alarm – the same feeling that is achieved when a roller coaster descends rapidly down a steep incline. His arm shot out and his large hand grabbed the rain-soaked handrail. From strength, only obtainable through fear, he managed to prevent himself from tumbling all the way down by gripping hard on the wet metal surface.

He sat on the step with tears of despair threatening his eyes. His arm had almost been wrenched out of its socket and it hurt terribly but he had to be strong.

'Hope defeats despair,' he said aloud as he stood up. He continued his descent down the slippery stairs and headed for the reception from hell – so it seemed to Allan. He knocked on the sliding doors, not really knowing what on earth he was going to say.

'Excuse me, have you abducted my fiancée, tied her up and are you now torturing her?' he mumbled quietly to himself.

The curtain was pulled back and light flooded into his eyes. The patio door slid open and a woman's voice, in a thick American accent, which he presumed to be a Southern accent, said,

'Yeah?'

'Um,' he began nervously, 'have you seen my girlfriend – my fiancée actually?'

The woman's eyes looked up to the sky as she leant against the doorframe. Her doubtful gaze fell upon him as she watched the distressed-looking Englishman trip over his own words.

'I mean, I realise you saw her when we first came in,' he mumbled, 'but since then have you seen her? I went to the car and came back – now I can't find her.'

'No honey.' The woman chuckled without a hint of concern. 'Nobody's been here since you's two.' She began to close the door again.

'What about your husband?' he asked urgently, preventing her from returning to her television.

She tutted impatiently.

'Hon, he's in the shower. I would have seen her go in there, but if she's in there I think they're both in trouble, don't you?' She glowered at him.

'Oh,' he said simply as he turned away, really at a loss what to do. He heard the patio door close behind him and the light from inside faded away as she let the curtains fall again over the window.

What to do now? he wondered. He decided to check the hotel grounds and, if he was unable to find her, then he would have to call the police. His first night in America and he had managed to be careless and perhaps caused the abduction of his fiancée. He was left in a daze as he ascended the stairs once again.

'All–an!' A voice called his name, using two syllables.

The voice was coming from the top of the stairs. He turned to look upwards – it was Denise.

'Denise!' he exclaimed excitedly as he bounded up the stairs, ignoring the fact that he had fallen twice on them already. 'Is that you?' He ran successfully towards the outline of a figure standing in the open doorway, with the yellow light shining from the room behind. 'Denise, where, were you?' he spluttered when he reached her. 'I was worried that something had happened to you.' He paused as he held her tightly in her arms. 'Has anything happened?'

She tilted her head back slightly and laughed.

'Of course not, stupid.' She pushed him away gently. 'Anyone would have thought that you hadn't seen me for months.'

'Well, what was I supposed to think? I thought that I had left you alone in the room with potential criminals lurking about the area with guns. I thought the worst, and I was really worried. I thought something terrible had happened to you.'

She laughed again.

'You always think the worse, don't you, Allan?'

'No,' he replied indignantly. 'Listen, Denise.' He stepped over threshold and shut the door. The two of them were standing in the room by the bed. 'I was worried. The question isn't about me or how my thought process works, but where you've been for the past ten minutes.'

'And who do you think you are questioning me like that, Mr Dad?' she sneered. 'I can do what I want, when I want and I don't need your permission.' She poked his shoulder blade hard with a pointed finger as she finished her sentence.

'I'm not trying to tell you what to do,' he pleaded, harbouring offence. 'I was worried what had happened to you. I wasn't trying to keep you locked up.' He placed his hand warmly on her shoulder.

She shrugged off his affection, annoyed.

'Well, that's the way it seemed to me. I'm going out now,' she said haughtily.

'Where?' asked a bemused Allan, as he turned to watch her go.

'Oh, I don't know. I might try and get drunk, pick a fight with the local gangsters and get into trouble with the police. I'll probably see you in the morning – if you're lucky,' she said matter-of-factly as she opened the door.

'Denise, I'm tired. Let's have a sleep first, then we'll go out, eh?' he implored.

She paused.

'Fine, you stay here, wimp. I'm going out.' She disappeared quickly from his view.

He immediately followed her out of the door, locked it behind him and caught up with her.

'Sorry Denise,' he offered, seemingly hopelessly as he drew level with her, as she walked so briskly.

'Allan, you've done it again, haven't you? It's a good job that I can handle your moods. Any other woman would be upset by the way you act.'

He tried to get his mind around what she had said but could only repeat his question.

'But I was worried, Denise. Where on earth were you?'

Her laughter broke the silence of the darkness. The quiet side road that they were walking along, ran adjacent to the beach. They reached a small bar on the corner of the street, situated under the bright lights of the all-night shop and the abundance of streetlights on the main road where a regular stream of cars flowed.

'Buy me a drink and I'll tell you,' she teased as she now took his arm.

He felt dazed and confused. He did not know how she coped with his apparent mood swings but he certainly could not keep up with hers. When their relationship had started six months ago she had been most accommodating. For instance, when he suggested going out somewhere she would reply, 'I don't mind,' and smile sweetly. Over the past few months, since they had agreed to become engaged, he almost had to result to obsequious requests to cajole her into doing anything that he suggested. It sometimes appeared to him that she said the exact opposite of whatever he suggested.

He loved his beloved Denise and would do anything for her and he most certainly did not want her to be servile – but he did not desire to be subservient to her either. However, every time he tried to even the balance he exposed a sore nerve and made matters worse, upset her or made himself look silly in some way. Patience was one of his strengths and so he was determined to balance their relationship on an even keel, even if it meant taking a very gradual and sometimes painful route. However, with the luxury of hindsight, he should have begun their relationship as he meant to carry on, with an even approach that involved sharing.

'I *would* like an explanation,' he replied as he looked into the interior of the bar, and the thought of a beer and a cigarette cheered him considerably. He pushed open the door of the bar and they walked in. The interior of the bar was decorated entirely in light-coloured, polished wood. Bar stools lined the bar and a barman stood in the centre of the wooden structure. The ceiling was low, the lighting was soft, and the ambience pleasant.

'What'll it be?' the barman said, as he placed two paper bar mats on the counter and smiled.

'A beer please.' He turned to Denise. 'Denise?' he asked. She gave the barman her order and they each took a seat on a bar stool at the bar. The barman busied himself rummaging in the various metal refrigerated bins that lurked beneath the bar and soon placed their order on the paper mats. Allan took out his wallet and went to pay the man.

The barman shook his head and said, 'This your first night?'

'Yes,' he replied. 'How did—'

'A tab is run up through the night, Allan. You don't have to pay until you leave.' Denise interrupted scornfully.

'That's right.' The barman smiled as he placed an order slip below the bar where they were seated.

Allan contemplatively returned his wallet to his pocket.

'Silly,' she whispered in his ear.

'I didn't know,' he said dolefully as he raised the bottle to his lips and let the cold beer flow down his throat. He pulled a packet of cigarettes from his jeans pocket and lit the tip, surveying the other people in the bar. Apart from two or three couples sitting at tables, and a small group of people on the other side of the bar, Denise and Allan were the only other patrons.

He sighed a contented sigh. He had Denise by his side now, a beer in one hand and a cigarette in the other and he was comfortable.

'So where were you then?' He took another pull from his bottle and watched her set the glass down on the bar mat, which she fiddled with and plucked at the frilled edges.

'Well,' she said as she continued to pick at the paper mat. 'I was hiding.'

'Hiding!' he cried in bewilderment.

'Shhh,' she said as she noticed a few people turn to look at his exclamation. 'I was standing in the wardrobe, in the main bedroom bit of our room,' she said quietly.

'Whatever for?' he asked with incredulity and increasing volume.

She sighed.

'Well, you were banging on about locking the door for no reason, so I decided to give a reason – just to wind you up.'

He huffed, 'Well, you certainly did that. I almost broke my neck on the suitcase and then the stairs.'

'I know.' She held her hand over her mouth to stifle a guffaw. 'I heard you trip over the cases and then I heard you cry out as you must have taken a tumble down the stairs.' She giggled openly.

'That's a bit unfair. Didn't you think to check to see if I was okay? I could have been seriously hurt when I fell.' He examined the bruise that was forming on his leg and showed it to her. He was becoming increasingly aggrieved by what had happened and so he continued with the same tone. 'That's a bit irresponsible, I think, not to mention childish,' he rebuffed.

'Nasty.' She giggled when she saw the wound, 'but you're so serious.' She laughed openly now, having broken into a smile throughout his outburst. 'I was having a bit of fun, that's all. I found it funny. Can't you see the funny side of it?' she said wide-eyed and gesticulating with open arms.

'But you're twenty-six years old,' he continued. 'Those years of fooling around should have long gone, especially the pranks that could hurt your fiancé and lead him to no end of worry.'

'Oh Allan, lighten up, it was only a few minutes. We're on holiday. For goodness sake relax and enjoy yourself and stop acting like an old man.'

'I will, once you've stopped trying to give me a heart attack.' He sighed knowing that his display of concern was fruitless – and he was doing nothing to dispel her current opinion of him.

'At the age of twenty-eight, I'm sure you'll be okay,' she confided patronisingly as she patted his shoulder.

He laughed a singular token laugh, without a hint of humour. 'Well, I think you owe me one,' he said quietly into his bottle of beer.

She looked at him uncertainly.

'When we get back to the room I'll make it up to you,' she whispered in his ear suggestively.

His thoughts tumbled and jumbled as she ran heedlessly through his mind pushing him into an emotional blender, yet all he could manage to do was smile at his fortune as the world spun about him.

Chapter Five

Philip started walking slowly towards the bar, now that her slender back was facing the illuminated window of the premises. All of a sudden the continual rain stopped, as if the tap had been turned off. However, large droplets fell intermittently and impacted heavily on his forehead, sending an unexpectedly large river of water down the length of his face and dripping onto his already sodden shirt. His mind was working overtime and the excitement was erupting inside him like a venting volcano. He quickened his pace.

'Don't you dare,' came a stern, slow voice. 'I told you not to go near her, didn't I?'

He looked at where the voice was coming from – an area that was shrouded by shadows – and he stopped stock still. He stole a brief, protracting look at the lone figure bathed in the bright light of the bar and then just stared blankly into the gloom from where the voice had emanated.

'I was just going for a drink,' he suggested absently.

'Don't lie to me,' the voice came immediately and firmly. 'I want you to help me move something in the shop, so come with me – now.'

He paused and considered that going ahead with his plan, regardless of who saw, was indeed very foolish. 'I'll have a drink later.' He spoke angrily under his breath as he walked towards the voice.

Once he had reached her, she regarded him warily and they walked side by side along the puddle-strewn street that was now enshrouded in dark silence. She could sense that it was rather futile to try and do what King Canute had done but she had to at least try and do all that she could.

As she was contemplating these thoughts, Philip silently stewed over his missed opportunity to talk to Christine. The only significant challenge that he had been faced with, for as long as he could remember, was now frustratingly close but never within his reach – like a dream that involves running after a bus that seems to be waiting but which one can never reach however hard or fast one runs. In fact, the last challenge of this magnitude that he could remember was disposing of the body of his first victim. He was then at the tender age of sixteen and he could still remember with sparkling clarity the indescribable pleasure of choking the life from the equally young woman that lay beneath him.

Once he had relished the taking of life to its full, he discovered that he had the daunting prospect of disposing of the body without being caught by the police. Once he had thought about it carefully, he took the body to an even more remote part of the wood in the dead of night. He had wrapped the body in cloth and poured a small amount of petrol over it. Once he had dropped a lighted match to the fuel, he watched as the body burned fiercely at first and then as it burned slowly, for many, many hours. The small amount of fat in the body fuelled the flames and kept it burning all night and through to midday the next day – like a very slow burning candle.

The fire had been so intense, yet the flames so small that even the bones were turned to ash. Only the lower limbs and part of the skull remained intact because they were relatively devoid of surrounding fatty tissue. He had collected the remaining pieces together, which weighed only a few pounds, and tied them up in a hessian sack. He moved the charred topsoil into the bushes and then covered it with leaves from the surrounding area, leaving no trace of the body or fire. He then added rocks to the sack and rowed his small boat a short distance out to sea, dropping the sack off the side into the deep, dark ocean depths.

The local police had investigated the disappearance of the young girl and they had even questioned him, but he was so convincing in the interview that they believed him when he said that he and the girl had parted company on the beach. He had said that, after they had drunk a bottle of wine they had gone skinny-dipping. She never returned to shore and he had searched for her for hours in his boat, he had explained, and this was corroborated by witnesses who saw him rowing in the harbour. When asked why he had waited a whole day and not told the police, he explained that he was so distraught that he could not think clearly, and this was accepted once he had been examined by a doctor.

They never found the body of the girl and could only find witnesses who saw them in the sea together – and they had been in the sea, before they had come ashore and he had satiated his hunger for what he saw as the ultimate expression of power and control.

He had discovered over the following years of adolescence and then manhood, that he relished being in control. He learnt that he could manipulate people so that they would accede to his every wish and whim. He had found that he could negotiate business deals and successfully charm a woman into bed with varying degrees of difficulty, but never with any discernible trouble. Even when he was choking the final breaths from a woman, he watched in wonder as the light faded from her eyes, and she was completely and helplessly within his power.

The thought that would disturb any normal person actually excited his dangerous, almost primeval urge to control. He would sometimes smile at the naivety of the woman who, only moments previous to the final act, had trusted him so implicitly. To be confronted by a woman who struggled against him both physically and mentally would provide the most exquisite experience, and perhaps was the final experience that he was searching for. The deep thought that then flashed through his mind was, What would be his next challenge?

His silent walk with Mo passed along the desolate street. Only the tumbling leaves accompanied them and danced about their feet to the tune of the rustling wind. It was not long before they turned down the narrow tree-lined path that led to the rear of the shop premises. A small number of ornate streetlights barely lit their way as Mo unlatched the side gate that opened into the well kept garden. They silently negotiated the path through the flowers and shrubbery to the unlocked back door of the quaint looking premises.

'What were you going to do once you were with Christine?' she asked him, once the door to the kitchen was closed.

'What's that got to do with you?' he replied gruffly. He drew a chair out roughly from under the kitchen table and sat down.

'Because I think that you were up to no good.' She stood close to him and put her face next to his nose pointing at him with a bony finger that resembled a gnarled, thin branch from an old tree. 'If you even try to harm her then I'll make sure that you never live another day,' she proclaimed with absolute anger.

'Would I do such a thing?' he leered.

She almost sneered in reply, 'You may think that I'm a stupid old woman but I'm not.'

He looked dumbfounded as the frighteningly gnarled and wrinkled woman glared at him. 'And don't look as if you don't know what I'm talking about. I'm not asking you to answer me because I don't want to listen to your lies.' She was indeed so disgusted and repulsed by his presence.

He stood up abruptly, knocking the chair to the floor.

'You don't like anything I do, do you? I wish you'd just hurry up and die, you old witch, then I could get on with my own life and not have you fussing around me all the time. If it wasn't for you then—'

'Then you'd be in hell,' she interrupted.

He stared at her, at a complete loss for words, his fists clenched tightly.

'I'm watching you, and I'm watching Christine too. If anything happens to her then the police will be knocking on the door and asking for you. *No*, don't bother walking away,' she said, as he turned his back. '*I'm* going to bed. I'm tired.'

He watched her walk slowly from the room. He corrected the chair and sat down again, contemplating what she had said. Did she know? he thought silently. Had she been snooping around the boathouse? Anyway, he considered, he had been careful not to leave any evidence of his actions, even if the police did come looking or if she had been snooping. He concluded that the old woman was only guessing and in fact knew nothing. If Christine went missing then he would ensure that the old woman was in one place only – where he thought it was safe for her to point her accusing bony finger.

The dark water pushed against the length of the window and gradually rose higher and higher, threatening to flood through the open window. Mo looked through the panelled glass and into the ocean beyond her home. The swelling sea loomed so vast, so dark and so powerful that it filled her with an overwhelming sense of helplessness and dread. She could not fathom why the window had not been broken by the weight of the pressing sea. She let out a cry of fright when, like a waterfall, the ocean began to cascade through the open window, crashing loudly on the floor all around her and thrashing the furniture around the room. It soon filled the room completely and forced her underwater where she held on desperately to the precious air in her old lungs. It was then that she woke, gasping for breath.

She forced herself into a sitting position, and looked at the window above her bed and saw the trees being pushed and pulled by the wind in the darkness of the night. She could hear the loud rustling of leaves on the trees and bushes and heard the distant waves crashing on the shore. She lay back on her bed with a sense of blessed respite from the recurring nightmare of the ocean.

Christine looked skywards and nonchalantly observed the feathery grey clouds high in the morning sky, pursuing each other across the background of blue like children chasing after one another in a swimming pool. The racing clouds revealed small and fleeting tears in the moving, downy blanket, momentarily relinquishing a view of the glorious blue sky and a glint of warm sunshine. She knew that the weather was not going to change for the better for a few days, even a week, and that the auspicious conditions were deteriorating too. The many clouds gradually increased in magnitude and, no doubt, in latent rain capacity too. The breaks in the clouds were becoming few and far between and the duration of sunny periods becoming less and less. Just like yesterday, she realised as she walked along Duval Street. She longed for the clear skies and dry weather to return.

The pavements and roads were peppered with wandering tentative tourists, exploring the puddle-strewn town of Key West and wondering if the rain would hold off sufficiently for them to spend a satisfactory day sightseeing, fishing, snorkelling or following any other tourist pursuit. Tourists who were more experienced, concerned or knowledgeable regarding meteorological matters in this part of the globe, had taken the lull in the weather as an opportunity to escape the island in their cars, just in case, along the giant causeways that connected the island to the mainland.

The satellites and computers at the weather stations had calculated the build-up of a tropical storm in the low pressure in the Caribbean Sea, but the winds had been predicted to blow the storm further south towards Cuba and beyond, thereby causing the worst of the storm to forgo the south of Florida. The people who had evacuated the area did not have the confidence in the professional forecasters who attempted to predict the virtually unpredictable.

As usual, even though the weather was becoming increasingly inclement, the warmth and humidity of the day necessitated that she wore shorts and a T-shirt. Her long, shiny black hair tied back, through the fault of the gusting wind, meant that her head was kept relatively cooler than if the free flowing luscious lengths were irritating her face.

She approached Sloppy Joe's bar. The windows were dark and quiet in the morning following the boisterous night before – as was indicated by the man sweeping broken beer bottles from the road. She headed towards Mo's small shop, which was situated directly opposite Sloppy Joe's bar, with a small and unnecessarily discreet entrance behind one of the many standard Key West tourist shops selling a multitude of printed T-shirts.

The outside of practically all the buildings in Key West are clad in wooden slats, the majority of which are neatly painted white – Mo's modest premises being no exception.

Christine pushed the solid door of Mo's shop and a small bell jangled vigorously above her head.

'Hello!' she called through the dim light of the cluttered shop. Busy shelves lined the uneven walls, upon which stood various trinkets; carved wooden boxes; hand-crafted metal candle holders; very small paintings and ornaments made from empty seashells. Mobiles with moon and star decorations hung profusely from the dimly lit, low ceiling and a smell of incense hung heavily in the air.

'Mo!' she called again, as she trod along the creaking, old wooden floorboards.

'Mornin',' called a male voice from a hidden area at the rear of the shop.

Philip, wiping his hands roughly on a piece of cloth, appeared in a doorway. 'And to what do I owe this unexpected pleasure?' He grinned as he ducked under the assortment of hanging mobiles, and approached her purposefully.

She stiffened. 'Don't flatter yourself,' she derided. 'I came to see Mo. Is she here?'

'Not now, no. She went out earlier this mornin', at first light,' he replied matter-of-factly. He eyed her up and down, starting at her slender legs, continuing up her slender physique and shapely torso, resting finally on her pretty face and beautiful hair. 'Why don't you wait here with me and have a coffee?' he enthused, and abruptly took her arm.

Her body again stiffened instinctively and she pulled her arm away from him suddenly.

'No, it's okay, I'll come back,' she replied quickly, immediately turning to leave.

He caught hold of her hand and squeezed it hard, pulling her back.

'I insist,' he persisted with a determined, almost menacing, look.

'You're hurting me,' she said angrily and looked at him with wide-eyed disbelief. He released his grip slightly but not fully. 'And what part of the word *no* do you not understand?' she said. She studied the handsome face of Philip, yet she was at the same time repulsed by the barren stare that lingered in his dark eyes. 'If you don't let go,' she spat between gritted teeth as she looked down at his grip on her arm, 'I won't apologise for kicking you straight between the legs,' she glowered at him, 'repeatedly.'

'Oh yeah,' he scoffed, 'and you think I'll let you?' He laughed with an open gesture of his arms, he moved forward and encroached on her personal space. 'C'mon Chrissie,' he pressured as his face drew nearer to hers.

She stood her ground and positioned herself directly in front of him and smiled inches from his leering face, belying the fact that her instincts were screaming at her to break free and run from the shop.

He hesitated and looked at her benign smile, then gently but firmly held the top of her arms in his strong hands as he gazed as best he could into her expressively large, dark brown eyes.

'I knew you couldn't resist for too much longer,' he whispered as he leaned towards her lips to kiss her. He stopped as he was about to touch her lips with his own, then slowly lowered himself to the ground and knelt before her – his head at the level of her slim waist.

'I warned you,' she stated with a very satisfied smile, 'but you wouldn't listen, would you?' She held a clump of his black hair tightly in her fist and lifted his head abruptly, revealing his furrowed, grimacing face. 'Don't ever touch me again,' she spat defiantly.

Her actions surprised even herself and her voice wobbled with anger and fright, which was soon joined by the same feeling in her legs, leaving them almost useless. She could not have raised her legs with any force to either run or attack him again, even if she had decided that she wanted to.

The bell jangled and interrupted the ambience of the volcanic sight of a petite woman apparently forcing a well developed man – as the singlet and shorts he was wearing revealed – to the ground in a most brutal manner.

'Mo!' Christine said, with surprise, as she let go of Philip's hair and stood up straight.

He remained kneeling on the ground clutching the fly area of his shorts, apparently in a considerable degree of discomfort.

She felt slightly embarrassed about attacking the old woman's son but she quickly reasoned that she had warned him quite clearly and he had chosen to ignore her. This culmination of many, many months of apparently harmless flirtation on Philip's part had developed a sinister undercurrent, which had only now bubbled to the surface.

It was something more than she had initially perceived. Now, with hindsight, she could mentally piece together past events and conversations with him. She only now realised that they had been gradually leading up to this confrontation, primarily, because of the plain fact that his furtive pestering seemed to her to have become increasingly persistent and frequent over the months. There was not a particular incident or conversation that she could impart to one of her friends that explained exactly why she felt so repulsed by him. His general demeanour in his everyday dealings with the public and local people was pleasant, courteous and congenial. However, if he was talking to her alone, in her bar for instance – for she regularly turned down his advances and invitations for a date – his attitude quickly became almost intimidating, and his blank stare unnerved her when she could not help, but briefly, to try and penetrate the heavily frosted windows that looked into his darkened soul.

In the past she had ignored his attitude, but the moment that had just passed was the moment she had been waiting for – for it was a definite moment when she had justified her fears and feelings for him.

'I was just telling Philip how much I cared for him,' she mustered innocently as she looked at Mo.

'Not a great deal, I see,' she said quietly as she closed the door behind her. 'Get up, Philip and do something useful with your time,' she said angrily as she slowly negotiated the fallen man and disappeared through into the passageway at the back of the shop. 'Come on, dear,' she called out to Christine.

Christine was already heading towards the open back door that led to the passageway, leaving the crumpled man on the floor.

'You didn't need to do that. I'll have you for this, just see if I don't, you frigid bitch. I'll make you wish that you had never been born,' he whispered venomously and breathlessly through gritted teeth.

She placed her hand on the door jamb as she turned and paused. In an instant she purposely walked back towards the kneeling man and kicked him in the same place as she had kneed him a few moments earlier. He immediately sprawled on the ground and groaned. 'You can have that one just for thinking that you can get away with it, and in case you are in any doubt how I feel about you.' She wiped her hands with a satisfied clap and disappeared from his view.

She looked along the small passageway to see the back of old Mo disappearing into a room. She followed with a steady smile but with unsteady legs.

It was fortunate that sufficient anger had steeled her for the confrontation because regret was already seeping into her thoughts. Perhaps I was too harsh, she considered.

The room at the end of the passageway possessed a dominant, yet pleasant, smell of sandalwood and the air was quite heavy with the smoke from incense sticks – not so that the air was impenetrable to the eye, but there were definite layers of very fine smoke magically suspended in the air, accentuated by the intermittent sunlight streaming through the narrow bay window. The walls were lined intermittently with heavy bookshelves and oil paintings of the ocean, which created an intense feeling of a great swelling sea with an icy and powerful tangibility. The wooden floorboards held two cloth covered, small two-seater couches with a low coffee table between them. A small desk with a brass desk lamp with a green downlight was positioned carefully in one corner underneath a long, yet narrow, bay window, which afforded just enough natural light to illuminate the room together with the light from a tall standard lamp. The room, from its appearance to the unfamiliar eye, with creaking wood and views of a perilous sea, could have been the captain's room aboard a Spanish galleon.

Mo was in the final stages of manoeuvring herself onto a chair that was situated behind the desk, under the window that revealed the view of the overcast day.

'Sit down, dear,' she said cheerfully as she carefully parked herself. 'Take two glasses off the side there. There's tea in the pot there too.' She waved her arm in the general direction of a bookshelf occupied by the tea paraphernalia.

Christine smiled obligingly and took and filled the glasses that rested tightly inside individual silver-plated holders that had ornate finger handles. She carried them over to the desk and sat opposite Mo on a soft two-seater couch that had a profusion of coloured cushions. She set the two vessels down on the table and settled awkwardly amongst the softly coloured cushions.

'Has Philip been troubling you?' she asked adroitly and with impunity.

Christine collected a weakened smile, initially taken aback by the speed and openness of the question. She was grateful that a hostile air had not been created by Mo after she had witnessed the aftermath of the attack on her son.

After a short pause whilst she collected her thoughts, she replied assuredly, 'Nothing I can't handle.'

Mo smiled seriously.

'I thought so. You make sure you tell me, though, if he gets too much to handle. I have serious misgivings about my son and his indomitable self-belief. I realise that it's healthy to believe in oneself but certainly not to the point of omniscience, bordering on the arrogant – if that isn't inevitable, I suppose,' she ambled with displeasure.

Christine nodded in quiet agreement but thought it strange that a mother should be quite so critical and scathing of her own son – especially imparting *her* feelings to her as she was not even a blood relation to Mo. However, she welcomed the fact that Mo realised that it was not the fault of her nature or character, that had led Philip to believe that she reciprocated the fascination that he obviously felt for her. She had been shaken by the incident with Philip but more so out of anger than fright. She now understood her intense feelings.

She raised the cool glass to her lips with an unsteady hand. The refreshing smell of the tea, the sound of the ice cubes plinking against the glass and the coolness of the vessel made her feel more relaxed. This was assisted by the soft lighting, the smell of sandalwood and the powerfully peaceful ambience of the room.

She quickly reflected on the audacity that Philip had displayed, although subconsciously she had one day half-expected that an incident – like the one she had encountered in the shop – could happen. With the benefit of objectivity, she knew she could use the incident as an example of his behaviour, although she had surprised herself by her display of brutality that she hoped was not in character. She had resolutely dealt with the matter that had been building up over the months, though, she re-emphasised to herself, she felt that it had been justified to put an end to her mind dwelling on the matter. She was forever analysing her conversations and thoughts *after* they had occurred, and her frequent examination of the past occasionally lead to a somewhat distorted view that caused her unnecessary concern.

Christine decided she dare not tell her father about the incident because he would no doubt fly straight back to the island and with help from his friends, teach Philip a lesson or two.

Looking at old Mo, she felt that Philip had suffered enough for now. She would keep her father as a guard in reserve, just in case. So much for the quiet life, she mused as she took another sip from the refreshing iced tea.

'Where did you go this morning? Anywhere nice?' she attempted conversationally, not really knowing what to say to Mo.

'Everywhere in Key West is nice,' she answered impishly, making Christine feel somewhat abashed and almost leaving her wondering why she had felt so compelled to visit the candid old woman. 'Hurry up, dear,' Mo encouraged her with a kindly smile.

Christine removed the glass mug from her lips and wore a puzzled look.

'Oh.' She raised her eyebrows and looked at the tea leaves in the bottom of the glass. 'You want to look at the leaves?' she said aloud as she sat forward with anticipation of the esoteric reading. She had not had her leaves read by Mo for years, and she felt rather silly because she had thought that Mo had offered her a drink out of nothing but hospitality.

Christine drained the remainder of the tea. Mo nodded and smiled knowingly at how she delicately and carefully did not to allow the tea leaves pass her lips and into her mouth. Christine passed her the glass when the liquid had been drained and she took it and turned it upside down onto a plate, then removed the glass and intently studied the pattern that the wet tea leaves left on the white china. Not a word passed between the young woman and old Mo, for a number of minutes.

Christine looked at the narrow window seat that was situated immediately below the wooden framed bay window, and then beyond the window panes at the view of the small, well kept garden, full of blooming flowers, trees, ferns and shrubs. An old wooden bench was positioned on a small patio outside, where, no doubt, Christine imagined Mo spending many a pleasant hour sitting in the cool shade offered by the surrounding greenery.

The bright sunny spell ended abruptly and the shadows cast by the brilliant sunshine melted away. The enveloping dull light of the heavy sky was intrusive in the absence of the previous brightness, and Mo looked disapprovingly at the window. She irritably leaned closer to the desk lamp that she switched on.

'Interesting.' She broke the silence. 'A major change in your life is all that I see. I don't know what it is but it's some kind of upheaval or input into your life that's very significant.' She looked up from the tea leaves. 'As I suspected, this storm that is developing is carrying a hidden storm for many people to weather. I have told many local people to be on their guard.' She finished, but was still studying the plate intently.

'That's all?' Christine asked quite serenely, wondering if Mo had finished. She felt rather uncomfortable because she was almost amused.

'For now, that's all you need to know,' she contentedly explained. 'I'm sorry to have dragged you here only to be so vague. To be honest, I was worried about something when I was in your presence. Perhaps it isn't you after all. Perhaps it's Jim or your bar that is troubling me. Don't worry, dear,' she said as she noticed Christine's frown. She placed the plate of tea leaves on the coffee table. 'I'm afraid that I do not know what you can do to look after yourself but I do not believe that you have to be any more careful than you are already.' She smiled a satisfied and relieved smile.

'That's a relief,' Christine replied decently. She was not the type of person who studied the astrological snippets in the newspapers and magazines and followed them religiously, for she believed that the content was so vague that the meaning could be interpreted by the reader and be pertinent to many individuals in many different situations.

Her thoughts now quickly advanced to other matters of no real concern other than politeness.

'Who else have you seen recently? To read their leaves I mean.'

Mo looked thoughtful and was silent for a whole minute.

'If you see James, tell him that I want to see him – will you?' she added, apparently having pursued her own thoughts and not necessarily Christine's question.

'James?' Christine was puzzled. 'Oh, Jim.' she soon realised, 'Mo, I don't think Jim'll agree to visiting you. I'm afraid he won't listen to anything remotely mystical or astrological.' She gestured slightly to the plate of tea leaves. 'And I don't think he'll change his mind either.' She continued to look thoughtful. 'I'll think of something,' she said slowly and with a growing smile. 'Well, be sure to tell me before you try anything.' Christine smiled, but seriously believed that Jim would tease Mo and so she decided to be part of her plans so that, perhaps, she could expertly adapt the plans to be more acceptable to Jim.

Mo laughed.

'Oh, I will be sure to tell you first, dear.'

'Is there anything I can get you, or do for you in the meantime?' she asked, already trying to think of ways to help Mo to fulfil her current objective. In her experience, Mo's dogged determination required that all her wishes must be acceded to if a quiet life was the general requirement.

Christine's father was accommodating with Mo's wishes. This started when he had lost his wife, Christine's mother, in the first year that the family had moved to the area from Ireland. She had died from a sudden blood disorder and Mo had assisted the devastated husband and his young daughter, through the dark months that followed her parting. Having someone to talk to like Mo, who did not dwell on the past but looked to the future, had helped him considerably – rather than other people who, however well intentioned they were, extolled pitying sympathy that only served to remind him of his great loss.

As for the remainder of the community, they each had a different story that explained why they too had once been grateful for Mo's presence, however small and seemingly insignificant. Mo commanded a natural respect, even if her alleged mystic abilities were not taken seriously, and her kindness, wisdom and objectivity was acknowledged by the community's willingness to comply with her wishes.

'No dear, it's all right. I can look after myself and anyway, my Philip can help me if I need anything,' Mo said distantly.

Christine wondered again how it was that Philip was her son, because the age of the mother and son did not appear to make sense.

'Mo, I've been wondering, and I hope you don't mind me asking, but is Philip your natural son?' she asked suddenly. Her thoughts immediately took control of her mouth and she wished that she had not been so impertinent. She wondered if Mo would be offended, but she quickly considered that a personal question would not penetrate Mo's thick skin or seemingly pragmatic personality.

'In a way,' Mo answered cryptically, and after a contemplative pause, 'I'm sorry, Chrissie,' she slowly stood up, 'but I have to take over from Philip and look after the shop.'

Christine read from Mo the abrupt signal that she did not wish to talk further about her relationship with Philip.

'I do apologise, Mo. I didn't mean to pry,' she offered as Mo carefully walked to the door. 'I shouldn't let my curiosity use my lips.' She sighed.

'Perhaps another time,' Mo said, unabashed. 'I'll make time to explain.'

Christine stood up and walked to the door, where the likeable old woman was now standing. She bent down and kissed Mo softly on the cheek.

'Well, you know where I am if you need me,' she offered kindly.

'Thanks, dear.' She gripped her arm tightly. 'I'll see you soon. And make sure Philip keeps his distance. You must tell me or Jim if he troubles you.'

'Okay.' She wondered if Mo was referring to the incident in the shop when she had been seen attacking Philip.

Christine walked through the passage and into the dimly lit shop, still aware of the tight grip that the seemingly frail woman had exerted.

Philip was standing awkwardly by the counter and till, still clutching his crotch with one hand.

She headed straight for the door of the shop and opened it gently, allowing a warm breeze to curl around the wooden frame causing the mobiles to stir from their slumber and the wind chimes to ring softly.

She felt that she could not leave without saying more to Philip.

'Perhaps you won't bother pestering me any more,' she said to the angry looking Philip who stood glowering at her.

'If that makes you feel better,' he replied moodily, with a blank stare from his empty black eyes.

She considered kicking him again but calculated that he would be ready for her this time, and that trying to resolve situations by the continual use of violence was not the most effective way of concluding all disagreements.

Instead she countered, 'You're weird and disturbed man. You really should get help.' Believing that a personal and justified insult was more effective than further acts of violence, she opened the door and went outside, closing it firmly behind her.

Again, she felt slightly shaken by this second confrontation but she was accompanied by resolution and determination to get through Philip's dense thought processes and make him realise that she most definitely was not interested in him, or disguising any feelings for him. Although he did have the immediate appearance of a charming man, she could not erase the image from her mind of the look in his eyes that seemed to conceal an inherently dark and disturbed soul.

She began to walk briskly when she noticed that the grey clouds now had a considerably darker hue, then the large droplets of rain began to impact heavily on her face and all about her. The sound of distant thunder rumbled and she broke into a leisurely jog, to avoid being caught in a sudden heavy downpour. Her mind was bubbling with sheer rancour at the nerve displayed by Philip, even though she was trying to remove the matter from her thoughts.

Jim took a step back from the easel to survey the canvas that he had finished working on. The oil painting was of a typical harbour scene, with the masts of yachts, frozen in time, as they bobbed in the painted wind atop the heavy sea. The sea itself was replete with white horses immortalised in the act of leaping the sea defences, crashing onto coast roads and partially obscuring buildings in the explosion of spray. Houses and buildings on the adjacent land were cowering from the elements; the painted trees were leaning dramatically, exposing roots and soil to the artist and the observer. The scene had a cold and powerfully windy, grey climate that immediately demanded attention as it leapt from the canvas.

He was satisfied with his work and considered that he had included all the feelings that he had wanted to express on the canvas; dramatic effects of the weather on the sea, trees, buildings and infrastructure of one of the many marinas in the Florida Keys cowering from the natural elements that man thought he could control.

He removed the scene from the easel and setting it down on a table he stood pondering what type of wooden frame he should be setting it in. He scratched the untidy beard on his chin and lost himself in contemplative thought.

Jim had taken early retirement from the police force five years earlier, taking advantage of the fact that his age was becoming increasingly noticeable in a job that demanded a young mind and body. The golden handshake that he had been given by the force and the savings that he had accrued over the years, had allowed him to move to Key West, where he purchased outright, opened his shop and sold his soul in the form of paintings. Painting was a passion for Jim, which was followed by fishing, smoking his pipe and drinking the occasional beer.

He had chosen not to marry primarily because the possibility of children and a family had never really materialised in the form of an appropriate partner throughout his working life – and he had never bothered to put himself out either. He had experienced minor relationships in his past years, all of them short-lived and rather inconsequential. As time drifted by and Jim's life became immersed in the force, long-term commitment never became of primary importance and it even signified a rather petrifying prospect to him as the years passed quickly. Now that he was in his fiftieth year, he spent the days as blissfully content as any being on the planet, but the nights were sometimes lonely and missing an aspect that he had thus far never been able to grasp – or perhaps had never been unwilling to. Whatever the cause of his single status, he very occasionally wished that a happy marriage had blessed him.

He selected a blank canvas from the stack which he had produced two weeks previously and set it upon the easel. When Jim had decided to paint the scene of his previous painting, a multitude of thoughts and ideas had flooded his mind with ideas of a painting scenes with the same theme. Now the painting was complete, with ideas including the dramatic weather remaining clear in his mind's eye, he was eager to begin painting the next canvas. Most of his paintings were of scenery or had a nautical theme, and they were usually painted with the accompaniment of radiating warmth and bright sunshine but his current feelings did not include such thoughts.

He preferred to visit an area to sketch the scene first but the weather was not at its most suitable at the moment. He mused as he looked out of the window at the first heavy onslaught of rain of the day. He imagined that his sketch pad would blow away if he even managed to open it in front of himself – let alone keep it dry – so he quickly dismissed the notion of even attempting the procedure.

The day had started rather bright, he mused, but now the dark clouds rapidly invaded the blue and began to empty themselves through increasingly high winds, that caused a constant and loud tapping sound as the large raindrops struck the seaward second floor window of the whitewashed studio. He decided to watch the weather and commit to memory its effect on the land and sea – while he watched from a stool in Christine's bar. He smiled to himself as he collected a sketch pad and pencils, which he intended to take with him but not necessarily use.

He briefly wondered if he should stay in the shop and wait for customers. However, he did not need the money and the amount of tourists shopping in this weather would undoubtedly be very small, if there were any at all. With his conscience clear, he opened the door to the studio and slowly descended the wooden stairs to the shop, idly leafing through his sketch pad as he did so; which contained some good material. He happily approved to himself.

'Mornin',' a voice sounded from the bottom of the stairs.

Jim slowly looked up from the sketch pad, not initially interested in the voice because he had not recognised it or matched it to a face, and because he had become so engrossed in the surprisingly good sketches that he had forgotten about. Perhaps he did not have to sketch new material at all, he pondered.

His eyes finally connected with his brain and he registered that Philip, Mo's son was waiting at the bottom of the stairs – which he thought odd because Philip rarely made personal visits to the male population of Key West. He did not know Philip really, which was unusual because everyone in Key West knew virtually everyone else quite well, especially as families lived in close proximity to each other – for instance, those who lived on or around Duval Street. That Philip should now be standing inside his studio, meant he must either want something from him, have a message for him or want to buy one of his paintings.

'Philip,' he said frostily as he stopped at the bottom of the stairs. 'I was miles away then, what do you want?'

Philip visibly took a deep breath.

'I thought you may be able to help me,' he said eagerly. 'I know that we don't often talk, but you know Christine quite well, right?'

Jim nodded slowly and watched Philip's large hands as his fingers tightly interlocked in front of his midriff – so tightly, in fact, that his knuckles turned white.

'Well,' Philip proceeded after he had acknowledged Jim's nod, 'you're not going to believe this, but I'm going on a date with Chrissie and I thought that you may be able to help me to surprise her.' He chuckled softly.

'You,' he said incredulously, 'on a date with Christine? You're quite right, I don't believe you.' He laughed scornfully.

'Is it so difficult to understand?' Philip replied. 'I *am* goin' on a date with Christine, Bob's daughter from the bar,' he said with exaggerated pronunciation.

Jim disliked being spoken to in such a patronising tone, and the implication that he was deficient in some way, to whatever degree of joviality, made him tetchy.

'I understand what you said,' he replied curtly. 'Christine despises you. Do you understand that? What possibly could have changed?'

Philip smiled thinly.

'That was just an act that we recently finished. She really likes me but didn't want to admit it. After all, Jim, what woman can resist me, eh?' he joked arrogantly.

Jim studied the smiling young man before him: with his strong chin; tousled black hair; tanned skin; six feet tall powerful frame and dark impassive eyes. Women were attracted to this man's body and appearance, he mused, and Christine had been adamant in her denial that she was attracted to him, when he had spoken to her in the bar the previous day. Perhaps Philip had broken through the same stoic barrier that he had used to protect himself over the past fifty years, he reluctantly pondered. Christine was far too beautiful and charming to spend her latter years alone like himself, he considered.

He gingerly settled on the idea that he should perhaps give Philip the benefit of the doubt. After all, Philip was charming, successful and a fine looking man with strong genes and an apparent liking for the family life – he did, after all, still live with his mother.

'What have you got in mind, young man?' He walked past him and towards the door at the back of the gallery. Philip followed.

They reached the small kitchen. The room itself, which had a low ceiling, was cluttered with hanging pots and pans, assorted utensils and used crockery.

'Well, keep it to yourself for now,' Philip began, as he seated himself on a chair at a square wooden table. He looked about his person disapprovingly while Jim busied himself by a kettle on the stove. 'As I said, I want it to be a surprise,' he continued. 'I'd like to get to know her better. I don't know, perhaps take her out for dinner or even cook for her – I'm a great cook, y'know,' he assured him. 'The problem is that she'll probably make some excuse. Seeing as though you know her quite well, I want you to try to put a good word in for me. You know, she really has got the wrong impression of me for some reason.' He looked offended.

'What do you mean?' Jim questioned, slightly flummoxed as to why the young man should confide in him.

'Well, take today, for instance, I was minding the shop for Ma and she came in. Y'know, we were chatting okay and she put her arms around me and kissed me. Ma walked in and her attitude changed completely. She didn't say another word, even when she left. It's as though she was ashamed.'

Jim reasoned that Philip was a good-looking man and Christine was at least as equally attractive, so the liaison that Philip had just detailed was not at all improbable. After all, her indignant rebuke of Philip earlier yesterday was, perhaps, too indignant. He became annoyed at himself for being so naïve when it came to relationships of the heart. He could easily inspect the true intentions of a murderer or a robber with a very fine brush, like an archaeologist uncovering a fossil in the sand. He could only unearth these matters of the heart, though, with a clumsy shovel.

'What did your Mo say about all this?' he tried. 'Besides, this coming from you sounds, well, sounds a little pathetic coming from a man like you.' He was becoming increasingly sceptical.

'Oh, I can't talk to Ma about things like this, besides, have you ever heard of me having woman trouble?' He chuckled. 'I've never met a woman who I haven't got along with and yet I've never met a woman who I like as much as I do Chrissie. Ma wouldn't understand that because she's my mom. I thought that you might have advice or an opinion, seeing as though I don't have an old man to turn to.'

'Me?' Jim huffed with surprise. He poured two cups of coffee from a pot on the stove and set one down on the table in front of Philip, before sitting on a chair opposite him.

'Affairs of the heart never were my forte. You shouldn't ask me.' He wondered who and where Philip's father was. He had never asked and made it his intention to find out. 'Hey, I'm no father figure.' He chuckled uneasily and there was an uncomfortable momentary silence. 'I hope you don't mind me asking but who was your father? Did you ever meet him?'

He looked at Jim impassively.

'No idea. I don't want to know either,' he said curtly.

'Didn't mean to cause offence. Just curious, y'know.'

'None taken,' he replied. He took a deep intake of breath and sat up even straighter. 'What I need, I suppose, isn't really a father figure but just someone to talk to. I just need a sounding board and you seem to me to be the ideal candidate.'

Jim reluctantly accepted his reasoning.

'So, what have you got in mind? What do you want to sound out?'

'Well, I need to borrow your kitchen for a night. I want you to invite Chrissie over and leave me to do the rest. You can stay upstairs, so there's no need to worry about us,' he suggested triumphantly. 'Perhaps she'll agree, as her behaviour today was less than civil. Perhaps this is the best time and she may be feeling guilty. What d'ya think?'

Jim scratched his chin thoughtfully. From a basic retired policeman's perspective he had his reservations about the young man's character, and he was concerned about Christine's future well-being. In using his shovel he could not see that his request was that unreasonable.

'What about your house, though? Why can't you do it there?'

Philip shifted his position in his seat. 'It's Ma. You know how well she gets on with Chrissie. If I do it there then Ma'll interfere and won't give us any peace. Chrissie will probably leave in a hurry without us sorting anything out for definite.'

Jim thought again, how in the past, he had been hesitant when it came to showing affection. Perhaps his cautious attitude had been the cause of his being alone at this stage of his life. He was reluctant to see it happen to anyone else – especially to the young woman whom he considered to be almost as his daughter. Philip was an experienced sailor and most respected on the island, for his boating and fishing skills had made him quite a wealthy man. His business acumen had helped him to build a fleet of powered pleasure craft that he rented to tourists. He took parties of tourists on motor boats and large fishing boats and recently he had set up a fledgling diving school. Jim looked hard at Philip. He had no reason to doubt him and thought it, perhaps, to be a gifted idea that would make Christine happy in the long term.

Christine's father would not have agreed to such a proposal unless he was in the same house, at the time of the proposed liaison. Seeing as though he would be in the same house as Philip and Christine, he reasoned that he would be acting responsibly. Her father was a man of principle and the 'mature' age of his adult daughter would not have entered the equation – she was still his precious little daughter and always would be.

Jim took a sip from the mug and contemplatively set it back onto the table in front him. He regarded the young man facing him, dressed respectably, as he was, in a black polo shirt and light brown tailored shorts. He smiled, once his clumsy reasoning had convinced him about Philip's proposed scheme.

'Okay, let's do it.'

'She won't know what's swept her off her feet.' Philip smiled as he raised the coffee mug to his lips. 'Just don't spoil the surprise.' He laughed affably.

Jim raised his mug to his lips and looked into Philip's dark eyes.

Philip quickly broke eye contact and turned to look out of the window.

'I just hope for a break in the weather,' he said distantly.

Jim was an ex-police officer with considerable experience, which allowed him to use an almost sixth sense to ascertain if someone was telling him the truth. Any other person would have been convinced by Philip, as Jim had been, initially, but the shifty intensity of his eye contact made Jim's highly tuned intuition instantly suspicious. He suddenly had a feeling of doubt, the same feeling of doubt that he had experienced in his days in the police service, when he had watched a dubious witness conduct an interview.

Some people avoided eye contact because they became embarrassed by a simple show of honesty, but Philip was not the type of person who was easily embarrassed by simple contact. It was almost as if his eyes would betray his true intentions. Now, Jim had the difficult situation of balancing, in one hand, Christine's long-term interests and on the other, balancing Christine's well-being, if indeed she was in any danger.

If Philip was telling the truth and Jim divulged his proposal to her, he would possibly be spoiling her future by spoiling the surprise. He did not want to be overprotective but he also had to consider her father. After all, Bob had asked him to keep an eye on her and he took the responsibility seriously.

Tentatively, Jim still decided to go along with Philip's idea, for now.

'When were you planning this for?'

'I thought about a few days time, y'know. All I want is for you to invite her for dinner at eight. Tell her to come round the back and I'll do the rest. If it's okay with you, I'll get here about seven and prepare the seafood and you can wait upstairs.'

'Okay,' Jim agreed. 'I'm going to the bar soon, so I'll invite her then.'

'Thanks, Jim.' He stood up to leave, 'And don't forget – don't mention my name or she won't come.'

'You just leave it to me,' he replied.

Philip said farewell and left via the back door, leaving Jim to struggle with the conflicting voices in his head. He was not an indecisive person, for once he decided to do something it was the result of considerable thought. Every possibility and every possible outcome, however impossible, would in turn be processed in his mind. He knew that he had much difficult thinking to do but his overriding responsibility was Christine's safety.

A group of four men sat around a table near the bar drinking beer, smoking cigarettes and laughing raucously. Jim eyed them with curiosity as he walked past them to the bar.

'This bunch behaving themselves all right?' he asked Christine when he sat down on a bar stool. He turned sideways and regarded their behaviour further.

'No need to concern yourself.' She smiled. 'They're taking their vacation and just unwinding. They're really quite pleasant, actually. Don't fuss,' she cajoled.

'Just checking.' He held his hands up in submission.

She poured him a glass of the usual and he turned to face her. She was, as ever, radiant.

'To be honest,' she continued, 'I'm pleased to have some trade today. A bit of company, you know.'

He thought of Philip's visit earlier and again thought of his own occasional bouts of loneliness. He had mulled the proposal over in his mind and allowed his subconscious to process what Philip had said. He had made a decision about the proposal, that he felt dealt with every issue and facilitated a predictable outcome that satisfied his conscience, Philip's request and Christine's integrity and safety.

She set the full glass, on a paper beer mat, on the bar.

'One of the reasons why I came in,' he began, as he contemplatively wiped the frosty residue off the outside of the glass, 'is that I had a visit not long ago from Philip. He came to my studio.'

'Oh?' she replied. 'Whatever did he want?'

'Yeah, I know.' He laughed. 'I'm not even a woman. No, he talked about you as a matter of fact.'

'Oh dear.' She winced. 'I saw him this morning and I was anything but civil to him.' Her mind had processed her confrontation with him to such an extent that she now almost viewed it as her fault.

'He said so,' Jim replied.

'I don't blame him for being mad but whatever has it got to do with you?' she asked, puzzled. 'And I don't mean to sound rude.' She touched his hand.

'No, I quite agree and that's what I asked him. He said because I was quite close to you and your father that I could speak with you. He's sorry for what has happened and would like to make it up to you.' He could not find the words to express Philip's reasoning. He again felt a pang of regret at his inability to deal with these matters.

She looked at him doubtfully.

'He's suggested cooking you a meal at my place. I'll be there too,' he said as he noticed her immediate expression of concern. 'He asked me not to tell you that it was him waiting for you instead of me – but I didn't like that idea. I thought that if I told you everything, then you could prepare yourself, whether you decided to go or not.'

'I don't think so.' She laughed defiantly. 'However, I wasn't very nice to him and I do feel slightly guilty.'

'I'm not surprised,' he said.

Her view that she had been wrong, was re-enforced by Jim's comment. She paused.

'I suppose I could go and see what he has to say. You're going to be there as well so nothing can happen, and I like to give people a chance, even if I don't particularly like them.' She tried to convince herself. 'It still doesn't seem right, though. A feeling in my stomach is telling me not to go.'

'Me too,' he replied, 'but I'm curious to know what he's up to. The thing is, he could genuinely be trying to make friends with you, despite what happened today,' he pressed.

'I do feel that I was a little harsh. I don't know why I did it, actually. It was one of those impulse reactions.'

'You don't have to explain.' He shrugged it off.

She was grateful and relieved at his dismissal of her actions.

'I reckon that we should go ahead with it, just to see what he's up to. I'm curious too, you know?'

'Perhaps you should ask Mo?' he suggested.

'I suppose I could.' She considered. 'I'll have to think about it, though, because I get the impression that they don't get on very well at the moment. I don't want to cause her any stress.

'Well, you think about it and do what you think's best.' He lifted his glass and took a large quaff as another burst of raucous laughter from the table of tourists filled the room.

Chapter Six

Allan crammed the suitcases and hand luggage into the boot of the car and shut it with a solid sounding clunk. Once he had checked to make sure the lid was firmly shut he then turned to approach the hotel, which was bathed in the warm morning sunshine. He walked along smiling broadly and contentedly. A car slowly pulled up behind their hire car by the side of the erstwhile, quiet road.

A man – who he perceived as an archetypal American citizen – dressed in blue jeans, T-shirt and a cream, cowboy-style hat, stepped down from the large indigenously popular American style pick-up truck and headed towards the hotel entrance.

'Morning,' Allan called out to the man – in an over-emphasised upper class English accent.

The man in the cowboy hat did a double take as he looked at Allan, then tipped the brim of his hat in apparent bemused acknowledgement, before disappearing from view behind a break in the hedge that fronted the hotel gardens. Allan smiled to himself at his deliberate accent and happily followed the man into the grounds of the hotel.

Today was the first full day of his holiday. The rain and clouds had gone, the sun was shining, the previous night's debacle was forgotten and his fiancée was in their room, dressing. Two weeks of excitement and enjoyment stretched before them in the *sunshine state* of Florida. First, though, their intent was to have some breakfast and then locate the apartment building that contained the residence for their two week stay.

He reached the outside of their room and pushed the door open. He was just in time to see the rear view of Denise, wiggling her slender hips and pulling a pair of tight blue jeans firmly around her waist.

'Are you ready?' he asked, as he forced himself to break from his lustful memories of the night that had just passed.

She turned to face him as she pushed her arms through a shirt that hung loosely over her shoulders and down to her waist. She fluffed her hair out from beneath the collar of the shirt looking at him seriously as she did so.

'Don't rush me.' She sat on the bed and opened her make-up bag.

She held a lipstick to her lips as he sat on the bed next to her and put his arm around her.

'Allan, don't sit so close to me and don't block the light,' she admonished.

He stood up.

'That's not what you said last night.' He laughed uncertainly.

She smiled superciliously before turning to look at him, managing to lessen her look before she did so.

'That was last night. Now is today and I'm trying to get ready with you jogging me, blocking the light and telling me hurry up as well. Give me a break, Allan.'

'I didn't...' he began, but decided not to pursue clarification of his earlier question, now almost forgetting completely their previous night of passion. He decided that this was a typical conversation where he need not antagonise her by pursuing significant, yet minor facts that she had misinterpreted. What he saw as critical, and what he meant to say, in the first place was completely ignored and repulsed by her, almost as if she *wanted* to take things the wrong way.

'Are you tired?' he suggested, thinking perhaps that this was the reason.

'Why?' she replied. 'Do you think I'm crabby?' she asked crabbily.

'No,' he replied defensively. 'I meant, are you suffering from jet lag? Did my idea of staying up late and drinking beer to beat the effects of jet lag work for you?'

He had speculatively, the previous night in the bar come up with the idea – even though he had been tired – to counter Denise's suggestion that he frequently exposed boring tendencies. He had found some rather weak logic in his somewhat curious suggestion that had eventually ended in the early hours of the morning. It had worked for him, even though he had a mouth that felt as dry as Gandhi's flip-flop, and the accompanying nagging need for a kebab or curry – even at this hour of the morning – was very strong indeed. He was impressed that he had adjusted to the different time zone in what he perceived as a rock'n'roll manner.

'I'm not tired,' she said abruptly in a strange voice, as she applied the light-coloured lipstick – that she managed to stretch into a circular shape – to her lips. 'But I have a slight hangover, which is your fault,' she said as she placed the cap back on the lipstick with a click and returned it to the make-up bag. 'I wouldn't have minded having an early night rather than spending a long night in a smoky bar with a crap guitarist playing stupid rock'n'roll and blues songs.'

'He was great,' he enthused. 'He played all my favourites, and very well he played too. That man should be a star.' He decided to forget to mention that it had been on her insistence that they went out in the first place.

'He should be *on* a star, on the other side of the solar system thing.' She waved her hand and laughed at her quip, which was rare indeed. 'Come on, I'm ready. Let's not discuss your rubbish taste in music now,' she said, as she stood up and walked out of the hotel room door.

He was about to point out that the only star in the solar system was the sun and that she should have said universe or galaxy, if she wanted to imagine a star farther away. However, this discrepancy was overshadowed by the fact that he could not believe what he perceived as Denise's ignorant and prejudiced view of music. He failed to understand how anyone – like Denise for instance – could prefer house and dance music that necessitated the use of mind-bending drugs to achieve a state of enjoyment when listening to it. When he listened to music he did not simply hear it, he felt its magical power too. He felt the lyrics stir his soul and the instruments reveal a multitude of emotions that the musician used to express him or herself. In his opinion, a sound could not be correctly termed *music* if it was not created through raw emotion, and in his eyes, creating sounds through a personal computer was tantamount to blasphemy.

He inspected the bathroom, the main room and cupboards for the third time – checking to make sure that they had not left anything behind – before he too, went outside and shut the flimsy door behind him.

'You'd better take the key back,' she called from outside, half-way down the stairs that led to the side of the swimming pool. Her high-pitched voice echoed around the small buildings and she was forced to hold her forehead due to the effort that had been made to raise her voice.

She did have quite a hangover, he mused as he watched her, but nothing could alter his cheerful state of mind as he made his way from the hotel room to the patio door of the reception.

Denise tried the car door, which was locked. She leant against the metal of the car and watched the sea as it crashed ashore, creating a generous amount of spray that twinkled as it rose high in the bright morning air. She heard the sound of footsteps crunching on gravel and watched as a man, dressed in jeans and a cowboy hat bounded through the opening in the hedge of the hotel grounds.

She looked wistfully as the handsome, powerful-looking man quickly climbed up into the pick-up truck and started the engine, which powerfully sprang into a throaty rumbling roar before he gunned the machine adroitly to the end of the short road. She watched as the dark truck glistened as it disappeared from view, leaving her wondering how she could make Allan appear more rugged and sexy.

'We're off!' exclaimed Allan excitedly with keys jangling in his outstretched thumb and forefinger as he veritably skipped towards the car.

She watched him with a dim feeling of regret and disdain, but also with an obscure whisper of hope for the future as she smiled weakly at him.

He unlocked the driver's door with the key and climbed in. She joined him as he was about to start the engine, holding his hand that was holding the car keys before instructing him to pull the roof of the car back before they got under way. She was expecting him to have to wrestle with catches, levers and poppers to accede to her wishes.

'I noticed it yesterday,' he said as he pressed a button on the dashboard, causing the roof to slide back with the accompanying small sound of a whining electric motor, far away in the boot of the car. He started the engine and they drove off into the sun saturated streets of Fort Lauderdale – the wind clearing their woolly heads and Allan daydreaming enthusiastically of an ice-cold soft drink.

'Allan,' she began, after they had been driving only a few minutes. She was forced to speak quite loudly to make herself hear above the sound of the rushing wind, 'have you any idea where we're going?'

'To have breakfast,' he replied. 'I'm so hungry I could eat anything.' He paused. 'Even carrots, and you know how they make me heave.'

A short silence followed. 'I think we should find our apartments first. I want to unpack my clothes and hang them up before they get too creased,' she said earnestly.

He was aghast – annoyed with her selfishness and extremely troubled by the fact that he was very, very thirsty.

'Denise, your clothes will be creased to buggery already. Another hour won't make any difference.'

'Let's go to our apartment first. We can take our cases in, unpack quickly and then go to have breakfast.' She ignored his reasoning and her tone of voice was very insistent.

'Denise,' he persisted, uncharacteristically. 'The dreams that I had last night were of ice-cold drinks, which woke me with such a need for a drink, you wouldn't believe. I am so hungry too,' he whined. 'My mouth feels like a gorilla's armpit.'

'Allan, you're sick – you look like a gorilla's armpit too,' she said under her breath, turning her nose up. Allan was indeed not looking his best. He actually looked slightly dishevelled with his untidy hair (made worse by the rushing wind), unshaven face and bloodshot eyes – he was in need of a shower too.

She was unwilling to parade him in public for people to turn their noses up at him and also, perhaps, at *her* – for the type of man she spent her time with. Although she liked a man to look rugged, if Allan looked rugged it was usually the same as a sports car that had a bolted-on, large spoiler on the back of it – it just did not look good and ruined the aesthetics.

'Stop at a petrol station then. I'll get you a bloody drink,' she conceded, reluctantly.

He was surprised at her accommodating attitude, and exceedingly relieved that his thirst was to be quenched within the next few minutes. He was willing to ignore the way she had remarkably conceded and not point this fact out to her – mainly because he was so taken aback by the fact that she had even said it.

'Thanks, Denise,' he said with continued surprise, as if he could not muster the courage to ask her to speak nicely to him anyway. He quietly noted that her act was uncommonly unkind at this stage of their relationship.

When they did pull up a petrol station and Denise soon returned to the car with two cans of ice-cold drinks in her hands, he understood her motives. He let her get comfortable in her seat and watched her as she put the seat belt on. How did she manage to look so immaculate always? he wondered.

He leant over and said loudly in her ear, 'How's the hangover? Thirsty too were we?' and immediately wished – when he saw the look of thunder that crashed onto her face – that he had not bothered to antagonise her.

'It *was* getting better,' she said, as she moved violently away from him to try to avoid the loud voice that had already left his mouth. She looked at him and said sternly, 'No thanks to you, gorilla features.' Anger seethed inside her at the thought of him belittling her, and she was disappointed at her choice of rebuke as it was rather less than childish.

He laughed as they pulled onto the main road and continued their journey. He had doused the unquenchable fire in his belly with the ice-cold soft drink, while Denise continued to seethe with annoyance and an unquenchable fire in her belly which was consuming her tolerance towards him.

'The hour that's just passed could have been spent having breakfast, when we could have asked someone where these damned apartments are.' Allan was hungry and exasperated by the fact that he had been driving for over an hour and they had not found their accommodation – which accounted for the fact that he then foolishly took his annoyance out on Denise.

'And I suppose that's my fault, is it?' she said nonchalantly as she looked out of the passenger window. She was still angry with herself and Allan, and she was eager to be as difficult as possible to reclaim her lofty position and force a certain amount of acquiescence from him.

He looked at her shoulder-length hair forced back by the motion of the car, at the black sunglasses that covered her small eyes and the immaculate complexion of her cheeks. To him, she looked very attractive and, aesthetically, she seemed more than worthy to be his partner. Her appearance made him value her quite highly and now he felt guilty at taking her for granted.

Silence fell between them as they continued their search down the large boulevards, and over the many drawbridges that spanned the abundant waterways, upon which floated lavish yachts. Large, opulent white houses situated in lush green grounds, fitted superbly into the crooks of snaking waterways. The sun bathed the area in an idyllic scene for them.

'There it is!' she exclaimed as she pointed at the windshield. 'I can see the name of the apartments on top of the roof.'

He smiled and drove the car towards where she had pointed, turning it into a small side road, which was adjacent to a large yacht moored in a quiescent waterway next to the apartment block. He stopped the car.

'At last!' He held his long arms above his head and stretched them.

She climbed out of the car and stood next to him.

'Is there any chance that *you'll* one day become a millionaire?' she said distantly as she studied the lavish yacht.

The sun blazed onto the surface of the calm water that mirrored the opulent vessel, villa and surrounding luxuriant grounds.

'Very unlikely.' He chuckled lightly as he pulled the suitcases out of the boot of the car. Denise said nothing in reply, which he noted and so continued more seriously, 'Is that so important?'

'Absolutely,' she replied firmly. 'I'd love to live here.' She looked wistfully about her at the sun soaked luxurious scene before them.

'So what you're saying is, if a rich man asked you to marry him you'd accept and dump me?' He set the cases on the ground and studied her face.

She looked momentarily startled and fell silent.

'No,' she said after a pause. She turned away to avoid eye contact with him and started towards the apartment building.

'Yeah, right.' He laughed.

She paused and faced him again – for she had only walked a few steps.

'So would you?' she countered. 'If a rich woman *came on* to you then you would dump me?'

He smiled.

'Thanks, Allan. Thanks very much. I obviously don't mean that much to you,' she whined.

'Hang on a minute,' he called after her as she stormed off in the direction of the entrance to the apartment building. He had not even answered her question and yet she had decided his response already. He was flustered. He picked up the suitcases, locked the car and quickly followed her.

It had been Denise who avoided the question first and turned it against him, he mused with increasing annoyance. He could live with being manipulated – put up with her occasional selfishness, foolishness, mood swings and her taking him for granted – but he was hurt by her making him feel inadequate, especially with the fact that she was blatantly materialistic. What was her goal in life and what did she like about him?

A heavy weight of confusion plunged upon his shoulders. He began thinking of Denise's unpleasant mother, who she would undoubtedly become, as the years added maturity to her person. He realised that she already revealed similar tendencies to her mother, and his father had always told him to ascertain what type of woman a potential mother-in-law was, because his fiancée, in all likelihood, would turn out exactly the same. Allan knew that when he spoke to his future mother-in-law she always appeared distant and disinterested, and in some ways she *did* fit the character of the archetypal, perhaps clichéd *dragon-in-law*.

He thought to himself that it was wholly necessary to justify his reasoning to doubt Denise and so she had to commit an act that he could use as an example to show how unsuitable she was for him. If he hastily broke their engagement or delayed their marriage, he would have much explaining to do to both families – even to himself if his reasoning was incorrect. If he was right, though, he recoiled from the thought of Denise's reaction to his potential decision to break off the engagement.

In the last twenty-four hours he had learnt more about her than he had in the past six months. He could not specify a time, though, when she had behaved as she had over the past day without taking into account his, perhaps, contributory behaviour. All of a sudden her attitude troubled him greatly – almost panicked him. Perhaps he would feel differently after some breakfast and more liquid refreshment, he mused unhappily.

He caught up with her, ignoring the brief conversation they had just brusquely imparted. Instead, he told her of his intentions towards having a much needed breakfast.

'Me too,' she replied gratefully, seemingly eager to make amends.

He was pleased that she seemed to want to ingratiate herself and the thoughts that he had had previously began to fade into the expanse of thoughts that occupied his mind.

They walked up the gentle slope that led to the reception. The narrow path was bordered by hardy-looking tropical plants with thick leaves to withstand the heat. Palm trees stretched upwards and passed the lower floors of the tall apartment building. The blue sky was now becoming peppered with white fluffy clouds that were being quickly dissolved by the blistering sun.

They reached the main doors, which opened automatically as they came near. The interior of the building was cool and quiet as they headed for the desk marked 'reception'. The sound of Denise's footsteps echoed on the polished marble floor. The receptionist had a welcoming smile for them when she looked up. Allan produced the necessary documentation to obtain the keys to their room.

Once the transaction had been completed, they had positioned themselves in the empty lift that was waiting. The lift doors closed.

'All women dream of marrying a rich man,' she said sweetly.

The matter had obviously been troubling her, Allan thought.

'Like all boys who dream of marrying a beautiful, slim woman with large breasts,' she added.

He laughed loudly.

'Well, if you put as trivially as that, then I suppose that what was said by the car was meaningless.'

'I take by that that you're not offended then?'

'Not now, no.' He continued to laugh, pleased that the situation was resolved but he was still empty with immense hunger.

The lift door opened and, as they tried to exit the narrow aperture together, the young couple became momentarily jammed in between the doors. Allan conceded and Denise passed through wordlessly.

'Can I have the key?' She held out her hand. He passed her what looked like a credit card. 'I said the key, Allan.' She handed it back.

'No.' He laughed. 'This is the key. It's a credit card key with our details on it.' He placed it in a bracket on the wall by the side of their room. An unobtrusive green light illuminated on the panel by the door and the digital reader accepted the card. He pushed the door open, bowing and gesturing for her to enter. 'There you are, madam.'

She disappeared inside and he followed, gratefully setting the luggage down in the hallway. The thickly piled plain carpet and the cool air conditioned air forced him to smile with pleasure. His immediate impression of their apartment was most pleasing. The lift had been small and hot and the exertion of carrying the suitcases had created sweat patches on his shirt.

'All these rooms. Two bathrooms, three huge televisions – one in each room,' Denise extolled. 'I can't believe it. This apartment is great, and the view! The sea, the beach...' she continued excitedly, drifting into an almost semi-conscious daydream. She stood next to Allan and regarded him with disdain. 'Phew!' she said as she waved her hand under her nose, soon returning to the real world. She quickly ushered him into the shower and vehemently explained that he looked a mess and needed to smarten up his appearance.

He was soon standing under the powerful stream of water that was soothing his back and massaging his fuzzy head.

Once dried and dressed, the thought of food quickly took over and remained prominent as he proceeded to hover about Denise's suitcases trying to help her to unpack as rapidly as he could – although she was being unusually pedantic. When she had finally finished, he virtually dragged her into the lift that carried them down the fourteen floors.

With urgent insistence as he held her arm, Allan hurriedly slammed the credit card key onto the reception desk and they left the startled receptionist to the remainder of her working day. They virtually ran from the apartment building and he led them to the first building that he recognised as being a bar/restaurant, which was only a stone throw away.

The bar/restaurant, in which they were very shortly seated, was situated halfway between the beach and hotel. The décor of the bar had a fishing theme, as was unmistakably evident by the large blue model of a marlin fish hanging prominently above it. The theme was further supported by a profusion of fishing nets hanging from the ceiling, sea shells behind glass table tops that served as display cabinets as well as tables, and a myriad of fishing paraphernalia adorning the walls. Waiters and waitresses busily and cheerfully buzzed around the tables with pencil and paper. They wore safari shorts and T-shirts that fitted the theme of the Beachcomber establishment quite nicely.

A short while later, Allan briefly broke his concentration from the large American breakfast placed before him. He took a slurp from his coffee cup, and he looked over the top of it at Denise. As he chewed a piece of toast, he said in a muffled voice, 'Nice, innit?' before continuing his assault on the contents of the plate with the flashing steel of knife and fork.

She held a full coffee cup in her hands, her elbows resting on the table and she watched him doubtfully as he zealously wiped the plate clean with his last slice of toast.

'Wow,' he said simply. He sat back in his chair wearing a contented smile. He stifled a burp with a cupped hand.

She tutted. 'Did you enjoy that by any chance?' He had demolished a hearty breakfast and then consumed vast quantities of coffee and cola and each time his glass or cup was replenished by a member of the cheerful staff almost as soon as it was finished. She eyed him with a certain degree of disapproval but he failed to take any notice.

He brushed the fallen crumbs and breakfast remnants from the front of his T-shirt.

'You don't know how much better I feel.' He smiled contentedly and visibly relaxed. 'So, what do you want to do today?' He sighed before he lit a cigarette.

She looked at him with continuing disapproval.

'Beach first, then a walk around the area, including a look in all the shops, and then a nightclub tonight,' she replied instantly. She pondered her words after she had spoken, wondering if she had missed anything out.

She had obviously been giving the matter some thought while he was troughing, he mused. 'So, what you're saying is, now that we have travelled thousands of miles and spent hours on an aeroplane and landed in a country where there's so much to see, *you* want to do what we could have done in Blackpool?' he said, inadvertently tempting her to metaphorically bite his head off.

'This is our first day, for God's sake. Let's just relax for today and have a bit of fun shall we? Tomorrow we are going to Key West, where I know you are dying to go and spend time looking around, and when we come back we're going to Orlando where you can enjoy all the kiddies' rides – and that's only in the first week or so.'

He nodded with distant agreement, conceding quietly that she did have a point.

'So, it's not as if we're wasting our time here, is it? I suppose if you had your way you'd be fishing, drinking beer from a bar on the beach and watching women go by in skimpy bikinis, followed by paragliding, powerboat racing and water biking,' she said sarcastically, 'or having sex in the apartment all day.' She finished unkindly and altogether unsuitably loudly, considering their proximity to other people – a few people nearby turned to regard them with a certain degree of interest.

He mustered a laugh and nodded enthusiastically.

'Wow, that is probably the best day ever.' He closed his mouth and cleared his throat unnecessarily. 'Sorry,' he said quietly, when he saw her that she was not at all amused.

She folded her arms across her white T-shirt and looked at him. He now sported tidy hair, clear eyes and possessed a fresh smell about his person. His dying need for sustenance meant that he had had no time for a shave while she had been unpacking the suitcases, but he nonetheless looked as good as he was feeling, she mused.

'Remember yesterday, at that horrible apartment, you accused me of being childish?' she said grimly. 'Well, today you're behaving like a teenage boy,' she said with disdain.

'No,' he said after a pause, 'I'm just behaving how all men behave, or how all men really think. If they aren't behaving like me then they are living a lie,' he said definitely.

She looked confused. 'What's brought this on?'

'Brought what on?'

'Your attitude.' She unfolded her arms and leant forward on the display cabinet-style table. 'You're talking like a man who spends his life with his mates, drinking beer and leering at women.' Her face changed from looking congenial to one of severe distaste. 'And I don't like it,' she added venomously.

'Denise.' He sighed after another pause, then carefully selecting his words, continued. 'I've been thinking, we really have been getting on well over the past few months. We're together for two whole weeks…'

She folded her arms tightly and looked at him incongruously.

He shifted uncomfortably in his seat.

'I think it's about time that I was honest with you.' He hoped that the ground would swallow him up as the bombshell of words formed in his mind and threatened to spill onto his tongue. Immediately his courage leaked away into the recesses of his mind like the tide from a beach. 'You should really buck your ideas up and not take me for granted,' was what he wanted to say, but he was most definitely not a protagonist, although it was an inner ambition of his.

'I'm waiting,' she said matter-of-factly as he struggled with his internal battle between honesty and cowardice. A surprise third party moved in and took control of his tongue.

'Do you really want to get married?' He winced.

She looked dumbfounded.

'Why? Don't *you* want to?' she scowled angrily.

'Of course I do.' He took her hand quickly in his. 'It's just, well, you seem to have been a bit offhand with me over the past couple of days.'

She withdrew her hand and glared at him. '*I* have? What about *you*? You've been impossible, and you started today by annoying me at the apartment before we left. You shouted in my ear in the car when you *knew* I had a terrible hangover, you dragged me down here and hurt my arm and now you're behaving like a chauvinist pig.' Her voice rose and she again caught the attention of nearby patrons.

As the silence fell around them, he half expected to hear the sound of a needle being dragged heavily across a vinyl record. Fortunately it did not, but he could not help noticing the many eyes regarding him accusingly.

'I'm sorry,' he pleaded quietly to her as he leaned forwards across the table – believing that these words were becoming meaningless because of the amount of times he found himself saying them, 'but I haven't meant to do anything to upset you. I don't know if I can be anything else but I'll try to think before I speak.'

'Believe me when I say you will change, if it's the last thing you do. You *will*, Allan.' She laughed.

'Sorry, I didn't mean it,' he said as he kicked himself. He had wasted a golden opportunity to explain to her how he felt, what his fears were and perhaps how she could help him. However, she had slammed the door firmly in his face and now, because of his relative weakness, the opportunity had passed. The future was unfolding before him and his options for altering how and when it unfolded were minimal.

'I'm going to phone my mother.' She stood up and held out her hand.

He gave her his wallet and took up his coffee cup with thoughtful expression.

She walked out of the establishment to the telephone booth across the street. As she walked into the warm sunshine she was also wearing a thoughtful expression.

As she pressed the numbers on the phone, he watched her and continued to watch as he silently smoked his cigarette. At first she dialled the number printed on her phone card and then dialled her home telephone number. She looked good in her shorts, with slender legs, neatly tied hair and fashionable sunglasses, he mused.

It was midday in the Beachcomber bar and seven o'clock in the morning in England. He wondered what she was saying to her mother and what she said in return. He imagined that she was asking if they had argued yet and whether Denise had called off the wedding. He smiled as he thought of running over to the phone and shouting all the names under the sun to his future mother-in-law before cutting her off – he could imagine his future mother-in-law's expression forming the face of a person sucking hard on a particularly bitter lemon.

Denise's face became animated in the conversation with her mother before she turned to face the booth, her back now facing the bar, and inserted a finger into her vacant ear to block the sound of a passing truck. Minutes passed and she eventually turned, faced Allan and waved. He could not imagine what the mother and daughter were saying to each other.

'Yes, Mum. I think he has got life insurance,' she said surreptitiously into the handset as she waved and smiled at him.

The bikini slipped from her shoulders and the palms of his hands fell firmly upon her breasts. His fingers slowly caressed and brushed her increasingly erect nipples and she arched her back, causing her long wet hair to fall softly and tickle her skin as she moaned with consequent pleasure. She eagerly positioned herself on the edge of the kitchen table and pulled his head closer. He responded and his mouth moved from hers and onto her breasts then down to her legs, where he removed her remaining small garment. She held his head between her legs and eagerly lay back on the table, dislodging a glass and plate that smashed on the tiled floor with a loud crash.

The suppressed excitement became intolerable and she feistily pushed him away. In one swift movement she whisked his shorts down to his ankles and physically forced him down onto a wooden kitchen chair. She impatiently straddled his erection and proceeded to ride him vivaciously until, eventually, breathing heavily and smiling broadly, they both collapsed in a tangle on the chair.

'Next time I ask you for a towel I want you to get me one, is that clear?' She kissed Tom firmly.

He pulled away breathlessly and looked at her.

'Actually, no.' He laughed. 'I'm never gonna get you a towel if that's what you're gonna do to me.'

'Well, perhaps I'll have to try a different way of getting what I want.' She stood up in front of him. He regarded her slightly tanned skin, her slim and toned physique and her beautiful long hair that reached halfway down her slender back.

The moment of passion had begun when she climbed out of the swimming pool in the rear garden of their home. When they had arrived home after the long hot drive from Orlando to Fort Lauderdale, the swimming pool offered an enormously welcome prospect and one that they had been talking about since they had left Orlando. They had dashed headlong from the car into the pool, then, once they had cooled down, Tom had refused to get a towel and she had then seen fit to chase him into the kitchen where the passion ensued.

'You can try to persuade me to do anything by whatever means you want,' he said, as he pulled his shorts up. 'I'll get you that towel now.' He smiled and disappeared up the stairs.

He returned to the kitchen and watched through the window as she showered naked by the pool, in the seclusion of the area that was surrounded by tall trees. She turned the shower off and wiped the water from her eyes when he went into the garden and tenderly draped the large fluffy towel around her.

'Do you feel like going out tonight?' She looked at him.

'Could do,' he contemplated. 'I feel like a few beers. Yeah, why not?' He smiled.

'Me too. We'll leave tomorrow at mid-morning. That'll give us enough time to get to the Keys, won't it?'

'Plenty,' he replied confidently.

The house that Tom and Tanya lived in was set in an opulent area of Fort Lauderdale. The long lawn that fronted the house had a gravel path that snaked from the house to the road. The house was sprawling in its construction and mostly single storey, except for the four bedrooms which were situated on the floor above the front door. The rear of the property contained a modest swimming pool surrounded by a secluded landscaped garden. At the bottom end of the grounds was one of the many connecting waterways of Fort Lauderdale.

Most people who lived in Fort Lauderdale had a boat of some kind or at least owned a luxury motorised yacht moored at the bottom of their garden. However, Tom, although wealthy, did not wish to become embroiled in a superfluous show of wealth. He knew that if he did own a boat he would never use it. Besides, if there was any money that he did not spend he would treat Tanya, himself or simply choose not to work a while until the money ran out.

When he was not working he enjoyed spending time with friends, Tanya and tinkering with an old motorbike that he kept in his voluminous garage adjoining the side of the house. He actually liked to spend time in his garage, where he had placed a stereo, pool table and a fridge full of beers. He liked nothing more than spending a few days not working but listening to rock'n'roll music and playing pool while drinking a few cold beers with friends.

Tanya would work elsewhere in the house so was not interrupted by the sometimes raucous behaviour that erupted from the den. She very rarely intruded into what she perceived as his space, and he rarely found it necessary to interrupt her while she was working either. They understood each other implicitly and petty arguments never arose from their living arrangements.

Later, once they had both dressed and unpacked, she pressed a button on the phone and ended the call. She curled her legs from underneath herself and stretched the length of the sunbed.

'All arranged?' he asked as he passed her a tall glass of ice.

She took it and smiled gratefully. 'Yup. I said that we were leaving tomorrow and he's looking forward to meeting you.'

He poured her a drink from the glass jug. The liquid cascaded into the glass and caused the ice to ring out a unique tune as it jostled under the waterfall of the falling fresh juice.

'Great.' He sat down on a seat next to her. 'I expect that you'll be glad to have someone else to talk to, after spending two whole weeks with me?' He raised his eyebrows.

She laughed. 'No.' She looked as though she was going to say more.

'And?' He noticed the look on her face so he leant towards her.

She jumped up, fearing that he was going to tickle her, from which she was always powerless to escape.

'Well, I'm looking forward to seeing a different face to yours.' She laughed and darted off as he lunged playfully towards her.

'So, you're fed up with me, eh?' he questioned slyly from one side of the barbecue.

She looked at him from the other side, ready to dart in the opposite direction. 'I didn't say that. What I meant was that I'm looking forward to seeing my uncle.' She laughed and she darted off again as he made towards her. He eventually caught her and wrestled her onto the thick grass. He pinned her arms down and sat on her legs. 'Ow!' she spluttered from a laugh. 'This grass is hard.' She wriggled but was unable to move. 'You're not offended are you?' She looked at him seriously.

'I don't know,' he said thoughtfully, 'perhaps I need reassurance.'

She raised her eyebrows, pulled him close and kissed him deeply. It was indeed fortunate that the garden was secluded, he mused, as they soon both felt the moist grass against their exposed skin.

Allan stubbed the cigarette out in the ashtray and drank the last of his coffee as Denise returned to her chair.

'Everything all right at home?' he said as he set the cup back into the saucer.

'Fine.'

'How's your mum?' he said, inwardly and distantly hoping that she had come to a painful demise.

'She's missing me already. Can you believe that?' she said rhetorically. 'I don't know how she'll cope when we live together. I expect she'll be around our house every five minutes.' She laughed.

He did not doubt her reasoning and immediately felt a rotten pang of dread kick his stomach repeatedly, but he did not impart his disdain to Denise. What she said had merely added to the considerable weight that had already taken root upon his shoulders.

'You wouldn't want that, would you?' he forced himself to ask her.

'I don't mind. We'll be at work all day, so it'll only be the evenings and weekends anyway.'

'That's all right then,' he replied drily – which was wasted on his parched fiancée.

She smiled at him for a whole minute, distantly, and it was something that he was not quite used to after the past months.

He responded to her with a smile too.

'What?' he eventually said, slightly perturbed by her attention.

'You know what I was saying earlier, about you being a chauvinist pig?' she said at length.

He sighed regrettably and pressed his brow with his fingers.

'Yes.'

'Well, I've changed my mind about part of it. How about we go back to the room and do it?'

'Eh?' Allan looked confused. 'Ohhh.' he said, at her clumsy terminology as realisation dawned upon him. He slowly stood up and placed money on the table to pay the bill and she stood up too, and they left the bar arm-in-arm.

His mind did not stop to try to ascertain the reason for her sudden change of mood – from frosty to that of almost warm and loving – but he was merely pleased that it had. He could not help wondering if it was something he had said. Perhaps it was something that she wanted, but she would never usually be backward in coming forward, he mused. Perhaps she felt guilty, but he could not think why. Perhaps she was softening him up for something that was about to happen, he finally thought. He concluded that, whatever the consequences, he was willing to make love to the woman who he loved.

In his indomitably deep and thoughtful mind he considered that each person was dominated by two halves, yet complete sections, that formed a perfect whole, in most cases – that is not to the extreme extent of a split personality or schizophrenia. He perceived that there is part of the mind where the conscience is situated and this deals with the deep thoughts, reasoning and the very deep thoughts – the soul, the inner self, the internal voice of reason.

The other part of the mind he perceived as being for everyday thoughts – hunger, work, play and physical needs, to name but a few. Each of the two parts of the mind need constant stimulation and yet only one of the two halves can be present at any one time. At this moment in time, despite his inner-self prodding him to give the matter more thought, the more dominant self was urging him to use his everyday state of mind and accede to her wishes.

Now his inner self had been temporarily banished to the recesses of his mind, where it continued to shout the questions at an increasing distance from the fore. They remained unanswered.

Over the years he had struggled to overcome a very self-conscious attitude to himself and life. Although his attitude was much improved than that of a decade ago, a certain degree of self-doubt still plagued him. However, during the adolescent years of low self-confidence he spent many hours, even days, thinking – he thought about himself, who he was, life and where he stood in life. Such was the depth of his internal probing of his mind, and after reading many books on the subject, he discovered that he had inadvertently learnt what had been taught thousands of years ago by Chinese philosophers. The fact that he was so right in his thinking, in the views of the ancient teachings, was now unknown to him because he was only really now concerned with how he could appear confident, even though, deep down, he was not. He was on the very edge of self-discovery but had never made the final step because of an opposing personality that would not allow him to probe further.

'What are you thinking about?' she said to him when they were back in the apartment.

'Oh, nothing much,' he confessed as he held her tightly.

She pushed him away and quickly untied his shorts.

'Come on.' She led him into the bedroom by the cord. Once inside the room she peeled off her one-piece bathing costume and giggled at his bulging shorts. He virtually impaled her as he pounced.

'No, not like that,' she eventually commanded and he eagerly positioned himself again.

She lay where she wanted and he immediately shuffled his position, doing as she instructed, even though he was not at all comfortable. Her long painted nails dug deeply into his back and he winced.

'I'm sorry Allan. Did I hurt you?' she said irksomely.

'Doesn't matter,' he said breathlessly.

Allan watched as the large cars glided almost silently past the beach on the adjacent coastal road, his chin resting on his hands as he lay on the large towel that was protecting him from the scorching heat of the soft white sand. Denise was lying beside him, smothered in sun cream and looking perfectly delectable in her bikini. He had watched her step into it after the passion that they had shared but an hour earlier. As far as he was concerned, she could now ask anything of him and he would accede to her every wish with gusto, if it meant that he was rewarded as he had been earlier.

'Do you fancy a swim?' he enthused.

'Oh Allan, I was just falling asleep then.' She tutted as she propped herself up on her elbows. 'No I don't. I've just put all this sun cream on. You go in. I'll look after our things.'

He sat up and looked at the surf curling underneath itself – repeatedly and powerfully dashing the sandy shore. The waves were not quite large enough for surfers, but the heads of other swimmers disappeared into the troughs between the crests of each wave, as the sun shone a shimmering light on the surface of the ocean, necessitating him to shield his eyes. The salty spray filled the bright sunlit air and the sound of the sea rhythmically rang in his ears like oceanic orchestral cymbals.

'Do they have sharks in the water here?'

She opened one eye and looked at him as she again lay flat.

'I don't know,' she said honestly, then added without hesitation, 'probably not.'

'I wonder if the water's cold. It looks cold, and rough.'

'Just go in, will you? Look, there are other people in the water,' she said, exasperated. 'For goodness sake, can I have a bit of peace?' She closed her eyes and stretched out again. She soon heard him run towards the sea exclaiming to himself repeatedly and distantly with the words 'Ooh' and 'Ahh' as his feet made brief contact with the scorchingly hot sand. She smiled and wondered if there were sharks in the water, before her mind drifted on to the thoughts of expensive yachts, large houses and a hefty bank balance.

The orchestral sound of the waves became distant and the sound of faraway excitable voices, heard on the gentle breeze, grew softer and softer as she sank from consciousness and into a light sleep. She did not even notice him dive through the pounding warm surf.

'What's that!' she exclaimed loudly as she sat up with a start. She had been asleep. 'Allan, you're dripping all over me.' For a moment her imagination pictured him – his face pale and his body ravaged with deep cuts and bruises – dripping blood on her from the stumps of severed limbs that had been ripped from him by a shark.

'Sorry,' he said, as he stood farther away from her on the edge of the beach towel. He dried his tongue with the corner of another towel and she looked at him with disgust. 'The sea is great – it's warm and the big waves are great fun,' he enthused, 'mind you, it doesn't *taste* all that great.' He grinned as he continued to wipe his tongue. 'Why is it that when you swim in the sea you always get a mouthful of salty water? It's as though the sea opens your mouth for you and forces some water in. Have we got any mints?' he said as he began to rifle through the rucksack that they had brought with them. He eventually pulled a packet from the bag and crammed a handful of sweets into his mouth.

She tutted with suppressed amusement as she watched him.

'No sharks then?' she said, with what seemed like disappointment.

He looked at each of his limbs in turn.

'Not that I noticed.' He smirked as he continued sucking the mints noisily, attempting to extract as much taste from the candy as possible. He continued to towel himself dry roughly.

'Allan, will you get me a drink from over the road? I'm thirsty.'

He looked at the busy road which had an almost constant stream of moving traffic. They had earlier experienced great difficulty when crossing the road to get to the beach because the pedestrian crossing did not seem to have the same meaning on an American road as it did in Britain. He looked on with trepidation. However, he thought of their earlier passion and smiled.

'Okay,' he said finally.

She closed her eyes and smiled.

A considerable time elapsed and he still had not returned. She eventually decided to sit up straight and she began to wonder where he was. She mused that she had dozed again for a while. She had read some of her magazine – that had passed some time as well – so she could not determine how long he had been gone. It was while she watched the cars slowly passing by that she noticed him, waiting in the middle of the constant stream of passing traffic and then she watched as he sprinted safely to the edge of the sand.

'What happened to you?' she asked as he approached, eventually, with a large frosted bottle of soft drink. 'You've been gone ages.'

'Have I? Oh, I knew that you'd probably gone to sleep so I went for a walk – found a few bars that we could try. We'll probably have to get taxis to them. No nightclubs nearby though.'

'Wait a minute,' she interrupted, as he sat down and passed her the bottle. 'While I was sitting here, worried about you crossing that dangerous road, *you* were in a bar, drinking beer and looking for nightclubs? I was becoming concerned! I could have been kidnapped or something.'

'I didn't stop in any bars,' he explained with incredulity. 'I just made a note of where they were and bought you a drink at a general store. Sorry if I took so long, but I was thinking of you all the time,' he crooned as he smoothed her soft, now shiny and sweaty leg. 'Kidnapped?'

She was torn between the intense affection that he displayed and the inner feeling of resentment that she harboured. She smiled before she raised the bottle to her lips, then passing him the bottle when she had finished she wordlessly returned to her horizontal sun worshipping position.

'You shouldn't sunbathe, really,' he said, as he pulled the bottle from his lips with a plopping sound. He looked at her. 'It causes skin cancer, you know.'

'Thanks, Allan,' she said irritably with her eyes closed. 'I needed that. I was just relaxing thinking that I haven't got a care in the world – then you hit me with that one!'

'You mustn't hide from the truth and pretend that it's not going to happen,' he replied somewhat pompously. He had remained buoyed up from his passionate experience earlier and his confidence was high enough to rebuff her mild hostility towards him.

'Just like the link between cancer and smoking,' she retorted, her eyes still closed.

He enjoyed discussing controversial issues and was surprised and pleased at her reasoned argument.

'So, if I give up smoking would you sunbathe anymore?'

'I only sunbathe for two weeks of the year and you smoke every day of the year. Smoking is disgusting and annoys non-smokers, whereas sunbathing doesn't interfere with anyone and isn't repulsive in any way.'

'Unless you're fat,' he replied seriously.

'Are you saying that I'm fat?' She sat up suddenly.

'No!' he replied as he rolled his eyes to the sky. 'I was playing the devil's advocate.'

'Well, if you want to smoke yourself to death that's your decision. Just *don't* do it near me, *don't* try to make me stop enjoying the sun and *don't* call me fat – or *that's it*.'

He was about to iron out a few discrepancies in her statement but quickly decided against it.

'Sorry,' he offered instead, disappointed that their potentially intelligent conversation had come to an abrupt end. He sat down quietly, anxious not to antagonise her further, his confidence melting as the powerful sun slowly passed across the sky. He wondered if the approaching night would harbour any surprises for him.

Chapter Seven

'Your red nose looks like one of those plastic joke noses that clowns wear,' Allan quipped as he regarded Denise's somewhat outrageous-looking nose.

'Thanks very much,' she said angrily, as she contemplatively looked at her reflection in the large bathroom mirror. 'That makes me feel so good about myself. You're about as subtle as a brick.' She dabbed ineffectually with a powder puff, trying in vain to reduce the shiny redness of her sunburned nose. 'Why do you bother saying these things?'

He ignored her question, or rather did not hear it because he was already thinking about something else.

'Why is it that, after a day in the sun, one always appears to be sunburnt when one steps out of the shower in the evening?' he thought aloud. 'I mean, in the sunlight one's skin doesn't look tanned at all. It's only after a shower,' he continued.

'I don't know, Allan.' She sighed waspishly at the reflection of him in the mirror. 'Why is it, do you think, that men are so tactless? Why is it that men don't think of the feelings of women?'

He paused for thought. He believed that, perhaps, people should be strong enough to look after themselves and not be so sensitive.

'Sorry,' he replied finally, not really knowing what to say.

'I would love one dollar for every time you've said sorry,' she said, as she applied an unusually large amount of foundation to her throbbing facial beacon.

Eventually, after he had waited another half an hour for her to blow-dry her hair and finish dressing, they rode down in the lift from the fourteenth floor and made their way to the Beachcomber bar that they had visited previously that day.

The evening was warm and the air turbulent with a strong, warm wind that swirled around them constantly. It was trapped by the surrounding buildings, trees and parked cars and, with a sound almost like running water, lifted fallen dried leaves and dashed them against everything static.

The few bars that lined the dark street were full of tourists who were quietly drinking or eating in a discernibly mature and sedate atmosphere – there were no bright lights, brightly illuminated advertising signs or loud, throbbing dance music intruding on the ambience. Due to the fact that the night was so warm, the front windows of each establishment had been removed to create an open, breezy atmosphere – the windows and frames were purposely removable.

The street itself was almost devoid of moving cars, mainly because it was a side street and did not actually lead anywhere; apart from the large apartment complex where Denise and Allan were staying. At each end of the small road was a rather busy road that was the main coast road.

The two of them walked the short distance of the side street to the bar and went inside the establishment.

The façade of the establishment was open to the elements and the breeze circulated freely and gently inside the bar, quietly disturbing paper beer mats and gently rearranging the hair on the heads of the patrons.

The majority of glass covered tables were occupied. There were stools and spaces at the bar and they sat there.

'I think we should try somewhere else,' he suggested after a while, having deduced that Denise was becoming bored, as was indicative of the way she sat quietly with her arms folded and her impassive eyes staring ahead.

'No, I like it in here. We'll stay for a drink or two then order a taxi to take us to a nightclub,' she said with surprising finality.

'We don't know of any nightclubs here.'

She said huffily, 'The taxi driver probably knows the area quite well, so he'll tell us.'

'Yeah, he'll probably take us to a nightclub at the back of beyond so that our fare is higher. I'll ask one of the staff here,' he said sensibly and ordered their drinks when a smiling member of staff asked him for his order.

The sound of guitar blues with a heavy harmonica riff suddenly filled the room. Denise turned in her seat to see where the music was coming from and saw that it was a live band – to which she turned her nose up. Conversely, Allan really enjoyed this genre of music – as did the other occupants of the bar – and the sound of the music caused him to turn in his seat and look on with obvious enjoyment. When the music had finished it was applauded and whooped vigorously by virtually every occupant of the bar.

'We shan't stay in here long,' she said as she looked with distaste at the musical scene before her.

Allan received the ordered pitcher of beer, which was placed with two frosted glasses on the bar. A sealed bag of ice cubes floated in the jug and he carefully poured the icy beer into the glasses – so as not to allow the bag of ice to follow the beer into the glasses.

She noticed his movement from the corner of her eye.

'Allan, what did you get all that for? We'll be going soon. Anyway, I don't want any beer. You know I don't like it,' she confided in a flurry and with obvious annoyance. She did admit to herself that the drink looked very cool and refreshing. It was not that she disliked the taste of beer, provided it was not served in a pint glass – which she regarded as being rather crass if a woman drank thirstily.

'I noticed that most people were drinking it here and so I decided to get one too,' he replied as he took a large quaff from the glass, draining half the contents thirstily. He could almost feel the heat being discharged from his body in a vaporous hissing cloud.

'Only because you like it,' she said. 'I don't want any. I want a short drink,' she commanded haughtily.

'Okay, okay. I suppose I'll have to drink all of it.' He smiled when he passed her the vodka that he had ordered in addition to the pitcher of beer. He thought about offering her the bag of ice cubes for her nose but he visualised her probable response and smiled broadly into his glass instead.

'You'll be drunk,' she said contemptuously.

He continued to grin into his glass. 'I'll try not to be.'

'I'm not drunk exactly,' he confided as the taxi drove along the grand darkened streets of Fort Lauderdale to the nearby – in American terms, for 'nearby' in Britain means that you can walk there – Trios nightclub. 'But I'm definitely on the right road.' His speech was slightly slurred.

'You're on a slippery slope,' she chided him. 'If you get drunk then I'm going home and leaving you at this nightclub. I can't stand it when you're drunk – you're really argumentative and embarrassing.'

'Looks like your girl's in for an early night.' The taxi driver chuckled quietly as he looked at Allan out of the corner of his eye, being careful not to take his eyes from the busy highway. The two men laughed together loudly and she folded her arms tightly as she quietly seethed on the back seat – Allan was seated in the front of the car.

Allan turned to look at her response to what the driver had said.

'There's no need to look like that,' he said with accidental buffoonery. He was about to remark on the fact that all he could see of her face was her nose glowing in the dark, but again he sensibly decided against it as he realised that she would be outraged. At this moment in time he did possess a small amount of Dutch courage but he most certainly had not drunk enough beer to induce a state of galloping stupidity.

After about a twenty minute drive, the taxi drew alongside the entrance to the nightclub and the couple climbed out – once Allan had paid the fare to his newly found friend and they eventually parted with more raucous laughter – and joined the queue.

The nightclub was housed in a two storey, rather unimpressive warehouse structure surrounded by car parks and various large stores in a retail park. The queue for entrance to the nightclub was approximately thirty-strong and was comprised of local people and tourists of equal number Allan presumed, by their evident dress sense.

'A friend of yours?' a man – with his female partner in the queue immediately in front of Allan – asked, as he studied him with obvious amusement.

'No,' Allan replied to the stranger. He looked at Denise for apparent approval, but she just glared at him with wide eyes and a look that dared him to say anything else to the stranger, who she thought looked decidedly disreputable, dressed as he was and sporting long hair and a goatee beard.

'He was just a funny fucker who was making me laugh,' he replied with a wry smile.

'Allan!' she said, aghast at his unusual use of alternative vocabulary, especially as he was speaking to an American couple who he had never met before and she did not want to create the wrong impression – even though she thought the man looked like a drug dealer or something equally criminal.

'It's awful, isn't it?' tutted the female half of the American couple. 'He swears often, sometimes even in front of my parents,' she said with good humour.

Denise looked surprised and looked down her nose at the couple.

'If he did that,' she said, as she nodded towards Allan, 'my mother would throw him out of the house.'

'Would she?' he asked with exaggerated surprise. 'I'll have to try that.'

Both Allan, and the man he was speaking to in the queue, laughed heartily.

'My name's Allan, by the way, and this is Denise, my fiancée.' He extended his hand politely, still chuckling.

'I'm Tom.' He shook his hand. 'And this is my partner, Tanya.'

Denise and Allan shook Tanya's hand and they all smiled politely.

'You're a polite lot you Brits, aren't you?' Tom offered.

'Bollocks.' Allan laughed loudly and Tom joined in. 'It's only when people first meet. After that it's a free for all.'

'Allan,' Denise hissed venomously, 'will you stop swearing and showing off.'

He tutted flippantly, annoyed that she had seen fit to patronise him.

'Just leave it,' she said quietly, and nudged him in the ribs with her elbow so he winced slightly.

'Where are you from?' Tanya asked.

'We're both from London. Well, Greater London,' Denise explained with an unusually precise English accent.

Tanya and Tom looked momentarily puzzled.

'Suburbs,' Allan explained, wondering if he should ask Denise to speak normally and stop showing off. He was puzzled as to why she had told him to be quiet, yet she saw fit to talk to the couple – presumably so that she could feel superior – he mused cynically.

'Have you been to England?' Denise asked.

'No, I've been to Europe plenty of times: Germany, Switzerland and Italy – but never England. I've always been meaning to, though. You haven't been either, have you Tan?'

Tanya shook her head and smiled.

'Those countries are pretty boring places to visit,' Allan explained. 'You want to go to London.' He smiled. 'That's where the fun is.'

'And you've been to those places, have you?' Denise rounded on him unexpectedly.

'I have actually,' he was pleased to reply, knowing that she was going to ask that question.

'I'm warning you,' she said quietly, not at all pleased that he had got the better of her for the second time that day. She turned back towards Tom and smiled thinly. 'Were you on your holidays when you went to Europe?' she asked.

The American couple looked puzzled.

'Vacation,' Allan interjected.

'Oh right.' Tom chuckled. 'No, I had to go to the American banks to sort out some of their computer equipment. I didn't get to see much really, just the inside of hotel rooms and the workings of computer equipment.'

He had provoked Denise's interest sufficiently for her to ask what he did for a living. It was now apparent to her that the American couple's appearance was misleading.

The queue had moved forwards quickly and they were already at the front. Tom allowed Denise to move in front of him so that she stood beside Tanya in the queue.

'Wow, man,' he said quietly to Allan, physically putting himself between Allan and Denise. 'She's a bit of a handful. Is she always like this? I mean, is she always needling you and trying to trip you up?'

Allan was not the type of person who became offended by frank and open questions, especially when alcohol made him so melancholy. In fact, he preferred people to be honest and say what they thought because then he knew where he stood with them. He considered the question carefully so that he could give a deservedly honest reply. 'Yes.'

'I couldn't be doin' with that, man,' he chuckled, 'however good the sex was,' he said as the two couples entered the club.

The interior of the club was dark and noisy, with the thumping bass sound of dance music distorting the atmosphere. Pulsing bright lights strobed across the darkness of the dance floor; dry ice billowed across the club and captured everyone and everything in a paradoxical slow-motion world. Allan looked up and noticed two levels of balconies, assuming that the nightclub possessed a further two floors that gave the establishment the name 'Trios'. The various bars were ultraviolently illuminated behind the optics and glasses so it was easy to locate them in the sombreness.

'What'll ya have?' Tom shouted in his ear to make himself heard.

Allan was not expecting to stay talking to the couple once they were inside but he was pleased that the man had asked.

'I'll get them,' he said appreciatively as they approached the bar. They ordered the drinks and took the women theirs.

'Make a night of it, eh?' he said in Allan's ear as he offered his bottle of beer as a toast.

'Good idea,' he replied and chinked his bottle against Tom's. 'Anyway, there's safety in numbers,' he said, as he looked at Denise who was engrossed in conversation with Tanya.

Tom laughed.

'Yeah, but wait until you get back to your hotel, she'll get you then – and then some,' he said seriously but with a hint of humour.

'I'll deal with that when it happens.' He sighed with serenity, then raised his bottle of beer again for a toast. 'Oh, bollocks to it!' he said, virtually inaudible above the noise of the tumultuous mixture of light, dry ice and the thumping bass of the music that pervaded all the senses and caused his jeans to vibrate against his leg.

Tom just about heard him and laughed but Denise could not have heard their conversation. Tom turned to face Tanya when she touched his shoulder, then she turned away from the two men and walked off with Denise.

'Where are they going?' Allan asked.

'Upstairs to 'the Seventies' floor,' he replied, 'Can't stand all that shit myself.' He waved his hand. 'Do ya wanna game o' pool or do you wanna join them?'

Allan pondered the idea for a second, and thought it strange that a nightclub should have pool tables included in the list of facilities but he quickly concluded that playing pool and drinking beer were preferable distractions to listening to the monotonous beat of dance music from *any* decade.

'What about the ladies?' he asked. The two of them made their way through the swelling throng and ascended the busy, darkened stairs. 'They won't know where we are.'

'Tan'll find us. She knows I like pool so they'll find us eventually – don't worry, man.'

He worried that Denise would be less than happy with the arrangement and, as a consequence, he would undoubtedly later receive a severe dressing down from her, which he would have to respond to with backbreaking apologies. However, he was steadily achieving an inebriated state which was affecting his decision making powers, and this was unfortunately numbing the essence of his knowledge concerning cause and effect.

He felt that he had already created a situation that was not acceptable to Denise and so there was no turning back in an attempt to remedy it. She was enjoying herself on the dance floor, he presumed, and so he decided to go for broke and enjoy himself however he wished – whatever the inevitable consequences.

They reached the collection of five pool tables in a row and set their beer bottles down by a table next to a free one.

'Won't Tanya be annoyed?' He continued to wonder anyway.

Tom looked surprised.

'Nahhh,' he replied as he arranged the balls in the shape of a triangle and offered Allan a cue. 'She's a real fine woman and a good friend too. If she's ever mad, which ain't often, she shouts and screams, bangs me with her fists, and then,' he said in an amusing gravelly voice, as he stepped closer to him as he was cueing up for the break – for the music was not as loud on this level of the nightclub, which Allan was relieved about – 'we get naked and have fantastic sex.'

Allan miscued the ball and launched it off the pool table and into the darkness. Tom's openness had become amusingly frank now. Tom laughed at what he had said, what had happened to the cue ball and then at Allan, who was still assuming the position he had adopted to strike the ball. Allan rested his head on the green baize and laughed too, causing his shoulders to heave up and down. He eventually laughed his way from the table and into the darkness before returning with the cue ball.

'What about you? What happens when *your* girl gets mad?'

He looked at Tom and, with an accompanying miffed noise from his lips that resembled a raspberry sound, raised his eyebrows.

'When Denise is mad,' he began with incredulity, 'she shouts, blames me, threatens me with leaving the relationship and then cries a lot until I present her with a profuse apology and an offer to go shopping.' He struck the cue ball smartly and widely scattered the pack of colours. 'Which is at least what I'll have to go through after tonight.'

'Man,' he replied as he approached the ball to take his shot. 'And that happens every time? I couldn't live with that. Good luck, man, that's all I can say.'

Allan took a large pull from his bottle of beer and contemplated Tom as he chose his shot. Tom was a tall man, with shoulder length, light brown curly hair, a small goatee beard and dressed in blue jeans and a white T-shirt. His abundance of confidence and natural, honest charm and pleasant demeanour was immediately apparent in these first exchanges. He had taken an instant liking to the man, for he represented to him, the type of man he would like to be allowed to be.

'Well,' he said, as he lit a cigarette, offering the packet to Tom, who took one. 'I sometimes wonder if it's worth it. I mean, I have to put up with a lot, but I do love her.' He lit Tom's cigarette for him.

'Easy.' Tom chuckled as he blew the smoke into the already smoky atmosphere, made more evident by the green covered light that hung over the pool table. 'Don't do anything and put up with nothin' that gives you hassles, man. What can't be changed must be avoided – period,' he offered candidly, 'No offence intended, but life's too short. A wise man seeks knowledge from others, an enlightened man seeks knowledge from within. Deep down, you know the score.'

The words rang heavily in Allan's head, like the familiar perpetual sound of crashing waves on the beach.

'You're right, I suppose.' He struggled, 'I have tried to encourage her, though, to be more relaxed about things but she doesn't seem to want to.'

'What she needs is som'at that makes her realise, that wakes her up to smell the coffee,' Tom offered.

'Like what?' he asked in vain, although pleased to receive sympathetic assistance and advice from any quarter, even from an apparently seriously happy man who he hardly knew at all. 'I have tried the easy-going approach – taking things slowly and gently pulling her towards what I see as the normal way of behaving.'

'You make it sound like she's deranged or som'at,' Tom said, turning his nose up. 'I'll get the beers, Al. Life's too short to be arsing 'bout. Go with *your* flow, man.' He struck him firmly on the shoulder and left him happily contemplating his situation.

Allan slowly pondered whether he should go in search of Denise to ensure that she had sufficient money. However, when Tom returned with the two bottles of beer he did not give the matter any further thought. The alcohol had lubricated his mind and allowed him to confront his inner feelings permitting him to vocalise them to a virtual stranger.

'I don't even know you,' he said, as Tom passed him the bottle of beer, 'and I'm telling you all my woes. Sorry, mate.'

'That's okay, man. Listen bud, I majored in psychology for two years before bombing out to work for my old man. Not only do I reckon I know what I'm talking 'bout, not only do I use common sense but us guys all across the world have got to stick together and eliminate troublesome women.' With another firm hand on his shoulder he reiterated what he had said before continuing with the pool game.

Allan pondered the gravity of what Tom had said. 'You're not suggesting that I get rid of her permanently, are you?'

'No, no.' He laughed incredulously. 'I can't condone that type of elimination – yet.'

Allan raised his eyebrows.

'What she needs is to see and experience what a true relationship entails.'

'Take her to the cinema and watch a gooey film?' he suggested with intended irony.

Tom laughed heartily.

'You Brits are too funny. No, man, real life experience, like me and Tan.'

The conversation rambled while they drank more beer and played frame after frame. They discussed everything from politics, favourite films, favourite famous women to music – and they discovered that their tastes were alarmingly similar. It did not take long at all for them to become firm friends.

'Are you on holiday here or do you live here?' Allan asked.

'I live here in Fort Lauderdale, with Tan. We're just loafing 'bout for a couple of weeks, taking a break from work. Sort of like a vacation in our hometown. My old man has just bought us a house by the water, so we've been sorting that out, man.'

Allan nodded.

'Well, then I have a proposition: Denise and I are going to Key West tomorrow. Why don't you two come with us for a few days? It'll be a laugh,' he said boldly.

Tom looked thoughtful as he pondered the idea, then he smiled. He looked distant, almost puzzled.

'Would you believe that me and Tan are going to the Keys tomorrow?' He slapped Allan's arm in surprise. 'Must be fate, man. It sounds like a real good idea.' Allan nodded as Tom enthused. 'I like the Keys, man. There's good fishing there, bars and plenty of nightlife.'

He looked thoughtful and increasingly attracted to the proposition.

'Great idea, Al. Hey,' he said as he held out the palm of his hand in the worldwide gesture for 'halt', 'what 'bout Denise? What'll she say about it?'

The gusting wind suddenly stopped billowing Allan's full sail: he regretfully mused that, lately, she was not agreeable to many things that he proposed.

'I don't see why not.' He pondered aloud, as he did not think that she would immediately disagree to the proposition but there was not really a reason for her not agreeing, and so he remained optimistic. She seemed to get along with Tanya, he thought, and she did not seem overtly hostile towards the American couple.

'We'll have a ball, Al,' Tom enthused. 'Drinking beer, smoking and having a real good time – and at the same time we'll try and see if we can't make Denise see the real life. Tan'll help too, right; if I explain to her. If it don't work out then I'll lend you my gun and you can threaten her,' he teased, as he pressed the cue into Allan's hand. 'Your shot, my man.'

Allan grinned and was lifted by Tom's suggestion about accompanying them to the Florida Keys,

'My round.'

Tom looked puzzled.

'Beers?' He gestured with his empty bottle.

'Cool,' he said, and Allan disappeared towards the bar.

They continued drinking at an alarming rate and playing pool for a considerable amount of time. Allan had developed a taste for the cold bottles and Tom was amusing himself by trying to keep up with him. Tom had a very competitive disposition and he would have maintained the drinking pace even if it had been detrimental to his demeanour – e.g., he would have continued drinking until he passed out before he conceded defeat.

'Don't you think,' Allan began slowly as they stood next to the table, clumsily chalking their respective cues, 'that if you're doing something while drinking then you don't get as pissed as you would if you were standing around drinking quietly?' he slurred.

Tom leaned backward dangerously, looking at him for further explanation.

'What I mean is, if we sat down now, after a few minutes we would feel really drunk and not just pissed as we are now, playing pool.'

'So, you reckon that coz we're playing pool we're not getting too drunk?' he reasoned carefully. He was slowly losing the thread of what *he* was saying and not really understanding what Allan was talking about.

'That's right.'

Tom completely lost the thread of what was being said and could not form a reasonable response, so laughed loudly instead.

'Hey you two,' Tanya exclaimed happily as she approached with Denise. 'Looks like you've been having fun.' She turned to Allan. 'Has he been making you play pool all night?'

Allan swayed slightly.

'My choice,' he said simply, not wanting to appear too drunk.

'Jeeze.' Tanya laughed. 'How many have you two had? Tom, you look a little drunk.'

'Hey, just keeping up with my Limey friend here.' He put his arm around Allan, who stood only an inch shorter. 'Hey, you'll never guess what, hon – Al and Denise are *only* going to the Keys tomorrow.'

'No way!'

'What's so amazing?' Denise asked.

'We're going to the Keys tomorrow too. We've had it planned for a while now. I've got family there.' Tanya explained enthusiastically, 'Me and Tom are going to stay there for a few days.'

He nodded enthusiastically.

'Well,' Denise offered, 'we'll have to meet for a drink when we're there too.'

Tom and Allan looked at her with mild surprise.

Tanya pre-empted both Tom and Allan. 'How about you come with us? We'll drive down together. It'll be fun. I want to hear more about England. Perhaps it might give me something to write about. Actually, I've already got some ideas developing that you can help me with, Denise,' she confessed.

Allan looked at Denise for approval.

'I think that's a great idea, don't you, Denise?' he said hopefully.

Denise looked thoughtful. She was slightly cynical when she thought of the friendliness of the couple and she wondered what ulterior motive they had for wanting to travel with them. However, she mused, despite the fact that Tom looked like a drug dealer, he seemed to have a good job because he travelled to Europe on business quite frequently.

Tanya was very attractive and seemed to be an intelligent woman, who had a strong belief in her ability to write. Perhaps one day she could say that she had travelled to the Keys with a famous author, she mused. She was also pleased that Tanya had expressed a need to talk to her about life in England too, for this gave her a feeling of relative importance.

The proposition quickly became settled in her mind.

'Well, why don't you drive, Allan?'

'Yeah, I'll drive,' he agreed. 'No, hang on, I don't know if everything will fit in the convertible, besides, it might rain. We should have hired a different car, Denise.' He laughed.

She shot him an angry look, which Tom could not fail to notice.

'I'll drive,' he interjected hurriedly. 'We'll fit everyone in our car easily, and the luggage too.'

'Judging by the state that you'll be in in the morning, I think I'll drive and Denise can keep me company in the front,' Tanya sensibly offered.

'Hey, even better idea. Me and Al can sit in the back with a box of beers and a packet of cigarettes,' he enthused.

Denise folded her arms and gave Allan a penetrating look as he took another pull from his bottle. She wondered what she had let herself in for and was already regretting her rather hasty decision.

The old woman turned restlessly as she lay under the sheets of the bed, eventually and rather chaotically manipulating the sheets until they tied themselves into an untidy knot around her ankles. She barely stirred from her slumber as the cloth began to restrict her blood flow and the movement of her horizontal person, despite her repeated attempts to remedy the situation while still half asleep. She discovered with increasing consciousness that she would have to wake fully and organise her bed properly.

The wind howled at the window, spattering raindrops heavily with each billowing gust and increasingly conspiring with the blanket situation to stir her from her agitated slumber. She was definitely asleep, though, Philip mused as he looked in from the open doorway, so he softly closed the door and quietly made his way out of the back door of the house.

Once outside he discovered that the night air was restless in the company of the wind and rain. As he progressed along the streets, the rain carried in the wind compelled him to walk close to the front of the buildings that offered minimal leeward shelter and protection from the weather. He neared the busy vicinity of Sloppy Joe's bar – which is the centre of commercial activity in Duval Street – and he casually observed that the puddle-strewn streets were full of tourists, still amiably wandering under the bright lights offered by the various bars and tourist shops that remained open until this late hour. He did not move aside or accommodate the tourists who were also sheltering from the wind as they walked close to the buildings, and his powerful shoulders barged solidly into those who were either too slow or too indignant to make room for the man who walked with such purpose.

His stride was not broken until he reached his most favourite bar, the interior of which was filled with happy tourists revelling in the unified community spirit that had been created by the inclement weather. He walked through the darkened bar and towards the rear of the establishment, through a door and into another bar area that was unknown to most of the tourists and instead was occupied by local people.

At this late hour of night the number of occupants barely reached double figures. The few who were present, were seated at various tables between the many brick pillars that divided and supported the low and undulating ceiling of the apparently makeshift structure – such was the seemingly lazy construction of the town. Soft lighting illuminated the bar but barely emanated to the scattered tables that were occupied by patrons, primarily because the lights were not powerful enough but also because the various nooks and crannies created by the abundance of brick pillars meant that, what light there was, could not sufficiently circulate.

The bartender rattled a bottle of empty beer on the counter. Philip nodded to him as he seated himself on a stool by the bar.

'How're things tonight, David?' he asked casually.

He instantly regretted being so familiar with the wispy-looking barman, who was dressed in loose jeans and a shirt that would have been filled out more by a coat-hanger. David the barman was a relatively young man in his early thirties and he seemed to have been hankering after a woman to share his life with, ever since Philip had known him at school. He remembered giving the young David regular beatings just for being a geek, and he remembered how he seemed to accept the fact that people disliked him for no other reason except that he was weak and easy prey. Eventually the beatings became less, as Philip became tired and bored with the uncomplaining resignation to every increasingly hard punch and kick that he dealt.

Now that they were both in their early thirties, David seemed to think that they shared some sort of friendship because of how he had been picked on by him at school.

'Fairly quiet in here tonight really,' he replied cheerfully. 'There were some pretty young women earlier but they've gone now.' He laughed singularly. 'Surely not, Phil? You not got laid today already? Jeez, you must be slackin' man.'

He glared at the weak-looking man behind the red darkened bar area – his impertinent familiarity and his eagerness to please, which seemed so contemptible to him.

'Sorry, man. Just foolin' with yer.' Noticing the smouldering anger of Philip's expression and realising that he had overstepped the line of familiarity, he hastily moved to the other end of his bar to serve another customer. He too remembered the beatings that he had been dealt by the eager hands and feet of Philip, and he remembered watching the gleeful expression on the face before him while he was being punched, until he saw the blood on his aggressor's knuckles through half closed eyes.

Philip continued to contemplate the man who had served him. David always gave the impression that he was an old-time friend of his and yet they rarely spoke. If they did, it was often about a most impersonal and irrelevant matter and would barely extend further than a single question. For the barman to have been so flippant with him within earshot of others – especially from someone who he saw as vastly inferior to himself – made him seethe with anger. He made a mental note to remind David of their childhood, and he smiled at the perverse pleasure that he would take from beating him again.

His mood drifted into different waters when he noticed a young woman walk through the door, and he smiled with the dawning thought that he had seen her somewhere before. The woman was not a local patron of the bar – he knew that much – but she was definitely a regular visitor to Key West, he realised with a self-congratulatory smile. He took a drink from his beer bottle as the small blonde woman approached the bar and stood next to him. He appraised her quickly but intently, studying the defined contours of her jeans and T-shirt.

It was at this moment that she sensed was someone looking at her – as one's own sixth sense can – and she turned to look at him. She appraised *him* rapidly and smiled, for his appearance was in no way threatening or distasteful. In fact, his appearance was the exact opposite to what most women do not appreciate in men.

'Hi,' she said with a smile that instantly revealed her openness and eagerness.

He smiled as his eyes fixed on her face – his mind wandering to other parts of her potentially naked body. He had already decided that he wanted her and yet, because of the way she looked at him with instant submission, he knew that she would not be much of a challenge. He briefly toyed with the idea of immediately suggesting uncomplicated sex to her, but decided that he would talk to her a little first because he liked to know his victims strengths and weaknesses so that he could maybe exploit them to the limit and beyond. He irritably noticed that her eyes dwelled on him for too long and her smile was the only part of her face that was animated.

She did not even feign disinterest or hide the fact that she found him appealing, he mused with disappointment. Although there was not a perceptible change in the expression of her eyes, it was the position of her eyebrows, her fixed smile and the general stillness of her features that allowed him to see straight into her soul and know her intentions.

To ensure that his five second appraisal of her was correct, he decided to engage her in conversation so that he could watch her when she was fully animated. Perhaps she would confront him with more of a challenge when he spoke to her, he contemplated hopefully.

The woman stood beside him displaying a receptive posture as she leant on the bar and continued to smile at him with the same look in her eyes and the same inanimate yet pleasant smile that was little more than lips slightly angled. It was not an unpleasant smile, like that of a bared set of teeth like a horse, and neither was the overtly seductive way she was standing – she merely stood with no obvious symbolic barriers that were subconsciously adopted by her limbs.

'Allow me,' he said, as he set his beer bottle on the bar.

'You sure?'

He nodded and smiled.

'Okay, I'll have a white wine soda. Thanks.'

He called out the order to the barman. 'You're not from around here are you?' he turned to her. 'But I know I've seen you here before. I couldn't forget someone as attractive as you.' He stifled a yawn as she preened in the glow of the cliché. He had intended it as a joke to break the ice. However, there seemed to be no ice to break.

'I'm Cathy. What's your name?' she asked.

He introduced himself and she held out her hand, which he shook firmly. He was surprised by her formality and lightly touched by her politeness. She seemed to him to be almost sweet and so – he thought to himself in the dark recesses of his mind – his grotesque pleasure would be greatly enhanced.

'Strong hand shake,' she commented with an approving smile.

All the better to choke you with until your eyes explode out of your head and you shit yourself when you gasp your last breath. A voice chuckled silently from the diabolically dark waters of his mind.

Cathy represented the dim light that would soon be engulfed by the overwhelming darkness, and the darkness was hungry for any light that it could swallow – like failing torchlight in the pitch blackness of the very deepest depths of the ocean.

Philip was very familiar with the bar staff in the main bar and they regularly invited select young people into the locals' bar so that it swelled the numbers and made the atmosphere more interesting for the regular local patrons. Provided that the tourists looked agreeable and were not troublemakers they were shown through.

It was also good fortune for Philip because it meant that he could turn his indomitable charm on the visitors discreetly and satiate his needs. He knew that – as the evening drew on and the bars closed – the bar would become full of tourists who wanted to continue drinking. It was then that the local people left and the tourists who remained were, more often than not, very drunk indeed.

From the other end of the bar David turned to look at Philip as he attended to his customer. He chuckled to himself and shook his head.

'How does he do it?' he said under his breath.

He had often witnessed Philip preying on women and secretly wished that he had his good looks and charm. He often dreamed about what he could do if he was the same man. What he could never understand was how he managed to charm a different woman whenever he chose and without them ever bothering him again.

David was a lonely man and curiously looked up to Philip as a very masterful and powerful person. He was keenly aware that Philip was not to be angered, as he had been on the receiving end of his frustration and temper on countless occasions in the misty past. Essentially he was a man who followed others, and in his mind Philip commanded instant respect by the use of a latent power, a power that most men are conscious of – the same instinct that animals possess is the same latent hierarchy within almost every circle of male humans.

Philip continued to study her face as he spoke.

'So, what are you doing here on your own at this time of night? Had an argument with your boyfriend?'

'No.' She laughed ardently. 'I've just got here. I flew in to Miami earlier today and drove straight down here in a hire car. I couldn't sleep after that drive. I'm dog tired but all that concentration has made me *too* alert – I can't sleep.'

'So you thought you'd have a few drinks to calm down and unwind?'

She nodded and smiled.

'You know, you should have had a hot bath. That would have been more relaxing.'

'Perhaps, but it isn't such an interesting proposition as coming here.' Her eyes fixed on him as she took a drink from her glass and set it down. 'So, what do you do?'

He told her what he did and she nodded in appreciation.

'I'd love that, working here in the sun, with my own business and the lovely relaxed atmosphere of the place. I came here to stay at my friend's house – she's gone away and I'm looking after her house while taking a vacation at the same time. I just wanted to get away from it all for a few weeks, you know? I live in New York and it's unbelievably hectic in the city. It's so good to come here and relax. I used to come here lots when I was a kid – with my mum and dad.'

He interrupted her and smiled, 'You sure talk a lot. Why don't you relax just for a minute, take a step back and contemplate things for a while. Have a few drinks,' he said in a soft almost hypnotic voice. 'No wonder you couldn't sleep. You're so tense. I bet your shoulders are all knotted.'

'They probably are knotted,' she confessed as she leant more casually on the bar and, without taking her eyes off him, took a long drink from her glass.

'You know, if I knew you better then I'd offer to give you a massage.' He continued to smile.

She remembered his strong handshake and shivered involuntarily as she imagined his strong hands kneading her flesh. A feeling deep inside her – like the sensation one gets when a roller coaster suddenly descends rapidly and provides the feeling that one's stomach is left way behind – told her that tonight was her lucky night.

'Well, who knows? After a few more drinks I might just take you up on your offer.' She laughed. 'Shall we sit down?' she asked as she raised her already empty glass.

'Why not?'

He drained the remaining contents of his bottle and studied her more closely as they went over to an empty table: she was of average height for a woman, about five and a half feet, with short dyed blonde hair – not as blonde as he had at first thought. She had small, unremarkable brown eyes and an anonymous facial structure. He could not fail to notice that she talked very excitedly and the words just spilt from her tongue like sheep spilling out of a cattle truck.

She was not at all a match for Christine, he mused disappointedly – not even comparable to the gum on her shoe. He could not help himself. Even though he did not find Cathy enormously attractive he could not pass up the opportunity of having her – of controlling her and ultimately ending her insignificant life.

To him, a woman was an object that he could pick up, use and discard at a whim. The more unobtainable the object then the more desirable it became – like a priceless painting or a rare sports car. The fact that Cathy was an average print or a common mass produced car was just a substitute for what he really wanted – what he felt that he really needed.

She returned to the table with the drinks and they continued talking, about what he saw as rather inane subjects, yet he knew that he had to allow it if he was going to finish their brief relationship how he intended. It was obvious to him that she wanted the same thing from the encounter, but he took a small amount of satisfaction knowing that she knew this but did not know what he was going to do to her eventually. After another hour of meaningless conversation he decided that they had talked long enough and so he easily encouraged her to go back to her apartment, where he promised that he would give her the massage that he had tempted her with earlier.

Cathy was charmed by his natural good looks, easy manner and honest face. She genuinely felt that she could trust him and was willing to allow matters to at least progress into a 'one-night stand'. She was tired but she had a little life left in her to, perhaps, see the night to a more than satisfactory conclusion than simply sleeping alone.

When he suggested that they go back to her apartment she was more than happy with the idea and readily agreed. After all, she mused, tonight could be the start of a long-term relationship. She had never had much luck with men and she was impressed by her success on this night. She smiled happily at her good fortune to meet an attractive and friendly man on the first night of her vacation.

David was even more dumbfounded when – an hour after the woman had first walked into the bar – Philip walked from the bar with her woman holding on to the crook of his arm.

'I wish I was like him,' he muttered under his breath.

'What was that?' said a middle-aged man who was sitting at the bar. He turned and watched Philip and the woman leave. 'You mean Philip?

David nodded.

'Well, he certainly has a way with women.' He chuckled. 'But there're rumours about him y'know.'

'Like what?'

'Well, as I said they are rumours, but some people say that he's got a problem – he's a sex addict.'

David laughed.

'I'm sure that we all are – given the chance.'

The two men laughed inanely.

'So, where do you live?' she asked Philip as they walked out of the back door of the bar, which was now a hive of activity – with the revelling drunken tourists and quietly watching locals.

'Oh, I live down by the marina. It's quite a way from here in this weather and without a car, even in Key West terms,' he lied easily.

'So how would you have got back tonight?'

'I would have walked.'

She smiled to herself. The fact that he had said the word 'would' signalled to her that he was intending to stay the night with her. She tried not to let her excitement get the better of her and instead she embarked on a conversation concerning her life in

New York. He was not at all interested but nodded and made sounds of agreement as his mind pondered torridly on the most satisfactory method of killing her. He was torn between removing her limbs while she was still conscious – then there was the problem of the mess and the screaming, and the matter of hiding her body once he had finished with it – and his preferred choice of simply choking the life from her at the exact time of ironic climax – which always made him smile.

He decided that he would take the body along the coast to the mangrove swamp that he had used in the past, provided that the weather held sufficiently to allow him to use his boat that he reserved for such journeys.

It had obviously been raining heavily, for there was an abundance of large puddles strewn across the road and sidewalks. For now, though, the rain had stopped.

'It sure must have been raining some for these puddles to be here,' she said excitedly as she skirted one particular lake.

Once back at his side she slipped her arm through his, which was a signal to him that she was now his. The voice in the dark recesses of his mind sneered at the thought that he had not even tried.

The thought of obtaining Christine again filled his dark mind and instilled him with fresh impetus – like dark flood waters saturating the sanctity of a hitherto dry place. Cathy would have to do for now, though, he mused again, but the thought of Christine excited him considerably and a surge of lust raced through his body.

It was not long before they climbed the small flight of wooden steps that led to the timber door of the two storey house. The porch was festooned with ferns and plants that they were forced to brush past.

'Needs a little attention.' She gestured as she brushed past the foliage and opened the unlocked front door. 'Come in,' she said, as she walked through the doorway and switched on the light.

The furnishing of the apartment was of simple fabrics; throws on the sofa; a wooden rocking chair and large paper-covered lamp shades that afforded soft warm light. A ceiling fan spun slowly, throwing a peculiar intermittent shadow from the ceiling, over the floor and walls.

'Drink?' she offered in the silence. She felt slightly awkward because she was not comfortable with progressing the encounter to the next stage, primarily because she was out of practise in initiating physical contact with a man and also because she did not want to appear too eager. In her native town she would have been wary of meeting a stranger, but in Key West she felt unusually safe – free from the dangers of the urban jungle of New York.

'No thanks.' He smiled as he neared her.

She looked up at his face as he stood directly in front of her. Her head tilted back as he leaned down to kiss her, thus dissolving her feeling of awkwardness. Her arms enveloped him as he pulled her close. Her body relaxed.

It was only minutes later that the consenting adults were almost naked in the bedroom of the holiday apartment. Philip was subjecting her to acts that forced her to squirm in sexual ecstasy as she crumpled the sheets and clasped them with vigour.

His need was being attended to but already he was becoming bored with the familiar and boring sexual procedures. He wanted a challenge and thought that Christine was now almost within his reach, if only he could keep hold of her for long enough. The woman beneath him groaned and her nails clawed lingeringly on his back and he thought of Christine when he entered her.

The heat in the room was greatly increased by the exertion, and small beads of sweat soon appeared on her forehead. Her eyes closed and his hands clasped around her throat when her excitement grew. She choked barely audibly and her eyelids burst open. She stared at him with wide-eyed incomprehension as his grip tightened and slowly crushed her windpipe. She tried to struggle but her strength was so weakened by her now rapidly disappearing pleasure that her arms barely moved, when, in the incredible grip of his strong hands, the critical components of her neck cracked finally. She stared at the ceiling – motionless. He looked down at her smooth, tanned naked body, and her ample breasts which no longer heaved with the beat of her excited heart. He did not know whether he had intended to kill her then or not, but he was so distressed at the woman beneath him not being

Christine that he had felt the sudden compulsion to take his frustration out on the unfortunate woman. He did not always kill the women who he had sex with because often he could not be bothered to deal with disposing of the body.

Almost every month he would drive to Miami and frequent the many nightclubs and bars, carefully choosing feisty looking women or prostitutes who would agree to his acts of depravity. If they would not satisfy him in the ways he wanted – it was then that he felt compelled to kill.

She would have to be dismembered though, he decided with a satisfied smile. The problem now was – he began to think as he pulled his clothes on – how was he going to dispose of the body without being seen? He fully dressed himself and then effortlessly lifted the body from the bed carrying her into the living room and putting her onto the sofa. He returned to the bedroom and smoothed over the sheets, giving it the appearance of an unslept-in bed. He opened the wardrobe and emptied the contents, gathered the clothes located inside the small chest of drawers, and placed them all in the suitcase that he had noticed was lying obtrusively under the aforementioned bed. He also checked the bathroom and carefully removed the items, throwing them into the open suitcase too, together with the clothes that she has been wearing – and then discarded so eagerly. This done, and when he had removed the car keys from the pocket of her jeans, he went to the back door of the apartment and opened it, listening intently as he slowly scanned the trees and bushes of the small garden. Apart from the wind and rain, he heard no sound and saw no movement. The way was clear, he presumed, so he walked quickly through the garden and then jogged the relatively short distance to his boatyard, through the puddle-strewn streets of Key West – this only took him about five minutes.

He climbed inside his pick-up truck and drove slowly and carefully back to the road where the apartment was situated. The usually minimal light offered by the moon and stars was obliterated by the racing clouds, and the sleeping night was silent and desolate in the company of the blustering wind.

Only the additional sound of creaking timber of trees and violently rustling leaves could be heard, as the dark outline of

Philip noiselessly placed the bundle in the back of the truck. Shortly afterwards he also stowed away another dark shape which was the suitcase.

He returned to the apartment and wiped clean the very few surfaces that he had touched, being careful not to wipe all the surfaces that he had not touched, through fear that he did not want the police to examine the room and believe that the apartment had been *cleaned*. He thought to himself, though, as he returned to the truck and drove to his part of the marina – where he parked the truck outside one of his empty boathouses – that the apartment would soon be let to other tourists and so fresh fingerprints would be placed throughout.

Her presence there would be unlikely ever to be discovered, he confidently presumed. The only person who would remember her being with him was David the barman, and he had decided that he would put him straight one way or another.

He turned off the lights and engine and scanned the area, watching for extraneous movement. After a few minutes he decided that the way was clear as there was nobody outside on this most diabolical of nights. He opened the truck door and smiled to himself as he unlocked the padlock on the wooden boathouse door before turning to approach the rear of the vehicle. He let down the tailgate and heaved the already cold and lifeless body into the dark interior of the spacious boathouse.

The sound of the wind rattling the corrugated roof and the rain dripping through the ceiling accompanied the sounds of him searching noisily for the light switch: knocking metal tools onto the concrete floor and dislodging empty cans of paint. He flicked the switch but there was no resulting light. The power was obviously not on-line, probably because of the storm. He swore.

Eventually and successfully he further rummaged in the darkness and found a torch. He flicked it on and scanned the large boathouse. The beam fell on a large sheet of green tarpaulin, so he gathered the stiffening body into his arms and dropped it heavily onto it – the lingering breath in her lungs being forced out suddenly and startling him for an instant.

He briefly wondered if she was still alive and therefore he would have to *kill her again*. He checked for a pulse, searched for her heartbeat and listened for her breath. There was no sound at all and her body felt cold. Her pupils – in her still surprised eyes – did not dilate when he shone the torch into them. She lay on the tarpaulin, frozen in time wearing a look of utter astonishment. He abruptly drew the edges of the tarpaulin together, covering her body and expression completely, and, with a small rope that was threaded through the holes at the edges, tied the ends into a knot soaking himself as he did so with the collected rainwater that had fallen from the ceiling and onto the sheet. He swore under his breath as he felt the coldness of the water stick to his legs through the cloth of his trousers.

He opened the trapdoor on the boathouse floor that led down to the fishing boat that was moored in the harbour immediately below the building. He dragged the tarpaulin to the trapdoor, carelessly forcing the bundle to drop into the hole. The falling body made a dull thud as it came into contact with the small wooden deck below – which was followed by another thud as the suitcase followed. He positioned himself feet-first at the edge of the trapdoor and dropped down the six feet onto the gently heaving deck, carefully maintaining his balance as he opened the second trapdoor that led to the engine room of the boat.

The sound of the waves against the wooden harbour door of the boathouse sounded loud and muffled, like the slow rhythmic banging of a large oceanic drum. He ignored the constant drumming and allowed the deadweight of the tarpaulin to drop again, and it thudded heavily onto the interior wooden hull of the vessel. He climbed down into the engine room of the boat and shone the torch until he found an overhead battery-operated light. He switched it on and untied the tarpaulin.

He tied her hands tightly together with a piece of rope and hauled her up into her vertical position, hanging her from a hook that was lashed onto a wooden beam. There she swung with her feet scraping on the floor, swaying slightly with the motion of the boat. With considerable effort he positioned a large metal tank under the body, so that however hard she swung she would always be swinging over it. Once he had dragged the wickedly sharp knife – that he used for gutting marlin – the length of each of her legs, ensuring that the deep gashes severed her veins, the blood cascaded from her body and began to fill the bottom of the tank.

He decided that he would dismember the body below deck when he was out at sea, disguising the fact that he had stopped by anchoring the boat and extending a fishing rod over the side. The blood should have collected in the tank and he would empty this slowly into the open sea by means of a small valve situated in the corner of the space below deck. By the time the blood had been drained from the body – when the time came for him to cut the body into pieces – he would not be covered in blood and so he could relatively cleanly insert the body parts into the roots of the mangrove swamp and wait for nature to take its course.

He decided that the suitcase would be burned in the furnace situated in one of the corners of the boathouse. He used it for smelting metal he needed for various fishing utensils and diving equipment. He would leave the matter for now though, as he had already dropped the suitcase onto the boat. He thought about sinking it in the harbour, but immediately feared that the suitcase and the items within were too light and could easily be washed ashore.

He resolved to remedy the situation the following day, for the sound of the waves crashing on the boathouse was becoming louder and this awoke him from his troubled thoughts.

Once he had locked the entrance to the engine room of the boat, he climbed the short ladder into the boathouse, closing the trapdoor behind him and locking it securely. Now that the body had been dealt with, and his truck thoroughly cleaned by the wind and rain, even intense probing by the police would provide no clues to her whereabouts – as if he would give them any reason to suspect him when they spoke to him, for he knew that his demeanour and social standing was totally convincing. They would not be checking his boat and the tank inside either, he reasoned, and even if they did, he would ensure that it was cleaned and then filled with fish guts to make the proposition wholly disagreeable and seemingly pointless.

There was only one matter left he had to deal with and that was her hire car. This fact leapt to the front of his thoughts and moved aside his contemplation of the diabolical scene in the bowels of his fishing boat – where the body of the woman was gently swaying while the erstwhile life-giving contents leaked through the horrifyingly butchered flesh.

He toyed with the idea of taking the hire car and leaving it somewhere remote so that it would, no doubt, be discovered by the authorities at a later date. However, he concluded that he would simply leave the vehicle where it was, and if ever the trail led to him and he was accused of causing her disappearance, then he would insist that she must have simply caused (faked) her own disappearance and had not returned the car. He decided that this was the least complicated course of action, for complicated actions meant complicated explanations which could be exposed by simple questioning. If he denied any involvement and there was no physical evidence to link him to her disappearance then he knew that he would be safe from prosecution, if not suspicion.

Feeling satisfied with his reasoning and comfortable with his story of complete denial, he made his way to the pick-up truck parked outside. He locked the door of the boathouse and turned to face the harbour – the rain stinging his face as the tempest tore at the land and everything that dwelled upon it.

He threw the small bunch of keys into the harbour, not seeing where they landed because the densely falling rain obscured his eyes, and forced him to squint to protect them. The darkness pervaded all senses; the vast ocean swallowing the remaining symbol of her existence.

Chapter Eight

Mo woke with a start. The nightmare of the thundering, enveloping clouds that filled her throat and choked her as she dreamt, still made her throat feel tight even though she was now awake.

The rain spattered sporadically on the window with each gust of the wind. The blustering air violently rustled the leaves and branches on the trees immediately outside the window, rhythmically striking the glass as if asking to come into the house.

She pulled the sheets back, slowly pulling on her dressing gown and stepping into her slippers before carefully walking to the kitchen. Once there, she began to fill the kettle with water. It was then that the back door to the kitchen suddenly opened and Philip walked in. She was startled and turned quickly. She massaged her throat and the pain subsided as she pondered.

'What are you doing up?' he asked with surprise.

She glared at him.

'And I ask you the same,' she replied. 'I couldn't sleep. What's your excuse? It's almost light and you are wearing the same clothes you had on yesterday.'

'I couldn't sleep,' he replied nonchalantly. 'I went to the bar and had a beer, but I think I will sleep now.'

'You're wet,' she said, as she looked at his soaked tan-coloured trousers. 'I didn't think it was raining that much in the bars around here?'

He tutted as he paused for thought, his mind working hard to expel the excitement of the night that had passed.

'Damn puddles,' he said eventually, then chuckled softly, 'I didn't see it, and it was so deep. I'd better go and change out of them before I catch my death.'

'You probably have already,' she replied quietly as she watched him. She promptly balked at his presence when he walked past her and an involuntary shiver ran down her bent spine as an almost inhuman will seemed to emanate from every cell in his body.

'What did you say?' He paused with intent as he suddenly bore down on her. There was a pause as he seemed to change his mind. 'Oh,' he suddenly composed himself, 'I see.' He was pleased that he had stopped himself from whatever it was that he was going to do. Instead he walked slowly and gratefully from the room.

She watched him leave, sensing an aura of death following him like the lingering smell of smoke from a wood fire – that clings to a person's clothes. She did not know what to do, what to say to him or if to say anything to anyone about her fears. She did not want to stay in the house and so she glanced at the kitchen clock deciding that it was too early to knock on Christine's door.

Outside the kitchen window that overlooked the neat little garden, the night was giving way to dawn and the night sky was peeling back to reveal the still-racing clouds and slithers of dark blue sky. She decided to wait for dawn to break fully with the undoubtable company of intermittent rain showers to fill the small island of Key West.

After she had listened for his feet clumping up the wooden stairs to his room, she seriously began to think that he had been a breath away from hurting her, perhaps even killing her. She sat down as the gravity of the situation pulled her down onto the seat. She had thought that she could keep him under control, but now that she was old she reasoned that she was no longer up to the task in hand and he was now running amok. She was powerless to stop him, and she could no longer account for or prevent his actions, she concluded with impending despair.

Christine busily swept the floor of the bar and thought of the night that had just passed. The previous night had been relatively quiet. Her friend had assisted her to serve behind the bar, thereby helping the evening to pass quickly with having someone to talk to. Her friend had left at around midnight, when there were only a few remaining patrons, who she then hurried along so that she could close for the night.

She had thought that she could take advantage of the situation and have an early night to catch up with her sleep, but the sound of the wind and rain had kept her awake and the nagging thought of spending an evening with Philip troubled her. She toyed with the idea of going to see Mo to ask her opinion but she did not want to cause any unnecessary problems between Mo and Philip. Besides, she had spoken at length to Jim and they were both confident that they could deal with the situation on their own without involving the frail old woman.

It was at that moment that Mo appeared at the front door of the bar. Christine looked at the diminutive old woman dressed in a waterproof mac, rainhat and wearing a broad almost toothless smile. Christine propped the broom against a chair and walked briskly to the door and unlocked it.

'You're early, Mo!' she said cheerfully, 'but I suppose that I can make allowances for you.' She beamed, genuinely pleased to see her. 'Actually, I've just been thinking about you.'

'Really? Well, I haven't come for a drink, dear. It's far too early in the day for that business. Dear me, most of the people around here haven't flossed yet.' She cackled uncharacteristically.

'Come in the kitchen then.' She locked the door behind Mo and they ventured to the rear of the establishment. 'What brings you here at this early hour?' she said over her shoulder, as the old woman followed.

'Philip,' she said simply.

'Why? What has he done?' she asked, when they reached the kitchen. She gestured to a chair by the kitchen table and Mo slowly and gratefully took a seat.

'I don't know. Maybe nothing, maybe something – I just don't know what to do for the best,' she confessed.

It seemed to her that Mo was unusually distressed, seeing as though it was her own son that she was concerned about, and she was now more concerned than ever about the forthcoming evening that she was due to spend in Philip's company. Should she tell Mo what they were planning or not? she pondered. She was now very tempted indeed to impart what she had been planning with Jim.

'Well, what do you mean? What has he done to make you... well,' she paused to find the correct word, 'suspicious, I suppose. I get the impression that you think that he's up to something.'

'Quite perceptive of you, my dear.' She sighed, 'Well, apart from the fact that I have never felt so awkward and nervous when in the presence of Philip than I did when he came in last night – well, the early hours of this morning really – he could not explain where he had been or what he had been doing. I just have an intense feeling that he has been up to no good – something that is the farthest from good as one can possibly be.'

Christine was taken aback by the almost melodramatic words and she tried not to scoff.

'Mo, he's a grown man. Why should he explain to you where he has been? With all due respect, he can do what he likes because he is old enough to.'

Mo sat motionless and fell completely silent, looking intently at Christine, fiercely staring at her with grey eyes with seemingly insurmountable determination and conviction.

'Perhaps you cannot understand the gravity of the situation after all.' She contemplated slowly. 'I'm not talking about anything as inconsequential as staying out late without telling me. What do you take me for? I find your chosen thoughts concerning me rather insulting in their meaninglessness.'

'I'm sorry. I didn't mean to offend you.' She back-pedalled hurriedly. 'I suppose that I'm not used to having this type of conversation, that's all. After all, there aren't many people that are, are there?'

She bowed her head, dimly remembering being chastised by her father when she was a child. She could remember once that she had lied to her father about where she had been and he had already secretly known that she had been at her friend's house. He had watched her and listened as she spoke a complicated web of lies, and then he had said to her, 'All lies lead to the truth…' It had only taken those six words that her father had spoken to make her understand the benefit of cutting through any hidden meaning by applying honesty, simplicity and truth. The instantaneous recollection of this incident suddenly appeared in the forefront of her mind and forced her to look directly into Mo's eyes.

'Well, be straight with me then, Mo. What are you talking about? What exactly do you think that Philip was doing last night?'

Mo sighed and bowed her head.

'Perhaps I'm just too old. Perhaps I'm just a silly old woman after all.'

Christine had never seen Mo lacking in self-confidence and evidently being plagued by self-doubt. She sat down on a chair opposite the old woman.

'Don't worry.' She touched the gnarled old hand that rested on the table and instantly felt the iciness of her mottled flesh.

Mo looked at her and offered a wavering smile of gratitude.

'Well, over the years I have watched Philip grow up. He has never had a father figure, never had a male role model to steer him through life's complicated web of relationships. He has only had me to learn from and I can't pretend that I am the most congenial person.'

She listened intently as Mo skirted around what she was trying to say.

'You don't have to justify to me why you think the way you do,' she said openly. 'Just tell me the crux of what you want to say and then we can discuss the rest.'

'Thank you for being so candid with me.' Mo sighed. 'Your strength is infectious.' She smiled and she raised her head and her familiar confidence grew. 'I cannot help but conclude that Philip has been preying on women. I do not want to explicitly impart my worst fears yet, because I cannot prove anything, but let me just say that once he has found one victim she will never be seen again.'

Christine remained silent as the words reverberated in her head. For some strange reason – although what Mo had said had not been backed up by any tangible evidence – she did not find what she had heard that hard to comprehend. The words seemed to fit into her own thoughts like a piece of a jigsaw, and the proposed rendezvous with him at Jim's suddenly seemed a very dangerous and stupid prospect. However, Mo had not explained why she had come to this conclusion.

'Mo, before we go any further, is Philip your natural son?'

She smiled.

'He isn't my son, as well you know. I took him under my wing many years ago. He was the son of a friend of mine who was sectioned in a mental hospital. She gave birth to him while she was in hospital but his father had already been long dead. God knows what went on in there or who the actual father is.' She looked blankly out of the kitchen window and sighed. 'She's dead now. Philip never knew her and he never speaks about her and does not want anyone to know either.'

'I had no idea.' Christine looked thoughtful. 'That must have affected him, I mean, his outlook on life and people.'

'Undoubtedly.' She pondered at length, then said with melancholy. 'The sad part is that his mother became incoherent over the years preceding her death. She was once a respected hotel owner with a husband and a home. He died and she became withdrawn – so withdrawn that she seemed to be grotesquely inside out almost. I did not see her for five years, until one day I received a letter telling me about where she and her newborn son were. I went to the hospital to see her. It was horrible to see the living ghost of an old friend. She was barely recognisable; her hair was grey, thin and long, her face and body terrifyingly gaunt. She asked me to look after her son because she did not want him near her. For a brief moment I glimpsed my friend of old but then she seemed to sink deeper into her mind and was quickly incoherent again. She died a few weeks later, leaving me all the paintings that I have in my back room.'

'Oh,' Christine said simply. She pictured with her mind's eye the many paintings that she had seen in Mo's house. She had often wondered who had painted them but had never thought to ask about the striking, haunting paintings of the sea. Now she was caught in the gravity of Mo's words – like a buoy in the mouth of a harbour surrounded by a heaving and expansive ocean.

For the first time in her life she did not know what to say. She did not know whether to try and soothe Mo or try to probe her with questions that brought the collective years of thoughts and feelings that she had to the surface. However, she did not know whether the risk of being overwhelmed by this sea would be beyond her social skills. She eventually decided that the latter was probably not the best option at that moment but a more gradual approach must be adopted if she was going to help the poor woman.

She decided not to tell her about the planned evening with Philip, as she thought that this would be detrimental to her proposed solution to Mo's problem.

'So, what shall we do about Philip? Shall we go to the police?'

'No,' she replied definitely. 'For one thing we have not got any evidence. I would never forgive myself if I was wrong about Philip. No, we'll have to watch what he does.' She touched Christine's arm and held her hand firmly. 'And it is you who must be most aware of him. I know that he is overtly fond of you and I am worried that he has taken a very strong and unhealthy interest in you.'

'I have noticed,' she said gravely. 'I'll be very careful.'

'Perhaps you should go away for a while. Perhaps visit your father in Ireland.'

Christine tried to lighten the atmosphere and she laughed singularly.

'Not an option. I'll ask Jim to keep an eye out for Philip. If the worst comes to the worst, then I'll ask his friends in the force to come and check him out unofficially – if that's all right with you.'

'It may be necessary.' She stood up slowly. 'I have to go now – see what he's up to,' she said gravely, 'I'll come back tomorrow.' She looked out of the window at the rain that was now falling in heavy sheets that travelled vertically past the window. 'Perhaps I should wait awhile.'

Christine kindly gestured for her to sit down.

'Try not to worry too much. Together we'll find out what he has been doing and what he is planning to do,' she said, as she quietly and nervously contemplated the forthcoming days.

The rain cascaded from the sky incessantly, splashing on the roofs of buildings, dripping from the leaves of the many trees and collecting in the lagoon-sized puddles that now proliferated the streets of Key West.

Philip stood in the shop and looked at the world outside in an apparent daze. His mind was turbulently playing through the scenarios pictured in his mind's eye to ensure that he had left nothing to chance – left no loose ends that the police might get hold of and find him at the end of them. He knew that Cathy had been renting a friend's empty holiday home that was due to be occupied by a family on vacation the following week – this was his last thought on the matter of loose ends. He was positive that the only other loose end was the dead body, festering, as it was, in the engine room of one of his boats in the boathouse.

The weather was currently too severe to allow him to venture out to sea and along the coast to the mangrove swamp to leave the body where the teeming sea life would dispose of the evidence for ever. However, he knew that he could tie this loose end as soon as the weather cleared – which would not be long at all.

He remembered the pleasure he had felt as his hands had squeezed the life from her, how he had gleefully imagined that Christine was the one that had been lying naked beneath him as he had reached the climax of his labours. He smiled with satisfaction, breaking away from his deep and dark thoughts into an even more lurid and foreboding light.

Once his inner mind had receded and he had returned to the present, he decided that no customers would venture outside in this weather and easily concluded that it was pointless waiting in the shop and, equally as pointless, waiting in his boathouse for customers – not that the dead body bothered him at all, should he decide to go to his boathouse. He decided to disregard Mo's request that he look after the shop and instead, made up his mind to brave the elements and visit Christine's bar, for he was almost certain that other local people and tourists would not face the weather – therefore he would be alone with her.

He remembered how she had insulted him the other day and now he was determined to seek retribution one hundred times as strong. Not only was he intending to make her wish that she had not done what she had but he was going to make sure that she begged for mercy when she was lying beneath him. Perhaps he could make her wish that she had never been born by breaking her spirit, but that would take a prolonged period of work on her and she would have to be under his complete control day after day with nobody else around. It was difficult to arrange this, he mused, but the options were endless and he was filled with expectation and excitement. Abduction was indeed an exciting option that was not beyond consideration, he mused.

He pulled on his yellow waterproof coat that hung on a hook behind the door and approached the front door of the shop and opened it. The wind immediately blew inside and sent the assembled wind chimes into their familiar musical frenzy. He hurriedly closed the door behind him and was forced to employ considerable effort against the powerful wind that was attempting to fill the interior of the shop. He then proceeded to jog the length of Duval Street, pulling the hood tightly around his face as his feet splashed through the river of rainwater.

Christine stood leaning on the bar with her head resting in cupped hands, watching with a degree of sullenness at the rain that fell incessantly from the sky. Mo had left a few hours ago. The bar was devoid of customers, as was usual in the past few weeks. She wondered when the weather would clear and the tourists return.

The sensible yet distant notion of locking up the premises until later in the day forced her to decide to close the bar now, and later in the day, maybe, the rain would ease somewhat and she could re-open. She lifted the latch on the bar and rested it against the pillar and walked towards the door.

A figure dressed in a bright yellow jacket rushed towards the door of the bar. The figure removed the jacket hood, revealing ivory white teeth and a static smile.

'Damn, it's wet.' Philip smiled a disarming smile that could have pacified a fundamentalist terrorist. 'You're not closing, are you?' he said, as he stood outside the half-closed door, the rain urgently pattering on the hood of his raincoat.

She paused, momentarily wondering what to do. 'Yes,' she replied curtly, with her hand on the door, ready to close it fully.

'I came to apologise,' he said, holding the door open with an outstretched hand, 'for the way that I've been behaving. I've been thinking while standing in Ma's empty shop, thinking what a rat I've been to you.'

'You can't help it. You'll always be like that.' She watched his pleasant smile and involuntarily shivered as she was caught in the dark pools that were his eyes. She stood up straight, bolstered up by her own judge of character and the fact that Mo seemed so concerned about Philip. She knew that she was not having unnecessary reservations about the man who stood before her.

'No amount of grovelling from you will change that,' she said sternly, forcing herself to return a stare into his dark, ominous eyes. 'So take your cheesy smile and go and annoy somebody else.' She closed the door but only as far as his boot, which he had placed in the doorway to prevent the door from closing. 'Get your foot out, now!' she said loudly as she pushed him, and because his leg was outstretched he became off balance and consequently staggered back onto the river that was once a road. She slammed the door and quickly locked it – her heart beating fast and hard against her ribcage.

He stared at her through the window of the door and pulled his hood slowly over his head, the rain lashing down all about him. He seemed not to notice as he continued to stare at her blankly, no longer smiling.

She shuddered to think what he was thinking in his horrifyingly polluted and murky mind.

'I'll see you tonight,' he called out loudly.

The words immediately struck her with dread and foreboding. In an instant she decided to alter the plan that she had agreed upon with Jim. In an instant she decided to arm herself when the evening came, and she decided to tell Jim to do the same.

With a strong degree of dread she turned and proceeded hurriedly to check that all the windows and doors on the ground floor were closed securely, and then she continued to check all the windows on the other two floors of the building. She paused at the window on the landing when she saw – from the corner of her eye – a figure in a yellow jacket standing in the rear garden by the pool – looking up at the window that she was standing by.

She screamed in fright.

Jim looked at the clock on the wall. He was always surprised at how the time flew by when he lost himself in a painting. Time seemed to suspend itself and become irrelevant as his mind and hand worked as one; the image in his mind slowly flowing from his neural pathways, through his nerves and muscles and on to the delicate movements of the brush. The painting was a complete and temporary expression of his innermost thoughts that necessitated the suspension of his own personal existence. He looked at the painting, which depicted a dark sky and a raging powerful sea wreaking destruction on the local shore. Such a forbidding painting fascinated him and he knew instinctively that it would stand out dramatically in his gallery downstairs in the shop. He believed that he had surpassed himself with his latest creation, believing that the meaning of life for him was painting a picture like the one that he had before him. Perhaps one day, when he was dead, his mind and innermost thoughts would be remembered and revered due to the legacy of his undiscovered paintings. He contentedly smiled at this thought because he had no children of his own. Even the thought of this possible legacy, however remote, filled him with pleasure and the warm feeling that his life had not been wasted. After all, every time he painted a picture he was painting a portion of his mind. In the future, when he was dead, people would look at his paintings and perhaps, if they looked hard enough, they would see the artist who had created them – they would see Jim.

An involuntary shiver passed down his spine with the realisation that he, like other artists, would live for ever – providing people continued looking and appreciating the thoughts and expression that had created the artistry. With these thoughts firmly in place, he looked happily out of the window to ascertain if the weather would allow him to take a quick break at Christine's bar.

He pulled on his yellow rainproof coat and made his way down the stairs. In his opinion there was nothing much more satisfying than collecting his thoughts and recharging his creative juices by sitting in his favourite bar, drinking stout and smoking his pipe. His face was smiling brightly as he stepped out into the torrential rain and shut the shop door behind him. His feet splashed heavily through the now shallow river that used to be Duval Street.

He ran carefully along Duval Street to Christine's bar, and he was greatly disheartened when he tried the door, only to find it firmly shut. He rattled the door unsuccessfully and knocked loudly on the wood. He pressed his head against the window shielding his eyes from the reflection, and peering into the unlit interior of the darkened bar. He was greatly surprised when Christine approached the door with a handgun in her comparatively small hand.

She smiled thinly as she unlocked the door.

'Thank God it's you,' she said as she let him in and locked the door after him.

'What have you got that for?' he blurted. He tried to take it from her but she calmly tucked into the belt of her jeans.

'It's all right, the safety catch is on,' she said soberly. 'I'll get you a drink and tell you all about it.' She steeled herself for the full explanation.

'I feel like death.' Tom sat on the edge of the bed and held his head in his hands. 'I think there's something in my head hitting the sides of my skull with a sledge hammer. And the taste in my mouth. Man…' He spat into an empty glass next to the bed. 'Well, I think that I must 'ave been drinking out of a drain or som'at'.'

'You were very drunk last night.' Tanya laughed. 'And your hangover serves you right – you never drink that much. Allan must be more used to it than you are.'

'Perhaps,' he conceded reluctantly as he stood up. He quickly lay on the bed again. 'That was a mistake.'

'What, drinking so much?'

'No, standing up.' He groaned into the pillow.

She laughed.

'I'll get you some breakfast. You'll feel better after that. Besides, it'll set you up for the long drive with your drinking partner and the woman from hell.'

'Eh?'

'Key West, with Allan and Denise,' she shouted next to his head.

'Ohhh,' he groaned. 'If I didn't feel like shit then I would get you for that,' he said irritably into the pillow. The alcoholic fog began to clear slowly and he remembered playing pool with Allan. 'Oh yeah, I remember now – Key West.'

His mind slowly replayed the events of the previous evening but with many blank spaces, and so, to him, the evening seemed rather disjointed. He remembered, with some clarity, the events and conversation right up until he and Allan had finished playing pool.

'Whose idea was it for them to come with us to Key West?' He lifted his head gingerly from the pillow.

'Yours, I think. No wait, it was mine. Well, you and Allan had already discussed it but those two had already planned their trip anyway. I only *suggested* that they come with us and we all agreed.' She sighed, 'It seemed like a good idea at the time. It's just a shame that we hadn't realised what she was like, otherwise I might never have offered. When I was speaking to her on the Seventies floor she seemed okay, if a little neurotic.'

'I remember them being good company,' he said, holding his temple.

'Allan is, and she was to start with. The thing is, you were both drunk don't forget.' She looked at him protractedly. 'Oh dear, can't you remember what happened later in the evening last night?'

He managed to sit upright and he thought hard – as hard as his head would allow – but he just could not part the alcohol impregnated furry fog that engulfed his memory of the previous night. He shook his head very slowly.

'We had great sex.'

She sighed.

'I didn't think that you could remember – we were talking, drinking and dancing all night and she watched as Allan became really, really drunk. Later in the evening she said that she was going to the 'ladies room' – but she didn't come back! We had to get a taxi back to their apartment block, helped him up to his apartment and there she was. She had just upped and left him because she was annoyed with him. Definitely a strange woman that one. I mean, how thoughtless and irresponsible, leaving your very drunk partner with two virtual strangers.'

'From what I can remember, he's a riot,' he said. 'Intelligent, dry wit and likes a beer and a smoke too. Seems like a great guy, although I think that I can remember that he's having trouble with her.' He finally managed to stand in a vertical position without falling back onto the bed.

'I'm not surprised.' She chuckled. 'She's okay, I suppose, but she's so serious all the time – talking about houses and marriage and stuff. She'd probably be all right if she lightened up a bit, had a good drink or smoked some weed or something – just to oil-up her dry bits, you understand. We'll have a good time, though, won't we, hon?'

'You seem to be unsure.' He held her closely and stroked her hair gently. Suddenly, he did not know whether he was going to be sick or not and his stomach gurgled ominously, causing his body to stiffen while he contemplated the turbulent feeling in his stomach.

'Eww.' She took a step back when she heard the rumbling emanating from his midriff. 'I just have a strange sense of foreboding.'

She laughed.

'Don't ever do that again,' Denise scolded. 'I could have been picked up by rednecks and raped out at the back of the club by a group of men.'

'You weren't, were you? Anyway, you chose to leave so don't blame me,' he replied moodily. She had angered him, which was not hard because he had a hangover. She was also, he considered, in a particularly grumpy mood. 'Have you got a hangover?' he probed, and squinted against the sunlight that streamed in through the open window that led to the balcony.

'No. I bet you have though.'

She was not at all impressed with him, he mused.

'No,' he replied too hurriedly. 'Well, a bit fuzzy headed but I haven't got a hangover,' he conceded.

'You deserve to have a big hangover. I can't believe the way you behaved last night. First of all you got really drunk; made fun of me with the taxi driver; had a laugh at my expense with Tom and *then* you embarrassed me because Tom and Tanya had to escort you home,' she castigated.

'Yes, but...'

'And, when we were on the beach you said that I was fat.'

'No...'

'Yes you did.' She blubbed as she sprinted into the bathroom and slammed the door behind her.

He inhaled deeply and exhaled contemplatively, before gingerly making his way to the bathroom door, holding his temple as he slowly crossed the thickly piled carpet.

'Do you want a coffee?' he called out, wincing at the subsequent pain in his head.

'No,' came the sharp response from the hollow-sounding bathroom.

'Breakfast?'

'No!'

'Look, I didn't maliciously make fun of you, I didn't have a laugh at your expense and I thought that we got on really well with Tom and Tanya.' He was going to add that it was her who embarrassed him but he decided to leave that part out in case he needed it later. 'I'm going to give them a call. I know I've got his number in my wallet somewhere.'

She did not reply.

'Right. I'm going to have a shower and get ready in the other bathroom, then I'm going to phone.'

Still no response.

'Just don't go without me.'

He winced as he crept to the other bathroom, half expecting her to emerge, at great speed, with some sort of blunt instrument and bludgeon him to death.

Denise looked in the bathroom mirror and viciously combed her wet hair into a ponytail. She thought about the previous night and how drunk Allan had been and how much she was embarrassed by his jokes that he thought were so funny. She was sure that Tom and Tanya were only laughing out of politeness. What was Tanya going to write in her article? she wondered. If only he had not been so drunk, she mused, perhaps they could have got off on the right foot.

She decided that Tom and Tanya would change their minds and would not be going to Key West with them after all.

She opened the door of the bathroom and walked inside the plush living room of the apartment, flopping onto the settee as heavily as her petite figure would allow. She picked up the remote control and turned the television on, flicking through the channels as she stretched out and made herself comfortable.

Allan, upon hearing the sound of the television, opened the door of the room and bumped through with the packed overnight bags.

'Take your time, Allan,' she said as she watched him struggle through the doorway. 'Be a dear and make me a cup of tea, would you?'

He looked at her in disbelief.

She returned the look. 'Go on, I'm tired.'

'But you've been asleep all night. I think I passed out when my head hit the pillow because I don't feel as though I had a wink of sleep.' He made his way to the kitchen. 'I'm not exactly full of life you know.' He snorted as he filled the kettle. 'Is there anything else, madam?' he called out sarcastically.

'I could do with a sandwich.'

He sighed in continued disbelief as he opened the fridge door, which was when the telephone rang. He waited for Denise to answer it.

'Allan, the phone's ringing.'

He shut the fridge door with as much venom as the rubber airtight seal would allow, and answered the telephone.

She watched him as he stood by the television set, speaking through the handset.

'Denise, can you turn the TV down? I can hardly hear Tom.'

She tutted as she pointed the small black box at the screen. She pictured Tom in her mind's eye, thinking wistfully of his tousled blond hair, tall well built figure and what she presumed as a hefty bank balance.

He ended the brief conversation and put the phone down.

'Great,' he said, as he looked at Denise. 'He's picking us up at two o'clock this afternoon. He's feeling a bit groggy too and reckons that I owe him.' He laughed.

'And they seem all right? I mean, they still want to go?'

'They sound as though they're really looking forward to it.'

'Well, I *am* surprised.' she muttered. 'Anyway, how come you aren't driving as well? We've got a hire car, don't forget,' she said from her horizontal position.

'Your memory must be failing you,' he said deridingly. 'Their car is bigger, remember? I was drunk and I can still remember that.'

'You can't do that. You've invited them, and now he's driving,' she countered angrily.

'He offered,' he said indignantly. 'Anyway, he doesn't seem the type of person to try and bluff someone with a meaningless offer. He insisted and that's that.'

'I suppose,' she said, 'but I wanted to see their house.'

'I see.' He clearly understood her reasoning now.

'Kettle's boiled, Allan,' she said, when she heard the loud click of the thermostat on the kettle. She then quickly returned the volume to its normal setting and continued to flick through the countless number of channels, consisting mainly of advertisements.

He shortly returned to her with a mug of tea, and a sandwich on a plate. She sat up and took the offerings, setting the mug on the table and inspecting the filling of the sandwich.

'I can't eat this.' She handed it back. 'Allan, it's got pickle in. You know I don't like pickle. It makes me feel sick.'

He tutted, for he had just sat down too.

'Denise, I'm shattered. Can't you do it?'

'Well, *you* made it. Anyway, I'm all comfy now and you've only just sat down.' She smiled sweetly as she stretched with an extended arm, and Allan noticed her T-shirt pulling tightly over her firm breasts.

He swallowed.

'Okay then,' he said, as he took the plate and shortly returned, and set it down with an amenable smile.

'That's the last time, Allan,' she said angrily. 'Why do you do it? You know it annoys me. I fail to understand you, you bastard.'

'Steady,' he replied quietly, reaching for his temple again. He looked puzzled, not realising that she hated pickle so much. He observed that her expression was still stormy. 'What's the matter now? Did I cut the bread wrong as well?'

'Sarcasm is the lowest form of wit,' she said, flabbergasted. 'And I'm surprised that you aren't nursing a fat lip and black eye too,' she said indignantly. 'I've remembered something else about last night that you probably can't remember.'

'What are you talking about?' he said, as he slowly moved his fingers from his temple and gingerly took hold of the coffee cup in front of him, slurping a small amount of the steaming contents. He looked at her as she began to explain, for now he knew that it was something more than pickle that she was upset about.

'That woman, when she asked for a cigarette. Not only was I not impressed but I don't think she or her boyfriend were either.'

The incident surfaced slowly and formed in his mind, gradually reaching virtual clarity. He remembered a woman asking him for an English cigarette, which he had readily offered her because he could remember that she was quite attractive. However, he remembered that he had clamped his thumb hard onto the packet, denying her the removal of the cigarette because he was suddenly convinced that she had finished her request with the word, 'dickhead'. 'What did you say?' he remembered asking her and she had repeated her request *without* calling him dickhead. He had allowed her to take one and she asked for a light, which he reluctantly gave her together with a long, hard, angry stare. The woman's boyfriend asked him if he had a problem – which was when Denise stepped in and managed to take Allan away from the predicament.

'Oh yeah.' He laughed distantly as realisation broke on the surface of his mind, his imagination picturing a newspaper with the headlines, DRUNKEN ENGLISH LOUT BRAWLS IN FLORIDA NIGHTCLUB. He realised that he had been so drunk that she had probably said nothing of the sort.

'It's not funny, Allan. I didn't enjoy looking after you last night,' she stifled a smile.

'Ha! You smiled.' He paused, confused; not really knowing why she smiled, where he was and why he was not in bed having a sleep in. 'Why's that then?' he asked tiredly.

'The woman's boyfriend was huge, really muscly and that. I reckon he would have made mincemeat of you.'

'And that's funny, is it? I could have been seriously hurt.' He comprehended with a renewed thumping headache at the thought of being on the receiving end of some heavy blows from a Neanderthal.

'Yeah, I know, but once again I saved you, you wimp. I don't know why I bother. I won't ever again.'

His head hurt and his pride was dented. However, it almost immediately popped cleanly back into place because he realised that he had never resorted to violence to resolve a situation – primarily because he had never been forced into the situation. If he was forced to, and there was no other option, he would defend himself and Denise, he mused. However, he concluded that discretion was the better part of valour, even the discretion of someone else.

'Never again.' He laughed.

'I may not give you another chance,' she replied smartly, as if she had been waiting to pounce. 'So just make sure you behave, Allan. These next few days are a real test for us.'

'Are we still getting married next year?' he asked, feeling as if he did not really have the casting vote in the matter. He again felt the weight that had rooted itself on his shoulders the previous day, and indecision leaked into his consciousness and filled his mind with self-doubt.

'I don't know.'

He paused for a moment, contemplating his headache but knowing that the previous evening would have been really boring if he had been drinking soft drinks.

'I'll only have a few then.'

She looked sternly at him.

'A few and no more. Next time I see you drunk then that's it – we're finished.'

He enjoyed letting his hair down and having a few beers too many, which, if she had her own way, would certainly put pay to the plans he had made with Tom. He imagined, though, that many opportunities would definitely arise where he could take advantage of the situation and drink a few more than a few beers. However, he wondered how far he could go before she finally broke.

Chapter Nine

Tom replaced the handset onto the telephone cradle with a clatter and he wandered into the kitchen.

'All set then, Tom?' Tanya asked.

He approached her from behind and towered above her, his arms warmly encircling her as he hugged her.

'Certainly am, hon. I spoke to Al and we're pickin' them up at two this afternoon. He's got a hangover too and wanted to drive, but I wouldn't let him,' he said as he picked a raw vegetable from the pile that she had cut on the chopping board in front of her and crunched noisily into it. 'You sure you don't mind driving?'

'I wouldn't have offered if I hadn't meant it.'

He discarded his concern and placed his hands gently on her shoulders. However, she still seemed quiet.

'Just think, Tan, we'll be in the best place on this planet to see a sunrise, which we can watch on the beach in each others arms while sipping an iced tea, and listening to the waves gently washing ashore.'

She laughed, turned to face Tom and kissed him on the lips. 'I want to go, stupid. It's just, well, I'm not looking forward to driving all that way with Denise in the car. I reckon she'll be a pain in the butt.'

'I've thought of that,' he said, as he bit his lip, stifling a smile. She looked at him quizzically and he continued. 'Let's make a cake. We'll eat it in the car on the way there,' he suggested triumphantly.

'Yeah, right. That'll do it.' She raised her eyebrows disparagingly.

He took a hard lump of dark matter from his pocket and carefully unwrapped the cellophane that had been around it. 'It was your idea, remember? Although *you* said weed but I haven't got any of *that* at the moment.'

'We'd best not put too much in, though,' she said wide-eyed, as she took a plastic bowl from the cupboard, 'otherwise she'll realise that she's under the influence of something.' She giggled as she started adding the mixture to the bowl. 'It should make her more reasonable and not so cranky, though.'

'That's right,' he said as he began to heat the dark lump of cannabis resin with a lighter and sprinkle it into the mixture. 'And if it doesn't work then it'll be hoot anyway.'

'Don't yer think it's a teensy-weensy bit irresponsible, though?' she said thoughtfully, without stopping what she was doing. 'And what about Allan? It's a bit well, a bit disrespectful.'

'Don't gimme all that!' He laughed.

'All what?'

'Pretending that your morals and conscience are ruling your sense of fun,' he said, smiling broadly. 'Okay, so it's a bit irresponsible but hey, so is driving over the speed limit, but people do it all the time.'

'This is a little different, Tom. Just 'cause everyone does it doesn't mean to say it's right. Besides, she could call the cops or somethin' like that.'

'Nah.' He laughed as he put a lighter flame to the lump and began sprinkling more of the substance into the mixture. He laughed loudly. 'She won't be bothered to get her butt off the seat.'

Their reservations were far outweighed by their determination to enjoy themselves. Besides which, they likened the act as far less irresponsible than spiking a person's beer with stronger alcohol – provided that the victim was not driving, of course – and they would not stoop to this level. They knew the effects of a hangover to be no laughing matter, and being drunk was overtly dangerous if a person was not aware of what was happening to them.

They understood the effects of cannabis and knew that there would not be a detrimental long-term effect and very little short-term effect. They had this understanding with the knowledge that alcohol altered a person's behaviour considerably – perhaps irreparably – over a period of time. However, one cake containing a small amount of cannabis was inconsequential, in their eyes.

The electronic pulse of the telephone rang suddenly, causing Allan to start and jump up from his seat in the lounge area of the apartment.

Denise walked into the room when she heard the sound.

'Who's that?' she asked rather unnecessarily.

Allan, who had not yet placed the handset to his ear, looked at her blankly as he picked up the phone and spoke into the mouthpiece. She stood immediately next to him and tried to listen – which he equated to being as annoying as somebody reading *his* newspaper from over *his* shoulder.

Piss off! was what he would have liked to have said but he did not have the gall, or the confidence that she would take the comment in the humour that it was offered. He simply turned his back towards her.

After a short conversation he replaced the receiver.

'That was Tom. They're down at reception. C'mon,' he said excitedly and picked up their large overnight bags.

'Have we got everything?' She fussed as they headed for the door.

'You must have checked about ten times already.' He groaned. 'Let's not keep them waiting.'

She followed him out of the door, which she locked behind her and checked half a dozen times.

'If you've forgotten anything then I'll blame you,' she said when she caught up with him.

'I have no doubt.' He was very eager to get under way and was looking forward to the trip, eager not to cause an argument before he had left the building. He urgently pressed the button to call the lift.

'I don't know if this was such a good idea.' She spoke aloud in the confines of the lift, not realising, until it was too late, that her thoughts had taken over her mouth.

'You could have taken the stairs,' he replied quickly.

'What?'

'Nothing.' He smiled to himself. 'It *will* be good, Denise – you worry too much. Just relax for five minutes.' He pressed the button and the doors slid closed.

He was buoyed up by the thought of spending a few days away where he could expend his time in a way that he saw as perfect: good company; a good time and with the woman that he loved. The thought that she too would enjoy their stay in the Keys made him feel confident that she could maybe change her own outlook on life and that he could, perhaps, empower her to enjoy her life more.

The increase in his confidence over the past few days was partly down to the fact that he was alone in a foreign country and the consequences of his actions seemed to have a lesser effect, and partly because of the thus far brief, yet poignant, influence of Tom. To Allan it seemed that the indigenous people of America were so confident in asking for what they wanted without embarrassment that he felt compelled to behave in the same way – otherwise he could risk being embarrassed by his lack of confidence.

In England, where the majority of people acted in a reserved manner, he felt strangely restricted and adversely influenced by everyone around him – more than he realised, until now. For the first time in his life he was beginning to feel at ease with himself.

His life and personality were turning a corner. Could Denise turn the corner and follow him like he had done? was his main thought. Conversely, he was mindful of how far he could go without losing sight of her.

The lift sounded an electronic 'ping' and the doors slid open. Tom and Tanya stood on the highly polished cool marble floor of the lobby, waiting to greet them, surrounded by flourishing green potted plants and slightly chilled by the ubiquitous air conditioning. Tom beamed as Allan and Denise emerged from the lift.

'Hey Al, Dennie!' Tom called brashly.

Allan looked towards him and raised his hand in a greeting.

'Morning!' he called out happily in an emphasised English accent. The two couples met halfway and Tom and Allan shook hands warmly. Denise and Tanya kissed each other on the cheek – coolly.

'How did you feel this morning, eh?' Tom asked enthusiastically, as he clapped him on the shoulder.

'A bit fuzzy – a bit of a headache actually,' he confessed, 'and sorry about last night. I must have been more drunk than I realised.'

'So you should be,' Denise interrupted.

Tom and Tanya glanced at her blankly.

'No problem. I felt like death this morning, man. I had such a hangover when I woke up but I feel better now that I've had some fresh air. Did you enjoy your early night, Denise?' Tom turned to her.

'Yes, I did enjoy it, thanks.' She avoided the intended question. She did not feel awkward about having left the three of them last night but instead she felt that it was *they* who should be apologising to *her* for the fact that all three of them were so drunk by the latter part of the evening. She pursed her lips, folded her arms tightly and looked out of the window of the reception at the scene outside: a young couple walking arm-in-arm as the wind played havoc with their hair. The woman was trying desperately and unsuccessfully to keep it under control as her long locks flowed persistently across her face.

Tanya looked at Denise's obvious display of her thoughts as on the previous evening, and she noiselessly sighed. Her face gradually grew into a pleasant smile as she placed her hand on the shoulder bag that contained the chocolate cake.

Tom did not pursue the matter of Denise's avoidance of her behaviour the previous night either. Instead he decided to pursue a path of quiet antagonism and urge Allan to do what he wanted to do, even if it meant upsetting Denise.

'Shall we?' He gestured towards the door that led to the car park.

'Did you have a hangover, Tanya?' Allan asked, as they walked from the lobby and into the apartment car park. The wind was warm and restless but the sun was eagerly trying to break through the many clouds that peppered the sky. It was a warm day and quite humid, causing him to break into an immediate sweat and creating an urgent thirst within him that was already antagonised by the fact that he was dehydrated from the night before. He licked his dry lips and could taste the salt-laden air blown from the sea – which made him feel even more thirsty.

'I don't suffer from hangovers,' she smiled.

'I hate people like you,' he objected jovially.

'It gets to me too.' Tom laughed. 'Do you get hangovers, Dennie?'

'No, I don't.' She forced a smile.

'Only because she doesn't drink much,' Allan interjected.

'I am *here* you know. You don't have to talk as if I'm *not* here,' she snapped.

He looked at Tom and winced before putting his arm around her shoulders.

'My apology – no offence intended.'

She looked at him doubtfully and pulled away.

'Nice car,' she remarked when Tom opened the driver's door of the large jeep. The strong smell of leather that emanated immediately from the interior made her smile because to her, it meant that the opulent vehicle was new and expensive.

He looked at the now smiling Denise with almost a sense of distaste.

'Thanks,' he replied offhandedly.

Tanya climbed into the driver's seat and smiled at him from the interior. He held open the passenger door too and ostentatiously gestured for Denise to enter the car before he and Allan climbed into the back of the vehicle.

It was stiflingly hot in the interior of the car behind the large glass windows. They settled into the comfortable leather seats and Tanya turned the ignition on starting the powerful engine, which caused the air conditioning to blast a continual stream of refreshingly cool air into the capacious interior. Tanya drove the car with aplomb onto the coast road that was peppered with sedately cruising cars.

'How long do you think it'll take to get there, Tom?' Allan asked as he opened the can of beer that was passed to him.

Tom opened his can of beer with an accompanying fizz and a small amount of froth spilled onto the top and onto his shorts. He slurped the area on the can clean and looked into the cool-box that was on the floor between the two drinkers.

'Almost the length of time it'll take to sink these beers.'

He smirked. 'You surprise me. I thought it'd take longer than that. So the faster we drink them then the faster we'll get there?'

'Ha!' Tom chuckled.

Tanya smiled.

Denise pursed her lips and turned to face Allan with a look of repugnance.

'Do *ya* want one, Dennie?' Tom regarded her expression with amusement as he held up his can.

She regarded him with much the same expression of silent distaste as she had Allan, but it seemed to have little effect on Tom, who continued to smile broadly, holding an open can to her face.

'Nice. You'll like it,' he pronounced.

'I don't think so,' she replied succinctly as she looked down her nose at him. 'And I shouldn't think that Allan will have many either.' She briefly stole a look at him, almost as if she could not bare to keep her eyes on her fiancé for longer than she had to. 'And I would be grateful if you refrained from calling me Dennie. My name is Denise.'

Allan looked at Tom and stifled a laugh, thereby causing the two men to stifle laughs like two little boys would who had been told off by their parents in a quiet room – there is nothing on this earth as amusing as laughing at a mildly funny situation when it is not appropriate to laugh, for instance laughing in the presence of the clergy when all is quiet.

'It's not funny,' she said seriously, without turning to face them.

She could obviously hear them sniggering and this fact caused Allan and Tom to burst into laughter.

'Men are so immature when they get together, aren't they, Tanya?'

'Sometimes, but they are harmless,' she replied with a wry smile. She looked at Tom who returned her smile, in the rear view mirror.

'Cigarette, Allan?' he offered.

He took one and thanked him.

'You're not going to smoke, are you?' Denise turned quickly in her seat.

'Sure am,' Tom said cheerfully, 'You want one of these too?'
'I don't smoke.'
'Too bad. In my car I'll let you do anything, except object to what I do, right Al?'
'Too right, Tom,' he replied. They bashed the beer cans together in triumph and then took long drinks from the cans.
'They're as thick as thieves, those two,' Denise said to Tanya. 'They're really winding me up already.' She scowled, beginning to wish wholeheartedly that she had not agreed to venture on this trip with Tom and Tanya.
'Don't worry, Denise. If they're having fun we can too.' She quickly looked into the rear-view mirror to get Tom's attention before calling out – without taking her eyes from the traffic filled road – 'Tom, get that cake out that I baked this morning, would you?'
'Already?' he said, surprised.
'Yeah, why not. It'll keep me going.'
Denise looked slightly bemused in her naivety. She simply assumed that eating cake on a long car journey must be the usual American custom. Like the transatlantic custom of eating ice cream in the middle of the night to remedy insomnia – she presumed that this was what Americans did, because this was what she had witnessed on the many American television shows that she watched at home.
After what seemed like an eternity of rummaging, Tom produced a neatly sliced piece of cake wrapped in a paper napkin.
Denise accepted it with thanks.
'Mmm,' she said as she chewed a small piece. 'This is nice.'
Tanya was looking at her intently.
'Good,' she said with a smile – her attention quickly returning to the road.
Tom sat back in his seat and offered Allan a slice before taking a piece himself.
'You wanna a piece, hon?' he asked her.
She laughed.
'Not while I'm driving, thanks.'
'You worried about getting it on the seats?' Denise asked.

Tom desperately tried not to choke on the contents of his mouth but he coughed ever so gently, causing a small amount of sponge cake to eject from his tightly closed lips. This caused even greater coughs because he was finding the whole thing very amusing indeed.

Allan looked at him with curiosity.

'Don't choke, will you, Tom,' he managed to say to him quietly through his mouthful of cake – which was when Tom was forced to spit out into his hand what he had in his mouth.

'Yep, that's right, it's the seats. It's quite a new car and I'm sure to make a mess,' Tanya explained with an acceptable smile and Denise accepted this without further question.

Tom tried the same mouthful again but found it hard to keep the contents in his mouth from spraying the back of the seats in front of him. He quickly took a drink from his can to assist his efforts with lubrication and eventually sat back in his seat with a relieved smile – and the onset of hiccups.

Allan savoured the chocolate cake and took a swig of his beer, amused at the most entertaining behaviour of Tom.

Tom and Allan had been laughing constantly for the past ten minutes.

Denise was talking at length with Tanya about life in England and Tanya was asking questions about life in London. Tanya was planning to write an article on what people from England thought of America, and Denise was being surprisingly complimentary. However, she mused, the laughter from the back of the car was most disconcerting when she was trying to concentrate on driving and talking about a serious subject.

The view of the City of Miami from the car window had passed long ago. Denise had been more than a little disappointed by the fact that the outskirts of Miami reminded her of Birmingham: polluted, grey and, in places, relatively run-down – not at all like she had seen on the television and at the cinema. This began to play on her mind.

'I really thought it would be different.' She offered her thought to anyone who would listen.

'What's that?' Tanya asked, as she continued to study the road ahead intently, as it was now being pounded by heavy rain and was throwing heavy spray six feet into the air. Only the faint glow of the tail lights of the cars ahead were visible.

'Miami. I had visions of sunny streets, plush high-rise buildings, expensive cars and big yachts filling the harbour,' she continued.

There was a pause accompanied by a silence.

'Hon, that was about two hours ago when we passed Miami. Have you been thinking about that all this time?'

'I don't think so. I can't remember what I've been thinking about. Come to think of it, what are we talking about now?'

'Miami.'

Tanya smiled.

'What about Miami?' she questioned seriously.

Tom broke into a fit of hearty laughter, causing Allan to follow his lead for no reason known to himself.

'What you laughing at, Allan?' he managed to blurt out in between gasps for air.

He stopped laughing and looked serious.

'I have absolutely no idea.'

'Shall we stop for somethin' to eat?' Tanya said loudly, trying to diffuse the somewhat obtuse situation.

'Yeah, I'm real hungry. What about you two Limeys?' Tom said, drying his eyes.

'Why do Americans call British people Limeys?' Denise asked. 'It's said quite a lot in films, you know.'

'C'mon, Denise, we learnt that one in primary school.' Allan said, drying his eyes happily.

She looked at him blankly.

He began to explain.

'When Britain ruled the seven seas and America was a British colony, the British seamen – who spent months at a time at sea – were notorious for suffering from a serious medical condition called scurvy. They found out that it was caused by a lack of vitamin C, which was remedied by the sailors sucking limes – hence Limeys.'

'Is that true?' Tom said.

'Apparently.'

'I didn't know that,' Denise said. 'That's quite interesting coming from you.'

The three occupants looked at her in amazement as the jeep turned off the main highway and headed for a small diner – almost striking a passing car as the manoeuvre was inattentively executed.

'I think that's where the word hangover comes from too.' Allan finished his can of beer and returned it to the cool box where they had placed the empty cans before.

Tom asked him to explain.

'Well, I was thinking that, perhaps, when the sailors were on long voyages they must have drunk serious amounts of rum because there was nothing else much to do at night. In the morning – when the movement of the sea turned their stomachs so much and made them green – they must have rushed to the side of the ship and hung themselves over to spew up – hence the term hangover.' He smiled triumphantly.

'Is that true?' Tom replied, genuinely thinking about the validity of the explanation.

'I've no idea. I was giving it some thought some time ago. It just seems to be a logical explanation. What else could be the origin of hangover? It can't be anything to do with the effects and so it must be something else.'

Tom scratched his chin.

'Y'know, I think you're right. Nice bit of thinking, Al.'

'Spare us the details of your boring mind,' Denise proposed.

Tom was about to argue in Allan's defence, but he quickly realised that he could not be bothered – and neither could Allan. Besides, he thought, Tanya needed to keep her concentration, judging by the conditions and coping with talking to Denise – who seemed to him to be momentarily stoned.

'Where are we now?' Allan asked.

'Just hittin' the top of the Keys.' Tanya brought the vehicle to a stop in a gravel car park and she continued as they climbed down from the jeep. 'We've got another few hours of hard driving, provided the weather holds out.' She looked up in the sky, at the massing clouds.

The areas of blue sky had all but disappeared, obscured by the large fluffy cumulus clouds that had white peaks and threatening black bellies. The clouds had the appearance of large, weightless glaciers floating in a calm, clear ocean.

The rain had now slowed to intermittent heavy drops that impacted heavily on their heads with a sometimes audible dripping sound.

'I was watchin' the weather channel this mornin' on cable,' she offered, 'and they were explaining 'bout a tropical storm centring on Cuba. Apparently it's throwing a few storms towards the Keys.'

'You are joking?' Denise said, concerned. 'Is it safe?'

'Course it is,' she assured.

'Sorry Tanya – could I interrupt with a bit of sidetrack?' Allan said.

She nodded and smiled tiredly, for the journey was already taking a toll on her usually gregarious nature.

'Here's one for you, Tom. Why are the Keys called the Keys?' He posed the question with gesticulated speech marks.

'I have no idea. Do you know, Tan?'

The four of them walked across the puddle-strewn car park and into the single-storey roadside diner, built haphazardly over a large plot of land. The construction consisted mainly of wood which was in dire need of re-decorating – or at least a great deal of fresh paint – the existing white paint was peeling profusely from the wooden exterior.

'It could be something to do with their *key* position in the ocean – being so close to the so-called trading post of the Colonial West Indies – or it could be the shape of the islands? To be honest,' she confessed, 'I've no idea either.'

Once inside the establishment, they chose a booth by the large window and sat on the red-cushioned plastic benches. Denise picked up a menu and eagerly read the contents, not even bothering to turn her nose up at the tacky interior of the featureless diner. Country and Western music suddenly piped softly through the hidden speakers, failing dismally to create an atmosphere in the empty room.

'Why are we going to Key West if the weather's going to be bad? Shouldn't we go back?' She spoke into the menu, her eyes fixed on the words and pictures in front of her.

'Nah, it'll be okay. The storm's right out at sea. The worst we'll get is a bit of wind and rain.' Tom dismissed it with a wave of his hand.

'Yeah, but they can move around quickly these storms, can't they? I mean, they can catch you off-guard because they can change direction without warning,' Allan said. 'And I'm not talking telephone calls or hand signals,' he offered to Tom as an aside.

Tom raised his eyebrows doubtfully and shook his head slowly. He was smiling, though.

'Don't worry, you two. If they thought there'd be danger a weather warning would have been given. Anyway, the storm has been blowing about the Caribbean for 'bout a week. It's probably run out of steam by now anyway,' Tanya offered amiably. 'Besides, I'm not turning back now.'

Allan and Denise relaxed somewhat, satisfied with Tom and Tanya's confident lack of concern.

A waitress – dressed in jeans and a red sweatshirt and carrying a small notepad and pen – approached the table. She flashed a heavy smile revealing a comparatively huge set of white teeth, (emphasised by thick red lipstick and surrounded by heavy make-up). She spoke very enthusiastically – like an aunt would to her favourite nieces and nephews who she had not seen for a number of years.

'Hey, good to see ya. You folks on your holidays?' She again revealed her piano-key-style smile.

To Allan, she looked strangely like an overpowering aunt, with coiffured hair, heavy make-up and a very attentive disposition. To him, her obsequious manner was most disconcerting and quite overbearing.

'Not really.' Tom smiled at her, amused by her almost comical appearance.

Allan would have left the conversation at that, as he did not want to be drawn into idle chit-chat with her because she looked like the type of person who suffered from verbal diarrhoea.

Tom continued perversely, 'We're just accompanying our friends here – from across the Atlantic – to the Keys for a few days.'

'Right.' She paused contemplatively. Her eyes suddenly lit in comprehension. 'So you're from Europe then? Hey, whereabouts?'

'London,' Allan answered succinctly, hoping in vain that her attentive manner was only a front for the fact that she could not actually 'give a shit.'

'Wow, I love your accent.' She sat down on the edge of one of the red plastic-covered benches.

Tom noticed Allan's look of discouragement and moved along the bench so that she would be more comfortable.

'Go on, say *tomato*,' she said.

There followed a rather pointless conversation, as Allan had feared. He gave as brief answers as he dared without seeming rude, for he never wanted to appear thus to a stranger, especially a foreign stranger. Tanya stifled her giggles and Tom egged the woman on as he noticed Allan's increasing awkwardness.

'Go on, Al, say something to make her melt.'

'Leave it out, Tom,' he said, turning to him, blushing slightly and relieved to have a diversion. 'Let's order,' he said, as he swiftly picked up and scanned the menu. 'I'm really hungry.'

'I am hungry too,' Denise said. 'I can't remember ever being so hungry.'

'Well, you folks decide what you're having and I'll get you some drinks.' The waitress took their order and veritably skipped off to the kitchens.

'I think you've made her day.' Tanya smiled once the woman had disappeared. She was obviously most amused by it all and by Allan's bashfulness.

Denise was looking out of the window at the rain, as it created puddles in between the small gravel stones of the car lot. She seemed not to be at all bothered by the conversation or indeed, that it had taken place.

'I think you're right, Tanya.' He looked at Denise. 'You all right, Denise?'

'Eh? Oh right, yeah I'm fine.' She smiled.

Her eyes looked lazy, she mused.

A momentary silence fell upon the group.

'Why?' she looked at him quizzically.

'You just seemed quiet, that's all. It's not like *you* to be quiet.'

'I was just watching the rain and thinking about food.' She giggled.

Tom kicked Tanya gently under the table.

'I'll get some cake for you out of the jeep if you want.'

'Thanks, I'll wait. I may have some later though, if that's all right,' she said appreciatively.

'Sure is, hon.' Tanya patted her hand that rested on the table.

'So, what are we going to do when we get there?' Allan asked, as the waitress 'beamed' over to their table and set the drinks down. She took their food order and disappeared again.

'Well, I've got an uncle who lives in Key West,' Tanya began, 'and he owns this art studio in Duval Street. That's the main street,' she explained, when Allan looked at her blankly, 'Anyway, he lives above the studio but he's also got a house that he rents out to tourists. I called him yesterday and he said that it's empty this week, so we can use it. It's big enough for all of us, if you *want* to stay with us,' she offered politely – not for a second expecting them to accept the offer.

'That was good of him,' Allan said. Suddenly he felt awkward because of her generous offer. 'Is the house far from all the action?'

Tom noticed his bashfulness. 'Don't decide now, if you don't want to. Wait until we get there.'

Allan nodded.

Tanya continued.

'The apartment isn't in the part of town furthest from the centre anyway. It's near to the sea, where we can go fishing and snorkelling and that.' She watched Denise looking out of the window again. 'What about you Denise, do you like getting wet?'

'Eh?'

'Swimming, do you like it?'

'Mmm,' she replied.

Tom looked at her and smiled.

'Fishing?'

'What about it?'

'Sea fishing. Do you like it?'

'I've never been fishing. Do you eat them after?'

Tom laughed.

'You can if you want. We'll have a go, eh?'

'Mmm.' She smiled dreamily, apparently thinking of food, so it seemed to Tom.

She *was* thinking of food.

'And then, of course, there's the beer. No doubt you two ladies might prefer browsing the shops then while me an' Al drink beer and shoot some pool.'

'Good idea,' Allan enthused.

'I would like to go on a boat trip,' Denise said, with her hand on her chin and her elbow resting on the table. 'I like the sea – when the boat tips and falls on the waves. The taste of salt on your lips and the wind blowing your hair.' She looked distant and smiled dreamily. 'I find the sea quite romantic.'

'And,' enthused Tanya, pleased that Denise seemed so agreeable for once, 'Key West is one of the best places in the world to see a sunset – if the clouds disappear, that is.'

'Why's that?' she asked with interest.

'It's something to do with its geographical position. It's near the equator and so you get a better view of the sun setting,' Allan explained, without reference to the clouds.

'You're a real encyclopaedia, aren't you Allan?' Tanya smiled.

'I pick a few things up,' he replied bashfully.

The waitress came over to the table – with the four plates balanced precariously, yet securely, along her arms – and set the plates down. She came back shortly with additional smaller plates.

'Enjoy. And if you folks want anythin', just holler. I'll be out back if you need me.'

'Thanks,' the quartet said, in unison.

'If this had been in Britain,' Allan said, 'the waitress would have been downright rude, even hostile. She probably would have thrown the food at us and not said a word. That's what I like about this country: even though the people don't really mean it, it makes a change for employees in the service industry to treat you as a valued customer.'

'On that basis, would you prefer to live here then?' Tanya asked in a journalistic mode.

'Not for that reason alone.' He paused for thought, his mind processing his thoughts thoroughly. 'It's quite a laugh actually, getting bad service.' He smiled. 'In Britain you can actually stand and stare in amazement at what people who serve you, *do* and *say* so rudely.'

Tanya smiled as Allan continued his comment on Britain, gesticulating enthusiastically, as he sometimes did with his hands, usually when he was drunk.

'I have heard that the theme parks here are run to cinematic perfection. Now, if that same park was situated in Britain, the attendants would be surly youths with the enthusiasm of a hippy in charge of a busy office in the City. The majority would stand around chatting to each other not adding any enthusiasm or excitement to the rides at all.'

'And that's your idea of fun?' Tom asked, puzzled.

'No, not fun. It's just amusing to compare the attitude of the people of Britain to the population of the USA. I suppose that the irony of 'what is funny' is that the reality is not amusing at all.'

'There're probably some good workers in theme parks in Britain. Don't forget that there're more people in the US and so there's more choice for employers: therefore more competition amongst employees. That's why people in our theme parks are more enthusiastic.'

Allan laughed out loud.

'In theory, Tom, you should be correct. When you come to England, you go to a theme park and justify what you said.' He laughed again. 'You'll eat your words, and that's why it's funny.'

'So, what you're still saying is that getting bad service is funny in Britain?' he replied, still bemused.

'Well, it's only funny when you compare it with service you get in America. The difference is so vast that it seems amusing.'

'Gotcha,' Tom and Tanya said in relieved unison. They were amused by the fact that he seemed almost eccentric when he was explaining something that he had been thinking deeply about.

The three of them looked at Denise, who in return was looking at them.

'What the bloody hell are you three going on about?' she said, more like her old self than the vacancy of the past few hours.

'We were discussing... we were talkin' about...' Tom paused and then frowned. 'What were we talkin' about, Tan? I've just lost my train of thought – period.'

Allan frowned deeply, his forehead wrinkling like a loose sheet of bedlinen.

'I've forgotten too, now that you mention it.'

'Never mind.' Tanya laughed as she bit into her burger. She chewed a mouthful and moved it into the side of her cheek and was about to explain – but Allan and Tom had forgotten to follow up even *that* part of the conversation and so she shrugged her shoulders.

Denise shook her head with incomprehension and cut into her burger with a knife and fork.

The rain emptied like a waterfall from the blanket of very dark grey clouds. It was so continuous and so intense that the view from the diner window was like looking through a frosted window.

'Jeez, would you look at that,' Tanya said, above the roar of the wind and rain against the window.

'I thought you said the storm was nowhere near us,' Denise said hopefully, as if the weather would suddenly change direction because it went against what she had been told.

'I did, and it wasn't,' he replied, as, with nothing more than curiosity he watched the weather.

'Nothing unusual on TV,' said the woman who worked in the diner, as she gathered up the empty plates. She refilled their mugs with coffee. 'You can stay here as long as you like, until the rain eases off. Can I get you's anythin' else?'

'We'll call you if we want anything.' Denise smiled curtly.

'Okay, dear,' the woman said, as she walked back into the kitchen, oblivious to Denise's surliness.

'You should get that cake from the car,' Tanya said to Tom.

'I will if the rain keeps on falling like this.'

'I won't be a minute,' Denise said, as she got up and went to the washroom.

Allan watched her as she walked purposely, yet slowly, towards the washroom.

'What's so special about this cake?' he asked Tom and Tanya in an unnecessary whisper. 'Is it a special cake?'

Tom looked at Tanya and she shrugged her shoulders. Neither of them was sure whether to reveal to him what was actually in the cake, and now they felt a little awkward. However, Tom decided that it was best to tell Allan the truth as honesty was his overriding concern, for if Allan somehow found out at a later date then he would not be best pleased. It was not because Tom was afraid of what Allan might do in return, but he was afraid of how he might view their friendship, even though he barely knew him.

'Don't have a cow, Al, the cake's got hash in it.'

'Hash?'

'Shhh. Yeah, sorry, Al, but we thought that Denise might need some to calm her down. You're not mad, are ya, Al?'

'I don't really know what to say. I haven't taken drugs before.' He looked thoughtful.

Silence.

'It's no big deal,' Tanya offered. 'I know that we probably shouldn't have done it without your knowledge but no harm has been done. Anyway, hash isn't as bad for you as alcohol or caffeine, (and that's not even classed as a drug) – not socially, anyway. Hash is legal in some states and some countries in the world too, you know.'

'So is hanging,' he said, and continued to look thoughtful. He knew that colleagues of his took drugs on a recreational basis at the weekends and he was not shocked by the mention of them. It was just that he was averse to taking them himself, and against people tricking him. Having thought about it, though, despite the fact that he had been duped somewhat, he felt no adverse side effects and Denise had been more amenable over the past few hours. In fact, he had rather enjoyed himself.

'I mean, you must have heard of a crazed drunk shootin' someone, or beatin' on someone but you will never hear of a stoned person doin' anythin' like that,' Tom cajoled.

'I suppose that's not what I'm worried about, Tom,' he said seriously, but calmly.

Tanya and Tom studied his composed features.

'What are you worried about, Al?' he asked, concerned that Allan was becoming very annoyed indeed.

'Well,' he replied seriously, as he looked each of them in the eye. 'When's the rain going to stop enough for someone to get the cake so that we can have some more?' He revealed a wry smile and they all laughed heartily, until Denise emerged from the closed door and approached the table.

'What are you laughing at now?' she said.

Allan kicked Tanya gently under the table as the three immediately quietened. Tanya threw a surprised look at Tom.

'Oh, just laughing about smuggling that cake in here,' Allan said.

Tom and Tanya visibly stiffened at Allan's feeble explanation.

'Oh,' she responded without interest, believing that each of them was being rather immature again – and she instantly felt superior to all three of them.

Allan did not add to the conversation and the tension visibly fell from Tanya's shoulders.

'Let's have another beer!' Tom slapped the table top.

It was not long before the rain had abated enough for them to decide to continue their journey. Once they had paid the bill and bade farewell to the friendly proprietor – who they all agreed was a bit 'too much' – the two couples stepped across the puddle-strewn car park, avoiding the deepest looking puddles as best they could.

'I've never seen so much rain fall in such a short time. In Britain it just rains slowly for days on end. Look at it now,' he said as he pointed to the sky. 'The sun's coming out over there…'

'Al, watch that…'

Allan, with his head tilted back watching the clouds racing across the sky above him, inadvertently walked straight through an enormous puddle and fully submerged his trainers.

'Shit,' he said as he stood still and looked at his feet beneath the water. Had his reactions been quicker then he may have stopped himself sooner than he had and prevented his trainers becoming fully submerged.

'Well, don't just stand there, you idiot.' Denise fussed from the other side of the lagoon-like puddle.

Allan started to laugh – so much so that he bent double.

'Now what are you laughing at?' she castigated.

'I don't know what to do!' he spluttered, as he continued laughing.

Tom, upon regarding the scene before him, soon joined the laughter too with his own deep chuckle.

'I knew that I was walking into a puddle but I couldn't stop myself. I'm right in the middle now.' He looked about himself like a lost boy.

'I can't stand it when he's drunk, he's so stupid,' she said earnestly to Tanya, who was standing next to her and watching Allan with considerable amusement.

'Just walk round it, hon,' Tanya called out.

Allan held up a finger in recognition of her relatively quick thinking.

'Oh dear, my feet are all wet.' He giggled as he stood beside the open car door. 'Now, we can either continue our journey with my feet sticking out of the window or I'll take my trainers off and you can all smell my feet – your decision.'

'Hold on, Al, give us time to think,' Tom said.

Allan hesitated as he waited for him to answer. 'Take your trainers off and get in, Al. Denise'll suck your toes until they're fresh and clean again.'

'Um, if your feet come anywhere near my face then there'll be trouble,' she warned adamantly – without a hint of humour.

'Good idea, and then she can have some cake to take the taste away,' he said to Tom, ignoring Denise.

She started to cry.

'Good grief,' Tom muttered under his breath.

Tanya wore a look of quiet disbelief as she turned wide-eyed towards Allan. She mouthed the words '*do something!*'

'What's the matter?' Allan said to his fiancée as he climbed into the car, holding his trainers as far away from her as he could. 'They don't smell. Here...' he said, as he thrust his shoe towards her hand-covered face.

'It's got nothing to do with your feet or your stupid trainers, you idiot,' she spat.

'That's a relief. I thought you could smell them.' He tried a joke, seeing that it was barely noticeable that Denise was crying except for her whimpers.

'It's you, Allan. *You* are making me upset.'

He looked at Tom, who shrugged his shoulders, then he looked at Tanya who also shrugged her shoulders. He could find no answer from within himself or from the occupants of the car.

'Not now, Denise, you're overreacting. We'll talk about it later,' he said quietly.

'Fine,' she replied, furiously turning in her seat. She struggled with her hands, doing something in her lap. 'You'll be wanting *this* back,' she said, as she threw her engagement ring at him.

He looked with utter surprise, not knowing what to say. Presumably, he pondered, she was waiting for a profuse apology from him.

'Thanks.' He paused. 'Sorry about this, Tom, Tanya. When we get there I'll sort this out when we're alone – Denise and I, that is.'

'Don't worry yourself, man,' Tom reassured him.

'It'll sort itself out,' Tanya said, as she patted Denise's arm. She started the engine and gunned the jeep along the straight highway that led to Key West – at a considerably faster speed than she dared before they had reached the diner.

'The weather doesn't seem to be getting any better,' Denise offered magnanimously. 'Perhaps we should turn back.' The dark clouds massed around her thoughts.

'There's absolutely no way I'm going back,' Tanya scoffed. 'Anyway, we've only got another hour to go until we get there.'

'Yes, but I'm worried, especially as we're going along this long bridge in the middle of the sea.' She looked out of the car window at the sea that stretched uninterrupted to the horizon – on both sides of the bridge – with neither land nor feature to interrupt the interminable expanse of water. It was the view that one would expect to see from an ocean-going ship but certainly not from a car. The wind buffeted the car strongly and lashed heavy rain onto the windscreen, as if the weather was punishing the occupants for daring to travel on the long causeway through to the Keys.

'It'll be okay,' Tom reassured her, as he reached forward across the headrest and placed his hand on her shoulder.

'I still think we should turn back,' she said again, being awkward as much as she was concerned.

She probably did not want to be in the car – with the atmosphere that had been created – and she no longer wished to stay in Key West, where, because of the presence of Tanya and Tom, she could not be in the lofty position to blame him sufficiently for their faltering relationship, Allan thought silently. However, he knew that as soon as he parted company with Tom and Tanya she would verbally tear him apart. He had to relish the time he spent with Tom and Tanya before she could get her claws into him.

'It'll be all right,' he said to Denise, knowing that it would be anything *but*.

He could not think of anything else to say to comfort her, and the dark clouds that surrounded her made him feel threatened. His heart sank and his bowels clenched as the awkward realisation dawned upon him.

'Like *you* would know,' she rebuffed sternly.

He shrugged his shoulders resignedly and sat back in the seat, taking a large swig from his can of beer.

'Why don't you two make up?' Tom said cheerfully.

'As silly and childish as this sounds, Tom, *I* don't have the problem. As far as I'm concerned the ball is in Denise's court. It's down to her now,' he replied with a detectable slur in his speech. Dutch courage was indeed digging him a deeper grave.

'That's the idea, why don't you speak about me as if I'm not here?' she snarled, as she rounded on him.

'Well,' he actually sneered in reply, caused by the Dutch courage, 'in case you are interested, I will explain that this phrase originates from the fact that some Dutch merchantmen would courageously ferry gin across the North Sea to Britain during the Great Plague of the seventeenth century. 'You treat *me* as if I wasn't here, so from now on that's how I'm going to treat *you*. Anyway, why don't you at least be civil to me until you can really have a go at me – when we're not around to embarrass Tom and Tanya.'

'Al, you're making it worse, man.' Tom whispered helpfully.

He laughed. 'I'm already up to my neck in shit, Tom, I just might as well say what I mean.'

'You're drunk again, Allan. I'm not going to stand for it anymore. I told you what would happen if you got drunk again,' she said in a high-pitched voice.

'You were bluffing,' he said calmly.

'No I wasn't!'

'Okay, Denise, I'll call your bluff.'

'You're drunk. You don't know what you're saying. We're getting married later this year and so I can't be bluffing.' She looked surprised. Tears welled in her eyes.

'Precisely.'

'I'm confused, Allan. We'll talk later.'

She seemed to calm somewhat. Perhaps the realisation that she had gone too far had made her back-pedal so suddenly, or probably because she could not fathom what he was talking about, he mused. He knew, though, that it was the quiet before an almighty storm that would leave a devastating trail of destruction.

'Good idea,' Tanya said with a sigh.

'Have some cake, Denise.' Tom offered the open tin over the front seat.

'No thanks, Tom. I don't think cake will help the way I feel at the moment.'

Tom coughed away a chuckle, Tanya smiled and Allan scoffed.

'What's up with you now?' She abruptly looked at Allan.

He briefly toyed with the idea of telling her what had been added to the cake mixture.

Tom looked at Allan, wide-eyed with surprise, silently begging him not to tell her.

Allan was close to being in a rage and telling her everything just to tip her over the edge and make her really mad.

'Well, I'm going to have some,' he said with a smile instead. Tom sighed with relief.

'Right then, let's start again – a clean slate,' Tanya said calmly. 'Do you agree, Denise?'

She nodded sullenly.

'What about you, Allan?' she continued.

'Yes, Mum.' He laughed. The thick atmosphere that had hung in the cabin of the car seemed to lift somewhat and they all laughed with relief, except Denise, who remained stone-faced with pursed lips that refused to break into a smile.

If she folded her arms any tighter she would cut off her circulation, Tanya thought to herself.

'Are your parents still around?' Tom asked Allan conversationally.

'No, my dad died five years ago.' He looked at Tom sadly.

Tom held his head in his hands. 'I did put my foot in it. Sorry Al, I was just making conversation.'

He tried to feign affront by silently looking out of the window at the passing countryside.

The straight road passed small pockets of buildings that were separated by long stretches of dense forest and swamp that lined the coast road. The pockets of buildings predominantly consisted of deserted petrol stations and shops advertising fishing tackle and diving equipment for sale or hire. Due to the weather it seemed that these businesses were not at all busy.

'I haven't upset you, have I, man?' Tom asked gingerly.

Tanya watched Allan in the rear-view mirror and noticed the smile that broadly crossed his face.

'No, not at all. I am used to him not being here now, so no, you didn't offend me.'

'My mom and dad aren't alive,' Tom said mournfully.

'Stop it you two,' Tanya said seriously. 'You mustn't make light of the matter of death, y'know. Tom's father and mother *are* still alive, Allan, and so are mine – stop trying to make each other feel like they are putting their size tens in the conversation.' She looked at him seriously but her voice and smiling eyes gave away the fact that she was slightly amused.

'Too right,' Denise said moodily.

'Well,' Allan started, 'as Oscar Wilde said, there are only two things certain in life – death and taxes.' He contemplated what he had said, 'No, it wasn't him, was it? It was someone else.'

'I think *that* phrase has been attributed to many famous deceased authors,' Tanya offered.

He nodded. 'Anyway, I am not mocking the death of the people that I once loved – and I'm not afraid of talking about it with a certain degree of frivolity either.'

'You swallowed a dictionary as well as an encyclopaedia?' She smiled.

He ignored her with a bashful smile. 'It's going to happen whether we like it or not.'

'Allan, you're so morbid sometimes,' Denise said, as she looked out of the window. 'I don't want to talk about death because it scares me to think that one day I won't be here.'

'Are you concerned about this holiday ending?' he asked.

She paused. 'Not really. The holiday is for two weeks and I know that I've got to go home when it's over.'

'So what's the difference?'

'Shut up,' she mumbled.

'Wasn't it Oscar Wilde that also said something like: 'Nobody ever lay on their death bed and wished that they had spent more time in the office.'?'

'That was Ernest Hemingway, wasn't it?' Tanya joined in. 'He lived in Key West for some part of his life, you know.'

'Every deceased author probably wrote that one too. Anyway, whoever said *that*, was indeed right.' He took a drink from another can of beer that Tom passed him.

'I'll drink to *that*.' Tom joined in.

'How can you be so flippant, talking about death like that,' Denise said seriously. 'I mean, surely it's not healthy.'

'On the contrary,' Tom said, 'It's very healthy. A person should not hide from the truth any more than they should try and disguise it. I reckon that people who dress things up so that they are more believable are in real danger of causing intense psychological problems – look at political correctness, for instance. I believe that people who are overtly PC are, for instance, just like people who have an unhealthy interest in only one part of their life – people who live for only one reason and that reason alone is their meaningless existence.'

'You're losing me, Tom.' Allan looked puzzled.

'Me too,' Tanya said. She turned to Denise and said quietly, 'He studied psychology for a few years and thinks he's Sigmund Freud.'

She nodded with disinterest and continued to look out of the side window. She had initially tried to move them off the subject but now that they had ignored her she was not even listening to what they were saying.

Tom continued.

'What I'm saying is, for instance, take a woman who has children. Those children grow up and they mean the world to her. As the years pass by, then maybe so do her other interests in life – her friends, career and the things that she liked to do before the birth of her children. Now, depending on her basic structure of her mind and her reasons for living, as the children grow up they'll become increasingly independent and require less and less of their mother's attention. In turn, this'll affect the mother and make her more possessive, and *this* will drive a wedge between her and her children. Eventually the children could reject their mother and her reason for living will be shattered. This would tip her over the bounds of sanity and she will be susceptible to alcoholism, neurosis and a varying degree of psychological disturbances.'

'Are you aware that there are many large holes in your argument?' Allan countered.

'Not to mention a certain amount of chauvinism,' Tanya added. 'What about the father of this hypothetical family?'

'Oh sure, I know there are holes – because each person's mind is so complex you cannot apply a rule that extends to the accepted norm. There're so many other factors to take into account – too many to mention. I was just emphasising that it is unhealthy to lie to oneself and selfishly live your life solely for your own purposes. I suppose that I'm being a little sexist but I'm using these extreme examples to illustrate my point. Well, take a man then: he may work hard all his life at the office. At the age of sixty he may be forced to retire, having spent an active and healthy life. As soon as he retires you can be almost certain that he will die sooner than he would have done if he had stayed at work.'

'I think that you have strayed from the point,' Tanya said. 'Too much beer and cake,' she dared, as she thought that Denise was no longer listening, besides which, she decided that Denise would not make the connection anyway.

'Perhaps I have, but my point is still the same: as long as you have plenty of things to occupy your life – like friends, a career and interests – if one aspect falls by the wayside then you'll still have plenty more to keep your mind healthy. However, if you live your life and worry simply about death then you'll undoubtedly become unhealthy, unhappy and unloved, maybe even obsessed.'

'Oooh, strong words, Tom.' Allan contemplated, 'What about people who do have a family and they stay by their side for the rest of their life?'

'Then they're lucky because, like anything in life, if you expect something to happen then you can almost guarantee that something will happen to change it all – the best laid plans will always stumble when applied to real life. Here's an example: when you were younger, did you ever plan a conversation with a girl who you wanted to date?'

Allan nodded.

'Well, you must remember that you spent hours planning the conversation and trying to predict what she would say. I know that this is a very simplistic illustration, but I can guarantee that nothing went according to how you planned it. Am I right?'

'I'll drink to that, Tom.'

'Thank goodness we haven't far to go,' Tanya said quietly.

'And here we are!' Tanya announced triumphantly, as they eventually came to the end of the causeway – many miles in length – and continued along the main coast road of the island of Key West. She felt relief bounding towards her like a happy dog, with the thought that she would soon be able to escape from the strained and uncomfortable atmosphere that still pervaded the interior of the vehicle. The situation that had arisen in the car had been made worse by the fact that there was no escape, but at least if Denise and Allan acted badly again in Key West then she would be able to leave the room or wherever they happened to be. She regretted suggesting that they share the accommodation with Allan and Denise and hoped that they would decide against it now

– which, given their current behaviour she assumed they would decline.

'That took a while longer than you said, Tom,' Allan slurred.

'Eh?'

'Well, we finished the beer half an hour ago. We're late,' he said.

'You yanking my chain, Al?'

'Idiot,' Denise whispered, as she folded her arms tightly.

'Here, Denise.' Tanya passed her a piece of paper. 'The directions are on this. Read them out to me, would you?'

'It's a good job you didn't ask Allan. He couldn't navigate his way out of a supermarket,' she replied provocatively, as she took the map. 'He got us lost on the way to the airport in England and we could have missed our flight.'

He was about to object because they had come nowhere near missing their flight, but Tom offered him a cigarette and he decided that he could no longer be bothered to argue – when he had the alternative of nicotine refreshment. He knew that she had deliberately baited him and was disappointed that she had not received a response – but he really was just past caring now.

Denise successfully read out the map instructions to Tanya, which was probably the most amount of words she had spoken throughout the entire journey since they had left the diner a few hours earlier. The coast road of Key West was relatively short in its overall length and so it took comparatively no time at all for them to reach their final destination.

The rain had abated to a drizzle, bringing a welcome break from the constant and frantic movement and noise from the windscreen wipers. Allan looked out of the window, at the tall palm trees that lined the golden beach. It was being lashed by the heavy grey and white sea that reflected the equally bleak sky as it crashed ashore. He watched as people ran – from cars to bars, from houses to cars – with brightly coloured waterproof garments held tightly about their heads, fighting to wrestle them from the grip of the gusting wind. He watched the wooden buildings go by, clustered together in small plots of land that were lavished chaotically with overhanging, multicoloured green trees and shrubbery.

The horizontal wooden cladding of the houses – invariably painted either white, green or brown to blend in with the soft, natural colours of the surrounding flora and fauna of almost jungle proportions – often reached from the ground to the tiled roofs.

He instantly liked the quirky arrangement of the town, the narrow streets and the uncomplicated yet interesting buildings. He was instantly comfortable in his surroundings yet he could not help wondering why an area of the globe, that was frequently hit by forceful winds and rain had its homes, shops, businesses and bars made of wood. He spoke this thought aloud for his fellow travellers to hear.

'It's probably because they get damaged real easily and get blown down so regularly that it's more cost effective to rebuild wooden homes,' Tanya suggested.

Denise shot a look at her.

'You're joking, right?' He laughed rather nervously.

Tanya laughed, unconcerned.

'No I'm not. It's more than likely to be true. I expect that the houses here get destroyed whether they're made of bricks or wood. Look,' she said, as she pointed to the sea, 'there is no protection from the sea and the island is at sea level anyway. Perhaps wooden houses are better because they *float*.' She chuckled.

Denise maintained her arms in a tightly folded posture and looked nervously at the sea.

'There's a plaque on the wall of that house mentioning Ernest Hemingway,' Tom said inconsequentially as he continued looking out of the window as they passed an unremarkable row of wooden houses – it was in fact a row of tightly spaced houses without a single front garden.

'Who's Ernest Hemingway?' Denise asked nonchalantly.

'Who *was* Ernest Hemingway you mean – he's dead.' Allan scoffed. 'He was only one of the most famous American writers of the twentieth century – nobody special.'

'Well, I didn't know, did I?' she answered abruptly.

'We did mention him earlier,' he offered tiredly.

'Not everyone knows, Allan. Anyway, you're just a swot. Nobody likes a clever dick. I bet you were one of those kids at school who never misbehaved and always had his head in a book. Did you get bullied at school? Did the bigger boys pick on you for being a swot?' She tore into him.

'Well, *excuse me* for being a clever dick,' he slurred, as he took a swig from his can, 'I wasn't a nerd at school but I wasn't one of the elite kids either – you know, the one's that got all the girls.' He turned to Tom. 'I was in the middle of the two and didn't get involved with either group so I didn't get noticed or bullied.'

'You surprise me,' she said under her breath, as the hot air was expelled from her mouth once more, only to begin imperceptibly building up again for the next confrontation.

Just as the rain started plummeting heavily from the heavens, Tanya guided the vehicle gently to a halt and said, 'We're here.'

'Let's wait and see if the rain eases a little before we go in,' Tom suggested.

They all readily agreed.

Allan looked at the house. They had pulled up alongside one, which was one of many houses situated in a typically small plot of almost wildly planted jungle vegetation. The house was a two-storey affair that was covered in whitewashed horizontal wooden slats, with wooden sash windows, a wooden stoop and a wooden staircase at the side of the structure. The building leaned slightly to one side, making the windows slightly out of line.

'It looks like an interesting house,' he mused absently.

'Allan, you are boring. How can a house be interesting?' Denise scoffed again.

'No, it *is*, Denise,' Tanya said quietly. 'Apparently it's furnished real nice and the floors slope unusually, on account of the building subsiding 'bout fifty years ago. You'll like it.'

'Oh,' she replied simply, slightly embarrassed.

'The rain doesn't look like it's going to stop, Tom. I'm going to make a run for it and see if my uncle's in,' Tanya offered. Tom agreed and she opened the car door.

'Jesus Christ,' they heard her blaspheme when she stood in the rain and slammed the door shut. They watched as her legs splashed in the puddles, running towards the stoop. She knocked on the door with her knuckles. She waited a few minutes but nobody came to the door. The occupants of the jeep watched silently – as she sprinted back, the rain sounding heavily on the roof. She quickly climbed in and slammed the door shut.

'He's not there.' She puffed and pushed back her very wet black hair from her forehead. She blew away a collection of raindrops that had run down her smooth skin to the end of her nose. She quickly reclaimed her lost breath. 'We'll try the studio,' she said, as she started the engine.

'Tanya, is it still raining? You look a bit damp.'

'I don't really know, Allan.' She smiled. 'Why don't I stop and let you get out and see?'

He sat up in his seat and with feigned reluctance replied, 'Nah, I reckon it *is* raining and you're just messing about.'

'Shut up, Allan,' Denise said impatiently. 'Tom and Tanya have had to put up with your silly attempts at jokes all the way. You're drunk and I don't like it and I told you what would happen if you got drunk again, but we won't discuss our break-up now.'

'It's all right, Allan, you make *me* laugh,' Tanya said honestly.

Denise fell silent and was vexed at being rebuffed so openly.

'British humour is great, Al. You know with all that irony, dry humour an' all. Some people just don't get it.'

Allan was not sure if Tom was directing the comment to Denise but it made no difference to him at this moment in time. It seemed that his relationship with Denise was definitely doomed.

'I'm not used to these narrow streets,' Tanya confessed as she drove along the deserted roads. 'And this rain isn't helping. I can hardly see where I'm going.'

'I told you we should have turned back,' Denise offered.

'Our roads are like this all the time – wet, narrow, full of parked cars – except they're really busy with other road users as well,' Allan explained. 'I never expected that roads in America would be like this. It's probably because this island is so small, like our country. There's no room to have big roads?'

'Very true, Al,' Tom said loudly above the din of the rain falling on the roof. It sounded like somebody dropping a box of nails onto the roof from a great height. 'You know, Al, I think that you spend most of your time thinking about stuff. Would I be right?'

Allan thought about it.

'I guess you'd be right.'

'It's a pity you don't think of me more often,' Denise added.

'I thought you two were having a truce?' Tanya interrupted.

Allan groaned.

'We were, but now we're here the truce is almost over. She's warming up for the big one.'

'Well you can stay with us, Allan, until Denise comes to her senses,' Tanya ventured boldly. She had had enough of Denise's attitude, her constant baiting of Allan, and attempts to belittle and order him about. Now that escape from the relatively small interior of the car was imminent – and because Tanya was not one to mince her words when the situation allowed – she decided that she would speak her mind. Tanya was an intelligent woman, a tolerant and surprisingly subtle person but her patience had been worn out finally and the consequences of her actions were no longer her concern.

Tom covered his forehead with the palm of his hand with an accompanying slapping sound.

Allan smiled blankly.

Denise fell completely silent and scowled, furrowing her brow deeply and obviously seething with anger while she deliberated her next choice of words.

Tanya brought the large jeep to a halt once more.

'I'll just go and see if he's here.' She climbed out and quickly shut the door before sprinting over to the entrance of the shop. She went in, leaving the occupants in the car to an uneasy silence.

'Hello!' Tanya called out. There was no reply. She called out again but received no response from the dim interior of the small gallery-cum-shop. Paintings of the local scenery, the harbour, the streets and the sea haphazardly adorned the walls. Miniature carvings and ships in bottles were on display in small cabinets that lined one of the uneven walls from the timber floor up to the low wooden ceiling.

She started towards the wooden stairs with the intention of climbing them. However, she saw a piece of paper taped to the banisters and so took it up in her hand, reading it quickly. She put the piece of paper in the pocket of her jeans and returned to the uneasy silence of the car.

The car was filled with cigarette smoke now that the air conditioning was not working – on account of the engine being turned off. Tanya took one look at Denise's furious expression and decided not to turn the engine on for a minute, just to ensure that she became more uncomfortable in the polluted atmosphere.

'He's at the bar along the street,' she said, waving the note in her hand as she turned in her seat to face the two men. 'He's expecting us to meet him in that bar over there.' She pointed down the street. 'You up for a run, you guys?'

'What about me?' Denise said indignantly.

'Well, I'm not going to carry you so you can run with us, unless you want to stay here,' Allan advised her curtly.

'Well, you can go first and I'll follow when I see you go in. I don't want to stand in the rain if there isn't anyone there,' she said bitterly.

'You stay here, then,' Tanya said.

The remaining three opened their respective doors and slammed them shut.

Denise tutted as she watched the three of them sprint towards the bar. She turned her nose up as she noticed that Allan still had a can of beer in his hand. She heartily regretted meeting Tom and Tanya and she could not see a way out of her predicament. She was upset that she now seemed to be alone. Allan's attitude towards her had changed notably. She sighed and real tears welled in her eyes.

'Jees–uss!' Tom exclaimed as they ran. 'I can hardly see where I'm going!' he shouted.

Allan laughed.

'What are you laughing at?' he questioned him when they reached the leeward shelter of the building.

'You might have drowned – shouting and running in the rain like that. I have never seen rain like it.'

Tanya peered through the window of the bar and knocked on the door frame. The three of them peered through the glass into the dim interior of the bar.

'There doesn't seem to be anyone in, Tan. You sure this is the right place?'

Tanya pulled the note from her pocket and looked at it.

'Yeah, this is definitely the place. Look, he's drawn a quick map and all.'

As soon as Christine watched Jim disappear into the rain to leave a note for his visiting relative, the overhead lights in the bar flickered and hummed their protest. They went dim and faded completely. The sudden darkness caused her heart to leap into her throat. However, she managed to remain sufficiently calm. She moved to the bar and tried the coffee machine which was below the many optics that lined the shelf in front of the obligatory long bar mirror. The coffee machine was not working either and so she quickly concluded that the entire electric power must have been cut off – presumably by a felled power cable or a lightening strike.

So that she could be sure of her conclusion, she made her way towards the back of the bar and up the stairs that led to the accommodation area of the building. She heard, and thought she felt the house move slightly when the strong wind buffeted the sides, and the windows rattled in their frames as gusts of wind pushed past them and eerily whistled a soft moan. The wooden stairs creaked as she slowly climbed them, her mind alert for any additional noises amongst the cacophony of moans and rattles – if she had been a child then she would have expected a ghost with a ball and chain to walk through the building.

She reached the landing on the first floor when movement from the view of the small window at the top of the stairs barely caught her attention. She stopped and peered through the rain-streaked glass – which obscured her view because of the rivers of rainwater that snaked down the pane and created a near goldfish bowl effect.

She again caught a fleeting glimpse of a figure wearing a yellow coat disappearing behind the trees and vanishing from view. Her heart took residence again in her throat. She swallowed hard and continued to watch.

She had definitely seen the same figure earlier, but she wondered if she had imagined it because it had been a very fleeting glimpse on both occasions, and her view was obscured by heavy rain on the window – she could not see anything now. She remembered that she had left her gun under the bar and wished that she had it with her now, because it gave her the feeling that she was able to defend herself. She had never used a gun before, in that she had never fired a weapon and believed that she would not be capable of ever shooting a person – but she knew that she would feel safer if she had the heavy cold steel in her hand.

She listened to the sounds of the house, and after seeing the figure in the garden her imagination had broken loose and was running amok in her erstwhile level mind. It was then that she heard a loud banging sound from downstairs. It was too regular and of a short burst to be anything but somebody at the front door. She stopped in her tracks and then turned and slowly descended the stairs – her heart still in her throat. She reached the bottom of the stairs. She stopped again and listened.

The banging sound was coming from the bar, so she wearily approached the door that led to it with the intention of peering around the door without stepping into the bar area – to keep herself hidden from view. Her head rounded the door and she quickly scanned the bar for movement. Nothing moved, but something in the area by the front door caught the corner of her eye. She slowly turned and looked at the door seeing three figures standing outside – and rather wet they looked to her too.

She decided to let them in because she was so unnerved by the weather and the potential threat of who, she presumed Philip, was lurking outside. Having company would make him go and allow her to feel more secure, she reasoned. She walked into the bar area and approached the front door, smiling thankfully and quickly unbolting it and opening the door wide – allowing the wind to blow briskly through the opening together with a torrent of rain. She gestured them in and the trio quickly and gratefully stepped inside. She closed the door, shutting out the noise of the wind and rain.

'It's raining you know,' Allan said, as he ran his hand through his soaking wet hair. He smiled and looked at Christine – instantly appreciating her long dark hair, her gently curvaceous figure and her beautiful face. Her eyes glowed with clarity and contrasted purely with her pupils. He smiled, enchanted and captivated by her aesthetic charm.

'I had noticed,' she said, relieved.

'Don't mind him.' Tanya smiled. She introduced her partner and Allan. 'My name's Tanya. I'm Jim's niece,' she said, as Christine made her way to the bar. Christine moved behind it and introduced herself before offering them drinks and they gratefully gave her their requests.

'I know Jim, sure. He's been expecting you. In fact, not long ago he left here and posted little notes for you all over town so that you knew where he was.' She laughed briefly, buoyed up by her new sense of security. 'I guess that dodging the weather on foot takes longer than in a car,' she said conversationally, as she poured their drinks.

Allan nodded and smiled, transfixed by her appealing appearance – and now by her accent.

'It was one hell of a drive here,' Tanya explained to her amiably. 'The weather was getting worse with every mile that we came south. I'm glad we made it in one piece actually.' She sipped her drink and then sighed with relief. It had been a strain driving all the way from Fort Lauderdale, keeping her (much needed) concentration while all about her there was danger.

'I don't doubt that,' Christine replied, now *very*, *very* pleased to be in the company of others. She looked momentarily quizzical.

'Jim said there would be four of you. Did you lose someone on the way?'

Tom and Tanya turned slowly to look at Allan.

'What?'

'Remember Denise? You'd better go get her,' Tom said.

He shrugged his shoulders.

'No, she said that she would follow us in when she saw us actually walk through the doorway.' He sipped his pint of stout.

Tanya frowned.

'No, Allan. Just poke yer head out of the door and see if you can attract her attention.'

He looked reluctant.

'You know what'll happen if she comes in here in an hour's time and you haven't made the effort.' She looked at him and nodded knowingly.

He smiled at her reasoning.

'Now, that's a good point,' he said and then, turning to Christine, 'I'm going to get my fiancée now. Now don't be offended by her, she just gets my back up and we argue a lot and she can be really rude too.'

Christine looked wide-eyed and slightly amused.

'She's harmless really, just awkward and difficult to get along with.' He smiled.

'And she's your fiancée?' she asked incredulously.

He snorted and approached the door without verbally replying to her question. He could not even determine if he still wished to marry Denise, primarily because he could not find it within himself to let her know of his obvious reservations surrounding marrying her – which in itself was evidence enough of his uncertainties. However, it was already becoming clear how he felt and so the fact that their marriage was in question would not be a surprise to either of them. He opened the door and the wind gusted into the bar. He struggled to keep the door open as little as he could as he poked his head out of the aperture which he had afforded himself.

The three of them watched him at the door as he closed it and came back to a stool by the bar.

'Well?' Tom said.

'I can't see well enough. I waved a lot, so if she didn't see me then it's tough. At least she can't say I didn't bother.' He took another sip from his drink when he had reached his previous position at the bar. He smiled.

Tanya shook her head in despair. She was about to explain to Allan that he was wrong – but she had had enough. She concluded that, as much as she liked him, his relationship with Denise was not *her* problem. She was not going to venture into the rain to get her either, not even if the rain abated and the sun shone brightly.

Besides, they had only known each other for less than twenty-four hours, and so she did not feel particularly beholden to either of them.

'When the rain eases off a bit I'll go and get her,' Tom said. Not even Allan in his drunken frame of mind could be so blatantly brutal to Denise – surely, he mused. After all, she probably could not really help her actions. He had concluded that she could have spent a misguided youth in the presence of domineering parents. However, as soon as he reached this conclusion he was mindful of Tanya frequently reminding him not to judge people, and so he decided to give her one last benefit of the doubt.

'Jim will be back in a minute. He'll go and get her because he's dressed for a walk in the rain,' Christine offered.

They all agreed that this was a good idea and settled down on bar stools.

'So whereabouts in England do you come from, Allan?' Christine asked.

'South London suburb. You probably won't know it unless you have been to London. Have you?'

'I have been, actually. I lived in Essex when I was young but I left with my parents when I was eight years old. We used to go to the West End of London at weekends.' She smiled. 'I'll always remember Covent Garden at Christmas time: the atmosphere there was wonderful, with happy people spilling from bars; street performers and large crowds; the smell of roasting chestnuts in the streets that were lined with soft falling snow.'

'I see.' he nodded and smiled. 'Happy memories then.'

'The rain has eased a bit, Allan. Shouldn't you go and get Denise?' Tanya suggested persistently.

Her concern remained greater than her dislike for Denise, although she was not sure how long it would last. What she did resent was feeling responsible for her when Allan was the one who should be concerned – whether or not they had had an argument. She decided that they were both being as immature as each other and now she was irritated by it all.

She had even given her a chance, by agreeing to travel with them but it seemed that she did not want to help herself because she had made no effort at all – the previous night she had left the nightclub in a hurry without telling anyone and today she was sulking like a spoilt child.

Allan looked thoughtful as he held the pint glass in his hand and continued to look out of the window.

'I suppose,' he sighed as he climbed off the bar stool and set the glass on the bar, 'with a bit of luck the wind will have blown her away.' And with that he casually, and with a certain amount of dejection, walked to the door.

The three people left in the bar watched him leave.

'It's weird, you know, how two people can plan to get married, go on vacation together beforehand and not realise that they're not at all suited. I mean, it's a good thing that they found out before they got married. If they had, then she'd take him to the cleaners in a divorce court,' Tom puzzled aloud.

'Perhaps it's a love–hate relationship?' Christine offered.

'No way,' Tanya said confidently. 'Their relationship was doomed from the start.'

'How do you know?' Tom said with good humoured incredulity.

'It's obvious. Denise is a shallow and false person, whereas Allan, although intelligent, has been quite an introvert and almost weak – until now. He was virtually living a lie but he has almost seen the light. If he *does* marry her he will *definitely* be living a lie – caused by his inability to face reality. If he had been strong and known his own mind in the first place then this would never have happened.'

'That's pretty damning and bitter, Tan.' He paused for thought as her words hit home. 'I suppose you could be right, though. Do you reckon it's because he's drunk?'

'Don't you forget it.' She laughed.

'Everything happens for a reason,' Christine added.

Allan opened the door as he returned to the bar, then struggled to force the door closed against the gusting wind.

'That's strange,' he said, as he faced the window, looking at the gusting wind and rain. He turned to face the bar. '*She's not there.*'

'What?' Tom and Tanya said in unison.

'She's not in the car. I don't know where she's gone.'

'Well, what shall we do?' Tom lifted his arms in bemusement as he looked at Tanya.

'Well, I know what I'm going to do,' Allan said, as he approached the bar.

'What's that then?' Christine asked.

'I'll have another pint please.' He smiled back at her. He drained the contents of his first glass and set it firmly back on the bar. 'She's just doing it to make me feel guilty – trying to make out that I've been horrible to her and it's all my fault. Well, not this time. If she wants to be childish and immature as well as obnoxious then that's fine by me. I can't believe that I have put up with it for so long.' He stood erect and looked completely resolute and confident. 'If I hadn't come on this holiday with her then I would never have seen her for what she is. Phew,' he exclaimed, 'getting this out into the open has made me feel like a free man.'

'I could have told you that.' Tanya looked relieved.

Christine wondered if Tanya had overstepped the mark by speaking her mind, and she mused that Jim would have done exactly the same. She smiled involuntarily.

'What are you going to do, Al?' Tom frowned.

'Nothing,' he replied succinctly. 'I don't care if it seems harsh. I want nothing more to do with the silly cow. I have never seen my life as clearly as I have now. Let's celebrate my second birth.' He raised his glass.

Christine looked at Allan with concern.

Tanya looked thoughtful, as a deep feeling of fear crashed onto her consciousness like a breaking wave on the beach.

Chapter Ten

Denise watched Allan, Tom and Tanya run through the dense falling rain as a strong degree of anger and resentment bubbled inside her. She reasoned that Allan needed her – and she needed him to need her – so that she could perceive the relationship to be working.

She strained to see through the curtain of falling rain, as she watched the three simultaneously press their faces to the large windows of the bar frontage, and then she watched as the door eventually opened and they disappeared inside. She watched as Allan took a brief look back at the car – and then he disappeared.

The minutes passed and she wondered what to do. She decided against following Allan into the bar too soon as it would give him a certain amount of satisfaction, knowing that she was following him around. The thought of Tom and Tanya also angered her, and the fact that they seemed to be siding with Alan against her. The anger was now bubbling quite vigorously as she turbulently pondered whether she was still going to be married to Allan later that year. She had half a mind to proceed with the marriage, then have a child and then divorce him if necessary, forcing him to support her financially. She smiled thinly, but she was far from feeling happy.

She distantly daydreamed but after a short while she could not fail to notice the open door of the bar a hundred feet away. She watched as Allan peered from the door of the bar and then, as he waved both arms wildly in the direction of the car that she was seated in. He could have at least bothered to come and get me, to see if I am all right, she considered. She fumed.

She decided that if he had made the effort then it would have given them a chance to talk and perhaps resolve their differences without Tom and Tanya interfering. She chose to ignore him, calculating that eventually he would come to the car and plead with her to go with him to the bar. She hated bars. However, she knew that he was useless at playing the waiting game and she would take satisfaction from eventually winning.

The sound of the rain emptying from high in the sky onto the roof of the car reached a frenzy. The din was so loud and intrusive that it disrupted her lengthy thoughts of Allan. Her attention was drawn to movement on the other side of the road. She watched the lone figure walk purposefully along the road wearing a bright yellow waterproof jacket and holding the rim of the hood tightly so as not to allow the wind to wrench it from the wearer's head.

She initially marvelled at the boldness of the person confronting the extreme natural elements so casually, but as the thought lingered in her mind the idea of mild admiration soon turned to the opinion that the person was obviously stupid and reckless. The figure eventually reached the bar and went inside. She pondered the idea of following the lone figure but she decided against it. After all, why should she run after Allan? He was the one who was in the wrong because he was drunk again.

She could not help herself dwelling on the possibility that Tom and Tanya were polluting his attitude towards her by making him act against her. As far as she was concerned, she was getting along very well with Allan – until they met Tom and Tanya. Now, it seemed that all three of them were in collusion against her and she did not like it at all, or understand why the situation had reached the point that it had.

'You all right in there?' came a loud voice above the din of the falling rain.

She was momentarily startled and turned to face the side window and saw a face peering in. It was a kind and very handsome-looking face, she immediately thought, and so she rather capriciously – because she was feeling quite rejected – pointed to the rear passenger door.

The figure ducked towards the door and opened it to let himself in.

'Jeez,' he exclaimed, as he wiped the water from his face.

She looked at his handsome strong features, his powerful chin and undoubtedly muscular frame beneath his wet clothing and yellow waterproof.

'I didn't mean to startle you but what are you doin' out here on your own?' he asked.

'That's okay,' she muttered, then continued more audibly, 'I am having one hell of a day. I feel like the weather – rotten.'

'Why?' he looked at her.

She failed to make contact with his eerie black and lifeless eyes.

'Oh, my fiancé. I'm having second thoughts.' She found that her fears were easy to express to a complete stranger and she amazed herself by her own frankness.

'Well, he's a silly guy passing you up – splendid English rose that you are,' he tried to say, with a poor attempt at an English accent.

She laughed.

'I know, but now I just hate him. He's gone in that bar over there and left me outside in the rain – the bastard.'

'What, that bar over there?' He gestured to Christine's bar with surprise.

She nodded.

'You *don't* wanna go in there, or let your fiancé go in there. The woman who owns it is a maneater. She won't leave me alone, so if your fiancé is in there then you'd better get in there quick and keep an eye on him.' He watched to see what kind of reaction she gave to these words.

'Really?' she said, surprised and angered. Her shoulders dropped as she looked at him and sighed. 'Oh, I don't think that I care anymore. Do you know of anywhere else I could go?' She fished for him to suggest something.

He studied her face. He usually felt and could visibly see an aura that surrounded a woman that compelled him to win her into his confidence and then abuse her trust by exerting his indomitable power. However, from the woman who sat in the seat in front of him, he sensed and saw no aura at all but he could plainly see the usual obvious physical attraction that she displayed towards him – she displayed no amount of fear but he did sense something from her, but he knew not what. His mind quickly processed the sensation of anger. Raw powerful anger and bottled emotion invaded his senses and forced him to be curious.

'What's your name?'

'Denise,' she replied, and followed it with a well rehearsed smile that she reserved for such occasions.

'I'm Philip.' He held out his hand and she shook it.

She smiled at him as she failed to notice his clammy hand – which was attributable to the fact that she felt very attracted to him and noticed nothing except for his admirable physical features.

'And what do you do for a living, Philip?'

'I own a local pleasure-cruise business. We get one hell of a lot of tourists here.'

'Oh,' she answered thoughtfully, suitably impressed. His appearance was smart but casual and he seemed to exude confidence and composure. She confidently judged his character because she always judged people by what they wore, how they looked and what they did for a living. She had unwittingly acquired a highly developed but almost perfectly useless tool.

'Do you live around here?'

'Yeah, I live in a house down the street, past that bar that we've mentioned and round the corner. It's not far.' He watched her reaction, which appeared to be suitably interested, in that she was looking at him expectantly. 'Would you like to come back for a coffee?' he suggested casually, not sure whether she would readily accept – but he did not reveal his reservation by asking the question obsequiously.

She did not have to think very hard or at length, especially as she was so angry with Allan and his new-found friends. Her intention was to ensure that her fiancé became very jealous and sorry for what he had done – and perhaps jolt him into wanting her back.

'Thanks, I'd like that,' she said immediately. A small voice inside her mind let out a sound of surprise and another voice in her mind asked her what she would do if she had to choose between Allan and Philip.

As she climbed out of the jeep and watched Philip smile at her, she instantly realised that she would choose Philip every time – unless something better came along, which was very unlikely indeed. Allan was a good option while it lasted, but now her mind was already racing with thoughts of what *could* be hers if only she tried. She decided that she would try her best to appear as appealing as possible.

'Do we have to walk past the bar?' she asked.

'Yep.' He looked at her as the rain lashed down on her and forced her hair onto her forehead. She looked stressed and distraught when the wind and rain was making her appear so dishevelled. She tried in vain to keep her hair in some semblance of order amidst the driving rain and gushing wind.

'Shall we go a different way?' he said, 'so you don't have to walk past the bar?'

The wind tussled his short black hair. She noticed that he looked like the type of man who would look totally delectable in anything and in any situation – reminiscent of a model in a catalogue.

'I would prefer going another way, if it isn't too far out of the way. I don't want to run into my fiancé. I want him to realise what he has done. I want to hurt him, I think,' she said, and instantly regretted that she even had a fiancé and regretted that she had mentioned it again to Philip.

'It's not far,' he said, as they walked on briskly to the house that he shared with his mother. His mother had gone to the bar – he had not long ago seen her when he was making his way back there himself from the boathouse – so he knew he had to be quick with Denise. However, unlike all his previous encounters with women, he did intend to have sex with her but, unusually, he did not have the desire to kill her yet. He hoped that he would change his mind soon enough, though.

In the past when he had driven up the coast to Miami and cruised the streets, picking up women who populated the seedy bars, he would drive them individually to a secluded spot and have sex with them. If he did decide to kill them then he would usually strangle them so he could watch the light in their eyes flicker and fade. He always tried but so far had been unsuccessful in reading and feeling his victims final thoughts when they were overrun by sheer terror as they stared wide-eyed back into his unlit eyes.

With Denise he felt a certain companionship; something that he had never felt before. There was an anger and cold calculation about her and this aspect of her persona strangely excited and at the same time unnerved him. To kill Denise would be different, yet highly exciting and a new experience, Philip decided. Anyway, he thought cheerfully, if he decided that he wanted to kill her in the future he could always change his mind – there was nothing that she could do and she posed no threat.

He looked at her face, at her rather stern but nevertheless rather pretty face. He could not see her petite figure beneath the thin waterproof coat that was not affording her much protection from the elements. She was wearing shorts and on her feet were trainers, and he could see that her slender legs were cold.

'We'll get you dry when we get to my house,' he said when he surreptitiously finished studying her.

'Thank you. I'm wet right through,' she said.

He calculated that he had about an hour before Mo returned, so if he did decide to kill Denise he would have to be very quick indeed, which was a shame because he preferred to take his time – and he especially wanted to take his time if he did decide to kill her.

The house was secluded from the street and was located in a small alleyway surrounded by wooden fences and dense bushes. He knew that their approach to the house would not be seen by anyone, and even if a neighbour was looking out of the window, the falling rain was so heavy that it would severely mask his appearance to the point that he would be indistinguishable – if not completely invisible.

The enchanting appearance of the leafy tunnel – that was the alley that lead to the house – caught her attention and she momentarily marvelled and appreciated the beauty, even though the rain saw fit to try and ruin the scene. They passed quickly along the winding garden path and to the back door of the old wooden house that stood sullenly in the failing light of the already dreary day. He opened the heavy wooden door of the house and went inside. She followed him through the doorway that opened into the large kitchen.

A large, old, cast-iron kitchen range occupied the wall under the small window and antique pine cupboards lined the walls. Jars containing pickles, preserves and spices littered every available surface. Above the table that was in the centre of the room hung various pots and pans, suspended on a wooden rack that could be lowered by an adjacent pulley. Although the room looked rather chaotic, and appeared very homely indeed she knew that the kitchen's use was wholly functional. She thought it strange that a man, who presumably lived alone, would have such a kitchen.

'Do you live alone?' she asked curiously.

'No.' He smiled. 'I live with my old mother – she still likes to cook.' He gestured around him at the same time as he filled the kettle with water and placed it on the kitchen range. She relaxed in the knowledge that – even though she found his appearance pleasing and was not at all troubled by Philip – she now had evidence that he was also a kind and obviously a caring man. This just about silenced the small voice in the brightly lit recess of her mind.

'I'll get you somethin' to dry yourself with.'

'Thanks,' she said after him as he left the room. She peeled off her waterproof jacket and hung it on the back of one of the wooden chairs situated under the table in the centre of the room. She wiped her hand along her arm and felt the saturated rainwater slide off her skin. She was cold and she shivered.

'Come through!'

She heard Philip's voice from another room. She walked through the doorway that led to a small passage. The dimly lit passage had a strong smell of flowers and she sniffed appreciatively.

'I'm up here!' he called from further in the house, and she assumed that he was on the next floor of the old house.

She approached the polished wooden stairs that creaked as she ascended them. The rickety banister joined the creaking noise as she held on to it traversing the unsteady flight. As she reached the top of the stairs she saw him move behind the door of a room that joined the landing.

Her heart began beating faster and faster with increasing expectation. What she was intending do was something that she had never done before but she had often thought about it in her dreams. The excitement of the circumstances caused the adrenalin within her to rush her body headlong into the situation, without a thought to the possibility that she may come to harm. She entered the room.

Philip held a towel out in front of her.

'Thanks,' she said softly as she slowly dried her face and studied his features intently.

'You'll probably want to take those wet clothes off,' he said as he stood in front of her.

She hesitated momentarily as she watched his warm smile. She slowly unbuttoned her blouse and let it fall gradually from her shoulders, before unbuttoning her shorts and letting them fall to the floor too.

'I'm cold now.' Denise bit her bottom lip and folded her arms across her chest – now feeling very awkward.

He moved close to her and slowly untangled her arms. He pulled her close to him and kissed her firmly on the lips as he effortlessly lifted her onto the bed. The awkwardness left her as she surrendered herself to him. He dextrously removed her remaining garments before removing his own. He watched her face as he caressed her body; his hands stroking and probing all over her slightly tanned, smooth skin.

A little more than thirty minutes had passed since they had first met and now Allan was but a fading memory in her otherwise occupied mind.

She closed her eyes as she felt Philip's hands caress her. She wrapped her arms around him and intentionally clawed his back as his hands moved to her shoulders and gently stroked her neck.

The tiny voice that had lingered in the depths of her brightly lit mind turned its back and disappeared for ever.

She briefly arched her back, and slowly shook her head with acquiescence.

Chapter Eleven

'Would you like a drink,' Philip asked her.

Denise looked puzzled.

'After that I have a surprise for you,' he offered.

She nodded then, rested her chin on her hands as she looked at him wistfully. He was internally repulsed by her apparent and immediate adoration but he did not show the disgust that bubbled inside him. Wearing only a pair of shorts, he left the room, and descended the stairs and walked into the kitchen.

Had he been in the act of trying to seduce a woman then he would have taken up a bottle of wine. However, she had served her purpose for now and he was left with a feeling of disappointment. Instead he poured her a glass of juice and then went to a cupboard in the pantry. He took down a small bottle that was hidden behind a loose brick and added a few drops of the thick liquid to the glass before quickly returning the small bottle to its hiding place. He then poured himself a glass of juice and ascended the stairs to the bedroom.

She waited for his return as she lay naked on the bed; she was proud of her physique and had no qualms about a relative stranger seeing her thus. When she was with Allan she rarely left herself uncovered, for it was rare that she felt the need to offer an inducement to someone who doted on her already. In her opinion it would only serve to lessen what she saw as her attractiveness to him – after all, familiarity breeds contempt, her mother always told her.

Philip re-entered the room and passed her the glass and he smiled.

She took it from him gently.

'What's this?' she asked, half expecting the drink to be an exotic cocktail. She sipped it.

'Freshly squeezed orange and passion fruit,' he said, omitting to point out that that was what was printed on the carton. 'It's good for you, have some more,' he urged her kindly.

She drank from the glass and he observed her as she drank deeply. He knew from past experience that the drug would not take long to have an effect.

She sighed as she looked at the soft colour of the liquid in the glass.

'I don't know what I'm going to say to Allan,' she confessed matter-of-factly.

'Does it matter?' he replied gruffly. He was annoyed with himself for not ending the life of the naked woman on the bed. Now he was angry with himself and felt a compulsion to arrange an end to her swiftly and cleanly. He had no time to clear up any mess, though, because Mo would return soon, he mused.

She placed the half-empty glass on the table beside her and altered her position to allow him to lay down next to her.

'Are you coming back?' She patted the crumpled sheets close to her.

'In a minute.' He watched her eyelids draw closer together. 'You look tired. Perhaps you should have a sleep first.'

She tried not to yawn.

'I am a bit tired, actually,' she said lazily. 'Perhaps the day has finally caught up with me.' She smiled coyly and set about draining the contents of the glass in small gulps. She eventually finished the drink and placed the glass on the bedside table. 'What's this surprise then?' she asked, expectantly repositioning herself on the bed.

She lay completely horizontally on the bed now, but suddenly her attitude changed completely and she mumbled something incoherently. Her eyelids flickered open and shut before they closed tightly.

'The surprise is that you'll wish that you had never woken up,' he said malevolently. He studied the comatose woman lying on the bed. He had already decided what to do with her and so he quickly gathered the sheet around her and joined the four corners together before heaving the body from the bed. He struggled out of the door with the awkward shape of the sheet containing the woman, carelessly banging her against the stairs and walls of the narrow aperture and staircase. He went into the kitchen and opened the back door slightly, listening intently – the rain was falling heavily and the wind was gusting strongly.

The night had come quickly and there were no extraneous sounds and seemingly no people about. His pick-up truck was parked only a hundred yards away at the end of the alley and so he walked briskly with the body swung over his shoulder.

He arrived at the truck and swung the sheet into the back with a thud. He arranged a sheet of green tarpaulin to cover the body and then climbed quickly into the cabin of the vehicle. He looked about the street to ensure that nobody was looking; he could see nothing moving apart from the falling rain and swaying trees and bushes caught in the gusting wind. Large droplets of water began to explode on the windscreen as they fell from the sky in increasing numbers.

He drove off in the direction of his boathouse, with the intention of tying her up and leaving her in the hold of his boat with the putrefying and decaying body of his previous victim. Keeping two bodies on his premises was not desirable, he mused, but decided that if a woman was stupid enough to trust a complete stranger so implicitly then she must be prepared to take the consequences. He would have preferred to kill Denise swiftly and without a fuss but needs must as the devil drives. She would pay dearly for her mistake, though, he mused gleefully.

He soon arrived at the boathouse and he could not help but notice the tumultuous sea. He regarded the angry spray of the ocean that shot high into the air with an accompanying booming sound when the waves thudded against the concrete jetty. The power of the sea made him wary and he wanted to be away from the area as quickly as possible. He threw back the tarpaulin and heaved the deadweight of the body from the open rear of the vehicle. He had parked adjacent to the entrance to the boathouse, which he unlocked and he went inside.

Once inside, he sniffed the air in case the decaying body in the engine room of the nearby boat was noticeable. There was no smell. He switched on an oil lamp that he had brought with him and he lit the wick before covering the strong flame with the glass cylinder. He placed the body near to the trapdoor that opened on to the boat and then searched the boathouse for a piece of rope and a section of fishing net.

He found a large roll of thick nylon fishing netting and laid it on the floor next to the unconscious woman. He dragged her from the sheet and onto the net, not caring about the fact that her delicate flesh was grazed by the rough concrete. Once he had bound her hands and feet, he tied a rag tightly over her mouth and a knot firmly behind her head before he pulled the corners of the net together tying them securely.

Satisfied that it was securely tightened, he opened the hatch that revealed the moored boat and let down the bundle onto the moving deck of the ageing craft. He too, dropped and balanced himself as the deck undulated with the harbour beneath him. He carefully opened the hatch that led to the engine room of the boat and steeled himself in case the nauseating smell of death threatened to invade his nostrils and make him gag. He discovered that the smell was unpleasant but it was bearable. The sooner he dismembered the body, he mused, the sooner he could be rid of it.

He decided to complete this procedure in front of Denise, when she was awake again and she could silently witness the full horror of the mutilation that he was intending to inflict on her.

He heaved the second and most recent victim enclosed by the nylon net into the hold of the boat. He sadistically let it drop the six feet to the floor of the engine room and heard the sound of bones breaking when she landed. He climbed down into the dim and dank bowel of the small wooden vessel and allowed his eyes to adjust to the gloom. Some light from the oil lamp that was positioned by the hatch in the boathouse above was pouring into the open hatchway of the engine room and he could see the outline of the *human catch*. He found a battery-powered light and turned it on.

He lifted the collected ends of the net onto a hook that was attached to the wooden beam that held up the timber deck of the boat. It was there that he left the second body, gently swinging with the motion of the sea that swelled beneath them. He watched her swaying calmly and peacefully as he heard the waves crashing loudly against the seaward entrance of the boathouse.

He had been so engrossed in his labour that he had not noticed the urgent noise of the boisterous sea. He switched off the battery lamp and quickly climbed from the engine room, padlocked the wooden hatchway on the deck and then ascended the ladder that took him into the boathouse. He made his way from the old building, blowing out the oil lamp flame and then securely padlocking the door behind him.

He paused in the streaming rain, searching the area with his eyes to ensure that he had not been seen. If he had been seen he was seriously considering eliminating any loose ends – however dangerous the proposition. As far as he could determine, though, nobody had seen him. In any case, he considered, the boathouse entrance was not visible from the nearby houses; the boats that were moored in the marina were the only place that the boathouse entrance was visible and nobody was stupid enough to be inside a boat that was being tossed about on the sea like a matchbox in a washing machine.

He climbed into the cab of the pick-up truck and started the engine. He drove into the driving rain and smiled a satisfied smile. He knew that Denise should never be allowed to speak to anyone ever again and so he would have to devise a method of eliminating her without a trace – once he had finished with her. She would have to be sent to Davy Jones's locker, dead or alive and never be allowed to see the sun shine again, never speak to another soul, laugh or smile at anything. Never again, he mused, would she see anything but his boat and what was already inside it.

The latent confidence had been dormant in Allan's mind but it had never managed to surface in his self-conscious youth, and as a consequence had never had a chance to mature in his relationship with Denise.

There obviously was a period between his adolescence and his meeting Denise but this was a desolate period where he was not significantly influenced by another personality. He simply muddled along by drinking, having fun and partying with his colleagues from work – without the need for his confidence to awake. Since his persona had been significantly dominated by Denise it had awoken an inner voice of indignation inside him and now this dominated his personality and was being propelled by an inner sense of renewal. However, although the heavy cobwebs had been dusted from his personality, the discarded old persona of Allan still held a small amount of office in the new and somewhat improved Allan.

The problem was that Denise now represented the cobwebs and dust of the past and now he was desperately trying to be rid of her; to fastidiously keep himself clean, so it seemed to him. It troubled him greatly even to think of the situation that, up until an hour ago, he was part of. He really was eager to dispel the memories of the past even if it meant forsaking the memory of Denise – who he had once loved – and this last fact made him resent her even more.

Tanya considered Allan as she watched him playing pool with Tom; he seemed not to have a care in the world. It was as if he had never known Denise and her disappearance was as inconsequential as a single wave landing on the beach. She had noticed the change in his attitude in the way he actively held himself now; the way he assuredly stood up straight and looked at the person who he was talking to and especially the way he spoke succinctly and saw no reason to explain himself further than his decision.

It seemed to her that he was extremely reluctant to even acknowledge his previous self that Denise was a part of. She wondered if the cannabis cake had anything to do with the situation reaching crisis point, but she quickly and self-assuredly reasoned that the cake could not have been the sole cause and should not be attributed to what had already developed between Allan and Denise – albeit as it was in a previously dormant state. Perhaps the alcohol and cannabis could have accelerated matters, she concluded, but she was not sure if she should feel a small amount of regret because of this.

She resolutely absolved herself of any lingering guilt and her doubts were banished when she acknowledged that she felt no regret. Denise's disappearance was another matter, though, and she would not want any harm to come to anyone – even people she did not care much for.

'He seems happy enough,' Christine said quietly to Tanya as she followed her thoughtful gaze. 'Do you think he's putting on a brave face?'

'No,' she replied definitely. After a reasonable pause she continued, 'I honestly don't think that he gives a shit. I must admit, though, however much I dislike her I am concerned about where she's got to. I mean, where could she have gone? It's probably real dangerous out there now, you know with the wind blowing objects around and the sea probably crashing ashore where she could be walking. As well as all that, the rain is so heavy she could lose her way if she has stupidly gone for a walk.'

Christine shrugged her shoulders.

'I have no idea – but it is worrying.' She began wiping the surface of the bar with a cloth. She had the habit of wiping away any liquid rings left on the bar by the customers' drink glasses – with the fastidiousness of a house-proud mother. The irony of this was that, although the bar was pristine, her room was a mess of clothes and books, and she also had a tendency to forgetfulness that almost contradicted her apparent fastidiousness in the bar department.

'From what you've been saying she sounds like the type of person who sulks. Perhaps she's sheltering from the rain somewhere and she's just making him sweat – just like Allan said she was. After all, he knows her better than any of us.'

'All the same, I can't help feeling a little concerned,' she persisted, wondering perhaps, if deep inside she did feel a small amount of guilt. 'When did Jim say he would be back?'

Christine remembered seeing the figure in the rear garden and how relieved she was to see Jim when he had called in earlier. She had told him what she had seen and explained why she felt the need to have the gun, which she had left in a drawer under the bar now so that it would be at hand in case she needed it. Jim had left shortly before the three guests had arrived.

'He should be back real soon.' She looked thoughtful, 'Where are you staying? Have you got somewhere yet?'

'Well, Uncle Jim has got an apartment. We were going to stay there.'

'Oh.' She looked initial disappointed. 'I was going to suggest that you stay here. Never mind.' She smiled, already feeling very comfortable in Tanya's company and relishing the companionship and security of them all being in the bar.

Tanya noticed her disappointment.

'We can stay here for a few nights if you like, or until the storm passes and the tourists come back.'

'I didn't mean to sound so pitiful.' She contemplated. 'I mean, I am all right on my own but I would like the company.' She pondered her recent troubles and fears. 'You see, I was due to have dinner tonight with this man.'

'Oh yes.' Tanya became intrigued and leant on the bar. 'Come on then, tell me more. Who is he?'

'He's this local man, Philip.' She sighed. She noticed Tanya's empty glass and took it up in her hand and turned to face the optics. She was about to continue explaining. Suddenly, when she turned away, the door of the bar swung open and the wind rushed in, accompanied by a torrent of rain. All the occupants of the bar looked up and expected Denise to be entering the bar with a face like thunder.

'Mo?' Christine exclaimed, 'What are you doin' out in this weather now?'

She scoffed. 'I was bored,' she lied, as she firmly closed the door. 'I wanted company.' She looked at the two men playing pool and then at Tanya seated at the bar. She cleared her throat gently as she slowly approached the bar and raised a gnarled cupped hand to her mouth, stifling a sudden heavy and guttural cough.

To Tanya she said, 'And what brings you here? Not the weather.'

Christine gave the old woman a look of concern as she stood in front of the bar, but Mo just gestured impatiently for a drink.

'No, we came to see my uncle. He owns the gallery and studio down the street. Jim's his name. Do you know him?' She studied the wrinkled and gnarled face of the old woman who resembled a small wizened character from a seminal science fiction film. Her eyes were bright though, and her expression firm and confident. In many ways she also resembled an old bonsai tree, obliviously bothered by the ravaging effects of time.

Mo looked thoughtful as she paused.

'I know Jim all right,' she said slowly. 'He's the one that thinks he's a comedian – always poking fun at me he is. I hope *you* are more respectful of your elders.' Her gaze bore straight through her as she shuffled closer.

'Pleased to meet you,' Tanya said.

Mo looked at Tanya's extended hand as she offered it for her to shake. She looked again into Tanya's deep brown eyes and smiled warmly, revealing very few old teeth indeed. However, she chose to ignore the gesture of Tanya's extended hand.

'Hold my hand while I climb onto this stool,' she commanded. Her initial impression of Tanya was that she was kind, warm and sharply intelligent. She knew that her expressive blue eyes were honest and without prejudice – unlike Jim's almost flippant demeanour.

It was obvious to Tanya that assisting the old woman onto the stool was more practical than shaking hands in a meaningless greeting. She steadied Mo's arm as the old woman helped steady her small frame onto a large stool that had small wooden arms and an inadequate amount of back support. She intelligently guessed that Mo would not tolerate any inkling of patronising and she reasoned that the old woman was undoubtedly very strong in mind despite her apparently frail appearance, and so she did not persist or think any less of her for not shaking her hand. She actually admired her apparent single-mindedness.

'Mo, you haven't said why you've braved this foul weather,' Christine persisted with daughterly concern.

She took a sip from her glass.

'I came to make sure that you were all right, dear. *Are* you all right?'

'Well, I should ask you the same, but yes I am. Why shouldn't I be?'

'I don't know,' she replied. 'I just couldn't settle. I thought that something wasn't quite right. I can usually be more specific but today it's different.' She sighed.

'And you thought that it was me?' she remarked almost scornfully.

'No, you misunderstand dear. I thought that you were in danger but I can see that you are all right. You've got these people about you.'

Christine looked bemused. She thought again about the figure that she had seen earlier in the garden. She was almost certain that she had seen Philip but she could not be one hundred per cent certain – that was why she decided not to tell Mo. Besides, what could Mo do about it? She decided, once again that the best course of action was to cause the old woman as little stress as possible.

'There is something isn't there,' she said, as she scrutinised Christine's thoughtful expression.

She looked surprised and she felt somewhat awkward.

'Well yes.' She recovered her thoughts, 'I was just thinking whether you came here out of sheer determination or recklessness,' she said, as she lowered her head and studied the weathered old woman, smiling at her own audaciousness.

Mo did not look convinced but she did not take offence either.

'And what else were you thinking about? Have you seen Philip today? Now tell me the truth please – I have seen that expression of yours before.'

She resignedly explained to Mo that she thought she had seen someone lurking in the garden at the back of the house.

'Do you know who it was?' Mo enquired.

'No,' she answered uncertainly.

Mo raised her eyebrows quizzically.

'Well, you do have an idea though, don't you?'

She paused, wondering whether to say anything more to her.

'I think it was Philip but I couldn't see properly. The clothes were the same as his and I think that he was quite tall. I can't be sure. Anyway, there's no harm done,' she said, in an attempt to disarm the situation with a flurry of words.

Her words did nothing but enhance Mo's curiosity and concern.

'If it was him then he had no business frightening a woman on her own,' she said angrily. She made as if to leave her stool and return to the elements.

Tanya listened with surprise and immediately wondered if this Philip character was the same local man that Christine had mentioned earlier and she wondered what he could possibly be doing to create such suspicion. She did not entirely believe that Mo had anything specific to divulge but she definitely had something else to say on the matter – which she was withholding.

'Will you stay for a while?' she said to Mo. 'You can't leave in this weather. Look, I think it's still getting worse.'

Mo thought about the situation and the fact that, in this weather, she would not be able to find Philip if he was not in the house. Besides, she concluded, the prospect was too dangerous. She eventually smiled.

'I think I'm going to like you,' she said. 'Thank you.'

Laughter erupted from the vicinity of the pool table, causing the three women to look at the two men.

'Are those two with you?' Mo asked Tanya.

'Yes.' She laughed. 'The one with the longer hair is with me, and the other is a sort of friend of ours. He's an Englishman, here on his vacation with his fiancée.'

'I see,' Mo said, as she slowly turned her head and scanned the bar area. 'And where is she then?'

'We don't know.' Tanya and Christine replied in unison.

'Did she come with you?' she asked incredulously.

'She did *come* with us but we left her in the car while we ran through the rain to see if this bar was open. When Allan went back to the car to get her she was gone. My Uncle Jim left a note for us at the gallery telling us to meet him here, you see.' Tanya looked somewhat surprised. 'Actually, he has been gone a long time. He should be back soon.'

'Jim's on his way,' Mo interjected, 'I think I saw him heading towards his gallery not long ago,' she said slowly and deliberately. 'He called out to me and said he would be here soon. There was something he had to do before he came here – said that he had something for you.'

'Oh,' Tanya said thoughtfully, wondering why Mo had not mentioned this fact already. She certainly did not give anything away this old woman, she smiled to herself. She decided that Jim probably had a painting for her mother. He was her mother's brother and family members do sometimes give gifts to their families if they have not seen them for a long while – as a sort of peace offering.

Tanya could remember looking at her uncle's paintings when she had been very young. In fact, his paintings formed her earliest recollectable memories: she distinctly remembered a painting of a boat being thrown across the peaks of a raging sea and ever since then the sight of an angry sea had chilled her heart. She involuntarily shivered at the thought, as a familiar feeling of dread – quickly and with only a small amount of provocation – flooded into her consciousness, then, as quickly as it had come, it drifted swiftly and calmly away into the deep open ocean of her mind.

She broke from her deep thoughts and was confronted by the wrinkled aged face of old Mo studying her intently.

Mo nodded her head slowly and smiled at her knowingly.

'You feel it too, don't you, dear?' she said rhetorically.

Tanya did not know what the old woman was talking about, because the feeling of dread had surfaced and sunk so quickly that she barely had time to register it.

'*Feel what?*' she practically challenged the old woman.

'Something powerful; something dramatic is afoot!' She ignored the fact that, for an instant, Tanya sounded like Jim, 'Have you seen the sea? It's angry. Have you seen the sky? It's a portent of doom. Not for us, perhaps, no, but all is not right with this place. Something is afoot,' she assured her quietly.

Not even Christine heard what the old woman said.

'What shall we do then?'

Tanya was a pragmatic person, even if confronted by something as strange as offered by the wizened and baffling old woman who stood before her. Many people would have made attempts to hurry the conversation along so that they could get away from the woman. Tanya, though, was a deeply thoughtful person and was willing to hear what she had to say. It did seem possible to her that the old woman was slightly mad but she was sufficiently interested in her to continue the conversation so that she could try to fathom the old woman's apparent rambling.

Mo laughed, almost cackled.

'There's nothing we can do yet, dear. We must all wait and see what is coming. When it *does* finally come we must approach it with care, and strength and take leave of our emotions. We must do what is practical – not that, if you like, which is deemed morally correct.'

'How do you know this?' Tanya replied with a smile. Her mind was now balanced in favour of the old woman being slightly mad.

'I don't know for sure.' Mo pondered. 'I just feel; I can feel the weather, the sea and the atmosphere all around but I cannot be more specific. I can apply my feelings to my knowledge of the world and its people but I cannot receive clear and defined answers – they must be interpreted.'

'Mo's a mystic,' Christine interrupted, catching the tail end of her pronouncement. She had approached their end of the bar and was leaning on the counter and had been listening since Mo had cackled. 'She can read your cards, tea leaves and palm for you, can't you Mo?' she smiled.

'Would you?' Tanya asked her. She was not a cynic on this matter but she was not of the ilk who strongly believed in mysticism either, yet she was interested in the subject and she intended to listen with an open mind. She believed that religion and mysticism both had some substance, but that the actual truth was something far beyond normal human comprehension. What people said and believed on these matters – in her opinion – was only the interpretation of a comparatively ancient and primitive race of beings who, in all probability, had naïve, simple and fanciful reasoning for everything from thunder and lightening to why people die of old age.

With the knowledge that had been afforded to her by modern science and tangible facts printed in books by scholars, she enjoyed scratching the surface of these mystical matters. She could assess their credence and marvel at how blind faith and fear had allowed the beliefs to survive for centuries. However, she did not dismiss them out-of-hand and knew that if she did break the surface, she would only make a small scratch and could one day be overwhelmed by her discovery. However far-fetched this notion seemed, the possibility still intrigued her.

She understood that the human mind was not capable of removing the veneer from the 'table of truth', and that having faith alone was an unreasonable, unjustifiable and impractical assumption anyway. To some people, it seemed, the capacity of faith was a necessary distraction from the possibility that life was indeed without a higher purpose – some people needed that crutch to remain sane when all around them there was madness, chaos, death and suffering.

She was content with the knowledge that life was meant to be a fulfilling and worthwhile experience, so that nothing or no one person could say, after her life had ended, that it had been worthless or wasted. For instance, if she went on a vacation she always enjoyed it right up to the last minute and appreciated the fact that one day she would leave and perhaps never return to the place she had visited. She did not become down and despondent when she neared the end of the vacation but instead, ensured that she did the opposite – and neither did she spend each day thanking the tour operator for arranging the vacation.

Tanya felt the bones of Mo's hand firmly twist her palm to face the ceiling. She looked down and expected to see that her hand was in the grip of the cold bones of a walking skeleton. Mo spoke the usual patter concerning her lifeline and how many children she would have and Tanya listened kindly.

Christine watched, listening to Mo's familiar phrases that she reserved for her readings.

Tom and Allan continued drinking and playing pool. However, Tom noticed the curious huddle of the two young women and the old woman who was perched on top of the stool.

'What 'cha doin'?' he called out.

Tanya turned her head and called out to her partner.

'Mo here is reading my palm. Would you like her to read yours?'

'No thanks.' He dismissed it with disinterest and instead, immediately positioned himself to take his next shot.

Tom, like Tanya, was sceptical when it came to the matter of mysticism and religion – but to a even higher degree. However, unlike Tanya he was not willing to give the subject any credence, despite his usual tendency to carefully consider anything that he heard from others or read in books – and he did read voraciously.

If he did elaborate on the matter of religion or mysticism he would usually be forced to say, 'I know all about it and I have made my decision – now piss off.'

His opinions had been formed in his youth and were partly due to the fact that his parents had been devoutly religious and had forced him to attend church school on Sundays. He had learnt all the parables that school children are taught and he attended Sunday school weekly, but as soon as his parents divorced, the hypocrisy was exposed and he never attended the church again. He believed that being seen to do the 'right thing' was not conducive to being a Christian. As far as he concerned, religion was a farce and had little to do with his belief in God.

When confronted by mysticism of any kind he could not help but be cynical, especially towards people who charged money to others who wanted access to their, 'mystic powers'. In his eyes, there was no tangible evidence to prove anything from Stigmata to Spontaneous Human Combustion, apart from scientific evidence that conclusively disproved it. As for crystal balls and palm readings, he perceived these to be as specific as tabloid astrology.

'Would Mo read my palm for me?' Allan called out, as he carelessly chalked the end of his cue, managing instead mostly to chalk the palm of his hand. Credence was not a concern in his current state of mind but passing the time in an alternative and entertaining way was always a worthy consideration for him.

'In a minute. Wait until Mo has finished reading Tanya's palm. I'll holler.' Christine smiled.

'What d'ya want that nonsense done for?' Tom laughed disparagingly, as he paused from taking his shot.

'Shhh, she'll hear and turn you into a frog or somethin'.' He laughed. 'Well, it's a laugh isn't it?' he finished drunkenly. They were both drunk.

Tom raised his eyes and slowly shook his head. His expression broke into a smile and he played his shot. The balls cracked together with a flurry of clean-sounding clicks, that mixed in the air with the sound of Mo's slow and deliberate soft voice.

Outside the wind pushed and pulled the windows in their frames, causing them to gently rattle rhythmically in their wooden supports. The rain persisted and fell heavily against the large windows, creating a distorted view of the outside world. It had been falling so continuously that the noise was no longer noticed as anything other than a background noise by the occupants of the bar – like when one is drifting off to sleep on a tourist-filled beach and the sound of a jet ski can be heard powering along the shoreline, it soon becomes unnoticeable and drifts into the background noise of voices and the waves crashing on the beach.

Allan sat down heavily on a chair and let out a long sigh. He smiled and leant back against the wall, lifting the front legs of the chair dangerously off the ground, and steadying himself on the wooden floor with the cue.

'Aren't you worried 'bout Denise?' Tom said, as he noticed his somewhat lackadaisical demeanour.

'Who?'

'Man, you're leathered. When you're sober you won't be talking like that.' Tom snorted.

'We'll see,' he answered nonchalantly. He stood up slowly to take his shot and potted the black ball surprisingly adroitly. 'Your round, Tom.' He beamed.

'Allan?' Tanya called out, 'you still want your palm read?'

'Coming,' he replied, as he unsteadily made his way over to the bar where the three women were watching him approach.

'You worried about Denise?' Tanya asked, as she looked intently at his expression.

He swayed slightly as he stood next to her.

'Who?' he said reticently.

'You'll be sorry you thought this way when you're sober,' Christine offered.

'That's what Tom said.' He smiled. 'I'll cross that bridge when I come to it. Now, about my palm…' He held out his hand and smiled broadly.

Mo looked at him, at his tall and upright stature, and his almost athletic frame and could not help but notice his very amiable disposition.

'Your name is Allan, am I right?' she said, when she took his hand abruptly, studying it intently.

'She's good,' he mumbled with surprise, as he tried to maintain a straight face.

Mo ignored him because she could smell alcohol on his breath.

'I sense that you are a *new* person.'

'I'm twenty-eight years old.'

'That's not what I meant,' she said tiredly into his palm. 'You've undergone a change recently. You've come to a crossroads in your life and chosen a route that has changed everything about you. You are now on the road that is true – but not necessarily the easiest road to travel.'

He looked thoughtful, as did Tanya. Although she did not know Allan at all well, she related what Mo had said with what she already knew of Allan's relationship with Denise and his recent drunken rejection of her. Although Mo had been specific in Allan's case, she concluded that she could have picked up on what she had been saying about him earlier.

Tom approached the bar and Christine attended to his order. He listened to what Mo was saying to Allan and observed Tanya listening intently.

'The old woman is a bit of a character,' he said to Christine.

She looked at Tom and smiled.

'She sure is. I've known her nearly all my life and she always seems to have been as old and idiosyncratic as she is now.'

'And she lives 'round here?'

'Oh yes. She lives with her son, Philip,' she explained.

He studied Christine's face as she concentrated on pouring the pint of beer. He appreciated her soft and shiny, long dark hair that looked as soft and flowing as gently running water; he admired her delicate features and he smiled inwardly at her musical Irish lilt. To Tom, who was never a bad judge of character, or so he believed, she seemed reserved yet had an obviously hidden potential for passion. She was beautiful without being overtly or ostentatiously attractive – the sort of person, perhaps, who would go unnoticed in a crowd of faces yet would be the most attractive person in that crowd.

She seemed to Tom to be a closed book of wonderful and magical delights and he could only imagine how she read. That too was part of her mystery: the fact that she had the attractive demeanour and an infectious presence – the type of person who is always pleasant to be in the relaxed company of – yet she was not intentionally or conspicuously flirtatious, false, shallow or manipulative.

His eyes focused on her downward-concentrating dark brown eyes. The softness and contrast of the pupils with the remainder of her eyes was as delectable as the sight of the head and body of the pint of stout that she was pouring, he considered.

She finished pouring and looked up, noticing Tom's intense gaze and blushing ever so slightly.

'Sorry,' he said honestly as he noticed her embarrassment. 'I wasn't staring at you. I was admiring your eyes.' He laughed as she now looked decidedly uncomfortable. 'I apologise again, Christine. What I mean is – and I'm not coming on to you – it's a compliment,' he said in normal conversational tone.

At the sound of voices Tanya looked up and looked at Tom. He felt his partner's gaze and decided that it was best to involve her in the conversation because he had nothing to hide.

'Tan, wouldn't you say that Christine has the clearest eyes you have ever seen?'

Tanya frowned and Christine squirmed even more, not wanting Tanya to think that she was flirting with Tom because she most definitely was not.

'She caught me looking at her eyes and so I had to explain,' he reasoned.

Tanya laughed.

'Don't mind him, Christine. He's not trying to come on to you. It's just that, well, he embarrasses people without thinking sometimes.' She looked directly at him. 'Tom, leave the poor girl alone and stop embarrassing her,' she finished firmly, resolutely believing what he had said because he would often embarrass people without knowing that he had – so great was his confidence.

He took the drinks in his hands.

'Christine, you are almost as beautiful as Tanya.' He smiled.

'That's better, Tom.' She laughed, 'Christine, just hit him next time he embarrasses you. Hey,' a thought bit her lips, 'he just paid a back-handed compliment to you.' She continued to smile. 'Why don't you hit him now?'

She smiled, relieved that Tom was not making matters awkward and that Tanya bore no malice towards her.

'If he does it again I'll tell you, and *you* can hit him.'

'Thanks. I'll look forward to that.' Tanya punched the top of his arm playfully, forcing him to quickly compensate by extending his arm in various directions and thereby causing a little of the contents to spill from a glass. 'What's going on here then?' he said, as he eventually passed Allan his umpteenth pint.

'Well,' he said, with a slur and drooping eyelids. He swayed on the stool and quickly steadied himself with his hand on the bar as he turned to face Tom and took the glass from him. 'Mo here reckons that my lifeline is broken.' He stabbed at the palm of his hand with his finger. 'It starts here and then stops,' he explained, as he turned to Mo – who was still studying his palm intently – and said, with considerable familiarity for one not well acquainted, 'What does that mean again, Mo?'

She sighed and looked at him uncertainly.

'Sometime in your life you will reach a point which will determine whether you live or die. I don't know when, and I don't know how. I just know that you must stay on the path of truth; the path that is true to you.'

'Providing there's no interference from Beelzebub, I should have three kids, a marriage and a successful career.' He beamed drunkenly.

'That's all right then.' Tom clapped him firmly on the back, momentarily threatening to knock him from his stool.

It was then that the group looked up as they heard the door of the bar open. The wind rushed in and deposited a large amount of rainwater on the floor by the door. The figure – dressed in a large, yellow waterproof jacket with a hood covering the face – shut the door firmly and looked towards the three women at the bar. The face of the wearer was enshrouded in shadow, as the lights flickered and then went out for the second time that day, depositing a gloomy light in the late afternoon of the bar.

Christine involuntarily inhaled sharply and her heart pounded against her ribs as she remembered the figure in the garden wearing seemingly, the same yellow-coloured waterproof.

Tanya tried to make out the face under the hood and Allan reeled across the bar, his balance losing out to the limited amount of light now occupying the room.

'Hey!' the figure exclaimed, 'is that you, Tanya?'

Christine let out a sigh of relief.

'Jim, you scared me.'

'It's me, Uncle Jim.' Tanya jumped down from her stool and ran across the room and hugged him, dropping at least a decade from her age in a single moment. She kissed him on the cheek and hugged him warmly.

Jim approached the bar with Tanya holding his arm tightly. She introduced Tom and Allan.

'And Tom's the man with you, right?'

'Sure am.' Tom shook Jim's hand firmly. 'Pleased to meet you, Jim. It sounds like a cliché but I have heard a lot about you.' He smiled easily.

'And I've heard about you too, from my sister. She says that you're *the one*.'

He laughed at the slight embarrassment caused by family members fishing for information.

'Perhaps,' he said coyly and winked at Tanya.

Jim read the situation and their apparent reluctance to divulge any further information concerning their current personal or intended status. He fully understood their wishes, in case they enquired about his personal affairs. The decades had passed and moulded him into a very private person, especially when it came to talking to members of his family.

His initial impression of Tom – for this was the first time that they had met – was a police officer's opinion; he did not much like the young man's long hair or the goatee beard. However, he was intelligent enough – and not yet too old and set in his ways – to put appearances aside.

Tom redeemed his appearance by providing a firm handshake and a respectful look in the eye, but not a stare that displayed a personality too eager to please. His voice was not too loud and he did not seem to feel awkward in the presence of an ex-police officer – as some people that he met often did. Overall, he was pleased with Tanya's choice.

Jim turned to Allan, who was engrossed in Mo's words. Neither Mo nor Allan had broken their conversation to talk to him: which he had expected from Mo but not the stranger. This act of accidental impoliteness in Jim's eyes instantly set Allan on the wrong path.

'So who's this guy then?' he said ambivalently, as he nodded at Allan.

'Allan's on his vacation. He's from London, England, and he's a bit drunk. His fiancée left him only a few hours ago. In fact, no one knows where she is,' Tanya offered with concern.

'What? And she came here with you two and him?' He nodded at Allan again. 'How can you lose someone like that?' He snorted.

'That's right,' Tom said, noticing that Jim seemed somewhat annoyed by the fact that Allan had not yet introduced himself. 'Hey Al, come and meet Tanya's uncle, will ya?'

Mo eventually turned to face the three of them and addressed Jim, 'I have finished now.'

Allan approached Jim.

'Hello, I'm Allan.' He swayed uncertainly. He shot out his arm and shook Jim's hand too eagerly. 'Where are my manners?' He laughed. 'I must apologise again, I seem to have had too much to drink,' he confessed loudly.

'I can see that.' He smiled thinly at the man before him who appeared to be an open book, in which he instantly read no danger or intent. 'But then you've had a busy day, young man.' He entered easily into police officer mode. 'I understand that you've lost your fiancée?'

Allan paused uncertainly before he found the solid surface of the bar to hold on to, then he laughed openly.

'That's right, she's disappeared! Hopefully she's been blown away by the wind or washed out to sea,' he added distantly, before taking another drink from his glass.

'Oh Allan,' Christine interjected with continued disappointment, 'you're beginning to upset me now. How can you say something like that?'

Tanya nodded and Tom started to say something in reply.

'Easy,' he slurred firmly, 'you may think that I'm just saying that because I'm drunk but I'm saying it *because* I am drunk.'

The four of them looked as puzzled as each other.

'What he means is, you think that he's making a mistake saying these things about her but he's saying these things because they are the truth and the alcohol is allowing him to speak the truth: his inhibitions have been dulled and he speaks the truth,' Mo confidently offered. Without waiting for affirmation from Allan she returned her glass to her lips and silently looked out of the window.

Jim sighed and shook his head.

'I don't think so, Mo. Besides, you hardly even know the man.'

'Maybe not, but she's right.' Allan smiled. 'I don't give a toss where Denise is.'

'So you won't help us to look for her then?' Tanya pinned the question on him, evidently preparing for a confrontation with his heartless reasoning. She believed that he still had a certain amount of responsibility, whatever his feelings.

'I'll come with you to help you look for her,' he replied certainly.

'Good.'

'So that when we find her I can give her a piece of my mind for behaving like a child,' he uttered with contempt.

The day had rapidly progressed into dusk and the light in the bar was now very low indeed, especially as the power cut had descended again.

'It's getting very dark in here,' Jim commented.

'You'd better get some candles ready before it becomes *too* dark,' Mo suggested.

Christine was already searching under the bar.

'I don't think I've got any.' She checked the drawers under the counter. She found an empty box of candles and the heavy revolver, but nothing else. Apart from the fact that she was often quite untidy she was also somewhat forgetful when it came to domestic matters. 'Nope. It seems that I forgot to stock up on candles.'

'Well, rather than sit here in the dark, I propose that we wait at my house,' Mo offered.

'We could do. Actually, we could split up on our way there,' Jim said, looking warily at the darkening sky and observing the relentless rain. 'I have seen it worse than today and the wind has dropped quite a bit. Why don't Tom, Tanya and I check the car and Duval Street whilst Christine and Allan take Mo home – if you're up to a walk, that is.' He looked directly at Allan. 'Perhaps Mo'll give you some strong coffee.'

'Of course I'm up to it,' he replied scornfully, desperately trying to disguise the effects of the alcohol by trying to speak clearly and stand up straight. However, he swayed slightly and his speech was too precisely pronounced to be natural. At least he was trying.

'Jim, will you come to Mo's when you've looked around?' Christine suggested. 'Is that all right, Mo?'

She smiled and nodded.

Jim looked at Allan and nodded with carefully considered agreement.

'Don't come looking for us if you find her. We'll all meet at Mo's just as soon as we can,' he said. 'I'll leave a note taped to the inside of the window on the door here,' he pointed to the front door of the bar, 'so if she comes this way then she'll know where we are.'

'Come around the back of the house when you arrive, then,' Mo explained. 'I'll have a hot drink ready to warm you up.'

Christine gathered her keys together and they each prepared to venture out into the rain. She disappeared for a few minutes and conveniently returned with a cagoule each for Tom, Tanya and Allan.

'I seem to collect the things that people leave in the bar in case they ever come back for them,' she explained as she passed a garment to each of them. 'It may be a bit big, Tanya, but at least it should keep most of you dry.'

Tanya watched her arms fail to reach the end of the sleeves. She smiled in agreement and each of them thanked Christine for her thoughtfulness.

Once Jim had taped the note to the inside of the door so that it was clearly visible from outside, one by one they forced themselves out of the door and into the rain. Outside, the wind was billowing strongly, pushing the heavy drops of rain firmly into their faces and creating a loud constant pitter-patter as the torrent of water struck their waterproof clothing.

'See you all a bit later – and be careful,' Jim said, as they parted company.

Allan silently followed Mo and Christine.

'You all right, Allan?' Christine asked him, as she turned her head. The sidewalk was not wide enough to accommodate all three of them in a line.

'Oh yes,' he said confidently, with the accompanying feeling that the fresh air had made him slightly more alert. It was as if the wind and heavy rain were expelling the effects of alcohol through sheer force, partly because the strength of the elements was awakeningly powerful.

'We'll check the car first,' Tom said loudly, forcing the level of his voice above the sound of the wind that was trying to blow his words into the distance. 'And then what?'

There was a pause as Jim and Tanya mulled over the question.

'I suppose we can have a quick look up the street to see if we can see this wayward Limey, stop off briefly at my studio and cut round the back streets to Mo's. Apart from that, there's not much we can do till tomorrow,' Jim offered.

'I wish we could do more,' she said.

'Jim's right, Tan,' Tom replied. 'We can only do our best. Anyway, perhaps Al and Christine have already found her.'

'Well, she's not in the car,' Tanya said, as she peered through the window of the jeep. She opened the door and checked inside the vehicle just to satisfy her own thorough mind. She was always the type of person who checked thoroughly and followed procedures fully so that she could be certain and not allow her mind to suggest 'what if's'. In her opinion, her present was too precious to allow her own past to interfere – which had already had its time and should not be allowed to intrude again.

'C'mon,' Jim said. 'Let's go check my studio and then head off to Mo's. I had a painting ready for you to give to your mother. I'll give it to you before you go, because the rain might ruin it if I bring it outside now.'

She smiled appreciatively at how safe and predictable her uncle was.

He set off at a fast pace, leaving Tom and Tanya having to catch up to him (once she had locked the jeep) and so she did not have time to question him on his life in Key West. The other matters of the present were also so pressing that it seemed to her to be rather inappropriate, for now.

Jim opened the door and, followed by his niece and her partner, went inside his shop.

'What else have you got to check on?' she asked, as she removed her hood and wiped the rainwater from her face.

He walked into the back room.

'I was arranging to meet someone here tonight,' he confided when Tanya and Tom stood next to him in the kitchen. 'But I suppose he decided not to venture out in this weather.'

'I think you're right,' Tom said. 'Local is he?'

Jim nodded.

'Well, I expect that you'll catch up with him tomorrow.'

'Right.' He smiled. 'Let's go to old Mo's.' He held up his hands and said her name in a deridingly ghoulish manner.

'She does seem to be a bit mad,' Tom suggested.

'No, maybe not. She seems rather eccentric,' she added as they approached the front door of the shop. They pulled their respective hoods onto their heads, 'I think that she's interesting. It's unfair to say that she's mad.'

'Okay Tanya, *you* spend day after day talking to her and then tell me that she's not mad,' Jim said wearily. 'After a while she really warms up and positively gets under my skin. I'm telling you, she is quite off her trolley.'

'Wait until we see her in her own environment,' Tom suggested. 'Then we can see who is right. People feel more confident in their own environment and their true nature becomes more apparent,' he explained to anyone who was listening.

Jim opened the door and the warm wind rushed in. The street was in darkness, except for the candle and battery lights, afforded by those living in rooms behind the windows of houses and shops that lined the narrow street. He shut the door after his two companions and locked it securely before he led them through the back streets to Mo's house.

The streets were deserted, except for the mournful howl of the strengthening wind; the abundance of rain and the multitude of leaves; small branches and litter flying through the shadows and dancing to the tune of the storm as it played with increasing vigour. The trio did not meet a single person on their short journey – not even a slowly passing car or a cowering feline.

'Let's check Sloppy Joe's bar first, in case she's waiting in there,' Jim suggested.

Tanya was hopeful that Denise would be in there, because she could imagine that Denise would insist that she had been in here all the while and would then claim that she did not see them enter Christine's bar.

The three of them continued walking through the sodden streets until they eventually went through a tree-lined courtyard. They passed through this feature consisting of interesting wooden premises and trees, and then onto Duval Street itself. From there they walked across the street to the corner of a junction where Sloppy Joe's is situated. The lights from within failed to shine through the shuttered windows. However, Jim firmly tried the closed door and it opened easily. The three of them quickly walked in and immediately shut out the wind that tugged forcefully at the door in its frame.

'Evening folks.' A young barman smiled as he placed three bar mats on the bar, 'What'll it be?'

The bar was full of people: almost every table was taken and standing people lined the fringes of the room. A myriad of candles of different shapes, sizes and colours were situated on all these tables, casting shifting shadows all across the large room and creating a veritable silhouette of the guitarist and singer, who were performing on the small stage. Almost all the patrons were animated by laughter and listening intently to the witty songs.

Tom turned about his person and looked at the occupants of the room in disbelief. The barman instantly noticed.

'It's a weather party,' he explained. Tom looked puzzled and smiled uncertainly at the happy barman, who was dressed in shorts and a T-shirt and smiling. Tom did not have to say anything however, to make the barman explain further, as the meaning of the party was clear.

'When the weather is real bad we all have a party. There's a big cellar in the basement and so this is one of the safest places in case it gets real hairy.' The barman laughed unnecessarily and too loudly.

Tom nodded his reluctant approval of the idea and smiled at the barman's need to explain to the three of them – without pointing out the real and obvious fact that most of people in the bar were quite concerned about the storm and the fact that having a few alcoholic drinks took their minds off it.

'Have you seen a young English woman in here today?' Jim asked.

Tanya explained what Denise was wearing to the man to assist him, in case a bus full of young English women had passed through Sloppy Joe's that day.

'No, I haven't seen her. Hang on, I'll ask the others.' He disappeared to ask his fellow bar staff.

'This is a great idea,' Tom said to them both as he continued to look about him. 'If we find her then we should all come in here. Al would love it in here.'

The barman returned. 'Sorry, there've been no English women in here today, or anyone matching the description you gave me.' He smiled intently at Tanya.

'Thanks anyway.' Jim sighed. 'We have to be goin'. If she does come in here then direct her to Mo's. No, wait a minute, you tell her to stay here and you send someone to get me,' he said seriously.

'Okay, Jim,' the man said assuredly, pleased that he had been entrusted with such an important responsibility.

They left the bar – Tom reluctantly – and crossed the street again and walked down the small alley that led to the rear of Mo's shop.

'I thought that we were going to find her in there: all prim and proper – as she sometimes is – standing at the bar and complaining that she doesn't like going to bars on her own,' Tom remarked.

'I thought she would be in there too.'

'Well, perhaps the others have had more luck,' Jim offered, quickly and easily having resumed the authoritative role of a police sergeant.

The alley at the rear of Mo's was darker than the street and the sound of the squelching mud from the unkempt path echoed off the sides of the buildings and dense foliage that lined their way. The rain had abated somewhat but the wind was being channelled through the alley quite forcefully and it ruffled their hair in each and every direction – like a rough invisible hand.

'Here we are,' Jim said, as he pushed open a low wooden gate. The light from the kitchen window illuminated the neatly kept garden and the path to the door.

'This is nice,' Tanya exclaimed. 'It's just how I imagined it, like a secret garden – enchanted almost.'

Tom laughed. 'Okay Tan – looks like a garden for the terminally insane. I expect that there is a statue made from the baked entrails of cat behind the bushes.'

Jim laughed.

'Shhh,' Tanya hissed suddenly. 'Mo'll hear you,' she whispered angrily. She was not amused at the two of them ridiculing the old woman.

It did not take long for Christine, Mo and Allan to return to the shop, despite the fact that they had to detour widely around puddles – that they had no idea of the depth of – that spanned the width of the road and reached the uneven curbs, in spite of the deep camber of the road. The puddles were indeed more like lakes and interconnected temporary waterways.

The rain started to fall in large droplets that exploded around them.

'Here it comes again,' Allan said as he noticed the preceding large droplets that – with his limited experience – signified that a heavy downpour was on it way.

'We're almost there now,' Christine said, as their pace quickened as fast as Mo's old frame would allow.

'That's right,' Mo chirped. 'It's just down this alley.'

They turned into the alley, which was considerably darker than the street that they had just come from.

Mo paused at the gate and looked back from where she had come.

'What's the matter?' Christine asked her.

Mo paused in silence.

'Mo?'

'It's nothing,' she answered resignedly – obviously keeping something to herself.

Had they been a moment earlier they could have said hello to Philip and Denise. However, because of the darkness that was retained by the alley, they failed to see Philip at the other end of the leafy tunnel as he arranged the tarpaulin to cover the body.

Mo headed the trio as they approached the door of her home. It was widely assumed to be the rear of the premises but she regarded the front of the shop as the rear of the building as it was not the main entrance to her home, so, depending what part of the building she was in, she was both at the front and the back at the same time.

Once inside the kitchen she called out, 'Philip?' and then a second time – but there was no response. 'I wonder where he is,' she mumbled.

Christine's shoulders relaxed slightly when he did not reply.

Mo lifted the kettle from the dated kitchen range to ascertain the amount of water within the vessel.

'You two sit down and I'll make us a hot drink.' She fussed kindly and pulled the chairs out from under the old, oak wooden table.

Allan sat on an equally old oak chair and looked at the pots and pans that hung from the low-beamed ceiling. The jars of jams and pickles that lined a recessed wall and the dried flowers arranged in small bunches on each of the uneven walls gave the appearance of a quaint and homely dwelling.

'This is nice,' he complimented. 'You could be forgiven for thinking that this was a country kitchen in England.'

Christine nodded thoughtfully.

'Thank you, dear.' Mo said. 'When I was young I stayed in Kent for a few years. Perhaps I was more influenced than I realised,' she said matter-of-factly.

'I didn't know that you'd been to England,' Christine said, surprised. 'What were you doing there?'

She looked distant and smiled.

'That was so many years ago now, it's difficult to recall.' She was silent for a minute. 'I think that… that's right, it was just before the Second World War and my father was working for the US Government. We lived in London for a while but when the war started he moved my mother and me to the country. When the Germans started bombing Kent too, then we were sent back home to America.'

'Can you remember it well? I mean, how old were you? Pardon my rudeness.' He smiled, acknowledging that it was rude to ask a woman her age but, in his opinion, the question changed from being rude to being something to be proud of when a person reached a very seasoned age.

She smiled and warmed to his politeness.

'That's all right, dear. Well, I must have been in my twenties. In those days it was still unusual to be travelling with your parents but I wanted to see the world before it was destroyed.'

'So, where else have you been in the world?' he asked.

Mo placed two mugs of black coffee on the table. She sat down with her own mug and carefully sipped the steaming liquid.

'I have been to every continent and visited almost every major city that you can care to name – and I'm proud to say that too. There're not many people alive that have seen what I've seen and been where I have been.' She smiled. 'You two should see as much of this world as you can – travel broadens the mind. You must not be content in your own safe world where everything is conveniently close.'

'That's why I'm here,' he said triumphantly.

She laughed softly. 'A two week vacation is hardly the same thing, my dear. In my opinion, following the separation with your fiancée, you are now more of a free spirit – seize this opportunity that has been given to you,' she said, as she gripped his hand – as it lay on the table by his mug of coffee – with her cold bony fingers. 'You may not have another chance.'

'Oh, I intend to,' he assured her.

'Hold it a moment,' Christine interrupted. 'Allan and Denise might make it up and get back together – Jim and the other two may come back here soon with Denise and you can discuss this in the morning with her,' she said, flabbergasted that Mo had written her off already.

'I admire your optimistic outlook,' he replied, 'but I don't want to – as if it's going to be an option anyway.'

She looked at him perplexed. 'Don't you even want to try? If she walked through that doorway then wouldn't you be pleased to see her?'

'No.' He snorted.

'I just don't understand men sometimes,' she confessed, as she shook her head and looked away in apparent disgust.

'Listen, you don't know what she's like. It's only now that I realise that she has made my life a living nightmare over the past six months.'

'You must be exaggerating. Why would anyone put up with being the partner of someone who they don't get along with? If you didn't like her, then how come you planned to get married? Were you going to wait until it was *your* turn to say, "I do"?'

She was becoming impatient and annoyed with his disregard for Denise's well-being. She could not fathom how somebody could be so cold to a person they were close to only the day before.

'It does happen y'know – perhaps you have been living on this island too long and you need reminding of the real world,' he explained, confident that he was no longer feeling too drunk. His thoughts were now more cohesive and he felt very strongly that his current state of mind was the most honest and true that he had ever realised. 'Anyway, I really don't have to explain myself. I'm confident and my heart tells me that I have made the right decision.'

'That's as may be, but that doesn't alter the fact that Denise is still missing. For all you know *she could be dead.*'

'That's enough, Christine,' Mo interrupted. 'I don't want this discussion to turn into a row that reflects the elements. Christine, respect Allan's thoughts and accept them – it's not your place or that of anyone else to judge another.'

'I wasn't judging him.' She looked back at Mo, who was looking at her most intently. 'Well, I confess that I was about to.' She looked into the steam that was rising from her mug – the pleasant aroma from the coffee drifted into her nostrils – however, the situation had made her unusually tense.

'You look tense, dear,' Mo said. 'Here…' She passed her a small cigarette case of already hand-rolled cigarettes. Christine took one and lit it with a lighter that she found in the case. She blew the smoke into the air as silence fell.

Allan watched her with surprise as the sweet smell filled the room. He was not particularly annoyed with her for questioning his attitude. He wished that he could explain to her how Denise had been so hard to please, but he knew that it would be difficult to explain to anyone just what he had had to put up with. It shocked him to realise that he could not offer any tangible evidence that he could use as an example of how she acted – because it was the combination of events, over the past six months, that had led him to the way he felt now. Why was Christine smoking weed – which had been offered to her by an extremely old woman – so openly, he mused? He was astonished and mildly amused.

Christine noticed that Allan was looking at her.

'What's the matter? Don't you agree with smoking?'

'Not at all,' he replied jovially, noticing that her expression was rather challenging.

'Here…' She passed him the cigarette case.

He looked at Mo for approval and she smiled and nodded. He took a cigarette from the case and lit one.

'Thanks,' he said, as he blew the smoke into the room, which was steadily being occupied by layers of blue-grey smoke that hung magically and drifted sedately. He sat back and relaxed as the quiet atmosphere lost the tension in the clouds of smoke. 'What do you reckon I should do if we can't find her tonight?' he said at length.

'There's no point in planning for something that hasn't happened. Wait until tomorrow and then decide – when the time comes.'

'Mo's right,' Christine added. 'Jim'll help anyway.'

There was knock at the door.

'That'll be them now.' Christine stood up and opened the door. 'Any luck?' she said as she gestured to the three of them to enter.

'I was going to ask the same thing,' Tanya replied as they entered the kitchen.

Mo busied herself with some more mugs and coffee.

Tanya sat on the remaining seat and the two men sat on stools that they pulled out from under a sideboard.

'I see you've made yourself at home, Al,' Tom said jovially, as he regarded him relaxing in the chair, and sipping his coffee and smoking casually.

'Well, I was feeling drunk earlier, but now, with the help of local hospitality, I'm helping myself to relax. Besides, what else can we do? Has anyone got any more ideas?' He looked at Jim with a questioning look that involved the raising of his eyebrows.

'We'll have to see what tomorrow brings,' he confessed reluctantly. 'I reckon the worst of the storm will have passed by then. We can organise a search party – well, *I* will organise a search party.'

'Sounds ominous,' Allan said, as he carefully flicked ash into an ashtray.

Everyone remained silent as they inwardly agreed with Allan. The matter did not need verbal affirmation, partly because the outcome did not seem favourable given the current climate, but mainly due to the fact that the entire situation seemed futile – especially now that it was very dark outside.

Outside, the wind blew strongly and rattled the door rhythmically in its frame. The constantly falling rain was repeatedly blown onto the small window with each gust of wind, as were the tiny branches of a small tree that was growing immediately outside the window.

The relative silence was abruptly shattered when the door swung inwards and Philip burst in quickly shutting the door after him. He looked at everyone in turn.

'I didn't know we had company.'

He smiled.

Chapter Twelve

'Where have you been?' Mo demanded caustically. She was angry and unsettled by Philip's sudden appearance in the room.

Tanya observed that Mo seemed anxious. Her attention quickly turned to Philip, and she was immediately struck by how handsome he was. She then watched as Christine eyed him warily, almost as if she was intimidated by him. She had expected that Christine's offhand mention of him in the bar earlier in the day was but a thinly veiled attempt to disguise the fact that she did, in fact like him. However, she could see and sense her distrust – which contradicted this thought – quite clearly.

To her, Christine seemed intelligent, level-headed and was undeniably attractive. She also appeared to be more than capable of dealing with difficult situations. Tanya therefore decided to respect Christine's judgement, as it was plain to see that her opinion of him was based on experience and not casual observation or the impression given by a simple dislike. She smiled at her own weakness and at how easily she was swayed by the appearance of a person.

'I've been seeing to my boats, making sure the boathouse is secure.' He poured himself a mug of coffee.

She watched the way he held himself, at the confident and slow movements of his obviously well built frame. He was as tall as Tom, but broader. She looked at Tom, who seemed quite disinterested in the man because he was helping himself to one of Mo's cigarettes, which held infinitely more interest to him, she smiled to herself.

'The sea is wild and the boathouse is being pounded. It should be okay, though.' He wondered if his confidence would be enough to hold his secret together. He looked at Christine, who seemed very pensive as she sat upright in her chair, 'Are you okay, Chris? The weather unsettling you?' he said, as he moved over to her side of the table and stood next to her. He placed a hand firmly on her shoulder. 'Don't worry. It'll all be over by tomorrow.'

She brushed his hand from her shoulder.

'The weather isn't the thing that's bothering me.'

Silence descended.

The atmosphere in the kitchen suddenly changed from being almost serene to that which mirrored the weather.

He looked unconcerned and replaced his hand on her shoulder.

'There's no need to be like that. I was only being kind.' He smiled, revealing the two rows of perfectly white teeth.

It was then that Tanya picked up on the problem that Christine had with Philip: it was the fact that he was handsome and charming almost to an imperceptible degree of smarminess – and this was how she decided to initially perceive the man who stood behind Christine.

Christine reddened with anger but Mo quickly interjected strongly.

'Why don't you stop pestering Christine. This young man here,' she turned to Allan, 'is from England and is looking for his fiancée. They arrived here a few hours ago with their friends, Tom and Tanya.' She introduced them and they each shook hands with Philip. 'Denise, Allan's fiancée, arrived with them but went missing from their car. You haven't seen a young woman wandering the streets have you?' She looked at him intently, watching his every movement and expression.

He slowly removed his hand from Christine's shoulder and noticed Mo watching him so intently; he decided to be careful not to display any of the surprise that he felt. He almost found it amusing that only a few hours earlier he had had this man's fiancée naked in his bedroom and now she was hanging drugged and bound in a net, in the engine room of his boat.

'No, I haven't. Have you tried Sloppy Joe's?' He impressed himself with the speed and deftness of his recovery.

Mo, however, had noticed a faint smile that appeared on his face for a brief second.

'We tried there,' Jim said. 'They're having their usual weather party and no one there has seen her.'

'Hey, they're great,' Philip enthused, grateful for the change of subject. 'Who wants to go there this evening? Chris?'

'Not with you,' she replied, outraged.

'Do you reckon we should have waited in your bar?' Tanya suggested. 'What would happen if she came back and we weren't there? And we've locked the jeep.'

'I'd better go and check the car and the bar once more.' Tom said reluctantly, looking at Allan to volunteer as well.

'I'll come with you,' Christine said. 'I'll unlock the bar.'

'I'll come too,' Philip said eagerly.

'No you will not,' she retorted angrily.

'I'll stay here,' Allan offered, as he lazily blew smoke into the room.

'No, Al. You come with me and Jim,' Tom said. '*We'll* check the bar and the car. Here Christine, give me your keys and I'll check the bar. You three can stay with Philip. We'll be back just as soon as we can.'

'Here you are then, Jim.' Christine passed him a set of keys, which he took and looked into her eyes for additional confirmation of the proposition. She nodded.

Allan reluctantly looked out of the window and could see the rain being dashed on the window pane as if buckets of water were being thrown at it.

'That woman is a pain in the neck, even when she isn't bloody here,' he said, as he stood up reluctantly.

'You be all right here?' Tom said to Tanya.

Tanya eyed Philip suspiciously as he observed Christine intently. She took into account the fact that Christine had seen fit to have dinner with Philip, so it was not as if Christine thought he was dangerous, and this was supported by the fact that he did not appear dangerous to her either. She knew that she was strong enough to fend off anyone, besides which, Mo was also in the room.

'Sure, no problem. You be careful, though.'

'We will,' they said in unison.

Allan slowly raised himself from the chair and the three of them left the house. The almost distant sound of the wind and rain increased abruptly before the door closed firmly behind them.

'Well, this is nice,' Philip said, as he sat down on the remaining chair. He looked at Tanya, who he instantly pigeon-holed as attractive and worthy of being explored and examined. He noticed, however, that she seemed to have a very strong personality and that she was surrounded by a strong aura of determination and power; that was not to say that Christine did not also have strength, but hers was more fragile and seemed more easily penetrable.

He smiled and enthusiastically tried to think how he could have his way with both women, or at least Christine. The obvious problem was that Mo was in the house and the three men would only be gone for half an hour at the most.

'So where do you come from?' He looked at Tanya and wondered if his gun was loaded.

'Fort Lauderdale.' She noticed his black eyes for the first time, almost startled by the impenetrable lifelessness contained within, and was suddenly uncertain.

"Retirement city', isn't it?' He laughed.

'It's quiet, sure.' She did not know why she was explaining herself but she felt that she just wanted to pass the time quickly. 'I travel a lot, with Tom.' She reiterated Tom's name because she noticed that he was unwrapping her with his eyes. She folded her arms and glared at him. 'I'm a journalist,' she added, answering his question succinctly before he had had a chance to utter it.

'Could you do a piece on Key West?' Christine asked. 'You know, the weather party at Sloppy Joe's and Denise disappearing?'

'I don't know about an article, this seems more like a novel to me.' She laughed. 'I mean, where could she have got to?'

'She left me quite happily,' he said, as he rested his firearm on the table, 'and unless you two ladies don't do as I say then I will shoot you,' he said calmly.

He looked first at Tanya and then at Christine. They wore the same look of utter disbelief, as if the gravity of the words that he had spoken were in some way humorous.

Mo made an attempt to grab the gun. He saw her move and quickly extended his arm so that the gun was out of her reach and then brought it down abruptly on the back of her head. The dull thud of metal on bone sounded hollow as she slumped onto the table. Her legs kicked the chair backwards and then her body slipped from the table and crumpled in a heap on the wooden floor.

'There, to show you that I'm serious I think that I've just killed my mother. Well, I *say* she's my mom but she isn't really.' He smiled. 'Shall we?'

Christine quickly moved from her chair and knelt next to Mo's crumpled body. She felt for a pulse in her neck.

'She's still got a faint pulse but she needs a doctor.' She took a seat cover from one of the kitchen chairs and carefully stretched Mo horizontally resting her wounded head on the soft cushion.

'What have you done with Denise?' Tanya shouted angrily.

'That's right, I remember her name now.' He laughed singularly. 'No, I haven't done anything with her. I just offered her a place to dry off and she took all her clothes off and virtually threw herself at me, and after that she dressed and left, muttering something about her fiancée; who I assume was the English guy in here earlier. Anyway, enough of this small talk. We have to go. C'mon.'

'Yeah, right.' Tanya sat down thinking rapidly how she could stall him long enough for the others to return. She quickly judged that it would be futile to attempt to overpower him and it was obvious that he knew this. 'Perhaps you would like to wait until poor old Mo bleeds to death first?' she spat.

'Don't misunderstand me,' he replied with a smile. 'I don't want to kill you. Anyway, even if I did shoot you then you wouldn't die straight away – I'd make sure of that. As for Mo, well, she's old and probably the best years of her life have already been lived. Why not die with dignity, that's what I think.'

'What gives you the right? Not only the right to wound a defenceless old woman but why should we do what you say? The men'll be back soon and then you'll have them to deal with. I'm not going to do anything you say,' Christine said defiantly.

'That's right, so you'd better tell us where Denise is and then you'd better run while you can,' Tanya joined in. She stood up in defiance.

Philip laughed. 'You're forgetting something: I have the gun and so even if they do come back then they will be eliminated straight away. The best thing that you can do – if you don't want innocent people to get hurt – is to do as I say and come with me – I'll take you to see… what was her name?' he asked as he chuckled. 'It's funny, you know, I've seen her naked but I can't remember her name.'

'That's real funny, Philip.' Christine rose from the ground and stood next to Tanya. 'But I'm not coming with you because – at the end of the day, if you try and kill Jim, Tom and Allan, as soon as the first shot is fired Tanya and I will jump on you and try to stop you. You won't be able to kill the three of them one after the other, with that old thing.'

'I'm getting tired of your smart remarks,' he hissed venomously, his attitude changing intensely. 'Mo stays here. Perhaps the others will come back and save her. In the meantime, we three are going to take a trip whether you like it or not. If you won't come willingly then I'll shoot you both in the legs and drag you with me.'

Tanya's mind raced with the possibility that he was bluffing. However, she could not take that chance. If he was not bluffing then she would be disabled and defenceless, and therefore unable to forewarn Tom and the other two when they came towards the house.

If they did as he said then at least that would buy them some more time.

'What are you going to do with us then?' Tanya asked. Christine looked as if she was going to launch herself at Philip and Tanya held her arm firmly.

'I'll decide when we get there.' He stared at Christine, eyeing her up and down.

'What about if I came with you and you left Tanya here?' Christine offered desperately, realising that attacking him would not work like it had done for her two days previously. 'You only just arrived here and I think it's me who he wants revenge on,' she said to Tanya.

'No,' she replied. 'If you go with him then I'm coming with you,' she objected resolutely.

'It's pointless, Tanya. I think that whatever he's going to do to me will end in my death. At least if you stay here then you can tell the others who has abducted me.'

'That's enough!' he commanded. 'I don't want you both fighting over me.' He sneered. 'You're both coming with me.' He grabbed Christine's arm and swung her with considerable strength towards the door. Her feet were not ready for the sudden and swift movement and she crashed into the door. Her head struck the wood solidly and she slumped to the floor, unconscious.

He watched her fall.

'Whoops. How careless of me.' He levelled the gun at Tanya and moved closer to her digging the gun into her ribs. 'Now, I want you to pick her up, you look strong enough.' He gripped her biceps. 'I believe in equality,' he whispered hoarsely.

'No,' Tanya said firmly, trying not to take his threatening demeanour seriously. In a sudden act of bravado she gambled on the fact that he was bluffing and hoped that she could stall him long enough for the men to return.

'That's quite brave of you, if not a bit stupid,' he said. 'I have got a gun stuck in your ribs.'

'Yes, but if you kill me then you'll have three bodies to deal with.'

The gun went off suddenly and the smoke from the discharge filled the room. Tanya slumped heavily to the floor.

'Stupid woman. I may come back for you if I've got time.' He easily picked Christine up from the floor and placed her over his shoulder looking down at Tanya as she lay on the floor. Blood had seeped through her T-shirt and was spilling onto the floor as she desperately tried to stem the flow with her hand. 'Actually,' he said, 'I don't think that you're going to last that long. Besides that, I don't think you'd survive what I'm going to do to Christine, and necrophilia doesn't seem appealing to me today.' He opened the door. 'Nice to have met you.' And with that he shut the door.

Tanya was in pain but she felt surprisingly alert. The pain was only on the surface and she wondered whether the bullet had passed through her body and missed her organs instead, exiting her back. She wiggled her toes and moved her legs slightly, then immediately stopped when the pain in her side sharpened excruciatingly. At least he missed my spine, she thanked her luck, then groaned at the fact she had not had much luck over the past few days: first the trip with Denise; her acrimonious split with Allan; then being shot and the two people who she had been in contact with over the last two days being suddenly abducted by a psychopath. Her train of thought subsided as the pain intensified and she slipped from consciousness.

'What do you make of that Philip character?' Jim asked Tom as the three of them hurried along. The rain was falling heavily and the warm wind was still gusting strongly but no worse than it had been already.

Tom let out a puff of air as he thought.

'I can't say. I mean, I don't know him. First impressions are quite good,' he said matter-of-factly. 'I wasn't impressed with his handshake, though.' He turned to Allan, who was walking behind them. 'What about you, Al?'

'Philip? Not sure really. He seemed a bit of a smarmy git – probably a hit with the women though.'

'I think you've summed him up quite well,' Jim said. 'That's all he seems to care about. Still, I don't think you've got anything to worry about. Between Mo, Tanya and Christine I reckon that there's plenty of spirit, determination and grit to deal with anything on this earth.'

He remembered Philip's visit to his gallery the day before yesterday and reflected on the fact that, although he did not trust Philip, he did not imagine that the successful and charming businessman was violent in any way. He assumed that Christine's fright earlier in the day – with the figure that she had seen in the garden – was in the mind of a frightened young woman on her own.

'You're right.' Tom laughed. 'You two check the bar then,' he said, when they drew level to the doorway, 'and I'll check the car and meet you back here in a minute.'

She was not waiting, as they could see when they were walking up the street. Jim jangled the bunch of keys loose from themselves and eventually found the key that fitted the single lock. He opened the door and pulled out from his jacket a pocket torch, which he switched on needlessly, for there was nothing to look at but an empty bar. An empty bar to him seemed a most lonely, somnolent and desolate place.

Tom returned and entered the bar, slightly breathless from running.

'She's nowhere around the car.' He wiped the collected rainwater from his face.

'I bet you wish you had never met me.' Allan sighed.

'Not your fault, Al. Besides, it's an experience to tell people at parties. We'll look back on these relatively dark days and you'll probably laugh – presuming we find her, that is.' He noticed Allan's most serious expression.

'I wonder where she could be?'

'Let's get back to the girls.' Jim sighed. 'We'll take a detour around the block on the way back, just in case. Then we'll definitely have to wait until tomorrow to start the search again.'

They walked briskly along Duval Street, now disregarding the detours that they had previously seen as necessary around the lake-sized puddles. Despite their rather flimsy waterproof garments that covered the top half of their bodies, they were soaked through to the skin and their feet were saturated.

They walked around the block but saw nobody.

'You two go on to the house and I'll just have a quick word with the people at Sloppy's,' Jim said, as he left them standing in the alley that lead to the rear of Mo's.

Tom and Allan silently agreed and made their way to the back/front door.

'She may already be in there,' Tom said, as he opened the gate.

'I doubt it very much,' Allan said honestly. 'I expect that Tanya has ripped Philip apart, though.'

Tom raised his eyebrows.

'Don't get me wrong, Tom: that was a compliment. What I mean is that Tanya is strong-willed and confident. I just imagine that being on the wrong side of her is probably not the best place to be.'

He laughed.

'You do seem to have a knack of summing people up.' He opened the door to the kitchen and the two of them stepped inside. He stood in the doorway and his eyes connected to his brain in excruciatingly slow recognition of the scene of Tanya lying in a small pool of her own blood.

'I seem to have had a small problem,' she whispered breathlessly.

'I'll say,' Allan said, as he knelt next to her. He looked up and noticed Mo lying on the floor on the opposite side of the table. 'I haven't had any first aid training, have you Tom?'

Tom shook his head. He was struck dumb with horror.

'Well, I know that you're not supposed to move people when they're injured. I'll get some blankets for them both and find something soft to prop her head up. I'll check on Mo too.' He stood up quickly and then knelt at Mo's side. 'Where are you supposed to check for a pulse?' He removed his sodden jacket and felt around her wrinkled neck. 'I don't know whether it's me or if there is a pulse at all.' He listened for her breathing and heart beat but he could not hear anything. *'I think she might be dead.* Shit, there's a hell of a lot of blood coming from the back of her head,' he said, as he noticed the blood-soaked cushion.

He stood up and hurriedly walked down the passage that was located at the rear of the kitchen. The passage was incredibly dark and he stumbled into the wooden stairs and stubbed his toe. He swore and ascended them and found a room at the top. A small amount of light was filtering in from the window and he went to the bed and removed two pillows and the crumpled sheets. He found the blankets in a cupboard and quickly bundled them under his arm too.

He carefully descended the stairs and entered the kitchen, passing Tom the blankets and pillow, which he positioned behind Tanya's head and laid the blanket over her to keep her warm.

A blouse fell to the floor from the bundle of blankets. He recognised the garment, and picked it up to examine it. How could it be? It looked like Denise's.

The door opened and the wind blew strongly, chasing leaves onto the wooden floor of the kitchen.

'No!' Jim exclaimed when he stood in the doorway. 'What the hell's happened here?'

'Tanya's been shot and we think Mo's dead,' Tom uttered, choked and almost in tears.

Jim went over to Mo's body and felt her neck.

'Yes, she's dead.' He went over to Tanya. 'Can you hear me Tanya?' he asked.

'Yes,' she whispered.

'Where have you been shot?'

If the situation had not been so serious then Allan would have laughed at the question. Tom carefully pulled down the blanket and showed him the wound.

'Okay, we've got to stop the blood. Allan, get some hot water and some more clean sheets.'

When he returned, Jim took a sheet and tore it into strips and dipped it in the water that Allan brought him. He carefully cut her blood-soaked T-shirt away from her body and cleaned the wound.

'Point blank by the looks of it,' he said. 'Judging by the angle I reckon that the bullet exited her back. Tom, see if you can find the bullet. If we can, then she will have been lucky because we don't have to remove the bullet.'

There then followed a few anxious minutes as Tom searched.

'I've got it!' he shouted, and passed the bullet for Jim to check. It was fresh with blood.

'Tanya, you're a lucky woman. It looks like you're gonna be okay.' Jim smiled as he smoothed her brow. 'Nice work, Allan.' He patted his arm. 'Now what went on here? Do you fellas know?'

'Tanya just said that it was Philip, and he's got Christine,' Tom said, bewildered.

'I think he's seen Denise too,' Allan said. 'I found her clothes upstairs.'

Silence.

'You sure it's hers?' Jim asked.

'Well, it's not got her name in but I don't think there are many British stores with this name in this part of the world.' He showed them the garment.

'They could be someone else's,' Tom suggested.

Allan laughed. 'That's a bit of a coincidence, seeing as how *Denise* is missing.'

'Well, let's not get too far ahead of ourselves here.' Jim's experience was unbelievably helpful. 'Tanya, did you get any idea where Philip was headed?'

Tanya shook her head slowly – her eyelids now closed.

'You rest, hon.' He stood up and looked at Tom and Allan in turn. 'I'm going to get help from Sloppy Joe's. I'll send a few more bodies over here in case he comes back: although I reckon that he won't.'

'What if he does?' Allan asked.

'Lock the door from the inside and get something heavy to use as a weapon. I'm going to get that bastard before he does any more harm to anyone.' And with that he opened the kitchen door and went quickly into the night.

Allan locked the door securely and took a rolling pin down from a shelf.

'If he comes near me I'll twat him.' He thumped the pin into the palm of his other hand. 'I hope Jim catches him and beats the fuck out of him.'

'If I see him again then I'll finish it,' Tom added.

'I don't blame you, but you heard what Jim said – at least Tanya will be okay and she's the most important thing to you.'

'What about you? What about Denise?'

'I wouldn't wish her dead,' he said. He paused. 'But, seeing what he's capable of I reckon that finding her alive does seem unlikely.'

'So you do feel something for Denise and you've been making out that you couldn't give a shit,' Tom countered. 'Why couldn't you have just admitted it rather than keep a stiff upper lip? Now you'll regret falling out for the rest of your life, that's if she has met some really bad luck.'

'I don't regret anything,' he replied impassively. 'It was her who had the problem and she expected me to come running. It was her who was foolish enough to go with a stranger who turned out to be a psychopath. It was her who made the decisions that led her to this and not me – everyone's life is a result of all the individual decisions that they have made. I refuse to feel any guilt for something that I could not possibly have done anything about.'

'You're so stubborn and cold, man.' Tom looked saddened.

'I'm a realist, Tom, I'm not cold-hearted. Besides, the concern now is to look after Tanya and catch that bastard and make him pay – as well as to find out what has happened to Denise. After all, there're not many people who deserve to die and I agree that Denise isn't one of them.'

There was a knock at the door.

A voice said, 'It's me, Jim. Open the door.'

Allan stood up and slid back the bolt, opening the door abruptly, the rolling pin raised above his head and ready to strike – just in case. As the door opened fully he realised that it was Jim and he stood back from the doorway allowing him to enter, followed as he was by four other burly-looking men. A rather wispy man came after them, followed behind by a man carrying a first-aid box – as was indicated by the large red-cross motif on the side. All seven men carried rifles or shotguns and they held them with purpose.

'Right, you three stay here with Tom and Allan, and you three follow me,' Jim said. 'And if you see him then shoot first: he's armed and proved already that he's dangerous.' He passed a shotgun to Allan. 'Do you know how to use one of these?'

He looked at the weapon uncertainly.

'I have never even seen a shotgun before.' He snorted. 'I think the best that I could do is hit him with it but I don't think that I could fire it.'

'Well, take it anyway.' Jim sighed.

'I can use one,' Tom said, as he stood up and allowed the wispy man with the first-aid box to tend to Tanya. Allan passed the gun to him and took up the heavy-looking wooden rolling pin again.

Tom checked that the barrels were loaded with cartridges, primed the weapon and looked stern as he held it purposefully across his midriff.

'As I said, I don't think he'll come back. Anyway, David here will see to Tanya. The local doctor is on his way – he only lives a mile away. Us four are going to search the bar and there are two other groups who are patrolling the streets. We should find him, but the weather is really kicking up and if it gets too bad then we're all going to meet up here.'

'Shouldn't someone check the boathouse?' Tom said. 'Tanya mumbled something about it earlier.'

'Philip's got a boathouse in the marina,' David said. 'Perhaps he's there?' He somehow felt released from the childhood tyranny of Philip, now that he had discovered what the man was ultimately capable of. However, if he had stood up to him in the past then...

'Okay. We'll check the bar first and then the marina,' Jim said.

The man with the rifle opened the door and the four of them entered the maelstrom that now occupied the air surrounding Key West.

Once Philip had closed the door to the house he quickly went over his options as he hurriedly made his way to the truck with his prize slung over his shoulder. His choices, as far as he could see, were to go to Christine's bar or to the marina. He reckoned that Jim and the Englishman and his friend had left the bar by now, but as soon as they returned to Mo's and saw that Christine and Philip were missing one of the first places they would check again would be the bar. The marina was too near the raging sea and so he decided to get into his truck and start driving.

He decided that he would try to make it off the island, for he knew that his life in Key West was over – but his obsession with Christine had grown so strong that nothing else mattered. He wanted her more than anything in the world and he would do anything to make sure that his obsession was satiated – even if it meant forsaking everything that he had.

The rain was pounding as hard as ever as he jogged down the alley. He arrived at his pick-up, opened the passenger door of the cab and carefully placed Christine's limp body on the seat. He ran around to the driver's side and opened the door and climbed in. He started the engine and slowly drove down the road – the frenzied activities of the windscreen wipers mostly ineffectual against the constant downpour.

He looked at Christine as she moaned softly and stirred; as she held her temple and blinked slowly. He took the gun in his right hand and pulled the vehicle over to the side of the road bringing it to a complete stop.

'Ahh, welcome back. I told you that you were coming with me.' He smiled.

She looked about her and realised that she was no longer at Mo's. She looked down the barrel of the gun.

'Where am I? Where are you taking me?' Confusion gave way to tempered panic.

'Away from here, where we can be together.' He took his hand from the wheel and moved along the front seat towards her. His free hand reached out and he touched her cheek with the tip of his fingers. 'I've waited a long time for this.'

She shrank towards the door and frantically searched for the handle.

He saw that she was trying to escape and pulled her viciously away from the handle and slammed her onto the soft seat. He was far stronger and heavier than her and she could do nothing to push him away as he lay on top of her.

'You can't get away, Christine.' He laughed as she struggled beneath him.

'You evil bastard.' She collected what she had in her dry mouth and spat viciously in his face. 'What have you done with Denise? Where's Tanya?' she screamed.

'Don't worry about them now.' He kissed her neck and she struggled to kick and punch him. He held her arms tightly and manoeuvred his legs so that they prevented her from kicking him.

'Where are they!' She screamed and pushed him away with all her might.

He pressed down even harder on her and she gasped under his crushing weight.

'If you stop struggling then I'll tell you. If you don't, then I'll hurt you,' he said calmly.

She struggled to remain composed but somehow managed to stop struggling, although her mind was racing, desperately trying to think of a way to gain the advantage and escape.

'That's better.' He sat upright but held her wrists firmly on the car seat. 'Now, before I tell you where they are I want you to do something for me.' He smiled at her, his lifeless eyes taking on the appearance of pools of deathly thick, suffocating oil – like that which washes on the beaches of the world and prevents the flight of the birds of the ocean.

'And what if I refuse?'

'Well, not only will I not tell you but I will have my way with you whether you like it or not. If you co-operate then I won't kill you.'

Christine did not have to think hard about her choice: she would rather die. However, she suddenly and boldly decided to try her luck for one last time. If it did not work then he would kill her, but if she did not try then she would suffer. Her father had said to her when she was a child, 'Do not regret what you have done in the past; only regret what you haven't done'. She steeled herself and sighed.

'Okay, I'll do as you say.' She strained.

'Good.' His voice revealed surprise and excitement.

'What do you want me to do?' she said.

The rain pounded heavily on the roof and windscreen. The streetlight – that was on the sidewalk immediately adjacent to the car – went out and a pitch blackness filled the cab.

'You know what I want,' he whispered. His hand fell on her breast and he gently squeezed. His breath was short and sharp and he lay the gun on the dashboard as he fumbled with the buttons on her jeans.

Still she did not struggle, although intently she searched the darkness for the gun with an extended hand. She noticed the shiny metal on the dashboard as he began removing her jeans. She reached out and her hand clasped the metal: only succeeding in pushing it further from her reach.

He undid her jeans and began to remove them from her slender body. He was still not looking at what she was doing, only at what she was no longer wearing, and so she shifted her position so that she could reach the gun easily. With relief, her hand clasped the handle and gripped the cold metal. She raised the gun to the full length of her outstretched arm and brought it down smartly on the back of his head. Again and again she struck him until blood soaked her hand and forearm. She was breathing heavily with the exertion and struggled to free her legs, kicking him onto the floor.

Her jeans were now more off than on and so she hurriedly kicked off her shoes and jeans, opened the car door and jumped to the ground. She fell awkwardly and she lay face down in a puddle. She managed to drag herself to her feet and then groaned and winced in pain. She froze in terror as the streetlight flickered on and she saw Philip's bloodstained face staring at her through the window of the truck.

Jim unlocked the door of Christine's bar. He was accompanied by one of the men and the other two had rounded the back of the house in case Philip was lurking in the rooms at the rear of the building. He stepped inside the bar with the shotgun cocked and ready, his partner quietly closing the door behind him was poised in the same manner.

Jim scanned the room and listened for any extraneous noise: the gun following his vision as he scanned the shadows lurking by the tables and chairs, the pool table and the bar. All he could hear was the howling wind rattling the roof tiles and the rain pounding on the windows.

His partner carefully checked the washrooms and they silently nodded in satisfied agreement that there was no one else in any of the rooms on the ground floor. The two of them proceeded to the door and the flight of wooden stairs that led to the living area of the bar/hotel.

The other two men were already waiting at the foot of the stairs and they started suddenly when Jim and the other man approached. He silently signalled with his hand to ascend the stairs and the three men followed him. Jim winced when – with every step – the floorboards creaked.

The noise of the roof tiles being stripped from the roof was louder now; the wind finding its way into the loft area and pushing against the ceiling the pummelling rain. Water dripped through in places, and in some areas quite profusely. He concluded that it was impossible to mask the sound of their approach, but it was unlikely that anyone could possibly hear them above the din anyway.

He kicked open a door and stood back behind the door jamb and the wall. One of the men quickly knelt in the room and another scanned it with the torch positioned above the gun. There was nothing inside this room and so they proceeded to the next, and the next and until every room had been searched.

'Is it worth checking the loft?' one of the men said.

They found the hatch that led to the roof and unlocked it. A set of loft ladders gently slid to the floor, accompanied by a waterfall of rainwater that soaked each of them.

'Great,' Jim muttered, as he watched the water cascading about them. He then carefully ascended the ladder. He pondered whether Philip was waiting up there, waiting for his head to appear, which he could strike with a blunt instrument.

With a sudden burst of bravado, mixed with recklessness and an urgency to find Christine, he quickly ascended the ladder and scanned the loft area with his torch. He felt a blow to his head and his feet almost lost their footing on the ladder when he slipped. However, his arms held onto the rim of the hatch and he recovered the momentum that was threatening his position. Slightly dazed and sickened by the blow, he picked up the torch that had fallen from his grasp and searched the loft – puzzled that he had not been struck again. He soon realised that the loft was empty. At least half of the roof tiles were missing and he could see the rain being lashed around the loft area, threatening to continue its attempt at destroying the building. He quickly descended the ladder.

'That was pretty stupid, Jim. He could have been up there, man.'

'What was it that hit me? It could have been him!'

'It was this, Jim. We saw it hit your head and then fall down here,' one of the men said gingerly, as he showed him the broken roof tile.

'We haven't got time. C'mon, we have to check the boathouse. The storm is really going for it now and we have to get there before it gets even worse.' He was filled with rage at what Philip had done to Tanya and the fact that he had taken Christine. He *had* to find him before anything else happened to anyone else.

The four men ran down the stairs and through the passageway that led to the back of the bar. They ran straight past the full swimming pool, exiting the gate and headlong into the street. None of them noticed the approach of the drenched woman who ran headfirst into them and knocked Jim to the ground.

'What the...' he said as he landed heavily in a large puddle. 'Chrissie?' he enquired as he made to grab the struggling wretch.

She suddenly recognised him and dived into his arms, sobbing and holding him tightly.

'Let's get her inside,' he said, as he lifted her legs and carried her through the gate and into the kitchen. He sat her on a chair and ordered one of the men to get her some clothes. He saw a robe hanging on the back of the door and draped it over her bare legs.

'It's okay, you're safe now.' He cradled her head into his chest.

'You have to lock the door. He's injured but he's mobile. He could be on his way here,' she gasped, as she shivered violently from fear and the coldness that she felt.

One of the men returned with a pair of jogging bottoms, some socks and a sweater. Jim ordered two of the men to lock the front door and the other to lock the back door. This done, he set about drying her feet and telling her to get dressed while he made a hot drink.

Christine slowly calmed down and warmed herself; the fear and coldness gradually being expelled from her body with the aid of short term anger and concern.

'How're Mo and Tanya? What has he done to them?'

'Mo's dead,' he said solemnly. 'I'm sorry.'

She hung her head and wept quietly.

'But Tanya's okay. She was shot but it's not too serious. They're at Mo's and they're safe. I think half of Key West is in the house.'

She managed a smile.

'What about Denise?'

He sighed.

'No luck. We may have to wait until morning. It's pretty dangerous out there, not only the weather but there's an injured psychopath on the loose with a gun. I'm all for staying secure until first light and then resuming the search for her.'

'No, you must keep looking. I think that he must have killed her.'

'We will keep looking for as long as we can. There are parties of four and six armed men searching everywhere for her.'

One of the men – who was guarding the front of the bar – walked into the kitchen.

'We've just heard: Philip's boathouse at the marina has been taken by the sea.'

Chapter Thirteen

The blue morning sky looked peaceful and calm and the sun shone unrepentantly. The devastation from the storm of previous days was evident: the proliferation of branches laying on tarmac and parked cars; roof tiles strewn around gardens and pavements; the occasional collapsed building that was too old or too weak to withstand the heavy assault of wind and rain.

The harbour was almost devoid of boats, that had initially been left in the water when the bad weather started, unbeknown to some of the owners that the storm would take a sudden change of direction and the edge of it scrape heavily across Key West. The boats that had once been anchored in the harbour or moored in the marina had been dashed against the harbour wall and were now flotsam and jetsam in the choppy water or were lying stranded on the coast road.

Over the past week the collective force of the waves had been so great that they had breached the sea defences and licked some of the buildings that were positioned near to the sea, causing considerable damage even at the end of their long reach, even after such a long journey that had started many miles out at sea.

The boathouses that immediately stood by the sea were now gone. Only the occasional vertical wooden plank forlornly reached for the blue sky. The remainder of the structure was now at the bottom of the ocean or floating with the wreckage of the boats.

A motionless man watched from the jetty as the boat, which was in the throws of death, was sinking: his black, lifeless eyes searching the water. The water had been gradually filling the hole in the wooden hull, just above the water line. The laws of physics meant that the boat was no longer able to float and so it gradually sank. The escaping air, pushed out forcefully by the water, bubbled violently around the dying vessel, as it sank lower and lower still, until the roof of the wheelhouse was lapped by the waves, and then it was finally consumed.

Disbelief.

It must be a nightmare and I will wake up any minute. Her mind screamed alarm, disbelief, despair and utter confusion.

She looked above at the small amount of light that was afforded by – unbeknown to her – a missing plank of the wooden deck.

Where was she? The sky was all blue, so the storm must be over and the morning had arrived. Her head was heavy and her thoughts ponderous, but where was she?

Why was she tied up?

What was that awful smell? Her confused mind and thoughts were quickly overrun with unimaginable terror, as she felt the water lapping against the bottom half of her naked body. She realised that she was being rocked from side to side and up and down – quite roughly.

She held her head up as high as she could, as the cold water quickly rose up her body and soon slipped around her neck. Still the water rose to her chin and then her nose. She held her breath in a futile attempt to stop the ocean breaching her mouth and nose.

She looked at the sky as the water blurred her vision and the makeshift coffin sank slowly into the dark watery depths of the sea. Her lungs burned when she could no longer breathe. The last thing that she saw was the blue sky slowly disappearing into blackness, as death breached her lungs and clouded her mind. She had no time for regrets, no time to savour the world for the last time and *no time*.

Her insignificant life ended unseen by all except the dark pools of blackness that were watching impassively from the water's edge. Her passing was a fortunate release for one watching and the regret of few.

The man looked about him to see if anyone had noticed the ocean claim his secret.

It seemed to him that everyone in the area was too busy – with clearing up their damaged homes – to be interested in a man looking at the devastation of the marina. He had seen the groups of armed men searching the area and he had heard them mention his name, so he guessed that they were looking for him. However, he was alone – for now. Nobody apart from him had seen the boat sink and no one would know that it was lying at the bottom of the deep harbour that was filled with strong currents.

'Stop!' He heard a voice call out. 'Put your hands in the air and get down on the floor!'

He immediately recognised that the voice was Jim's. He was livid that he had been stupid enough to be caught, but he had had to check on the boat that had contained the two bodies. He reasoned he now had two options: he could turn, remove the gun from his waistband and try to shoot Jim before he fired, or he could just surrender. The first option would never work successfully and the second did not warrant further consideration at all.

He felt unbelievably pressured and could taste the bitter taste of despair because of the fact that he had lost all his power, his life and his future. He had not achieved his goal and Christine was now far out of reach. Perhaps being shot was preferable.

Perhaps not.

Jim watched Philip standing still and was about to issue another warning before shooting him in the leg. However, when he watched Philip lunge forward and dive into the sea he quickly pulled the trigger and the shot rang out.

'I don't think you got him,' the man next to Jim said as they ran along the relatively short concrete jetty to the spot where Philip had entered the sea.

Jim scanned the water, waiting for him to surface and ready to shoot again. He scanned the shoreline and looked out to sea but he could not see Philip – alive or dead. He failed to notice the blood on the jetty before the ocean had washed it clean with one of its infinite outstretched hands.

'How are you bearing up?' Christine smiled when Tanya gingerly walked into the room.

'I'm a bit sore. They told me to stay still for a few days but I just couldn't stay indoors. These stitches are really tight.' She winced as she moved her arm. 'but the wounds are healing.' She smiled warmly. 'I am *so* sorry about you losing Mo. She seemed such a peaceful and interesting old lady.'

'I'm sorry too.' She retained an expression of immense sadness. She immediately felt very uncomfortable sitting in Mo's study – the place where Mo used to sit. She remembered when Mo had read her tea leaves and smiled as she remembered Mo becoming annoyed at the sun disappearing behind the clouds and how she had irritably moved closer to the desk lamp.

'I'll come back,' Tanya said, noticing that tears were welling up in Christine's eyes.

'No, please don't go,' she said quickly, as Tanya placed her hand on the door handle to leave. 'I appreciate you coming. It's just, well, so much has happened and I'm finding it hard to find peace at the moment. Perhaps I need to be alone, though.' She reconsidered, not really knowing what she wanted.

'No, you don't want to be alone.' Tanya came to her side and warmly held her hand. The paintings on the wall caught her eye and she looked intently at the scenes of the sea.

Christine noticed that she was looking at the paintings.

'Mo's friend painted these pictures you know. She was a very talented painter and Mo was very fond of them. These are all I have to remember Mo by now: together with my own memories.' She stood up and looked closely at a painting: at the tumultuous sea and the tortured vessels caught in time.

'What else is more emotive than a painting created by a tortured mind.'

Tanya stood next to her and studied the painting.

'She obviously had a strong relationship with the sea.'

'She did. It's something that I have been thinking about over the years and was something that I discussed with Mo once.' She sighed. 'She believed that each person's mind is like an ocean: with deep dark depths; warm shallows; raging storms and tranquil and peaceful waters too. Each ocean is filled with one's dreams, desires, determination, drive and devotions – which regulate the depths, the shallows, the storms and the peace. It seems that she was frightened, the artist, of her mind and had to paint it to keep it from her. She must have been deeply troubled about something in her life – she was never the same after her husband died, apparently, but Mo said that it was his death that had completely broken her composure and her grip on reality.'

She looked distant.

'It only takes one incident in a person's life to transform it into a raging and self-destructive storm.' She paused and her eyes were swelling with tears as her memory held her in the past. She did not cry but instead continued as her mind was deep in thought of the present. 'Mo told me that she had been having nightmares about the ocean bursting into her house. It turns out that the warnings were for her.' She moved along to the next painting, 'Philip was an evil man and has taken many secrets with him, which deep down I knew he had but I still do not know what they truly are.'

She looked at Tanya with her large brown eyes, almost pushing her against the wall her look was so forceful.

'Don't make the same mistake. Don't be afraid to explore the depths, play in the shallows, ride the storms and let others join you in your ocean. I never understood what Mo meant until now. She always said that there are *three* things that you should remember if you want to lead a full and meaningful life: each person's mind is an ocean: but beware, the ocean minds.'

Her voice grew fainter as the waves crashed on the not-so-distant shore: her thoughts becoming lost in the sea of her departed friend.

Epilogue

Bright sunlight filled the busy bar and highlighted the layers of smoke that hung happily in the air. The general hubbub of voices was pierced with jolly laughter. Glasses clinked, chairs scraped on the wooden floor and pool balls clicked together.

'So, what happened when you saw her mom?'

'Christine, you couldn't believe how much I didn't want to face her. The police had already been around to the house and said her daughter was missing – presumed dead. Apparently she became hysterical and screamed uncontrollably. Eventually they had to call a doctor to have her sedated. When she had recovered – a few weeks later – I knew that I had to see her: it was necessary even though she hates me.' He sighed. 'Y'know, at the end of the day I didn't like Denise but she didn't deserve to die.' I wish that it could have been different but it was out of my control. Events just conspired to make it end like that.

Christine looked as though she was about to say something.

He pre-empted her.

'No Chris, they found all her clothes floatin' in the harbour and there had been no sighting of her since her disappearance all those months ago. I know there's no body but she is *dead*, you know that as well as I do.'

She nodded begrudgingly.

'They found some clothes and a suitcase floating in the harbour. They belonged to another woman too, and they couldn't trace her whereabouts either. There was talk that he had something to do with that too, because there are witnesses who saw them together *and* they discovered an abandoned hire car.'

'I can't say that I'm surprised. Perhaps there's much more that they don't even know about?'

'The police are going through missing persons files that are ten years old and have been doing so for months now.'

'Enough about that, it's so disturbing and distressing. So, what happened when you went to see her mom?' she repeated.

He sighed again and sat up straight.

'The police knocked on the door and a relative of hers let us in – me and two detectives. When her mum saw me she went absolutely ballistic. She threw a vase at me – which exploded on the wall behind me – and the police had to wrestle her to the floor to stop her from attacking me. As a few of the police sat on her to keep her down, she screamed that she was going to sue me and then kill me – like I had killed her daughter. She then raged on that if I hadn't been so inconsiderate and thoughtless to her daughter then she would never have run away in the first place.'

'Damn.' She wore a distressed expression. 'Whatever did you say to that?' She imagined that he must have felt a degree of guilt having received those words from Denise's mother.

'What could I say? She was hysterical. She was in such a state that the policewoman suggested that I leave. Perhaps it was my fault in some ways, but she made the choices that led to this. I cannot be responsible for them. Anyway, next month they're holding an inquest into Denise's disappearance but her mum isn't fit to travel. She's in hospital now in a coma – she took a huge overdose last week.'

Christine looked surprised.

'Denise was her only daughter and now she's gone. I suppose it seems to her that life isn't worth living – what a waste of two lives,' he continued gravely. 'They could have done anything, been anything they wanted and they just drifted through their shallow lives, filling them with trivialities. Ultimately, I suppose, they both died because of themselves.'

'You always did seem a bit harsh,' she offered sombrely, surprised at his evident lack of remorse. 'So what happens now? I mean, what will you do?'

He looked into the deep, dark liquid of the stout. 'I've given up work. I can't stand it now. I mean, how can I go back to a normal life?'

'It must be hard.' She bit her lip. 'I'm sorry Allan, I really don't know what to say.' She looked slightly distressed.

'That's okay.' He smiled and took a sip from his glass. 'You don't have to say anything. I just thought I'd tell you what's happened since I left after the storm. Anyway,' he managed a smile, 'what else has been happening here? How're Jim, Tom and Tanya?'

'Ask him yourself.' She smiled and nodded towards the door.

'Hey, Allan. How are you?'

Allan turned on his stool and saw Jim, dressed in his usual shorts, T-shirt and flip-flops.

'Good to see you, Jim.' He shook his hand warmly.

'What's been happening with you then, Al? *Like the hair.*' Jim smiled and pulled Allan's ponytail gently.

Christine smiled and moved to the other end of the bar to serve waiting customers.

Allan relayed the whole story from when he had left Key West, the story of Denise's mother and returning to England.

'So what are you doing with yourself? How come you're back here?'

Well, I'm living on the money that I was going to spend on the house that we'd bought. I've sold it now and I made a tidy profit. I thought I would come back here – a psychiatrist suggested that it may help to cleanse my memory, although I don't reckon that it is in need of much cleansing. I don't know what I'm going to do.'

'Well, you're welcome to stay here for as long as you like.' Christine smiled, as she stood pulling one of the beer pumps with her hand.

'That's right,' Jim added firmly. 'I'll phone Tom and Tanya. I'm sure they'll come down to see you. When you left, Tom and Tanya spoke highly of you and said that they wanted to see you when you were up to it.'

'Surely not, after what I put them through.' He puffed.

'Something is not the result of any one single thing,' he said, 'but everything that happens is the culmination of a myriad of conversations, situations, reactions and occurrences. A wave landing on the beach began its journey long ago.'

Allan smiled. 'You sound like someone I once knew.'

Jim's expression slowly screwed itself into a frown.

'What do you mean?'

Allan laughed.

Whatever you want it to mean.' He listened to the almost imperceptible sound of the waves crashing on the distant beach.

'Whatever you want.'